About the Author

Andy Howden grew up in the Yorkshire Dales and read English Literature at the University of Sheffield before setting out on a career in market research which took him to London, Paris and Hampton Wick. He has worked for a number of companies, not all of them entirely sane.

Melting in the Middle is his first novel, started on a MA in Creative Writing at St. Mary's University, and was long-listed for the Exeter Novel Prize.

Andy lives in South West London with his wife and has two grown up children who have left home but fortunately keep popping back to see him.

MELTING
IN THE
MIDDLE

A novel

Andy Howden

Matador
9 Priory Business Park,
Wistow Road, Kibworth Beauchamp,
Leicestershire. LE8 0RX
Tel: 0116 279 2299
Email: books@troubador.co.uk
Web: www.troubador.co.uk/matador
Twitter: @matadorbooks

ISBN 978 1800460 645

British Library Cataloguing in Publication Data.
A catalogue record for this book is available from the British Library.

Printed and bound in Great Britain by 4edge Limited
Typeset in 11pt Baskerville by Troubador Publishing Ltd, Leicester, UK

Matador is an imprint of Troubador Publishing Ltd

In honour of my dear mother, Thelma Howden,
who always encouraged me to write,
and my beloved wife, Caroline Ewart, who made sure that I finally did.

The important thing is this:
To be able at any moment
To sacrifice what we are
For what we would become.

Charles Dubos
Approximations, 1922

Part One

Late November to December 2014

Chapter One

Stephen Carreras gazed into his screensaver. His two children looked back at him, heads inclined towards each other in a show of sibling affection for the camera. Kate in her swimsuit, smiling from an awkward ten-year-old body. And Jake, still a podgy eight-year-old, proudly flaunting his ice lolly, with lips of lurid orange. Summer holiday in Cornwall, little more than four years ago. Just before he screwed up.

'Steve would doubtless see the sense in these budget cuts, if he was paying attention to my presentation.' Oscar Newte, wearing a pink open-collared shirt and a smug expression, stared at him from the front of the meeting room.

'Don't bet on it,' Stephen said.

He had no idea what draconian measures Newte had been proposing. It was true, he hadn't been listening. So agreeing might be signing his own death warrant. And anyway, he liked to disagree with the man as a point of principle.

It was tempting to let his mind drift back to those happy days at the beach while Newte was presenting his financial review, a dish served with lashings of pessimism and a sprinkling of pomposity. Stephen glanced around the other board members of Grimley's Confectionery, sinking ever deeper into their meeting chairs. Discarded coffee cups, toffee wrappers and the curling sandwiches from their working lunch, as unpalatable as the profit warnings on Newte's charts, littered the rectangular Formica table. Jim Jeffries, arms folded, head lolling forward slightly to reveal his bald patch, was dribbling a little; a gentle, rhythmic snoring emanating from his nostrils. Nobody gave him a nudge.

So much for an 'Away Day Energiser' in this beige Molitor hotel, whatever a molitor was, on a building site somewhere near Cambridge.

But Stephen needed to focus now. He was on next. He reached for the one remaining bottle of mineral water, twisted it open and poured himself a fizzing glass. This was his chance to show everyone who was boss – or who should be. Interviews for the managing director role must surely be imminent. And Stephen was quite certain he was the man for the moment. Among this crew, Newte was the only possible competition. But he was again demonstrating he could bore for Britain. At long last, he put up what he declared to be his concluding slide. It looked to Stephen indistinguishable from those that had preceded it, a graph in which the lines were sloping gently downwards.

Newte opened wide his arms in a last appeal to his audience. 'Therefore, lady and gentlemen, I fear that my end of term headmaster's report is that you can and must do better.' A sinister leer spread across his florid features. 'And next year, of course, I'm sure that you will – or face the consequences.'

An unpleasant little reminder that Oscar Newte, for all his wind-baggery, currently had the power of the finance director – and a belly full of low cunning.

Stephen strode to the front. His rival needed to be taken down. And it was time to wake the rest of them up.

'OK, everyone, time for some *good* news,' he announced and launched into his presentation. It was, he felt, a tour de force – in the circumstances. A punchy demonstration of how as marketing director he had, if not exactly improved sales of Bingo Bars and Munchy Moments, then at least stabilised them. And even Little Monkeys, the problem child, had survived another year.

He was good at this stuff, shutting out those nagging doubts about the future while on his feet presenting, glossing over the sales data far too adeptly for this bunch to note the dodgier elements of his argument. Even Jim was sat bolt upright, wide-eyed and trying to follow the action.

But after a while Stephen became aware that now Oscar Newte was not paying attention to him. He could see his rival in the corner of his eye, playing with his phone, nodding his head in a knowing way, and murmuring, 'I thought as much,' just loudly enough to ensure he was heard.

Eventually Stephen was so distracted that he brought his presentation to a premature close.

'So, to sum up, this is the strongest ever marketing plan for my brands. Any questions?' He stared defiantly at his six colleagues.

Behind him on the screen, the final slide of *his* PowerPoint deck shouted out an optimistic proclamation:

LITTLE MONKEYS: LOOKING TO THE FUTURE

'I have a question,' Newte chirruped. Of course he had. Leaning back in his chair, he pushed his red-framed glasses onto his forehead and folded his hands behind his head, revealing a small damp patch under each arm.

'Do you seriously think Little Monkeys *has* a future? Or indeed any of these brands?'

Stephen hesitated. But only for a second.

'Absolutely, Oscar, you clearly haven't been following. You seem more interested in your phone. Anything you'd care to share with the rest of us? Don't tell me, a bad year for Pinot noir in your vineyard?'

Newte rose to his feet without responding to the barb.

'Indeed I do have very dramatic news. If I could have your attention please, everyone?'

All eyes turned to face him at the other end of the table, leaving Stephen with little choice but to sit down and concede the spotlight. Newte addressed the room. 'As you all know, there has been some speculation about the future direction of the company following the retirement of your... our... dear chairman, and I have needless to say, as your FD, been keeping abreast of developments. I have naturally been sworn to secrecy, but there appears to have been an – unfortunate – leak to the financial media, so I believe it's appropriate for me to read out this breaking news on *Business Live*, which I think you'll agree renders the Carreras master plan for next year somewhat irrelevant.' He glanced triumphantly at Stephen, then peering at his phone, cleared his throat in an exaggerated manner.

'I quote. The takeover of Grimley's by US confectionery giant Schmaltz has been completed today. A Schmaltz spokesman in Chicago announced the deal in an early morning press conference. Schmaltz has been voraciously acquiring European chocolate businesses over the past three years but its decision to take over Grimley's will surprise some analysts as the latter, still family-owned, has been in the financial doldrums in recent years.' This raised a dissenting 'bloody cheek' from Jim Jeffries, but Newte continued. 'The company's departing chairman, Gordon Grimley, last surviving family member in the business, was unavailable for comment. But a Schmaltz spokesman said the Americans would appoint a new MD for the UK business and a new senior leadership team imminently. He refused to rule out job losses at Grimley's East Midlands HQ in Middleton or their factory in Dumfries.'

And with that, Newte flipped his phone case closed and surveyed his audience.

'The Yanks are coming,' he smirked.

The room went quiet but for the whirr of the projector blowing a steady jet of hot air against Stephen's right cheek.

'I can't believe the media know about this before we do,' Stephen said. Although given how much of a car crash Grimley's was these days, it seemed entirely possible. 'It's probably pure speculation,' he ventured.

'Well, as I said, obviously a shame about the leak, but I can assure you it's true.' Newte looked at him pityingly.

Silence descended again, until finally it was left once more to Jim Jeffries, as the elder statesman, to articulate his feelings.

'Well, fuck me,' he growled.

'Thanks, Jim. I think I can safely say you speak for all of us,' Stephen said.

His chances of becoming the next MD of Grimley's were now officially zero. Whereas the odds on getting the boot had shortened considerably.

Newte turned to face him directly.

'So, Steve, I refer you to my previous question about your Little Monkeys presentation in particular. As marketing director, at least for the moment, are you certain that this brand, which hasn't made us any money since the last millennium, is going to cut the mustard next year? Do you seriously think Schmaltz, the sharpest operators in global confectionery, will let you continue with it? Little Monkeys? More like little lambs to the slaughter, old boy.' He looked very pleased with himself.

'Well, we'll just have to see, won't we, Oscar?' Stephen replied. It was important to maintain a bullish facade at least.

There was no appetite for the meeting to continue any longer. Phones were back on, earpieces in. Stephen surveyed them all, wandering around the room with hands thrust into pockets, resembling a group of lunatics allowed out for the afternoon, each muttering to some imaginary friend.

He checked his own messages. There were even more than usual. Clearly the takeover news had gone around the office, and lots of his team wanted a word, several sounding anxious already. There were three voicemails from his deputy Tony Perkins, each with a desperate request that Stephen should contact him urgently to discuss 'the bad news'. And just for good measure, there was a cheery message from Sandra, his PA, keen to let him know that meetings for the next three weeks had been synchronised in his diary. All the way to Christmas.

It was definitely time to go home. Calls from Perkins were never a pleasure. He made Eeyore sound like a positive thinker. He and the rest of them would have to wait. Cocooned back in his Saab estate in the hotel car park, Stephen took a deep breath and exhaled. At least the performance was over for another week. No more charades until Monday morning.

'OK, Alice, let's get out of here, shall we?' he said to his satnav. 'One and a half hours to get home, you reckon? In your dreams on a Friday, my dear.'

He left the hotel grounds. But he couldn't leave Oscar Newte. That man seemed to be actually relishing this takeover, as if immune from the fallout. He had always been suspicious of him since his arrival a couple of years ago. What was a posh ex-merchant banker doing at Grimley's in the first place? He recalled the lads in the pub speculating that either he had to leave the City because of some financial dirty laundry, or because underneath the Etonian exterior he was as thick as two short planks. But now Stephen wondered if he was in on this deal. After all, a merchant bank must have their fingers all over it and Newte was always name-dropping his friends in high places.

Of course, he had to admit the guy was right about Little Monkeys next year. Lambs to the slaughter was apt, with new owners hunting for sickly brands to sacrifice on their pyre of profit. There could be plenty of humans on there as well, with himself on top. But he still wasn't going to give the supercilious twit the satisfaction of agreeing. It was the brand he had always loved the most, even if it never made any money these days. He still remembered going into old Mr Godfrey's sweet shop after school, clasping his ten-pence piece. Eyeing up the Little Monkeys in one of those big glass jars behind the counter; a quarter pound for the weekend.

A car in his rear-view mirror flashed and hooted at him for drifting into the outside lane. He veered to the left, slowed down and focused on the road ahead, the naked trees on the horizon silhouetted against a sky drained of colour.

The temperature gauge on his dashboard read five degrees, and the weatherman on the radio was forecasting a damp, cold weekend ahead but with the voice of a man looking forward to spending it tucked up with his family. Stephen had no plans, unless you could call wading through the team's end of year appraisals a plan. Not his weekend to see Kate and Jake. What exactly was he driving home to?

At the next roundabout, Alice directed him left onto the motorway. But he had a sudden impulse to disobey her. He stayed on the roundabout and came to the right-hand exit, signposted to Cambridge city centre. But he drove past and went round again. After the third circuit, he still couldn't turn off in any direction.

Maybe this was his nervous breakdown.

The fourth time, gripping the steering wheel more firmly, he again ignored Alice and turned right, towards the city and a distant spire in the fading afternoon light. His phone was on the seat next to him, buzzing insistently. He switched it off. Alice, dazed and confused by the roundabout fiasco, was urgently imploring him to make a U-turn. He switched her off too.

Close to the centre of Cambridge, he pulled off a main road and found a parking place on a meter. As he got out of the car and rummaged in his pocket for change, a bite in the air hunched his back. Winter, sweeping in across miles of bleak, cold fenland from the North Sea.

Why was he here? He walked across a bridge into a street busy with late afternoon shoppers, found an inviting coffee shop and treated himself to a large cappuccino. He would not think about the American takeover. He would not think about Oscar Newte. Or losing his job. He lingered over the drink, enjoying the deep warmth in his cupped hands and the aroma of coffee beans. Until a girl and a boy in their early teens came in and sat at the next table while their mother went to order at the counter.

What would Kate and Jake be up to this weekend? And how exactly had Laura managed to outmanoeuvre him again, so that over Christmas itself he would get one measly Saturday with them before the big day, and then wouldn't see them again until New Year? All because she and bloody Tristran were going away to some swanky hotel for Christmas this year and taking the kids with them. What had happened to the notion of divorced couples getting together at this time of year for the sake of the children? He would end up spending Christmas Day with his sister, her jet-setting husband and their boys, and Mum of course. Their silent disapproval of the divorce still hovering over the Brussels sprouts, four years on. Watching his nephews opening their presents while his own kids were in some West Country love nest, two hundred miles away.

He walked back towards his car but paused at the corner of the side street on which he had parked. The Friday evening traffic was going nowhere. He walked on and turned instead into another road which appeared at first to be leading him out of town, past woodland, but then came to more open meadowland, with what looked like a college chapel soaring out of the gloom on the other side of the river. Early evening lights gently dotted the scene. When had he last been in a beautiful place, with no agenda? The only other onlooker was a Chinese tourist, a man of about Stephen's age, taking a photo of the colleges. They exchanged a modest knowing smile, complicit in their reverence. The chapel was drawing him in.

A gate indicated the entrance to Clare College grounds, and he could see that the path on the other side led across the meadow towards the river and the college itself. There was an entry fee, but nobody there to collect it. He passed through, feeling a slight thrill at breaking the rules. Two student cyclists idled by, pedalling gently, chatting, with leather satchels slung over their shoulders. He stopped for a moment and listened. Behind him the background hum of traffic. Ahead of him silence.

He pressed on over the bridge, and entered a courtyard with a lawn at its centre, a scattering of lights shining from college windows on all four sides. As he looked across it, in a room close by he could hear a woman singing. Her delicate voice was balancing on the tightrope of a complex tune and holding its line, slowly advancing.

> '*O come, O come, Emmanuel,*
> *And ransom captive Israel*
> *That mourns in lonely exile here...*'

A strange hymn, vaguely familiar from somewhere deep in his past – but he didn't know where. Maybe from when Dad had taken him to church occasionally as a boy.

He lingered and listened as the voice stepped carefully through the verses, until it had the tune well within its grasp.

> '*Rejoice, rejoice, Emmanuel shall come to thee, O Israel.*'

It had walked the tightrope, completed the journey, and here it was, at peace.

The door opened, and a young woman came out. She was the voice, he was certain. She had long fair hair, and was wearing a duffle coat and jeans, with a red and black college scarf loosely wrapped around her neck. Their eyes met for a second, and he smiled reassuringly. She looked across the courtyard, eyes searching in one direction and then the other.

A young man appeared at the opposite side and crossed the lawn, clutching a bottle of wine in one hand and pulling off a woolly black hat to reveal a tousled shock of dark curly hair. The young woman spotted him and with quickening pace, met him in the middle of the court and kissed him on the lips.

They turned and walked away, towards the far corner from where the young man had come. She laughed, her head tossed back, and he held her tightly around the waist, before they disappeared from view.

For a moment, Stephen felt their happiness – such beauty, such easy confidence. While Christmas seemed so far away to him, they were probably heading off to a college party somewhere.

He turned and walked back to the bridge, where he paused. Across the meadows, the mist was thickening, muffling the sound of the traffic beyond. He shivered and then kept going towards his car, and the road that would lead to his empty house.

Chapter Two

He reached out an arm and fumbled for his watch. Shit, half past seven. Why hadn't his alarm gone off?

It was Saturday, that was why. With a small sigh of dawning relief, he turned on the radio and curled into the duvet. Drifting in and out of sleep, he caught half-stories seeping into his brain. Until he heard the word '*Schmaltz*'.

'*So, John, that sounds like challenging times ahead for Grimley's, one of Britain's oldest manufacturers.*'

He was awake now.

'*Thanks Justin. And now it's time for Thought for the Day with the Reverend...*'

Stephen switched the radio off, got out of bed and drew back the curtains on soggy leaves, rotting in his driveway. He had a thought for the day. It wasn't repeatable.

He padded downstairs to make a cuppa, but his fridge was a desolate wasteland, and he groaned as he recalled finishing the milk last night. The weekly shop couldn't even wait until after breakfast.

When he returned from the supermarket, he gathered up the assorted free newspapers and junk mail which had accumulated during the week and threw them into the recycling bin. A small card had dropped to the floor. Keith and Michelle at number twenty-four, inviting him to a drinks party this evening. He hadn't noticed that earlier. The smarter end of the road. When had he last spoken to them? And they weren't friends, more just acquaintances. He stuck the invitation on the fridge door, and then crammed ready meals into the freezer – he would think about it later.

Munching his way through a worthy but dull bowl of high fibre cereal, he heard the pundit previewing the afternoon's football on the radio, explaining that the secret to Tottenham's recent success was their 'bouncebackability'. That was something he had always possessed – until now, maybe. He should leave the croissant till later and get out there for his Saturday morning run. He put on the new tracksuit his sister had bought him for his fortieth. It looked OK on him. No middle-age spread; a full head of hair. Things could be worse. And when he felt his breakfast had slid down sufficiently, he ventured out into a grey morning which had turned to drizzle.

Taking his normal route along the towpath by Middleton Canal, he fell into a rhythm. *Bounce-back-abil-ity, bounce-back-abil-ity.* Maybe Schmaltz would be the shot in the arm he needed, open up new possibilities here. Obviously he wouldn't get the top job now, but he might at least be able to hang onto what he had. But as he ran past a pile up of discarded supermarket trolleys, and another one with its nose protruding from the canal, the rain intensified and so did his doubts. What if they did get rid of him? There was nothing decent within fifty miles, if you discounted FastGro Fertilisers and Burton's Boilers. And he wanted very much to discount them, even on the remote chance that fifteen years marketing chocolate would qualify him for a career in compost or plumbing. But he knew what he risked if he had to move further afield. The fragile, limited time spent with his kids could be stretched to breaking point.

Back home, in his dressing gown, he threw his soaked running gear into the washing basket and gathered up the shirts, socks and briefs scattered around his bedroom. In Kate's room, under the crumpled duvet, he found the soft tartan pyjamas she'd worn last weekend, sitting next to him on the sofa, eating pizza and watching *Miss Congeniality*. Her night to choose the film. Jake's grumpy little face had relaxed eventually. He briefly buried his face in the pyjama top before adding it to the basket. The smell of Kate, and margherita pizza. He needed to stay here and make this takeover work somehow – assuming he was given a chance.

By eight o'clock in the evening, he had poured himself a second glass of Malbec and emptied another packet of Farmer's Market chorizo and truffle crisps into a bowl. Well, it was Saturday. But the invitation had followed him through to the sitting room and was perched on the mantelpiece. Keith and Michelle's do would be like any other neighbour's party. The couples would arrive with tales of the babysitter being late and make their excuses to leave at eleven because the babysitter needed taking home. Another old episode of *Lewis* was about to start. He could order a Chinese – they'd deliver it for an extra couple of quid. He stood up to close the curtains against the rain still spattering on the windowpane. And as he turned on the TV, he caught sight of himself in the mirror behind the invitation; unshaven, glass in one hand, remote control in the other.

*

He should have trusted his instincts on this one. Standing in the elegant Victorian hallway, with a glass of Prosecco, he peered into the crowded sitting room in search of a familiar face. He'd stuck it out thirty minutes already, most of it spent with Ron

Fletcher from number fifty-six bending his ear about signing a petition in favour of residents' parking permits. How soon could he go home without it looking odd? *Match of the Day* was on at twenty to eleven.

He put on a fixed smile, aimed at nobody, feigning enjoyment. What the hell, he would launch in. He spotted Cameron and Moira, the Scottish couple from down the road. At least Cameron was more likely to talk sport than parking schemes. And they weren't talking to anyone else. Twenty minutes' chat with them, and if it didn't lead anywhere more interesting, he would make his escape.

Cameron, muscular and ruddy faced, looked relaxed in a maroon and white hooped rugby shirt. Moira was petite and tense, with a dark, immaculately cut bob. She stood slightly apart from her husband, staring at her empty glass.

'Hi, Steve.' Cameron slapped Stephen on the back. 'Those Bingo Bars flying off the shelves? Not seen you for weeks.' It didn't seem like the bad news about Grimley's had reached this neighbourhood yet.

'All fine, thanks, Cameron. Been working too hard as normal but apart from that, all good. How are you, Moira?'

Before Moira could reply, Cameron interjected. 'Moira has just been haranguing me for not helping get the kids to bed before we came. You don't have that stuff to worry about, eh mate? Lucky man.' He winked.

'It doesn't seem to be a big worry to you, Cameron,' said Moira. 'You hardly know what the children's bathroom looks like.' She was still not looking at him. Cameron gave a shrug of indifference.

'Tell me, Steve, what do you think of this parking permit fiasco? First the bloody council put my taxes up, even though they only empty my bins once a fortnight, and now they want to charge me for parking in my own effing road.'

Stephen placed his glass on a side table. 'Actually, sorry, I'm just going to grab a plate of food before it runs out. I'll be back.' He needed to go somewhere, anywhere. The sanctuary of a locked toilet, just to regroup, then he could enact his escape plan.

He walked upstairs. This was a much grander house than his own, the kind he could have been living in by now if not for the divorce. At the end of the landing, a woman was leaning on a banister, checking her phone. A little younger than most of the partygoers, probably about thirty, and notably unadorned in contrast to the jewellery-fest downstairs, wearing a crimson blouse, jeans and ankle boots. She slipped the phone into a shoulder bag and turned towards him with the hint of a smile. Her jet-black shoulder length hair was tucked behind delicate ears.

'Hi, are you queueing?' he asked.

'I am,' she said, and then in a more hushed tone, 'Isn't it weird how long some people can take in there?'

He laughed. 'Oh well, on the bright side, I've struck up many a fascinating conversation waiting to use the bathroom at parties.'

Why on earth had he said that?

She looked amused. 'Oh, really? So where are you on the meaning of life, then?' She had a warm voice, with just the hint of a Northern accent.

'Well, good question,' he said, noting with relief that the bathroom door was opening. Ron Fletcher came out, fortunately without stopping.

'Ah, shame we didn't get very far,' she said.

When she left the bathroom, she smiled at him for a second, without saying anything, then headed downstairs, leaving the merest note of a vanilla scent.

Was that it? The one moment of potential in the whole evening, leaning on a banister waiting for a pee he didn't need? And he'd come out with a line like that?

Back in the hallway a gaggle of shiny happy people were involved in raucous conversation. She was standing there too, on her own. Holding a glass of orange juice and watching the people around her.

Stephen found himself at her side, shouting, 'Hello again. Where were we?'

'We were not getting far on the meaning of life,' she shouted back. He thought she looked relieved to see him. The noisy group were making their way through to the kitchen.

'I felt you were stalling,' she continued, more quietly. 'In fact, I reckon you were saved by the bathroom door opening.'

He laughed. 'No, I could have gone with it, honest.'

Suddenly he was alone with her.

'Have you tried the food?' she asked. 'It's pretty good.'

'No, I'm fine. So, how do you know Michelle and Keith?'

'I don't know them. I'm friends with Greg and Jane, neighbours of theirs. I'd planned to see them this evening but then they got invited to this. I did offer to babysit for them, but they insisted on asking Michelle if I could tag along.' She glanced towards the sitting room. 'I think they've got cornered by someone.' Suddenly she looked very much like a woman regretting her choice of Saturday night entertainment.

'Oh, right, I'm a neighbour as well, but I don't think I know Graham and Jane – where do they live?' He was boring himself.

'Number thirty-two. It's Greg, not Graham. He plays tennis with Keith.' A woman in a silver halter-neck top passed them to go upstairs. 'I think I've misread the dress code here – which isn't the first time. It's very glam in this road, isn't it?'

'Maybe at this end.'

'I'd just like to say that if I'd known it was going to be like this, I could have sparkled with the best of them.'

He didn't doubt it.

'Don't worry, it took me by surprise too,' he said. 'I mean, obviously if I'd known, I'd have worn my tiara.'

'But of course,' she replied, deadpan. She looked beyond him towards the sitting room again, tucking a strand of hair back behind her ear.

Try something.

'So, if you could only save one track on your desert island, what would it be?' he asked. God, where did that come from?

She turned back to him with a vague smile. 'Sorry?'

'I was asking, if you could only save one record, to play on your desert island, what would it be?'

'Ooh, let me see. That's a difficult one.' She was engaged now.

'Yes, I thought so. It's just that, so far this evening, I've only heard diverse views on the benefit of parking permits. I mean, I'll talk about anything, but I've got this hunch, I don't know why, that you might not be that interested in residents' parking.'

She raised her eyebrows. 'You've had that too? I'm an agnostic on that issue, I think. "Picture This" by Blondie.'

'Wow, I didn't see that one coming. Well before your time, I'd have thought.'

'Er, just a bit. My dad was a fan. It's my inheritance track, I suppose.'

'Well, good choice. Great lyrics,' he said.

'I agree. So go on, give us a verse then.'

'You really wouldn't want to hear me sing, believe me,' he laughed.

'That's a pity. When it sounds like you're familiar with Ms Harry?'

'Yeah, not personally. Is your dad still a closet punk rocker then?'

Had he gone too far? She'd said inheritance track. Her father might be dead for all he knew.

'I wouldn't call Blondie punk,' she said with a frown. 'More new wave, don't you think? Or at least they were at the time, I'm told. I do rather like the thought of the old man being a closet punk rocker, mind, but he's had to curb some of his wilder excesses, given the day job.'

'Why, what does he do?'

'He's a Church of England bishop. Or was – just retired. The General Synod is not a hotbed of punk – or even new wave.'

'Well, I'm pretty sure I've never met a bishop's daughter before,' he laughed. What was that old gag? She was only the bishop's daughter…

'Yes, that's what they all say.' She gave him a stern look. 'I've heard all the jokes, by the way, just in case you were thinking of one. What would your choice be?'

'Oh, I don't know. Let me think…'

'Hah, you put me on the spot, but you haven't even thought about it yourself?'

'Maybe "Babylon" by David Gray.' A memory of Laura, that holiday in Sardinia not long before Kate was born.

'Oh, very soulful,' she said, her brown eyes now more concerned. 'But mixed memories, I feel?'

'Yes, I suppose so.' Was it that obvious? He let the conversation lapse for a moment, regret still able to take him unawares.

Her face broke into a relaxed smile, acknowledging her friends returning from the sitting room.

'Hi, Rachel, are you going to introduce us?' the woman asked.

'Er, yes.' She turned to him, blushing slightly, with a questioning look.

'Stephen,' he said. 'Stephen Carreras.' Only his mother called him that. Why hadn't he introduced himself as Steve, like he normally did? He shook their hands heartily.

He sensed her – Rachel – watching him. She was the quietest of the group as he enquired about whether the tennis club was very popular, how often they got to play in winter, and several other things he didn't care about. He could still do this whenever he wanted to – switch on the charm.

Eventually Greg asked him, 'How often do you play then, Stephen?'

'Oh, I haven't played for years. Football was always more my thing, really.'

Rachel burst out laughing. 'I can't believe you've had us talking about tennis for ten minutes and you don't even play.' A note of mockery again, but he felt it was good-natured.

Greg checked his watch. 'I'm afraid we must be going already. Got a babysitter to take home. And we can take you at the same time, Rachel, unless you want to stay?'

'No, that would be good. I could do with an early night too,' she said, without looking at Stephen.

The couple walked into the kitchen to say their goodbyes to the hosts, leaving him with her by the front door.

'Well, it was good to meet you, and not talk about parking permits,' he said.

She laughed. 'Yep, definitely a relief. Enjoy the rest of the party. I should say goodbye to Michelle and Keith too.'

He was losing her.

'You're not staying with Graham and Jane for the weekend then?'

'No, going home tonight, and he's still called Greg.'

'Oh, yes, sorry. And do you have a nice lazy Sunday planned?'

'I wish. I'm helping to prepare lunch for about eighty people at church tomorrow, hence the early night. And then spending the afternoon rehearsing for the Advent carol service – and Lord, do we need a rehearsal.' She gave him a mischievous look. 'And men. We need men. I was thinking, with a name like Carreras…'

'Oh no, no way. Like I said, you really wouldn't want to hear me singing.'

'OK, it was worth a try,' she said, and he thought he detected a little knot of disappointment on her brow. He was struggling for a follow-up now. He didn't know anyone who went to church. Although she was the bishop's daughter.

'Which church?' he asked, as if it would mean something to him.

'Just my local, Saint Anselm's, over in Carnforth – the non-glam side of town.' She drank the last of her juice, her throat pulsing lightly above the one opened button of her blouse.

'So when is it, then? I mean just as a spectator, not a participant.'

She looked surprised for a moment, but then her face brightened.

'It's seven o'clock next Friday evening.' She hesitated. 'But it will be full by about quarter to. If you fancy it, just turn up. I'll keep an eye out for you.'

'Oh, right,' he said, trying to sound non-committal.

She checked him over with curious eyes for a moment more, before turning to join her friends in the kitchen. He watched her go, the scent remaining with him in the empty hallway. It was definitely vanilla.

Stephen opened the door and slipped out. He walked back along the deserted street; the rain had turned to sleet, lit up by the streetlamps' glow. At least he would catch *Match of the Day*. He might even have a nightcap.

Of course he wouldn't go to the service. On Friday evening he'd be picking up the children for his last full weekend with them before the scraps Laura had left him with at Christmas. So it wasn't an option, even if he wanted to go. Which he didn't.

Back home, just as he was about to turn the football on, he caught his reflection again in the sitting room mirror, shaking his head in amusement. Had a woman just asked him out? But it was to a church, for God's sake.

Chapter Three

'How are you doing out there this morning? It's Monday, the first of December – only twenty-four shopping days to Christmas.'

Stephen groaned at the DJ on his car radio, as he turned off the ring road towards Grimley's. He didn't need another Christmas reminder. Twenty-four shopping days? A hell of a lot of working hours, more to the point.

Sometime in the next three weeks he would have to give some thought to presents.

Jake had already declared that he just wanted money this year. It felt a bit mercenary for a twelve-year-old. Which Christmas was it when they spent the whole day together building that toy castle, son nestled up against father? Kate was more problematic. Laura had always been good at knowing their daughter's mind when it came to presents. That first Christmas after they split, she had agreed to still buy as Mum and Dad, keep up appearances. But as soon as Tristran got his feet under the table, she'd told Stephen he should fly solo.

The cheery jock escorted him into the Grimley's car park. *'Now here's an oldie but goodie. It's Phil Collins with "Another Day in Paradise".'*

Carol Coolidge was already by his office door, coffee in

hand, talking on her phone. She smiled at whoever she was talking to.

'Got to go, babe, speak later.'

The smile faded as she looked at Stephen. She was immaculate as ever, in a tailored dark suit, with her blonde hair tied in a matching ribbon.

'Morning. You look like you're waiting for me,' he said.

'Yeah, needed to catch you early.' She had always possessed a disarming ability to make it sound like her time was more important than his. He should have guessed Carol would be quick off the mark in wanting to establish the implications of the takeover.

She sat herself down in one of the chairs at the small meeting table and began tapping her foot, her face expressionless.

'So, how was the weekend? Do anything interesting?' he asked.

'Munich Christmas market. Sublime.' A smile flitted across her face at the recollection.

He could just imagine her in a boutique hotel in Munich. Stepping barefoot across the bedroom to throw open the shutters on a sunlit courtyard. He was sure the weekend in Germany would have been crisp and clear. And no doubt with the 'babe' she'd just been speaking to.

'So, what did you want, Carol?'

She slipped an envelope across the table.

'Sorry, this seems very old school to me, but I gather from HR it's still required. I'm resigning, to join Oyster Inc as a director. They want me to start as soon as possible, and I expect you'll want me to work my full notice period, so I wanted to get this in straight away.'

'Wow.' Stephen puffed out his cheeks. 'Are you totally sure about this? You did hear about the takeover on Friday, didn't you? Or were you in Germany already?'

'Yeah, I heard while I was there,' she said. 'Why do you ask?'

'Well, there could be big opportunities now here, with Schmaltz.'

She didn't look convinced. Then again, neither was he.

'No, I've made up my mind. I want a new challenge. And I need to be in London, not in Middleton.'

So that's how it was then. If she wanted out, he wouldn't stand in her way. She was the best he had, but she wasn't God's gift to marketing. Just thought she was. She hadn't done *that* well this year, since he'd promoted her to Munchy Moments brand manager, and could certainly have done more if she hadn't been so focused on her next career move.

'Well, I think you're making a big mistake, but obviously it's up to you. I can probably let you go early. I'll let you know in due course. Now, I need to get on, Carol.' He stood up to indicate the meeting was over. For a moment, her shoulders seemed to sag a little. But then she rose and with a terse 'Good, I'm glad that's settled,' she turned and left the room.

Stephen closed the door behind her and kicked his wastepaper bin, sending it spinning across the room. Sandra, sat at her desk on the other side of the glass partition, looked in at him for a moment, and then resumed her typing.

He plugged in his laptop and wandered out to the coffee machine, still brooding. More than four years now since it happened. The foolishness for which he had paid with his marriage and his kids and his house, while for her it had been merely a footnote in her career development. And now she was leaving him in the shit while she went on to bigger things. And at Oyster Inc, of all places. Grimley's own ad agency. They had a bare-faced cheek, head hunting among their own clients. He'd noticed at the summer party how Zachary Beavis and their other senior people had smarmed all over her. Now he knew why.

He returned to his office with the coffee to find her orange blossom scent still lingering. He wouldn't see her again, once she moved to London. Ever. He scrolled through his email inbox mindlessly, until the *Marketing Now* daily digest demanded his attention.

SCHMALTZ TAKEOVER LATEST

A middle-aged man with closely cropped hair and rat-like eyes stared at him accusingly in monochrome. He was seated on a wall against an urban skyline, arms folded, wearing an open-necked shirt and braces.

He looked like one mean bastard.

Stephen scrolled down to read the story.

SCHMALTZ EURO ASSAULT

Marketing Now can reveal that US confectionery giant Schmaltz has appointed Brad Hardman to spearhead its takeover of ailing British firm Grimley's.

Hardman will head up Schmaltz Europe, which will be operational from January, merging the confectionery businesses the Americans have acquired over the past two years, now across nine European countries. Paris will be the base for the new European HQ. According to industry insiders, Hardman is committed to integrating Grimley's troubled business into the European fold.

Hardman, 52, was recently named President of the Year by Business Week magazine, for taking discount pet food chain Pet's Paradise from near bankruptcy to become one of the most profitable retailers in the US market. He built his reputation as a ferociously tough operator at Paradise, introducing dramatic cost-cutting exercises and a cultural change programme to achieve their number one position.

An analyst at investment bank AGZ commented: 'It's a highly significant move by Schmaltz to recruit Hardman, who has an evangelical zeal for reform. It will be fascinating to watch him harmonise these European companies, and it will definitely not be business as usual. As Hardman takes charge across Europe, he will no doubt appoint his own man to manage the troublesome UK business.'

Stephen sipped his coffee, staring at the face. Once again, nice to have it confirmed by the trade press. And it might be fascinating for this investment banker, watching from outside the goldfish bowl. Inside the bowl, it looked like a piranha was about to come swimming.

Oscar Newte burst into his office. '*Alors*, your marketing rag seems to have got a story right for *une fois*,' he announced, throwing his printed copy of the story across the desk to reveal the news, oblivious to the fact that Hardman's face was still on Stephen's screen.

'How do you know they got it right? First I've heard of it.'

'Ah, *mais oui, c'est vrai, mon ami*. I've known about Hardman for a while, but I was sworn to secrecy. Was discussing him in Paris only a few days ago. Good news, though, eh?' He had a satisfied smile on his face.

So Newte was definitely in on this, as Stephen had suspected. The scheming bastard had actually been in Paris discussing the takeover, in advance of his revelation at the Cambridge away day. That explained his latest affectation of slipping schoolboy French into every conversation.

'What do you know about him?' Stephen asked, trying to remain calm.

'You must have heard about PP?' Oscar snorted.

'PP?'

'*Mais non*, you haven't heard of PP, *évidemment*.' His eyes rolled in disbelief. 'Pet's Paradise. The best performing stock on the Dow last year. What do you read, old boy?'

'Over the last twelve months, Oscar, I've only managed one badly written thriller. Got any recommendations?'

Newte wasn't listening. He was in full flow. 'This guy Hardman, he'll go through this place like a dose of salts. Hang on to your hat – it's going to be a bumpy ride.'

'Ah, another roller coaster. What a surprise. Care to be more specific about the implications? It says here he's going to be managing the whole shebang, but sounds like he has someone else planned for us specifically in the UK. Any idea who, Oscar, as you are presumably on the inside after your Paris trip?' Sarcasm was Stephen's only weapon, but it didn't penetrate.

'Heaven knows,' Newte said. 'But if you spent time following this stuff as you should, you would know that he ran PP as a famously lean operation. It's the classic back-to-basics strategy in extremis. Cut the crap and smell the money.'

'Sounds delightful,' Stephen laughed cynically. Newte, a man of distinctly rotund appearance, was joyfully embracing the idea of new owners cutting out the fat.

But now the pompous oaf was off, strutting around the marketing department as if he owned the place, waving the article in front of bemused faces, no doubt proclaiming the good news of Hardman's coming to one and all.

Stephen stood, hands in pockets, gazing out on his team through the glass. He wondered again how many of them would be here this time next year, himself included. The voice of a sports commentator, sounding suspiciously like John Motson, had been popping into his head recently with an ongoing analysis of his life.

'Oh my word, the boy Carreras is attempting something really difficult here, holding onto his own job and any remaining talent in the face of this Schmaltz takeover. In ice-skating parlance, it's very much the equivalent of a triple axel salchow, which has a particularly high

degree of difficulty. And to top it all, isn't that the company finance director holding him by the balls?'

Sandra knocked on the door tentatively.

'Sorry to bother you again, Steve, but lots of the team have been asking me if there's a plan yet for the department Christmas party. Remember you were going to get back to me? To agree a date and a venue? It's just we've left it very late this year and we're all worried we might struggle to find somewhere nice – like La Belle Époque again? And we're all hoping we can do it on Thursday the eighteenth, when we've got the salary reviews out of the way.' Her face was lit with optimism.

Salary reviews? Her naivety was touching. He scrolled through dates in his diary.

'Well, if it's to be in that last week before Christmas, it will have to be the Friday,' he said. 'That's the only evening I'm free, as I've got to be in the Dumfries factory on the Wednesday and Thursday.'

Sandra's smile evaporated. He knew they would all be angling for the Thursday night – and an excuse for a day off, hung over, on Friday.

'Oh, and will you book something, Sandra? But no more than about thirty quid a head. Somewhere a bit less formal this year.'

Sandra looked even more disappointed. 'I suppose we might just about get a deal on the upstairs room in the Old Ship for that,' she said doubtfully, probably hoping he would reconsider when faced with this prospect.

'Ah well, needs must. Don't want our new owners to think we're being profligate, do we?'

He knew Sandra would be perfectly happy for the new owners to think whatever they liked, just so long as it meant escaping plated roast turkey at the Old Ship.

Chapter Four

Stephen remained in his car, in the darkness. He could still
go home. He didn't need to be here. A couple and their two
teenage children, all wrapped up against the cold and chattering
to each other happily, walked past him and disappeared inside.
A further reminder of what he was missing. Typical Laura,
calling to say that he couldn't pick the children up tonight after
all because 'the whole family' had been invited to the Harrisons'
for Friday night supper. He was family, not bloody Tristran. And
the deal with the children was every other weekend, from Friday
evening to Sunday evening. She was twisting that arrangement
with increasing regularity these days, whenever it suited her.

The pub was still an option. Danny Allsop had stuck his
head round the office door at half five to say the Purchasing
lads were going for a starter in the Grimley's bar, but they would
probably be in the Crown by now.

The clock struck seven. 'I don't know why I'm doing this,'
he muttered into the chill night air, and walked head down into
the church.

'Good evening, welcome.' A bloke who looked about
sixty, and whose name badge on his blazer indicated he was
Terry, greeted him with a smile and an order of service leaflet.

Stephen's heart sank; the place was full, except for the front row. Had she said something about getting there early? He cast around desperately. No sign of her.

'You might want to sit down,' Terry chuckled, before a shuffling of feet and whispering from behind made Stephen turn around.

A stout grey-haired woman was staring at him fiercely through dark-framed spectacles. She was dressed in a white robe, but she didn't look very angelic. And she was at the head of a whole army of white robes, now rolling into the church through the open doors, their breath still steaming like a herd of cattle coming into the milking parlour. Shit, if he didn't move, he would be swept along to the front row whether he liked it or not, as that was clearly where they were heading, and they looked unstoppable.

There was one spare pew seat tucked away in the corner at the back, next to a guy on his knees in prayer. Or rather, half a spare seat. Stephen squeezed in, his neighbour opening his eyes to give him an inhospitable stare from behind a bushy beard. He looked a little younger than Stephen, and in his lumberjack shirt and jeans he cut a very different figure from the man on the door. Almost hipster by Middleton standards.

'Sorry,' Stephen whispered, manoeuvring for another inch of wiggle room but whacking his knee on the sharp pew ledge in the process. He managed to stop himself at 'f—'.

The toddler in front of him started to whine until his mother picked him up and held him over her shoulder, allowing him to fix Stephen with a beady eye and a furrowed brow, while sucking his thumb. The lights dimmed, and a headmasterly voice from the front of the church asked them to stand. The vicar, a dark-haired man of about Stephen's age and robed in white with purple adornments, was holding aloft a lighted candle, just visible between the toddler and a large bald head.

Visitors, he emphasised, were particularly welcome, and urged to stay for coffee afterwards. Stephen turned pointedly towards Mr Grump next to him. *There you are, mate, turns out I'm welcome after all, you uncharitable bastard.*

The vicar announced that they were celebrating Advent – a time of waiting, apparently. *That Advent calendar fiasco at work came flooding back. How could Perkins not have spotted that there was no window for the twenty-fourth before they distributed it?* He shuddered mentally at that embarrassing tabloid headline: *Christmas Goes Missing at Grimley's.*

'We're all waiting for something,' the vicar said. 'And I invite you now in a moment of silence to think about what it is you're waiting for expectantly.' *Silence was a bit of wishful thinking* as wriggle-bum in front was now moaning that he 'not like the man'. Judging from the disapproving frown aimed at Stephen, he didn't mean the vicar. But Stephen did manage to reflect for a moment on how he was waiting for Schmaltz to land like an asteroid on Planet Grimley and make everyone's life a bloody misery.

The vicar then explained that he was using the candle to light the first of four candles on a wreath, and that one more would be lit each week until Christmas. *Only three weeks away. There was a hell of a lot of water to flow under the bridge before this takeover.* Stephen's mind wandered to the backlog of staff appraisals he'd still not got round to, until a single voice brought him back into the church.

'O come, O come, Emmanuel,
And ransom captive Israel
That mourns in lonely exile here...'

He couldn't see the singer at all, as the choir was hidden by a pillar. But she sounded distinctly more cherubic than the malevolent angel who had led them up the aisle. And he had heard this strange, quirky tune somewhere else recently. Yes, about this time a week ago – the girl in Cambridge.

The voice sang the first verse alone: haunting, crystal clear. Then as the second verse started, the rest of the church joined in enthusiastically and the lights came up. The grumpy hipster next to him was well into it now, staring straight ahead with glassy-eyed fervour and singing lustily out of tune.

The toddler continued to eye Stephen accusingly, seemingly disappointed that he wasn't singing, but the service settled into a rhythm. A hymn, then someone from the congregation came forward to give a reading, then another hymn. Sometimes the choir sang on their own; on other occasions everyone was invited to accompany them – an invitation Stephen continued to firmly decline. At first the readings washed over him – nowadays he rarely stopped to listen to anything, his mind fast-forwarding to the next work hurdle. But then he heard the vicar say something about the Israelites being 'rescued from their infidelity'.

He glanced around. They were all listening with a complacent, contented look on their faces. Not much rescuing from infidelity required for this lot, by the look of it. Suddenly Laura was in his head again, avoiding eye contact in the divorce court, in that sober grey suit, her dark hair tied in a bun.

The choir processed along the aisle to the door of the church during the last hymn, still mostly hidden from his view. He couldn't spot her. She might have gone down with flu or something since last weekend. Or if she was here, she must be in some holy huddle, forgetting she had even suggested he come along. He was a fool.

He edged out from the pew while Mr Grump was still in reverent prayer on his knees. But it was difficult to make a quick getaway. Already, clusters of conversation were breaking out, blocking the doorway. Avoiding eye contact, he worked his way through the melee until he could feel the blast of cold air from the open doors. And a light touch on his arm.

She was wearing red boots this evening, just visible and incongruous beneath the white robe, and a bright red band held her hair firmly behind those delicate ears.

'So you're brave. You came.' She looked genuinely pleased to see him.

'Yes, hello again.'

Hell, that was vacuous. The words hung there.

'Sorry, I feel really bad because I said I would keep an eye out for you, and of course I hadn't thought about that being difficult, what with being in the choir.'

She was right, she hadn't thought it through, and had propelled him into this place where he knew nobody. But those brown eyes were seeking forgiveness.

'How out of tune were we, on a scale of one to ten?'

'I thought you sounded great. That soloist at the beginning was lovely.'

'Oh, yeah, Lila. She's brilliant, isn't she? Damn her,' she smiled. 'Ah well, I'm glad we got away with it.'

She glanced around, before her eyes settled on him again. 'I don't suppose you fancy staying for a drink, do you?' she asked.

He fancied her, not a coffee in a church hall.

'That would be great. Do you always do coffee after the service?'

'Um, yes... and we can stay for coffee if you want. But I was thinking you might prefer the pub around the corner.' She lowered her voice. 'I mean, I've tasted the coffee here.' She glanced down at her robe. 'Just let me slip out of this.'

Left alone to wait at the back of the church, he found himself trapped next to Terry, busily collecting hymn books as the congregation filed out.

'As you're standing there, can you give me a hand?' Terry's smiling face popped out from behind a pile of hymn books about to topple over at any moment.

'Actually, I'm just waiting for—'

'Thanks, that's great,' Terry said. 'Just over there.' He gestured with a nod of his head towards a cupboard. As Stephen took them from him, he spotted Rachel, now wearing a parka but still with her red headband, chatting with the grumpy hipster. He was transformed now, animated, making her laugh. With a loud and irritable 'Excuse me', Stephen made a path through a group loitering in front of the hymn book cupboard. He was a nobody here, marketing director reduced to book-carrier. By the time he had completed three trips back and forth, Rachel was no longer anywhere to be seen.

Terry beamed encouragingly. 'Nice job, thanks.' He shook Stephen vigorously by the hand. 'You want to help out on a regular basis? We can always use an extra pair of hands.'

'No, sorry, I'm just visiting, Terry.'

Maybe Terry could ask him why he was here in the first place, before trying to recruit him. Truth is, Tel, I'm a forty-year-old agnostic, and over the last few months I've started to feel ever more messed up. So if it's all the same with you, I will not be joining you for weekly evensong.

'Blimey, you're a fast worker.' Rachel reappeared, grinning. 'I can see you could be an asset to the local community.'

Now she was doing it too, daring to assume she had enrolled him to her clan. She cocked her head to one side and added, 'I was joking?'

*

It was rather a plastic pub which he'd never been in before – he didn't often venture over to this side of town. But nicely busy with a backdrop of convivial chatter. They pressed their way through to the bar, past a couple of middle-aged men who looked Rachel up and down. It felt exciting to be out with a woman again.

'What are you having?' she asked.

He couldn't remember Laura ever offering to buy the first round.

'No, let me,' he protested.

'No, you're all right. We like to incentivise first-time buyers here at Saint A's.' She smiled but only briefly. 'OK, I can see my jokes are falling a bit flat here,' she said, waving a tenner to try and get the barmaid's attention.

He needed a glass of wine. Maybe better make it a small one, not give her the impression he had a drink problem. She ordered herself an orange juice, same as she'd been drinking at the party. Didn't she drink? He scoured around for somewhere to sit, in vain.

'It's busy. Is it normally like this?'

'No idea. I'm not a regular. Anyway, we can prop this pillar up.' She raised a glass towards his. 'Cheers. And thanks again for coming. Blimey, it's warm in here.' She took off her coat, revealing a bright red blouse to match her headband.

'So did you enjoy the service? I love Advent, that sense of waiting, the symbolism of a light appearing in the darkness.'

She smiled encouragingly, but it was a pretty direct question. Stephen thought it best to overlook zealous Tel, the gloomy hipster and the wriggly kid.

'Well, it was definitely interesting.'

'Oh no, as bad as that?' she laughed, before a small cloud of hurt flashed across her face.

'No, I didn't mean "interesting" to sound negative. That one the choir sang about the apple tree, that was wonderful.'

'Oh yeah, that one always makes me want to cry. Not helpful when I'm supposed to be lead alto.'

'I'm going to make a confession here, Rachel. It's a long time since I've been in a church.'

'Mm, I always think it must be a complete mystery for the uninitiated. What took you to church the last time?'

Definitely not the moment to say it was his wedding. He hadn't told her he was divorced yet. 'You know, I can't remember.' Change the subject. 'I noticed you chatting to someone at the end who I happened to be sat next to.'

'Oh, Conrad? Yes, I've known him a long time. He was actively involved here a few years back. He's been living away, but he's just returned.' Her look suggested fondness for the uncharitable grump. 'He's quite a character, Conrad. And very keen – I mean as a Christian,' she smiled knowingly.

Stephen also had a feeling Conrad might be keen on something or someone else as well. He didn't want to consider that right now. Change the subject again.

'Anyway, Rachel, tell me what you do.' It was obvious ground, but he regretted it immediately, as she was sure to ask him the same. And he definitely didn't want to discuss his work on a Friday night.

She ran a small charity in Middleton called Action Stations, working with children and teenagers from broken homes. Stephen realised he was not listening very carefully to the detail, too busy thinking of the follow-up question, to postpone the moment when he had to talk about himself. It was something he knew he did when he felt nervous. He hadn't realised he was nervous. But there was evidently lots of evening and weekend work in Rachel's life, as well as the usual nine-to-five. Clearly someone who did good for a living. They were always intimidating. That sour-faced inner-city dentist at a party a few months back had practically accused him of single-handedly ruining the teeth of the UK population. And he'd had a sense of humour failure over Stephen's joke about keeping him in business.

'How about you?' She was scrutinising him.

'Sorry?'

'What do you do?'

'Oh, nothing so worthy, I'm afraid. I work in marketing.'

'What are you marketing?'

'Chocolate. Selling sugar to kids. Not very healthy.' He wasn't going to fabricate – she could think the worst of him.

Her eyes lit up. 'Ooh, Grimley's presumably? That's exciting. My uncle used to work there.' Mercifully it sounded like the takeover hadn't registered with her either. 'Any free samples?'

He laughed. 'Not on me, I'm afraid.'

'Seriously, if you did have any free samples, we could dish them out at After School Club. They need a sugar rush then. Or maybe I do. Although it does go straight to my thighs.'

He glanced down at her skinny jeans.

'Well, I'll see what I can do.' He was keen to move on again. Both their glasses were empty. He'd knocked that one back quickly.

'So, can I get you another orange juice?'

She consulted her watch. 'Sorry, Stephen, this will seem rude but I'm afraid I've got to be home in half an hour. My flatmate is finding life a bit hard going at the moment and I promised to do tea and sympathy with her over a bit of Friday night TV. But it's only five minutes on my bike from here, so I'll keep you company if you want a swift one. Although I know you've got to drive back.'

'No, don't worry, I should be going too. An early start in the morning.'

'What? On a Saturday?'

'Yes, well, it's complicated.' He was going to try and get some work done before he picked the kids up, but he didn't want to explain about them just yet either.

There was a moment's awkward silence. That moment before you asked for a second date – or didn't.

'Well, I hope you don't have to work too hard,' she said eventually. 'I'm so lucky, I get a week off now that tonight's out the way.'

'Don't tell me, some winter sunshine on a beach in Lanzarote?'

'Hardly. More like a damp week in Northumberland.' She hesitated for a moment. 'My six-monthly retreat.'

And there he was imagining her in a swimsuit. This was increasingly uncharted territory.

'Oh. Wow. What happens there, then?'

'Basically, I have a bit of a think and a pray. In the company of a few monks. Nothing too raunchy. Trying to think about the true meaning of Christmas and all that.' She pulled a face. 'Sorry, bit of a cliché. Just slipped out.'

It made his reflections on the flatlining Bingo Bars market share seem a touch shallow.

'OK, well, er, have fun,' he said. Was fun what you were supposed to have on a retreat?

It had turned into a foggy evening by the time he set off home, musing on the fact that as brush-offs go, providing a flatmate with tea and sympathy was pretty original. He could have done with some Chardonnay and sympathy.

Intriguing, witty and attractive. Very attractive, in fact. And not as pious as he'd feared, at least until that last comment about him driving. But still a God-fearing non-drinker, wedded to her good works. Shame. His parting shot had been a deliberately neutral 'thanks, that was nice'. But not 'maybe we can do it again' after that monk retreat thing, which was a bit weird. She had smiled and said she was genuinely pleased he had come along. He didn't think he'd offended her.

He ran through the conversation in his head, wondering if he'd said anything inappropriate. He was glad he hadn't answered that question about his last time in church, realising now that it hadn't been his wedding at all. His father's funeral. That would have been a bit of a downer.

As he focused on the white lines in the middle of the road, rising out of the fog to meet him one by one, he caught a glimpse of Brad Hardman's rat-like eyes in his rear-view mirror. And started to worry about losing his job, all over again.

Chapter Five

He hung his jacket and shirt on the back of the door, pulled off his shoes, and slipped out of his suit trousers, so that for a moment he was standing in nothing but a pair of light blue cotton briefs. From his computer bag he pulled out a pair of white chinos and a white shirt, ironed in haste at six this morning, but now crumpled again.

This was a tricky manoeuvre in a cubicle. He wriggled into the chinos, hopping from foot to foot, and put the same shoes back on. They didn't go with the outfit, but they'd have to do. After administering a quick spray of deodorant under each arm, he buttoned up the shirt and did the cuff links. It was probably the same shirt he'd worn to the party last year, the black-tie event at La Belle Époque. Bit different tonight. Last of all, he reached into the carrier bag Sandra had given him and pulled out the bright yellow scarf she'd run out to buy at lunchtime, along with the red floral-print umbrella she was lending him for the evening.

Stepping out into the empty washroom, he checked his appearance in the mirror as he washed his hands. Hopefully the five o'clock shadow around his chin and dark rings under his eyes were being exaggerated by the buzzing fluorescent light.

Well, it wasn't a bad effort, given that Sandra and her organising committee had only made the fancy-dress pronouncement two days ago.

The door swung open violently and Kevin Keeling, the sales director, burst in, whistling merrily. He put his hands on his hips, with a surprised grin on his face.

'Hello, Stevie mate, what's your game?'

'Department Christmas do, Kevin. Someone's bright idea to go for fancy dress. Come as your favourite cocktail.' He raised his eyes heavenward.

'Oh yeah?' said Kevin, laughing, as he unzipped and stood at the urinal, back to Stephen. 'What you going as then? Let me guess. No, on second thoughts, I give in already.'

'Pina Colada, mate.'

Turning his head, still in mid-pee, Kevin looked bemused. 'OK, mate, you're going to have to explain this one to me.'

'Pina Colada? White with a slice of pineapple on the rim?' He pointed to the scarf. 'And one of those twirly parasols?' He held the umbrella aloft. Was he really having this conversation?

'I wouldn't know. More of a lager man myself,' Kevin sniffed.

'Yes, so am I, Kevin,' Stephen said irritably. It was Sandra who had suggested the cocktail – and the outfit.

Kevin sniggered. 'Tell you what, though, I'm not sure you'll be pulling any of those women in your department dressed like that. But you never know, eh?' He gave a conspiratorial wink, zipped up and walked to the door, where he hesitated.

'Favourite cocktail, eh? Isn't there one called a long slow comfortable screw against the wall? I'd have gone for that myself, especially as a leaving present for Carol Coolidge.' With another wink he was gone.

What was it Carol had said about Kevin? *Five minutes in his presence and you feel like you need a shower.*

Stephen returned to his office through a deserted department. Fair enough. It was the last day for everyone before Christmas, and after recent events he could hardly blame them for heading off to the Old Ship already. Newte's all-staff email today had confirmed the building would be closed from now until Tuesday 6 January, for refurbishment to coincide with the Schmaltz takeover, and was strictly off-limits. The man was increasingly behaving like a tinpot dictator.

It would be a relief to be out of here, even if Christmas with his sister and brother-in-law wasn't filling him with deep joy. And of course, the extended break had at least been well received by the team. Some even seeing it as a sign of positive things to come from Schmaltz. But something about this refurbishment made him anxious. He had attempted to find out from Jennie Jacobs what was going to be changed, but she had played the classic HR director's straight bat.

He gathered the documents he needed to work at home over the holiday and went out into the cold, damp evening. He was grateful for the scarf, wrapped tightly around his neck. And as it started to drizzle, the floral umbrella might have been handy. But that would stay firmly under wraps until he got to the Ship. It would get too many odd looks in Middleton High Street.

He trudged towards the pub, wondering what the mood would be like. He'd done his best to toe the party line at everyone's salary review, carefully explaining that 'review' did not automatically mean 'increase', and that, although there would be no rise or bonuses this year, this was all about 'securing the health of the business as they embarked on this new adventure'. Newte had fed the other directors the lines they needed to use, and Stephen felt he had little choice but to follow them parrot fashion, minus the pomposity. At least nobody else had resigned in the last month, not since Carol. Although there would probably be a few pondering their future over the Christmas dinner.

The atmosphere was upbeat as he entered the upstairs room reserved for the party, unfurling the umbrella and a fixed smile. Sandra was first to greet him at the door in her role as party organiser, nicely lubricated already. 'Steve!' she screamed raucously, tottering towards him, practically bursting out of a fuchsia dress. Holding a glass of wine in one hand, she declared herself to be a Singapore Sling before grabbing both ends of his scarf with her spare hand and yanking him towards her for a kiss on the cheek under a sprig of mistletoe hanging from a beam. Still, before starting on the Pinot Grigio she had evidently put her initial despair over the venue behind her and made a decent job of commanding decorative operations. Streamers bedecked the room and flashing lights spangled from an artificial silver Christmas tree in the corner. 'I Wish It Could Be Christmas Every Day' was blasting out from a pair of tinsel-draped speakers.

Carol was leaning against the wall nearby, in conversation with her assistants in the Munchy Moments team. She was wearing a black mesh bodysuit that left very little to the imagination and strappy black sandals. He had no idea what cocktail she was, but of course she looked delicious.

'What exactly are you?' she asked him, sipping her glass of bubbly, a smile playing around her lips.

'I'm a Pina Colada, Carol. And you?'

'Black Russian. It gave me an opportunity to get this little number out. Not worn this since I was about eighteen.'

He looked around for the drinks. He didn't want to talk to her.

'I'll see you later, Carol,' he said tersely.

'Yeah, we're sitting next to each other at dinner. So we can discuss my news.' She raised a glass. 'Chin chin.'

He didn't know what she meant, and he didn't care. Grabbing a glass of wine, he started to work his way around the room. For a few hours, fuelled by alcohol, the muscle memory of how to play the extrovert marketing director would kick in. It was just a technique. He took the teasing over his outfit in good heart. Even when Tony Perkins became the umpteenth person to ask what he'd come dressed as, he suppressed his irritation.

'I should have thought it was perfectly obvious I'm a Pina Colada, Tony. What else could I possibly be? No, on second thoughts, don't answer that.'

And in turn he mocked the disappointing lack of effort by the other men, standing around in groups of three or four in their jackets and jeans, sipping pints.

Carol and her entourage appeared to have usurped Sandra as party hostesses, moving among everyone and refilling their glasses. By time they sat down to eat, he checked his watch for how long he had been there. Only an hour. How many times had his glass been refilled? He couldn't remember.

He had Sandra to his left and Carol to his right. He would have to talk to her.

'So, Carol, what's this news you wanted to discuss?' he asked, already thinking he was tripping over his words a little.

She looked surprised. 'Oh, I thought someone would have told you. I've turned Oyster Inc down after all, at least for the moment. I had a long discussion with Oscar this week and he's promised me an interesting opportunity here after the takeover. Said he's sworn to secrecy but seems to think I'll be pleased.' She sipped from her glass and licked her lips. 'In fact, very pleased. So Oyster Inc will have to wait. Zachary Beavis still desperately wants me, but I'll see how things work out here and if the new role doesn't tick the right boxes, they will still be there for me. I'm sure I'll have a stint on the agency side at some point in my career.'

Stephen stared at her.

46

'You really didn't know?' She laughed.

'No, Carol, I didn't.'

'Ah, sorry.' She shrugged her shoulders. 'I thought Oscar would have told you. I imagine he's been too busy to pass it on since we agreed it. I know he's been away again this week. Anyway, there you go. I hope you're pleased.'

Before he could reply, Sandra blew a pink party horn in his face and draped an arm round him. 'You're a good man, Steve,' she slurred, pulling him towards her so she could slap another big kiss on his cheek. And by the time he'd escaped, Carol had stood up and moved away to grab another bottle of champagne.

Turkey was served alongside a mound of mushy vegetables. Party poppers were let off, and everyone appeared intent on drowning the sorrows of not getting a pay rise. There was a whiff of fatalism in the air. Two of the young likely lads started flicking sprouts at each other, and then Slade's 'Merry Xmas Everybody' heralded the volume being pumped up further. Carol bobbed up and down from her seat, hectoring the bar staff, but whenever she sat down, her bare, bronzed back seemed to be turned towards him as she held court with the women to her right. And he really didn't want to know more about what Newte had offered her tonight. Sandra was shouting something to him, but he had no idea what it was. Christmas pudding appeared, along with a round of rainbow-coloured shots.

Several sparkly-topped women pushed a few chairs to one side and started waggling their hips to Beyoncé. Stephen joined the male jeans brigade at the bar, watching the women dance, as Carol joined in. The posse of young brand managers looked transfixed by her. It was more relaxing to join them in an animated discussion about what was wrong with English football, clutching his bottle of Euro beer rather than a pint of lager, a concession to Christmas. Until Sandra pulled him away to dance cheek-to-cheek to 'Happy Xmas (War is Over)'.

A couple of the old stalwarts from the media planning department slipped away. He could leave now without being a complete party pooper. Job done. And if he didn't leave now, he would be in no fit state for the kids arriving tomorrow afternoon for their brief pre-Christmas get-together.

It was time to pay the bill, and if they wanted any more to drink, they would have to pay for it themselves. Bloody hell, it was supposed to be a modest evening, but it was going to be astronomical.

The room was positively spinning now, and he took care to keep at least one hand on the back of various chairs and then hold the banister firmly as he made his way downstairs to settle up at the main bar.

Carol emerged from the ladies, holding a long, fur-lined black coat.

'Hello Carol, are you going already, Carol?' He took care to enunciate, fixing his eyes on her. She laughed at him.

'I am indeed. My man's picking me up. You look like you've been kissing all the women, or rather Sandra's spent the night kissing you. You might want to have a check in a mirror before you go home.' Her look of amusement faded. 'You don't look too good.'

'I'm all right. Although it's been quite a last few weeks.'

'Has it? Anyway, that's me done for the year. I'll see you in Paris, I suppose.'

'Paris? Why Paris?'

'The conference? You haven't forgotten? God, you really are well gone. Don't worry, you are definitely invited.' She gave a tight little laugh. 'So, see you then.'

He made a move towards her sculpted, perfumed cheek but made only faint contact with his lips. She wasn't looking at him. Her face broke into a smile, the cool reserve slipping.

'Hi, babe,' she breathed softly, and Stephen realised she was addressing a tall, muscular, olive-skinned man in a white jacket and a stripy open-necked shirt.

'Hi, you ready to go? I'm parked outside on a double yellow.' He looked at Stephen for a moment, then put a protective arm around Carol's shoulder and walked her out of the pub.

Of course he hadn't forgotten Paris. The conference on 5 January to launch Schmaltz Europe. On the first working day of the new year, before the office re-opened here. He had only been told about it a couple of days ago and felt relieved that at least he wasn't being fired immediately. But he had assumed it would be senior managers only. Now she was going too. What exactly had Oscar offered her?

'There you go, mate.' The barman presented him with the bill. Nearly three thousand pounds, and that didn't include service. Fuckety fuck. He fumbled in his wallet for his card and when the machine asked him if he wanted to add a gratuity he declined. The barman gave him a look. Well, tough, mate.

At last he was free to go outside, breathe in the fresh air and walk home.

'Hi there, it's Stephen, isn't it?' A man with thick-rimmed glasses was standing in front of him, holding out his hand.

'Remember me?' He took off his glasses and smiled with an enquiring look on his face, as if this trick would reveal all. 'We met at Keith and Michelle's party a couple of weeks back, remember? We live on the same road as you. We were talking about tennis?'

Rachel's friend, the one whose name he kept getting wrong. 'Oh, yeah, Graham. Hi.'

'It's Greg. Hey, fancy meeting again. Actually, Jane and I are here with Rachel, who you met. We're just over there.' He pointed to a table in the corner, but Stephen didn't look. 'We forgot when we came out that we'd be competing with the office parties tonight. It sounded pretty lively up there.' He was sickeningly chirpy. 'We're about to leave but do come over and say hello.'

This was an unbelievably bad idea. Stephen glanced across as Rachel took the last mouthful of what looked like orange juice again, before both women stood up and started putting on coats, ready to leave. But Jane spotted him and waved, then touched Rachel's arm to draw her attention. It would look odd not to go over now.

'Stephen's been upstairs at a private office party – so now we know who was making all the noise,' Greg laughed, clearly pleased with his discovery.

He really wanted to be sick now. He didn't want to look at Rachel, afraid of the reaction he would get in this condition. Jane's lips were asking him something about his work, but he couldn't focus. Her eyes seemed to be zeroing in on his left nipple, where a damp beer stain had appeared. He excused himself and went outside, taking deep gulps of cold, rainy air. But Greg, a buzzing wasp who wouldn't go away, was there again, car keys in hand.

'You look like you could do with a lift home, sir. We can drop you off.'

'No, honestly, the walk will do me good,' he muttered. And if needs be, he could throw up in a suburban hedge somewhere on the way.

'No, I insist, it's no trouble.' Greg smiled. 'You aren't exactly dressed for the weather, are you?'

Rachel was already in the back seat, her hands tight in the pockets of her parka. They didn't speak to each other. After the interior light went off, Stephen sensed her turn towards him in the darkness, but she remained silent while Greg burbled away about the pub being under new owners. What were the chances of her being in this pub tonight? Well, this one was over, before it had ever really started. It was five minutes' drive, that was all. He just had to get home.

Now Greg was asking questions. What company was it that Stephen worked for again? What did he do? He managed monosyllabic answers, until Jane leant towards her husband and said, 'Sweetheart, I don't think he feels like talking.' It seemed to take forever with Greg taking an odd route, choosing to go down a road with speed bumps, every one felt in his gut.

Finally they drew up outside his house, prompting a last interrogation. How long had he lived here? Did he have children? He stumbled out into the middle of the road, said thank you, closed the door, and spewed all over his shoes, splashing the side of Greg's shiny car.

*

He flipped each pair of leggings along the rail, not knowing what he was looking for. There were two girls of about Kate's age doing the same thing, sniggering together.

Another wave of nausea rolled in with the latest jabbing pain in his head.

He was forty for God's sake. But this was the hangover of his student days, after too many sherbets in the union bar and a late-night curry. Why had he drunk so much? Knackered for weeks now, dreading the American takeover, telling people there were no pay rises, worrying about his own job. It had all come out.

'After something in particular, sir?' asked a voice behind him.

She was standing with her hands on her hips, clearly amused. Wearing the same red boots as she had in church.

He realised he was holding a pair of rainbow-striped leggings.

'I think my primary need is painkillers, but I appear to be in the wrong department.'

God, it was good to see her smile.

'I'm not sure those are really you.' She gave him a doubtful look. 'I think maybe something a little more subtle?'

'Ah, do you think so?'

'I mean, would you like a second opinion?'

'Hell, yes. Sorry, I mean yes, please.'

'So who *are* you looking for? Assuming they aren't for personal use?'

'Kate, my fifteen-year-old daughter.' It was the first time he had revealed his family to her. And suddenly he felt liberated, that there was no point pretending. 'I'm seeing my children this afternoon – to give them Christmas presents.' He waited for a reaction to this declaration of his divorce, but Rachel was already rifling through the rails. So he carried on.

'I'm already in the bad dad zone, leaving it this late. When I spoke to her mother yesterday, she said she'd like some new leggings. Everything else on the list accounted for already. Of course, if I'd sorted it earlier, I could have got them in five minutes online. But here I am.' With a headache that was going nowhere quick.

Rachel looked thoughtful. 'I don't know quite how to ask this, but – is Kate a very... self-confident young woman?'

'Er, I wouldn't say so,' Stephen replied. He worried sometimes that she was anything but self-confident now, compared with the little Kate she had been.

'In that case, you definitely ought to check out something a bit more subtle. Do you know when she wants to wear them?'

'Not really,' he faltered. His head was throbbing. Rachel's look said she'd thought as much.

'How about these?' She had picked out a pair of black ones with a single white sporty stripe. 'I reckon these are pretty versatile. I mean you *might* be all right with the rainbow look but it's high-risk in my book. What size is she?'

'Ah, another good question. I think this conversation isn't really playing to my competencies, Rachel.'

She was holding them against her thigh. They would look good on her. 'Is she taller or shorter than me?'

'About the same – er, maybe slightly taller? I'm not sure. I'll text her. I don't suppose you have time for a coffee while we wait?'

To his surprise she agreed. They crossed the road to Alfredo's, the one decent coffee bar in town, and she found a cramped space among the hordes of last-minute shoppers while he queued for the drinks. As he brought them over, she looked up from her phone and gave him a warm smile.

'Rachel, can I just say sorry – about last night? I mean, clearly you didn't find me at my most coherent.'

'Ah well, *c'est la vie.*' She looked amused. 'I was trying to leave you in peace, but Greg can be on the chatty side. It is true that vomiting over his car wasn't perhaps the best way to thank him for a lift home.'

He had a moment of panicky recollection. 'Er, it was just outside, wasn't it? I mean, I had shut the door…'

'Yes, you're all right. It was all outside. I think. I might call him a bit later – leave it a bit.' She sipped her coffee. 'So, moving on, plans for Christmas?'

He told her everything, confirming that he would only see his children today rather than at Christmas itself. He played down his anger with Laura, and his sadness at being with his sister's children instead of his own. But he could see that she got it. She listened. When had someone last listened?

Rachel was going to spend Christmas with her parents in the Home Counties, catching the train down there this afternoon. She had been in town doing last-minute present shopping for them as well, and gently rebuked him for sexism when he said he'd assumed that last-minute was the preserve of males. She was an only child, and it would be a quiet Christmas, with just her father's eccentric sister as a guest for lunch on the day itself. Like him, Rachel seemed more resigned to events rather than anticipating them with delight, and he sensed there was something about the family relationship that wasn't entirely right, but she didn't seem ready to tell him more. Her real enthusiasm was clearly about going away with a group from church to stay in a cottage in the Lakes over New Year.

Kate texted back with her size requirements, so they finished their coffees and went back to buy the leggings.

'Well, good luck,' she said as they left the shop. 'I hope we chose the right ones. I'd better get home and then down to the station.'

They faced each other for a moment in the bustle of Middleton High Street. He wasn't going to die wondering this time.

'So, can we meet again? In the new year?'

Her look was benevolent, but she hesitated a second too long.

'Yes, OK, give me your number. I'll call you. When I'm back from the Lakes, maybe?'

It sounded like a question, not an assertion. And she wasn't offering her number in return. He couldn't read her. She could have walked past him this morning as he searched through the leggings, choosing to ignore the embarrassing drunk from the previous evening. But she hadn't walked past. In fact, she had saved his morning. Yet he still didn't know whether she would ever contact him again or was simply taking a leaf out of the Good Samaritan's book.

Part Two

January to February 2015

Chapter Six

Kate was watching his left leg as they sat in the traffic jam. He was doing that twitching thing again. She turned to gaze out of the passenger window, without removing her earphones. He stopped twitching, but started drumming his fingers on the steering wheel instead.

They were going to be late. He had promised to have them back by ten o'clock, but there was no chance. It was already ten to, and the queue to get past the roadworks was barely moving. Not that anybody was doing any road work on a Sunday morning at the start of January.

Why did he feel guilty? It wasn't his fault that he had to go to this conference in Paris on a Sunday afternoon, and he already felt cheated of the few extra hours with his children. And did it really matter exactly what time this morning he returned them to their mother? But it was typical of Laura to come over all self-righteous. He recalled her look of disappointment when he'd reminded her that he wouldn't be able to keep them all day today. Then her insistence that if he absolutely must return them early, he needed to make it 'properly early', by ten, so she and Tristran could get on with their plans for the day, rather than hang around waiting for him. God, she made him feel like a delivery company. And she made the kids sound like an encumbrance, getting in the way of life with bloody Tristran. Tristran with an 'n', not an 'm'.

The temporary traffic lights were about fifty yards ahead. Going from red to green... and back again. And he hadn't moved.

'This is ridiculous on a Sunday morning,' he burst out, banging the steering wheel with the palm of his hand. 'What on earth's going on?' He wound down the window to stick his head into the drizzle but couldn't see what the problem was. He gave an exaggerated sigh and looked to his daughter for sympathy. But Kate's repeated nodding was simply an appreciation of whatever she was listening to. In the back seat, Jake was tapped into something under his chunky headphones that had rendered him catatonic.

He had told Laura about this trip before Christmas, and her initial reaction had been to disbelieve him. Bloody cheek. Since when did he go to Paris on business, she had asked, unable to resist pointing out that during their marriage the furthest he had managed was that conference on a boat sailing round the Isle of Wight. He had mentioned the takeover too, hinting that after this initial adventure, the Job Centre might be a more usual destination in the longer term. But he knew she hadn't taken it in. Why would she, unless it had implications for her own domestic arrangements? What exactly was the law on paying alimony if he was fired?

Jake suddenly burst out laughing – what was amusing him? But Kate removed her earphones and touched him gently on the knee.

'Are you all right, Dad?'

His voice broke slightly in reply. 'Yeah, love, I'm fine. I'm sorry, it's just that you know I promised your mother I'd have you back by ten, but this traffic is awful.'

'I wouldn't worry – it's not your fault.'

She was growing into a sensitive young woman. Emerging from the empathy bypass just as Jake was entering it head-on, even though Laura worried about her moodiness and lack of confidence. He didn't want to burden her with his unhappiness, and yet he wanted to reach out, to explain a little of how it felt. She would be the only human being that week who would ask him if he was OK.

'I am sad that we couldn't spend the whole weekend together. Still, I hope you do something nice with Mum today, and I'll see you again in a fortnight.' He tried to sound cheerful.

Neither of them said anything for a few seconds.

'I think Mum and Tristran have some healthy Sunday walk planned,' she said, with a grimace. She never sounded too enthusiastic about going back home after a weekend with him, but was that just part of the sensitivity? Somewhere beneath those innocent blue eyes, what did she really want to say to him? 'You fucked up, Dad', maybe? A few weeks ago, she had just slipped it into conversation, the devastating one-liner: 'Tristran seems to make Mum happy.'

They were inching towards the lights now. Kate rested her earphones on her lap and started fiddling with the latch on the glove compartment.

'So, Katie Carreras, what was the best part of Christmas then?'

She hesitated before a smile of recollection lit her face.

'I guess the hotel was pretty amazing. We had a jacuzzi in the room.' She stopped abruptly. 'But the leggings were the best pressie,' she added.

At last they were moving. Kate returned to her music, tapping a rhythm on her knee, and Stephen was left alone until they arrived in the village.

'Here we are.' He turned into the gravelled driveway, with plenty of space to park next to the dark blue BMW and the smaller, light blue VW Golf, lined up neatly next to each other. Classy white Christmas lights adorned the front of the house. Laura had always been nagging him to sort out better Christmas lights. Another Tristran triumph, no doubt. Evidently they were still in festive mode here, after their New Year's Eve do with their pretentious friends.

At last Jake emerged from his headphones, his hair springing up in unruly fashion. He had a rather unpleasant zit on his chin. Stephen would still have kissed him, given half the chance. Or at least a manly hug.

'Cheers, Dad.'

'No probs, matey, have a good week. And it's not a crime to text me?'

Jake slung his rucksack over his shoulder as he crunched across the gravel. His shirt was hanging out, and as he rang the doorbell he was still the little boy arriving home from school. There'd be a growth spurt soon, no doubt. Kate's movements were slow and deliberate. She tucked her mobile away into her shoulder bag, got out of the car and paused to wait for Stephen. She quickly wiped her eye and smiled weakly up at him. Stephen wrapped her against his chest and kissed the top of her head. Jake was ringing the doorbell a second time, more insistently this time, and it was the tall figure of Tristran who opened it.

'Oh, hi kids, in you come.' He was wearing a bright pink T-shirt, boxer shorts and flip-flops. In January, for God's sake. He scratched his head of greying tight curls, yawning as he held the door open for Stephen. It didn't look like there had been any rush to get here. The kids dropped their bags and went up to their bedrooms, leaving Stephen alone with Tristran in the hallway. It smelt of varnished floors and his sickly-sweet aftershave. Behind his bland exterior he was like a rutting stag, leaving his scent all over the place, making it clear this was his fiefdom now.

Laura flounced down the stairs in a gold and black dressing gown, sweeping a hand through her hair, windswept like it always used to look after sex.

'Oh, there you are,' she said. 'Did you text to say you were running late?'

'It's illegal, texting while you drive. Didn't you know that?'

'You could have called then. Haven't you got hands-free?'

Tristran was still there, checking his phone.

'This is the point where you might want to go elsewhere, eh, Tristran, while Laura and I exchange greetings?'

'Mm?' he looked up absent-mindedly. 'Oh, yeah, sure thing.' He flip-flopped up the stairs.

'I could have phoned but I didn't want to disturb you.' Stephen's glance deliberately followed Tristran. Enough already – just leave it.

Laura informed him that she would let him know about arrangements for the next few weekends when she and Tristran had made some plans. Oh, how she was going to milk this 'favour' she was doing him.

Tristran shouted across the landing: 'Katie, Jakey, we'll probably go for a walk in about an hour's time. Your mother and I are just chilling for a while.'

'Remind me again why you get to go to Paris?' Laura asked.

'It's still for a conference, Laura.'

'Oh, well, lucky you.' And then just before she closed the door on him, she looked him in the eye for a moment. 'Behave yourself.'

As he drove away, he glanced back to see if the children were waving from an upstairs window. Of course they weren't. They were back in their own worlds. And Laura wasn't remotely interested in his life. When he had started at Grimley's, he'd always tried to get home early enough for the evening ritual, reading the kids bedtime stories after Laura wrapped them in warm towels from the bath and sent them through for 'Daddy snuggles' together on the sofa. Then, when the kids were kissed and in bed, the two of them would sit down with a nice glass of wine and recount their days to each other. They even made a point of eating in their candlelit dining room – where she would have been staring into Tristran's eyes on New Year's Eve. And she always wanted to know about the motley collection of Grimley's characters. In the early days. Before he got too knackered and too late, and TV dinners became the norm.

'Bugger,' he swore out loud. The same set of roadworks. He considered reversing down the road to take the turn he had just passed, but a large white van appeared in his rear-view mirror. The driver lit a fag, wound down the window to rest his arm, and wore an expression which didn't encourage negotiation. He was stuck – and the queue on this side of the temporary traffic lights was longer than it had been on the other.

Behave yourself. She never let him off the hook, Laura. One indiscretion, four years ago. Well, two, but with the same woman. Whenever guilt bubbled up to the surface, he tried to convince himself again that Tristran Wanker Wrigley might have already been on the scene even then. After all, he and Laura had worked at the same estate agents at the time, hadn't they? She denied it, of course.

*

In the concourse at East Midlands Airport, a large posse of Grimley's managers clustered around a woman with bleached blonde hair. She was wearing a smart chocolate-brown jacket and skirt, flashing a perfect smile, and holding aloft a sign which said 'Schmaltz UK'.

It was truly happening.

She was Taylor, and she was from Orlando. One by one, she recorded their names. If only they really were a bunch of tourists gathering for a winter break.

'Hi Steve, welcome to Schmaltz, here's your boarding pass,' she beamed.

'42B? How many rows are there?' he asked, but Taylor had already moved on.

Stephen reckoned there were about forty of them in total, and only now, looking around the group, could he verify exactly which members of his marketing team had been invited. Nobody had informed him beforehand. Tony Perkins was here, and Jerry Collins, his favourite brand manager, had made the cut too. But only a couple of others. And there was no sign of Carol. Had she changed her mind again over Christmas, decided to join Oyster Inc after all? He wouldn't put it past her.

Jerry was obviously delighted to be here, bouncing around like an excitable puppy, talking to everybody. Stephen felt pleased for him but couldn't share his pleasure. It should have felt like a big adventure for him too, his first business trip abroad after all these years, but all he could think of was Brad Hardman lying in wait. And the fact that it was four o'clock on a Sunday afternoon, and he was back at work for the year when he should have been at the cinema with his kids.

'Can't think why the fuck we have to go there on a Sunday afternoon. What bloody difference would it have made if we had flown over on Monday morning?' Danny Allsop had found him and echoed his own silent thoughts. Danny's beer belly was overlapping his belt a tad more after the Christmas break, and he was bleary-eyed.

'And a Happy New Year to you too, Daniel. I trust you had a relaxing festive period?'

Danny looked underwhelmed. 'Yeah, it was all right, I suppose. Too much time with the bloody out-laws as usual.'

Taylor walked past them, counting heads. 'Still, I suppose there are some compensations for being here on a Sunday.' He nudged Stephen. 'She's a bit fitter than your podgy PA.'

'Danny, where were you exactly when HR ran that course on respecting gender differences at work?'

'In the pub, I expect. Actually, you could be well in there,' he sniggered. 'Or are you going to tell me you finally met a gorgeous blonde over Christmas?'

Stephen ignored this question. 'Looks like the rest of your purchasing department formation drinking team have made it here,' he remarked, nodding towards a trio of middle-aged men, all stood hands in pockets, muttering to each other but ogling Taylor.

'Yeah, do you know where we're staying? A mate at the rugby club gave me the address of this Irish bar. We're thinking we'll go and have a few beverages. You on for it?' Danny asked.

'What, tonight?'

'Of course. We're back on the bloody plane by this time tomorrow. As I said, got to be some upsides.' Danny cheered up. 'In fact, given the missus was going on about some period drama she wanted to watch on TV tonight, things might be looking up considerably.'

'Well, I've no idea where we're staying,' Stephen said, 'but I think I'll give it a miss tonight, mate. I take it there's no dry January for you, then?'

Danny's neck jutted backwards in horror, his expression making clear just what a ridiculous notion this was.

Taylor concluded her headcount and declared they were all set.

'What about Carol Coolidge? Isn't she on your list?' Stephen asked.

She ran a perfectly varnished red nail down her clipboard and shook her head. 'No, sir, not on this plane.'

Stephen had noticed a couple of finance managers from Newte's team. 'And Oscar Newte? He on your list?'

She offered him another inane smile and without checking said, 'No, Mr Newte isn't either.'

'Is there another plane?'

She shuffled a little and avoided his eye. 'Not that I'm aware,' she said, before raising her voice to address the whole group. 'Follow me, please?'

He was sure she was lying.

On board, they filed slowly past business class, where an attentive steward was taking a passenger's jacket and placing it carefully on a hanger.

'Handy for the toilet,' he grumbled to Danny, before taking his seat between Tony Perkins by the window and Jerry in the aisle. Perkins started to interrogate him. What was the format of the conference? Where exactly in Paris was it? Who was going to be speaking? He stopped only when Stephen convinced him that he had no idea what was going on either.

Closing his eyes as they rumbled down the runway, he thought about his brother-in-law holding forth endlessly over Christmas about his recent luxurious business trips. And whether Singapore or Emirates had the more comfortable flat beds. When he opened his eyes again, the attendant with the drinks trolley was still at the front of the plane, working his way towards them at a snail's pace.

Now it was Jerry asking the questions, explaining that he'd never been to Paris before. Did Stephen think they'd be able to go sightseeing this evening? Or maybe there would be entertainment laid on? He professed his ignorance just as he had to Perkins, but more gently this time. He hadn't the heart to burst Jerry's balloon, but Brad Hardman didn't look like a guy who would be organising a riotous night at the Folies Bergère.

As soon as Stephen had paid for his gin and tonic and taken a first sip, the pilot cheerfully announced that they were beginning their descent into Paris Charles de Gaulle ahead of schedule. Whereupon the officious attendant demanded he drink up and fold away his table.

Taylor reappeared mysteriously at the arrivals hall, smile still glued on, and counted her sheep again before marching them off into the cold night air. They took their seats on a stiflingly warm coach while she exchanged a few words of halting French with the burly driver, then addressed them all again.

'It was a pleasure to meet you guys. Welcome to Paris and welcome to Schmaltz. I hope you have a great time here, and now I'll leave you with your driver, John Mark.' She escaped with a cheery wave. Where was she heading?

They appeared to circle the airport perimeter for twenty minutes and then the bus stopped. Stephen could make out through the window a neon blue 'Hotel' sign but nothing else.

'*Arrivé*,' the driver announced sullenly.

It took a moment for anyone to respond. Then slowly, as realisation dawned that this was indeed their destination, they shuffled off the bus.

The only other lights visible were from the airport in the distance and, in the drizzly black sky, those of another plane coming in to land.

'Fuck a duck,' was Danny's immediate assessment, as the driver threw their bags out of the hold onto the tarmac with a hefty thud.

'Mm, looks like a long way to the Eiffel Tower from here, mate,' Stephen said, an air of detachment his only possible alternative to despair. 'Is it just me or does this place have a certain Bates Motel chic?'

The turquoise walls and plastic chairs in the foyer of the Hotel Splendid weren't designed to immediately improve the spirits of the weary travellers, as the queue they formed to check in was quickly snaking back towards the hotel entrance. The staff seemed completely surprised by this sudden large influx of guests at seven o'clock on a Sunday evening. Which, given the hotel's ambience and situation, was in many ways an understandable reaction.

There was only one receptionist, a mournful woman with thin-rimmed glasses whose lank brown hair draped her face as she stared at her computer screen. Stephen and Danny were close to the back of the stagnant queue as she laboured through the hotel's check-in procedure. He could see that passports and credit cards were being handed over, but that clearly wasn't enough, as she was issuing a long list of instructions. She broke off a couple of times to pick up the phone, possibly for reinforcements, but none were forthcoming. The chattering excitement of three hours ago had well and truly drained away.

Eventually Danny snapped. 'OK, sod this, I need a drink. Eh, *garçon, où est le bar?*' he shouted at a passing porter.

'*Comment?*' The young man stopped and scoured him with icy blue eyes.

'*Le bar, ou ça?*' Danny asked, more aggressively.

'*Ah, le bar?*' Recognition dawned on the man's face.

'*Oui*, that's what I said.'

'*Fermé, monsieur.*' It was said with satisfied emphasis, and in a tone that suggested it wouldn't be opening any time soon.

Even though the same young man eventually came to help his beleaguered colleague on reception, it was nearly an hour before Stephen's turn came around. Danny had given up some time ago, enticed by his mates from the purchasing team into believing that it must be possible to get a beer somewhere. Stephen managed a weary smile to the receptionist, all energy to complain now spent. But she wasn't one for beguiling. Now he understood why it had taken so long, as she took him through her drill in monotone. *Passeport – carte bancaire – défense de fumer – attention aux travaux.* And various other announcements he didn't fully grasp. And the news of *petit déjeuner de six heures à neuf heures* was immediately followed by the revelation that 'the autobus will here at six and half'.

'*Pardon, mademoiselle, vous voulez dire six heures et demie?*' he asked, at least seeing an opportunity to try out his A-level French.

'*Oui*, this is what I am saying, six and half,' she replied from behind her hair.

Danny reappeared. 'This place is completely dry. They've been given some order that no alcohol is to be served to the Schmaltz contingent. Bloody Europeans. We're going to get a taxi somewhere. You coming?'

'Danny, if your pursuit of your career was as single-minded as your pursuit of a pint, you'd be CEO by now. I've had enough. I'm going to settle for the minibar.'

*

Room 213 had a panoramic view of the landing lights. And no minibar. He found the vending machine by the lift at the same time as Jerry, which enabled him to cadge a few Euros to get a packet of *cacahuètes*, which looked like peanuts, and a bar of chocolate called *Voom!* But not enough for a fizzy drink.

'I'm sure things will look up tomorrow,' Stephen said encouragingly, sensing that even Jerry's boyish enthusiasm was on the wane.

The room smelt as if it had been blitzed with bleach, although it couldn't completely mask an undertone of something staler. There was a small TV screen perched high up on a plain white wall, which was peeling in a couple of places and displayed a small but distinct grease mark just above the headboard of his bed. He flopped onto the bed, munching his peanuts, and discovered the only English-speaking channel on the TV was showing a programme called *Business Week*. 'Not tonight, Josephine,' he said out loud, and turned it off.

He tried to get started on the thriller that Kate had bought him for Christmas, but he couldn't concentrate. Nor did it have the soporific effect that trying to read in bed normally induced. It had felt like an exceptionally long day but was still only ten o'clock. Nine o'clock in England. Only twelve hours since he'd woken the children up in his house, gently nudging Kate's back, as it rose and fell gently under her duvet. Laura would be chivvying Jake towards bed now, with the start of a new term in the morning. Kate would probably be watching that period drama, curled up on the sofa with her – and Tristran. The thought of him in the same room as his daughter, their shared intimacy, knotted his stomach.

Rachel would probably have come back from her New Year's break and gone straight to church, surrounded by her church friends. She'd be home by now, doubtless offering more tea and sympathy to her needy flatmate. Or maybe she'd moved on to other good works.

He switched off the light and padded over to draw the curtains. Another plane coming in from somewhere, another load of human beings he didn't know.

He always felt like this before going back to work in the New Year, he reminded himself. At least for the last few years, since he'd been on his own. But this felt much worse. He kept staring out into the darkness, thinking of Brad Hardman, those eyes in that photograph following him.

Here was an inconvenient truth. He should be leading his anxious team into the brave new world tomorrow. But just at the moment, a tear was trickling slowly down his cheek.

Chapter Seven

The high-domed foyer of the Hotel Méridien was zinging with energy in contrast to the Hotel Splendid. Bellboys were wheeling enormous luggage trolleys; a group of exuberant American tourists, surrounded by huge cases, were engaged in noisy conversation; and Taylor, alongside a blonde twin called Lois in the same chocolate uniform, was beaming from behind a desk erected next to the washrooms. A white card stuck on the front had the words 'SCHMALTZ EUROPE' printed in bold brown letters.

As the Grimley's group stood awaiting further instructions, an explosion of guttural voices and *Guten Morgen*s announced the arrival of a large group of formally attired Germans.

Danny sniffed. 'See the Krauts have arrived. They'll have their beach towels on all the best seats, I expect.'

Stephen had woken determined not to fall into Danny's slough of despond. He shook his head as he put an arm around Jerry Collins' shoulder. 'So, Jerry, as you'll see there's a lot you can learn from our purchasing department's open-minded approach to being part of a European team. Not a whiff of 1980's racial stereotyping from Mr Allsop here.' Danny scowled and started to explain how this whole Schmaltz Europe thing was another EU stitch-up, while Jerry and Stephen laughed at him.

Lois marched them through into the hotel's business centre where a sign indicated that the Schmaltz Europe Conference would be in the Salle Marie Antoinette. Stephen couldn't resist reminding Danny what had happened to her. The *salle* turned out to be a large lecture theatre, with about thirty long rows of tiered seats. The British were first in and huddled together at the back of the class. But soon the room started to fill in front of them with managers from other countries. Danny was very clear on which country each group represented and provided a running commentary on their inadequacies as each one entered. The Italians? Not to be trusted. The Greeks? A drain on resources. The Spanish? Never did today what could wait until *mañana*. They were all noisier and more exuberant than the Brits. But all sat in their separate blocs, just as the Brits had done. Eventually there were probably about three hundred of them. Women were in the minority, but there were far more scattered around the other countries than in the Grimley's phalanx, where there was only Jennie Jacobs and three others. And Carol Coolidge still wasn't one of them.

The large circular stage below them was backed by a blank cinema screen, and at its centre was an empty black leather chair, picked out by a spotlight. In the surrounding shadows eight other chairs were just visible, arranged in a circle around the perimeter. As the multi-tongued hubbub continued, Stephen felt his stomach cramping. Too little sleep, the lack of a decent coffee, and rising apprehension. A poisonous cocktail. And it was only just gone eight o'clock.

Suddenly from speakers all around the theatre came the loud thumping opening beat of Queen's 'We Will Rock You'. The chatter quickly faded away, in collective anticipation that the show was about to begin. But the drumbeat was just on repeat, never progressing to the tune, just rapped out insistently and getting louder, driving into Stephen's head. Until finally the screen burst into life, a violent Day-Glo orange backdrop with a message flashing out in bold purple letters.

SCHMALTZ IN EUROPE
WE'RE HERE TO WIN!

If life at Schmaltz was going to be lived at this volume, he would have a permanent migraine.

The drumming stopped. A moment of sweet relief. Before a booming disembodied American voice filled the room.

'Ladies and gentlemen of Schmaltz Europe, please stand.'

Everyone struggled to their feet as the drumming started up again. And now those at the front of the room started to clap in time, in a wave that rippled all the way back to the Brits. Stephen found himself joining in. Only Danny kept his hands in his pockets, his trademark sneer now firmly back in place and directed at Stephen.

'Who're you expecting, Lady Gaga?' he shouted above the thudding beat.

The voice boomed again. 'Please welcome the man with your plan. Your leader and THE President of Schmaltz Europe, Mister... Brad... Hardman!'

The auditorium switched from rhythmic clapping to enthusiastic applause. 'I feel like a brainwashed Moonie already,' Stephen shouted into Danny's ear, as he joined in. This time even Danny crumbled and started clapping too, albeit with an air of surly reluctance. And from out of the shadows, the spectre which had inhabited Stephen's mind for the last month became incarnate, marching briskly into the spotlight, puffing out his white-shirted barrel chest.

Stephen looked up at the screen to get a clearer view of Hardman's face. Those mean eyes which had stared out of his laptop before Christmas were staring straight at him again now, the grey hair shaved tight to the scalp, the head pointier than he'd noticed before – like a bullet.

A podium rose automatically from the floor, but Hardman stood in front of it facing his audience, arms folded, as they continued to applaud. The narrow eyes didn't change their focus.

Only when the music stopped abruptly did the applause fade away. But they all remained on their feet. And soon any murmurs from the audience evaporated to leave just the silence, interspersed by the occasional cough. Still Hardman continued to stare at them. He was smaller than Stephen had envisaged, actually a bit of a short-arse, but with the air of a fit, squat sumo wrestler. He wasn't wearing a tie, although the dress code on the invite had stressed ties must be worn and every other man in the room was wearing one. And his sleeves were rolled up, suggesting a readiness to get stuck into something – or someone. No doubt he pumped a serious amount of iron when he needed some fun.

The screen behind Hardman burst into orange again. But this time, different purple words appeared on it, not flashing on and off, but frozen in place, as stern and accusatory as Brad Hardman himself:

WHY ARE YOU HERE?

Even the coughs were suppressed now. Everyone was looking at Hardman. And Hardman was looking at everyone. Stephen became aware of a pulse in his right ear.

'Anyone gonna tell me?' A gravelly drawl of a voice, straight from a John Wayne movie.

The silence lingered. Until a strong clue reappeared on the screen.

SCHMALTZ IN EUROPE
WE'RE HERE TO WIN!

Hardman raised his voice, this time with an edge of menace.

'Can't you fucking read, guys?'

'To win?' offered a small voice from somewhere near the front, sounding more in hope than expectation.

'Whassat?' Hardman shouted, marching to the corner of the stage, scouring his audience. The voice didn't try again. So now he went for the direct approach.

'You, fella, why are you here?' He thrust a pointing finger at someone.

'I'm 'ere to win?' came the reply in a possibly French accent, issued as a question, just audible from where Stephen sat.

Hardman beckoned with his little finger. 'Up you come, fella.'

A gaunt, balding man in a mustard jacket made his way onto the stage, head bowed.

Danny whistled under his breath. 'The man's a bastard.'

'OK, relax, fella,' Hardman barked in a tone hardly designed to elicit that response. 'You got the right answer. But here's some friendly advice on how we're going to get along. First, you'll find I like people to speak up when I ask a question. Nice and clear now. And second, you can call me Mr Hardman. Let's get off on the right foot, eh, fella? Now, why don't you turn to face your new-found pals here, and tell 'em why you're here?'

Just in case the cowed figure was still uncertain, the words were flashing now not just behind Hardman, but on screens all around the room, being hardwired into everyone's brain.

SCHMALTZ IN EUROPE
WE'RE HERE TO WIN!
SCHMALTZ IN EUROPE
WE'RE HERE TO WIN!
SCHMALTZ IN EUROPE
WE'RE HERE TO WIN!

And now, with his bewilderment projected around the room, the victim croaked, 'I am Thierry Haut-Brion, from Schmaltz France, and I am 'ere to win, Mr Ardman.'

'OK, O'Brien, you can go back to your place.' Hardman dismissed him with a flick of the hand and his eyes returned to his audience.

'Hey you, the guy in the third row with the red tie – yes, you, turn around and shout to your fucking friends, tell 'em where you're from and why you're here.'

'I'm Vassos Angelopoulos, from Schmaltz Greece, and I am here to win too, Mr Hardman,' Vassos proclaimed, with a little more self-belief than Thierry.

'Hallelujah!' drawled Hardman. And then he was off, bouncing up the centre aisle, randomly selecting his next victims. And soon Dirk from the Netherlands, Stanislaw from Poland and Hipólito from Spain had all solemnly declared that they too were here to win.

Hardman kept coming, mounting the steps to the back of the theatre, where the UK contingent were still standing like everyone else. Stephen looked along the row to see Tony Perkins biting his lower lip.

A smile came on Hardman's face for the first time as he addressed them. 'So, you guys must be the Brits.' Was it so obvious? Probably. He imitated a refined British accent to say, 'Jolly good show.'

Then he turned back to the rest of the auditorium, opening his arms wide, and reverted to Texan. 'Anyone else think there's a helluva lot of 'em?' There was a smatter of nervous laughter from lower down the hall.

Hardman had stopped next to Jennie Jacobs. He put a hand on her shoulder.

'We haven't heard from a lady yet. Say, lady, why don't you tell us why are *you* here?'

Jennie Jacobs, her voice quavering slightly, took the pledge, sounding like a well-groomed Conservative politician.

'I'm Jennie Jacobs, I'm HR director of Schmaltz UK, and I'm here to win, Mr Hardman.'

Hardman smiled at her, even creepier than when he was glaring grim-faced.

'That's good to hear, Jennie. Did you hear that, everybody? The Brits are here to win too.'

More obsequious laughter.

Now Hardman put his hand around her shoulder and whispered audibly into his mic, 'We'll discuss titles later, Jennie.' He gave her a squeeze and then he was bounding back down the steps. Stephen tried to catch Jennie's eye, to offer her a supportive smile, but her face and body were frozen in rigid misery. And Hardman was clapping his hands above his head like a gospel singer.

'Right, y'all got it? Turn to your neighbour. Tell 'em who you are, and why you're here.'

Stephen turned to Jerry, but before he could utter a word, his colleague, face now rabid with enthusiasm, bawled at him.

'I'm Jerry Collins, I'm from Schmaltz UK, and I'm fucking here to win, Steve!'

'OK, Jerry, OK,' Stephen replied.

'Now turn around and tell someone else,' demanded Hardman.

Stephen looked towards Danny, who was trying to rebuff the advances of an over-enthusiastic bear of a man from somewhere in Europe that wasn't England. He turned to Stephen with a grim look on his face.

'OK, Carreras, before you ask, I'm not here to win. I'm out of this shithole as soon as I can find a fucking shovel.'

But Danny was the exception that proved the rule. Stephen was soon surrounded by managers from other countries, all keen to shake his hand. And his Grimley's colleagues had caught the wave. Predictably Kevin Keeling was trying to sell himself to an elegant brunette who just had to be French, and who looked suitably appalled. And Stephen fixed a smile and told everyone he too was here to win. If you said it quickly, you could turn it into a meaningless greeting, just like saying hello. But he felt like the last sober man at a drunken orgy.

Feeling a light touch on his shoulder, he turned to be met by a tall man of about his own age, with thinning dark hair, intelligent eyes behind stylish dark-framed glasses, and a gently amused look on his face. He too offered his hand and gripped Stephen's firmly.

'Good morning. I'm Salvatore Carnevale, marketing director of Cioccolato Bonifacio in Milano,' he said proudly. 'You must be Stephen, the UK marketing director. I've heard about you.' He glanced around and then turned back to Stephen. 'What is that expression you have? The mad people are running the hospital?'

Stephen laughed. 'Yes, something like that. Nice to meet you, Salvatore.'

The Italian slipped a business card into Stephen's hand and put an imaginary phone to his ear. 'We'll talk soon, yes?' he managed, just before a burly wire-haired young man came between them, joyfully declaring, in case they hadn't got the idea by now, that he was Helmut from Germany – and he was here to win.

Hardman was resting on his podium, surveying the cacophony he had created, the master of all he surveyed. He clapped his hands above his head.

'OK, people, siddown,' he commanded, and everyone started to make their way back to their seats. He clapped again. 'I said siddown.' Now they all took the first seat available, a game of managerial musical chairs. Danny was still to Stephen's right, having not ventured far into enemy territory, but to his left Jerry's seat had now been filled by the considerable, heavy-breathing presence of Helmut.

Hardman loudly cleared the phlegm from his throat. The auditorium fell quiet.

'Right, I don't believe in long speeches that bore the crap out of folks. I'm gonna tell you about me, what I want, and how you're gonna help me get it,' he drawled.

For a few brief moments the tyrant was replaced by Uncle Brad, keen to be liked by everyone and to share the secrets of his success with them. He was particularly proud of the revolution he had achieved in his previous job at Pet's Paradise. One graph projected on the screen showed dramatic growth in sales figures for the last five years, the next plotted the simultaneous meteoric increase in share price.

'You wanna know what's the nicest thing anyone ever said about me?'

'That you're a big-headed wanker?' Danny offered in the softest of whispers.

But the alternative answer was on the screen in the form of a quote.

'This guy cares about what really matters – profit and shareholder value – more than any business leader I've ever known.'

'Isn't that beautiful?' he leered, without revealing who had said such a sweet thing. 'And guess what, folks? That's what you're going to care most about too.'

There was a distinct cry of 'all right!' from a lone voice. Stephen shuffled in his seat. It was good to know that Hardman cared about something, even if it wasn't another human being. Was there a Mrs Hardman? Next to him Helmut was enraptured.

'There's another thing you need to know about me.' The tone hardened again as the tyrant went on, pacing the stage. 'I learned all I know about kicking ass in business by first kicking ass for Uncle Sam. Youngest major in the US Marines, alongside storming Norman Schwarzkopf in the Gulf.' A large black and white photo of a much younger Hardman in combat fatigues, holding a rifle, appeared on the screen behind him.

'And you wanna know what I learned in the army?'

'No thanks,' muttered Stephen to himself.

'The value of discipline and giving orders, that's what I learned. Ya see, I'm kinda good at giving orders.' He smiled malignly. 'The US Marines, PP, everywhere I've been, people follow my orders, and we always kick ass. You wanna kick some ass in chocolate?'

'Yes, sir,' someone shouted. Had he planted this guy?

'I said, do you wanna kick some ass in chocolate?' he repeated, more threateningly.

'Yes, sir,' was chorused back this time, panto-style.

'So you gonna obey my orders?'

Stephen looked beyond Helmut, along the row at his colleagues.

'Yes, sir,' they all brayed again, even louder.

It was mass lobotomy.

Hardman's plan sounded disarmingly simple. He would cut huge chunks of cost out of the business, so he could lower prices dramatically. And by flogging everyone to sell more, he would turn Schmaltz Europe into a voracious money-making monster. And it was all delivered as fact, not aspiration.

'OK, people, on your feet.' He motioned them to stand with a raising of his hands. And Stephen rose in time with the rest of the room in a wave of obedience, a little light-headed now, his resistance ebbing away.

'The message is simple. You're gonna obey my orders and win for me, and we're gonna win big. You are gonna just – fucking – do it,' he bawled. And with the acronym JFDI now flashing behind him, the drumbeat started up again and the spotlight turned on a troupe of long-legged cheerleaders running onto the stage, all dressed in chocolate-brown bodysuits. They were led by yet another blonde woman twirling a brown sash above her head. Microphone in hand, she strode from one side of the stage to the other.

'OK, guys, I'm Christy, I'm here for Schmaltz, and I'm here to win. Let's make some noise.' Behind her, the words were back up on-screen:

WE'RE SCHMALTZ!
WE'RE HERE!
WE'RE HERE TO WIN!

And as the high-kicking girls clapped out the beat, the audience joined in, chanting and clapping in unison. Everyone was doing it. Including Jennie Jacobs, who had campaigned so hard to alter Grimley's antediluvian approach to recruiting women. In Hardman's new world, it looked like her Women in Management movement would be going underground. But as Stephen clapped and shouted, it felt so liberating, so easy. He was Schmaltz. He was here. He was here to win. Nothing else in life mattered. Right here, right now, there was nothing else. Nothing to do but obey.

Finally Christy dismissed the dancers and the spotlight returned to Hardman. 'I don't believe in management. I believe in control,' he barked, strutting round the stage. 'And here are the guys who are gonna enforce that control for me. My eight vice presidents who will be based here in Paris.' He pointed at his audience again. 'I expect you to take orders from these people, same as from me.' His face broke into a sinister grin. 'Of course, you should want their jobs too, because they'll earn a helluva lot more than the rest of you. That's the way I like it – nothing wrong with envy at work, folks. Because envy breeds hunger, and hunger breeds winners. And hey, if they want, they can try to get my job too.' Cue a further sprinkle of sycophantic laughter.

'OK, everyone,' Christy screeched, 'let's make some noise first up for the man who is your first Vice President Finance for Europe...' She hesitated to check the name in her notes. But Stephen experienced a strange quiver down his back. He knew it already.

'Please give it up for Oscar Nudey!'

There were a few sniggers from some of the Brits at the mispronunciation. But Stephen wasn't laughing. The beat of 'We're Schmaltz, We're Here, We're Here to Win' came in again, prompting more rhythmic clapping. But not from him. And then the fat bastard strode onto the stage, raising his arms in triumph.

Stephen felt faint. His body plummeted from hot to cold. He had to get outside.

*

In front of the hotel, Paris was going about its morning as if nothing had happened. The shellfish stall under the awnings was being hosed down, the boulevard was alive with the buzz of traffic, and a taxi pulled up outside to deliver a dapper man in a green jacket with over-long sideburns and a perfectly coiffured woman in a flowing black trouser suit. French, rich and carefree. Stephen took deep gulps of air and felt the spots of rain on his face.

In his two years at Grimley's, Oscar Newte had never shown any interest in anything but managing his own career. And now he had been rewarded. Finance Vice President for the whole of bloody Europe. Stephen had suspected something was going on before Christmas, that secret meeting the bastard had gone to in Paris. And now he was going to be living here. The war of words he had fought with Newte ever since he first clapped eyes on the pretentious wanker had ended in ignominious defeat.

'You all right, mate?' Danny was now beside him, with a look of concern on his pale creased face. He lit up a fag.

'Been better. Bloody Newte, Danny, Newte. How could they? I mean, of all the finance directors they had to choose from across Europe, how could they choose him?'

Danny sniffed. 'Yeah, what a prat. He's not been talking five minutes and already he's boring the shit out of everyone in there. Still, I suppose at least he's not going to be in Middleton. I thought he would end up as our MD.'

Stephen gave a dry laugh. 'Thanks for trying to look on the bright side of life for once, Daniel, but don't bother. You heard what Hardman said about how he's going to pay him. He's going to be earning a packet – and living in Paris, one of the most beautiful cities in the world.'

'Huh. It doesn't look that great to me. Have you seen West Bromwich recently?' Danny said, still valiantly sympathetic.

They stood for a while without speaking, as an ambulance flashed by. The smoke from Danny's fag made him feel a bit better, mingled with the aroma of the sea from the shellfish stall. Eventually Danny flicked his ash, sniffing again. 'Anyway, at least the tosspot won't have time to be bothering you.'

'Oh, yeah? What makes you say that?'

'Well, judging from what he's said so far, sounds like he's going to spend most of his time licking Hardman's arse.' He stubbed out his cigarette. 'So, should we go and get ratted, or are we going back in?'

Once inside, they hovered at the back like latecomers at the theatre. Newte was still blustering, his smug red face projected on screens everywhere.

'Now, *évidemment*, I will be based in Paris, but I will be a man on the move. I will be breathing down your necks, and

I will spare nothing to enforce the tight financial control that Brad wants to achieve. And you're going to help me, aren't you?'

He was presumably expecting a roar of allegiance like they'd given his boss. What he got was overwhelming silence. And as he presented rows of data which were impossible to read, the audience began to mumble. Hardman's vexed frown was captured on-screen, and then he stood up. Immediately Christy rushed back onto the stage.

'Great, thanks, Oscar Nudey.' She gripped Newte by the arm and ushered him towards one of the eight chairs encircling Hardman. 'I'm sure there'll be more time for you to explain it to the guys later.'

Stephen glanced at Danny, while shaking his head. If it wasn't so tragic it would be hilarious. Newte had just been told to sit down by a cheerleader in a leotard.

In turn, each newly appointed vice president came on to introduce themselves and present their wares. There was a Spaniard getting overly excited about the future of purchasing, and a German who knew all the answers for manufacturing. But Stephen just kept looking at Newte, leaning back in his chair, with a satisfied grin on his face.

Eventually, seven of the eight vice presidents had taken their seats, moons orbiting planet Brad. By now even Christy's incessant screeches of enthusiasm couldn't keep the mob at fever pitch any longer. Hardman strode to the front of the stage again to take control.

'OK, I got one more VP to introduce and I want to hear even more noise for her than everyone else. Yep, that's right, I said *her*. Don't want you thinking I don't like women. I love women and it's time we had a woman out here. She is also my youngest VP, but I heard great things about this girl, and as far as I'm concerned, if you're good enough, you're old enough.'

Now Stephen had a strange sensation of the power seeping from his body, leaving him numb.

Christy shrieked with joy. 'OK, you heard Mr Hardman. Be on your feet once more for the woman who is going to run marketing for the whole of Schmaltz Europe. It's the blonde bombshell, Miss... Carol... Coolidge!'

They were all on their feet clapping rapturously again. Helmut appeared positively orgiastic, an adoring smile on his jowly face. But this time Stephen couldn't applaud – or stand up. Nobody would notice. All eyes were fixed on her, stepping out confidently to the centre of the stage, dressed to kill in a navy pin-striped suit.

She was grinning at him directly from every screen. But he didn't hear what she said.

Four years he had spent mentoring her since it happened, resisting the infatuation that had cost him his marriage. And only a month ago he had accepted her resignation. Now this. The humiliation was complete.

The lips were still proclaiming their message. 'I have seen in the UK how outmoded marketing approaches have held us back,' she said, standing tall. They were eating out of her hand, enthralled. Of course, unlike Newte, she was playing it just right. Word perfect, concise and unflappable. She was going to unleash the full power of Schmaltz American marketing tactics onto the unsuspecting chocolate munchers of Europe. And Schmaltz advertising would be famous throughout the continent, she would guarantee that. The camera panned to Hardman, who for the first time seemed to wear a smile that wasn't malevolent, but signalled pride in his appointed one. After ten minutes of tightly presented ambition that left nobody in any doubt, she thanked them for their attention, turned and marched to her allotted place at Hardman's left hand, and the room erupted into the loudest and most prolonged applause of the morning. Now he would have to stand up – but he still wasn't going to clap. Newte was smiling at her, his sweaty face caught on the big screen for a moment. But in the row in front of him, Stephen caught sight of one other person not joining in. Salvatore, the Italian, hands behind his back, appeared to contemplate the scene with an air of serene detachment.

At long last, Christy granted them a lunch break, but with a finger-wagging warning that Brad wanted them back in for the afternoon session in thirty minutes. Such was the state of Pavlovian submission that Hardman had induced, Stephen didn't hear anyone else complaining as they poured out into the main foyer and snaked across to the Salon de Louis Quatorze. For a few brief moments he too had lost himself in the corporate ecstasy, but the sight of first Newte and then Carol on that stage had brought him back to cold white anger.

Ripped out of bed at six o'clock for an apology of a breakfast, sat on a cramped coach for an hour, forced to endure four hours of power-crazed egomania, topped off in his case by the most crushing defeats of his career – and now he was given thirty bloody minutes for lunch. As they filed past the hotel restaurant, he noticed those posh Parisians that he had seen arriving earlier, now sipping apéritifs and perusing menus. They glanced up disdainfully as the noise from the Schmaltz mob swept past them.

'Lucky bastards,' he snarled to Danny, now the only person in the world who understood him.

Chapter Eight

The old green neon Grimley's sign on top of the building had gone. Instead, in front of the main entrance, there was a huge white backlit panel emblazoned with gold lettering:
SCHMALTZ. BECAUSE YOU LOVE IT.

Dotty old Gladys, who had been on reception since the dawn of time, was no more. In her place, behind a gleaming new reception desk, sat Taylor in her chocolate suit.

'Good morning, welcome to Schmaltz?' she smiled, the inflexion turning it into a question. She clearly didn't recognise Stephen as one of her happy band of Parisian day-trippers.

'Guest or operative?' she enquired.

'I'm Stephen Carreras, the marketing director.'

'Mm, let's see.' Taylor consulted her screen. 'Yes, you are Stephen G. Carreras, marketing operative, and you are on the second floor.' Before he could respond, a loud drilling started up from behind the door to the Grimley's staff bar, which had a large 'Keep Out' sign on it. Taylor kept smiling, waiting for the drilling to stop before she handed him a single small white plastic card.

'This is your Work ID card. You need this to access all doors in the building and scan it on the card reader every time you enter and leave the Hive.' She dealt him another. 'And this is your Schmaltz World card and password. When you find a podium, just key this in to log into Schmaltz World. And this is your—'

'Whoa, slow down, slow down.' He raised a hand to try and stem the tide. 'What do you mean, when I find a podium?'

'Oh, don't worry, you'll see when you enter the Hive. And there'll be someone there to tell you what to do with the Eat Schmaltz card too. Have a nice day.' She had already turned to her next customer.

The drilling started up again. What was going on behind there?

Already feeling punch-drunk, he took the lift to the second floor as normal. But what greeted him was anything but normal. He was faced by an electronic gate, behind which was the office space that had always been the domain of his marketing team. All the desks and chairs had disappeared, and it was full of people not just from marketing but from all the other departments as well. Many of them were already standing tapping away at keyboards and monitors perched on glinting metal podiums. At the far end a cinema-sized screen was flashing out that purple on orange message:

SCHMALTZ IN EUROPE
WE'RE HERE TO WIN!

'Name?' Maureen Birtles, Oscar Newte's old PA, was standing by the gate, with an officious look on her face and a tablet in her hand.

'You know who I am, Maureen, for God's sake.'

'Can you just confirm your name, please,' she said, checking her tablet.

'Bloody hell, I'm Steve Carreras.'

'OK, Mr Carreras, there's no need for that sort of language. Just touch your ID card here to access the Hive, and then find yourself a workstation, key in your Schmaltz World password and off you go.'

'You cannot be serious,' he groaned, but found himself touching the card against the scanner as Maureen dictated. A message came up.

CARD NOT RECOGNISED

'Not that card,' Maureen said sharply.

He tried another card. Another message.

CARRERAS, S.
HOURS WORKED 00:00.
HOURS REMAINING 50:00.

Just in case he was in any doubt, an automated American voice announced, '*Time remaining: fifty hours and zero minutes.*' The gate slid open.

The Hive was an appropriate name. The orange floor was made of a material more suited to an indoor football pitch than an office, and conversation buzzed around the space, from those at podiums talking to their neighbours, but also from the many huddled in small, bewildered clusters around the edges.

'There's a space over there,' Maureen pointed out.

'OK, Maureen, I see it,' he snapped. She turned on her heels and greeted her next victim. There didn't seem to be anything for it but to install himself and enter his password.

His monitor welcomed him.

Carreras, S. You are ready to work.

No, he wasn't. He was ready to kill someone.

A solitary email from the IT department explained a series of hoops he was obliged to jump through to access 'Smart Schmaltz Worldwide Learning', whatever that was. He needed a pee and a coffee before he did anything else. The gents, mercifully, remained next to the lifts where it had always been, but this meant it was outside the Hive. And as he returned, the scanner informed him that he still had 49 hours and 55 minutes remaining.

'So peeing in my own time, is it?' he asked.

While he and his fellow 'operatives' were boxed in the centre of the floor with no natural light, there were still spacious rooms behind glass partitions, spanning each side of the building. His old office, with its window overlooking the playing fields, had been replaced by a meeting room with the word 'Ambition' on a shiny plaque by the door. Inside, close-up photos of Schmaltz's American brands covered the wall, and a dozen metal stools with ridiculous curves were positioned in front of a big screen perched high on the wall.

Alongside Ambition were three other identical meeting rooms – Discipline, Sacrifice and Winning. Weren't these the 'key Schmaltz values' that Hardman had hammered them with yesterday afternoon, way past the point when Stephen lost the will to live? He'd already forgotten the Grimley's values debated ad nauseam at a board meeting last year. Except for 'Integrity'. At least nobody was pretending about that any more.

Along another wall, accessible again only with his ID card, was an open-plan area with a large sign suspended from the ceiling, inviting him to 'EAT WELL, EAT SCHMALTZ.' So eating was in his own time too. Hardman had clearly got all the bodily functions covered.

A counter was laid out with fresh fruit and juice, and a salad bar, and just six of those uncomfortable-looking stools. But no coffee machine. Jerry Collins was there, peeling a banana.

'Blimey, all change, eh?' Stephen tried to sound positive. 'Have you checked if we still have the old cafeteria downstairs as well?'

'Nope, all gone,' said Jerry. 'Looks like a fruit and nut diet from now on – unless you want to sneak out to the chippy, but then they might set the dogs on you.' Jerry's evangelical zeal of yesterday had already been tempered by a healthier cynicism.

Stephen picked up a packet of Brazil nuts to take back to his perch.

'Excuse me, you'll need to load your Eat Schmaltz card for that.' A young man had broken off from filling a small fridge with juice cartons to deliver the reprimand.

Choosing one of his cards at random, Stephen's swipe across a card reader next to the counter was met by bleeping noises and another 'card not recognised' message.

'Pick a card, any card.' He held out all three in a fan.

'No, it's none of those. What you need is your Eat Schmaltz card.' The young man spoke slowly, as if addressing a geriatric. 'You get that from reception and then you need to get it registered by IT, and load it with money from your debit card, and then you can use it.'

'Tell you what, I'll just take the nuts anyway and sort it out later.'

'No credit, I'm afraid.'

Somehow he felt the line, 'Do you know who I am?' wasn't going to wash. Particularly when he didn't know himself. For the second time this week, he cadged a packet of nuts from Jerry.

'You had a look down the far end yet?' Jerry asked, handing over the nuts, the look on his face suggesting that Stephen's mood would not be lightened once he had.

Much of the far end was taken up by an enormous room with a nameplate outside reading 'President, Schmaltz UK.' So there was going to be a local boss after all. The glass frontage would allow the occupant to look out over the workers, as Stephen used to do from his own modest office in the past. But for now, the blinds were drawn.

Next door was another office, slightly smaller but still occupying a ridiculously large proportion of floor space compared with the heaving Hive. A handwritten card taped to the door said it was 'Reserved for N. Newte and C. Coolidge'. The blinds on this one were raised, revealing two large desks facing each other in the centre of the room, both with imposing black leather office chairs. To one side was a matching voluminous sofa. Why the hell did they need an office here? Weren't they supposed to be shacked up in Paris? Hell, those two shacked up. Maybe that was it; that was how she'd got the job. She couldn't have stooped that low, could she? The thought of Newte rolling around on top of her on that sofa. What an odious image that was.

The workstation where he had logged in before his walkabout had now been taken by a young woman he vaguely recognised as one of Newte's project managers from the finance department. At least five pay grades below him in the old regime.

'Hi, I was already logged on here,' he told her.

She smiled at him. 'Oh, I'm sorry. I think it logs you off automatically after ten minutes' inactivity. It's really easy just to log in somewhere else, though. It's great, isn't it? And all this fresh fruit too.'

Before he could reply, he felt a sharp prod in the back.

'Have you been round the ground floor yet?' Danny Allsop was apoplectic.

'Not yet. I'm just getting to grips with this floor actually, Danny. I'm not sure I can cope with any more surprises.'

'Well, the bar has gone, and guess what they are putting in instead?'

'Tell me, Daniel, please do.'

'Only a bloody gym.'

Danny's revelation was one of several unpleasant discoveries through the course of the morning, culminating in the distinctly limited fare available at Eat Schmaltz by the time Stephen ventured there in search of lunch at one o'clock. A weary banana and half an avocado and hummus sandwich, tasting exclusively of the cellophane that smothered it, wasn't going to cut it for him on a daily basis, as he explained to the disinterested cashier.

But worst of all, he was rudderless. What on earth was he supposed to do? Normally the first working day of the new year was taken up with starting to think about Easter promotions, the unrelenting procession from planning one period of seasonal indulgence to another. But today his only significant achievement was to locate the members of his shell-shocked team, scattered like lost sheep around the Hive. The same questions kept coming, echoing the ones he was asking himself. What was an operative? Did he still manage them now, and did they still have any brands to look after? He tried to reassure them that he was sure someone would tell them in due course.

Late in the afternoon, he noticed a small lever at the base of the podium where he had been standing for the last hour. He wondered if this would allow him to adjust the height and save his aching neck from further punishment. Which explained why he was on his hands and knees attempting a bit of DIY when he noticed that the buzzing backdrop of the Hive had muted.

Brad Hardman was standing there, surveying his worker bees. And he was giving Stephen a particularly questioning look as he rose to his feet with as much dignity as he could muster.

Hardman clapped his hands and shouted across the room, 'All right, people, gather round and listen up.' Everyone quickly formed a semicircle in front of him.

'For those of you not lucky enough to be in Paris yesterday, I'm Mr Hardman. The boss. Welcome to the new world. Like it?'

There were a few murmurs of assent.

'That'll be yes, Mr Hardman,' he said, fixing them with threatening eyes.

'Yes, Mr Hardman.' Stephen watched them bleating more valiantly this time.

'So, first up, I guess you might be wondering about your new job titles. Well here's the thing. I don't want you *managing* other people.' He spat out the words as if the very idea offended him. 'It ain't efficient. And I don't believe in a bunch of meaningless titles – they just confuse things. That's why I'm calling y'all what I called everyone at Paradise. Operatives. Those of you in Paris yesterday saw the eight European head honchos. I only need those people to control stuff for me, the rest of you need to focus on JFDI. That's just fucking do it, for those of you who don't speak my language yet.'

A rictus grin came across his face, which Stephen was fast realising wasn't necessarily a prelude to happy news. 'But to keep you on your toes, you're all gonna have two masters. One of those European guys, and then also a local country president. Just to make sure you hit the profit target in the UK. Let's see, why don't I give you a little example of how this is gonna work?'

He paused for a moment, eyes searching his audience. Stephen glanced around too at the herd, all looking at the orange floor. But when he looked back at Hardman, those eyes had settled unmistakably on the prey. Him. Hardman summoned Stephen to the front with one finger, just as he had that French victim yesterday.

'You, fella, come and stand here.'

He was determined to hold his head high as he made his way through the group to stand before Hardman. But even so, he felt a tightening in his chest. At close quarters, the beast emitted the scent of leathery aftershave.

'And who are you exactly?'

'I'm Stephen Carreras. I was the UK marketing—'

'So you're a marketing *operative*, Career-ass. Which means you'll answer to Carol Coolidge as your European Marketing Vice President, and then also the person I'm appointing to run your country.'

His humiliation was being played out to everyone in the Middleton office, and in particular his old team. Their former boss Stephen Carreras was no longer marketing director, and would report, like the rest of them, to the person that he used to manage. Career-ass. Too bloody right.

But Hardman wasn't done with him.

'Now, Career-ass, I guess you're wondering *who* I'm appointing to run your country?'

Stephen tightened his muscles and said nothing. He wasn't going to be sidekick in the bastard's Q and A game.

Hardman fixed him with a hard stare. But after a moment he turned to the rest of his audience. 'Is anybody else wondering that too?'

'Yes, Mr Hardman,' they chorused.

'Well, it's simple. One of my new VPs is Oscar Nudey, your old finance director, so I got him to give me the lowdown on you folks in the UK. And you know what he said?' Suddenly he had a big smile on his face, as if they would all enjoy the joke. 'Nudey said the UK sure needs some special treatment. In fact, he called it a basket case. That's what he called it. So guess what, guys? You're gonna get someone incredibly special as your UK boss.' He paused, then turned back to Stephen as his smile took on an even more sadistic dimension.

'You're gonna get me.'

Heads lowered in silence. Except Stephen was pretty sure he heard someone at the back of the room cough 'wanker'. And he was pretty sure he knew who the someone was.

Hardman appeared not to have heard. 'Yep, you lucky

people, I'm gonna double up for a while, heading up the whole damn European operation but also making sure you Brits in particular get your asses in gear. Now, I don't know what's been going on here the last five years. But frankly, I don't give a damn. The future starts here. And I got just two things to say to you, so listen carefully.'

He stuck two fingers up at them. 'First of all, from now on you're gonna need to work a lot harder. To turn this basket case around, you need to put in the hours. Some lady in the French HR department has been telling me about some fucking EU working directive or some such, but hey, you Brits never like taking lessons from the French, do you? So we won't worry about that here. I'm gonna be expecting fifty hours a week minimum from you people, and I mean minimum. You'll have noticed by now you check in whenever you enter this place. That's a little change I introduced to put a rocket up Pet's Paradise asses. It means I know at the end of the week how many hours y'all have done. Anyone dipping under fifty, they can explain to me. Good luck with that. Anybody dipping under fifty on a regular basis can go explain to their wife and kids, cos they'll be needing another job. Any questions on that?'

More silence.

'OK, point two. To work a lot harder, you're gonna need to be a whole lot fitter.' He surveyed them disdainfully. 'Most of you look like you need to work out a deal more – so I've only gone and bought you a gym!' He flashed his teeth winsomely. 'How lucky are you? Oh, and I've brought Madison with me from Pet's Paradise, as my Chief Energiser. You'll meet her soon enough, and boy, will she knock you into shape.' His face darkened again. 'And people, you really are gonna need that gym work. Because I gotta say, there are far more of you here than I need. So it's gonna be survival of the fittest. OK, let's get to work.'

And with a clap of the master's hands, they started to disperse back to their podiums. But Stephen didn't get far.

'Career-ass,' Hardman bellowed. 'In my office. Now.'

He was being singled out for special treatment already. Insubordination over the Q and A maybe. His chest was thumping hard now. And pressed against it, in his inside pocket, his phone was vibrating. Better turn it off before he entered the beast's lair. But there was a text – from Kate.

Hi Dad. Hope Paris was cool? See you soon. x

He needed to stay strong. And the malicious bastard was going to get his name right for starters.

Hardman had gone back into his office, leaving the door ajar. Installed just outside it now was Maureen Birtles, evidently the only other person apart from Hardman, Newte and Carol with a desk on the whole floor.

'You'll have to knock,' she smirked, without looking up from her screen.

Hardman was sitting at a broad, glass topped desk, facing out towards the window, so all Stephen could see through the open door was the back of his bullet head, just visible over the top of his bulky office chair. His knock was answered with a sharp 'yep', but Hardman's position didn't shift as he entered.

The huge office smelt of leather, like its occupant, but blended with the distinct aroma of sweaty feet. On one side of the room was a circular meeting table with just one chair in front of it, an L-shape sofa even larger than the one in Carol's office, and a huge wall-mounted screen. At the other end was Hardman's personal gym: a cross trainer, treadmill, bike, and a whole variety of tortuous machines for pumping iron. Plus a shiny steel fridge. It blew any hope that the tyrant might be only an occasional presence in the UK office. It looked like he was going to live here. The bench press probably converted into a bed – if he ever slept.

Finally Hardman swivelled round to stare at him.

'You wanted to see me, Mr Hardman?' Stephen said firmly.

Hardman inspected the notes he was holding, and lifted his stockinged feet onto a footstool, thrusting them in Stephen's direction.

'You said out there you were marketing director, Career-ass. That right?

'That is correct, Mr Hardman. Only it's pronounced Carr-AIR-ass.'

Hardman gave him a hard stare, sniffing phlegm into the back of his throat.

'Shit, so you are the guy responsible for this pile of crap.' He checked his notes again. 'What the fuck is Little Monkeys?'

'It's Grimley's, erm Schmaltz UK's oldest brand. And with the right backing—'

'OK, Career-ass, here's the deal. As you'll have gathered from yesterday and my little speech out there just now, I don't need a fucking UK marketing director, whatever it was you did. I'm paying that Coolidge woman to sort out my brands for me around Europe. And I don't need anyone else interfering, especially in marketing. As I told y'all out there, I've found that managers get in the way of people doing what I want them to do. But I do need people who know their way around here.' He paused. 'I assume you do at least know your way around here?'

'I used to think so, Mr Hardman.'

'Right. I need you to do two jobs for me. First off, these brands you got here in the UK. I've told Coolidge what needs to happen and to use you to help her do it.'

He looked up from his notes again. 'But I got another job for you too.' He leaned back in his chair and put his hands behind his head. 'There are swarms of you fuckers out there,' he nodded towards the Hive. 'Of course, Nudey tried to tell me marketing was particularly overstaffed, but I'm not stupid. He's a bean counter covering his own ass like they always do,' he grunted. Don't worry, I'll get rid of some bean counters too. But right now, I need you to wield the axe on the so-called marketing department. I don't know what the hell you've all been doing to amuse yourselves, but you need to cut it by half, and halve the salary bill too, by end March. You up for that?'

It was worse than he'd thought. Cut by half. Bloody hell. He mustn't roll over.

'Well, it's going to be a tall order to cut that much. I need a bit of time to think, Mr Hardman.'

'What the fuck d'you need to think about? I'm not pissing around here, Career-ass, and I'm not offering you an alternative.'

It was as if the man knew Stephen's personal situation. How he wanted to tell him what to do with his offer. 'Piss off' so nearly leapt out of his mouth.

He focused on looking Hardman directly in the eye. 'I need to know what the financial package is,' he said.

Hardman raised an eyebrow. 'Oh, really?' He consulted his notes again. 'It says here, if I halve your pay, you'll still be on 40K a year. That sound right?'

Again, even worse than he'd expected.

'It does, Mr Hardman, but with respect, it's a big job you're asking me to do here—'

'It's a simple job, firing people. Believe me, fella, I've done it before – it ain't rocket science.'

How far to push? Hardman had said 'need' at least twice. Maybe he didn't hold all the aces. Who the hell else would do his dirty work?

'I'll do it for sixty.'

'No fucking chance. I'll find someone else.' The American turned round again to face the window. Stephen continued to fix his eyes on the bullet head.

'That is of course your prerogative, Mr Hardman. But you need to know that I was Carol Coolidge's direct boss until three weeks ago. Nobody else knows her strengths and weaknesses like me. She's going to need a lot of help. And as far as cutting jobs here goes, there's no one else here who can best advise you on which ones to get rid of.'

Stephen's pulse was racing. It would be a crap job, but he needed it. Staying in Middleton close to the kids, paying the alimony, it was all on the line. If the ogre kicked him out, he was in deep shit. Even though shit might feel warm and comfortable for a few days, it was still shit.

Hardman swivelled back to face him. 'OK, fella, let's get this straight. There's no way I'm gonna pay you sixty thousand for this. I'll pay you fifty.' He pointed towards the Hive. 'And I still want the people out of here in three months.'

Hardman's axeman and Coolidge's lackey, working a fifty-hour week in a sweatshop. With no chair. And his salary reduced by 30K. No time to do the mental maths on the mortgage.

Not exactly a great result. But no alternative. At least it would buy him time to think.

'So?' Hardman stood up, hands thrust into his pockets, his eyes demanding an answer.

He'd got the bastard on his feet.

'All right, Mr Hardman. I'll do it.'

Chapter Nine

Danny Allsop joined Stephen at the urinals, with his coat on.

'I don't care about the fucking fifty hours. It's Friday night, and a few of the lads are going to the Crown to get pissed. You in?'

It would be a moan-fest, of course, and Danny would tell them he was going to leave for the tenth time this week. But Stephen had nothing better to do.

'Yeah, why not. I'll see you there. Just going to do another hour here first – one less to do over the weekend. I have a few more old agency contacts to tell that I don't have a job title or a budget any more. No doubt they'll lose interest in me after that.'

'You do as you like, mate, but I'm not going back into that war zone one more time tonight,' Danny bristled.

When Stephen returned, the scanner at the gate gave him a friendly little status update.

CARRERAS, S.
HOURS WORKED 41:25.
HOURS REMAINING 08:35.

Laura – that was what he was going to call this thing. Just like his ex: obsessed with time, always thought she was right, and refused to engage in negotiation. Over forty hours done in four days since returning from Paris. But he still wouldn't be seeing much of the weekend if he was going to get the full fifty in. He was actually relieved the kids weren't due – how crap was that?

Standing at his computer screen, he faced a newly installed digital wall clock. 18:05. Gone six on a Friday evening, but the Hive was still buzzing. A far cry from Fridays at Grimley's, where by this time most would have been in the bosom of their families – or on their second pint in the bar with Danny.

Another clock showed it was 12:05 at Schmaltz head office in Chicago. At least Hardman would be on his way back there on a flight from Heathrow by now, probably still cursing the fact that he couldn't get a direct flight from 'this godforsaken place in the arsehole of England'. After his first short week of wreaking havoc here, he had announced he was returning to the US just for the weekend. Any thoughts that his absence might provide a little relief had been soundly dispatched by his parting shot: he would be back by Monday evening and would contact Stephen over the weekend if he had need of him.

Stephen watched Tony Perkins pick up his coat, glance around, and then skulk out of the building. Fifteen to sack and Hardman wanted the names in less than three weeks' time. He was already forming a mental list.

He made little circular motions with his head, trying to ease the tension in his neck, feeling wrung out by Hardman's constant demands to see more and more data, which had continued from his chauffeured limo down to Heathrow. Sod it, he was going to be here tomorrow anyway, so he might as well head for the pub now. He checked his phone for missed calls and found there was a voicemail, left three hours ago.

'Hi, it's Rachel... Rachel Pearson? Er, I was just wondering how your first week back had gone and wondered if you maybe fancied catching up this weekend, but you're probably busy. Well, er, bye.'

She wanted to see him again. And he had her number now. He called straight back.

'Sorry, you're probably busy,' she repeated. 'And you've probably got the children…'

'I'm not busy, Rachel,' he interrupted. It probably wasn't cool to say he was free all weekend. 'I'm free all weekend,' he said. Apart from the eight hours work he had to fit in, obviously.

'Mm, I've sort of boxed myself in a bit for tomorrow,' she said. 'But I know this is short notice and you're probably busy—'

'I'm really not busy, Rachel.'

'Do you fancy coming round this evening? I can cook. Well, I can boil pasta, more accurately.'

Within the hour he had driven home, grabbed a decent bottle of red wine, shed his suit and tie for what felt like the first time in a week, and was driving round the ring road. Danny would be well into his moan-athon by now and wouldn't miss him.

He pulled up outside a Victorian villa that looked in need of a little TLC. She had told him it was the upstairs flat, and there was a light in the window with the curtains open. His heart was beating quickly. He didn't know her that well yet. Would he even still like her? And although he loved that thing where she tucked a strand of hair behind her delicate ears, and those expressive brown eyes that could switch effortlessly from amusement to empathy, her face wasn't fully formed in his mind yet.

She was on the landing, dressed only in a skimpy red vest and jeans – striking, if a little odd for the time of year. But it was OK. She still looked great.

'Hello, you found it then,' she said, looking rather flushed.

'I did. No problem.'

'Sorry, stupid remark. I mean obviously you found it, otherwise…'

He hugged her. He never hugged anyone these days, except Kate. She didn't resist – but she didn't exactly cling on either. God, he'd forgotten how complex first moves were.

The sitting room was a scene of chaos. Dominated by a piano, too grand for the surroundings, with piles of sheet music on top of it, and at the other end, a small dining table covered in magazines. A door led to a galley kitchen from where the aroma of fried onions wafted.

'As may be apparent, I'm not the world's tidiest human being.'

'Don't worry, I know what it's like by Friday evening, when you haven't had time to tidy up.'

'Mm, that's awkward, as this is me *after* half an hour's tidying up,' she said, hastily removing a pair of black tights festooned over a two-seater sofa.

'Honestly, don't worry, it's fine,' he said. Laura would have had kittens. But he thought about the ironing board still standing in his own hallway, and the trousers draped over his banister, and liked her even more. 'I really do know the feeling,' he added, hoping she could feel his empathy.

There was something more pressing he needed to know, though.

'So... I'm sorry, I've forgotten the name of your flatmate...'

'Beatrice.'

'Yes, Beatrice, where is she this evening?'

'Oh, she's gone home to her parents,' Rachel said in a matter of fact way, still holding the tights. 'She sometimes does at the weekend.'

Things were looking up.

Her face brightened. 'Come on then, I want to hear all about Paris. Was it exciting? Will you chat to me while I'm cooking? Not exactly gourmet, I'm afraid. Penne and ratatouille with just a hint of blackened onion.'

The compact kitchen was a hothouse, which explained her skimpy top. The small work surface was almost completely covered in pans and storage jars, but there was just enough room for a small chopping board where she had prepared a colourful collection of courgettes, tomatoes and yellow peppers. And next to it a glass of what looked like a berry smoothie, evidently her choice of apéritif.

'What would you like to drink?' she asked, without explaining his options.

She had put his bottle on the windowsill.

'Maybe a glass of wine?'

'Of course, good idea.' She looked a little sheepish. 'Sorry, I should have nipped out to buy some, but I got carried away with the cooking – and the tidying up, obviously. Give me five minutes, and I can nip round to the supermarket.'

'That's OK,' he said. Alcohol really was low on her list of priorities. 'Maybe we could open what I brought?'

'Oh yes, of course, that looks great thanks.' She picked up the bottle without consulting the label and opened a cabinet next to the cooker in search of a wine glass.

'Will you join me?' he asked.

'No, you're all right, but let me pour you a glass.'

There was an initial formality, as Stephen navigated towards a bond that had started to form on that shopping trip before Christmas. And he wondered again if it was madness, this fascination with a non-drinking do-gooder. Just not really him.

But then as Rachel sizzled away, smoothie in one hand and spatula in the other, he unloaded. The crappy hotel, the extraordinary conference, how a buffoon called Oscar Newte had got a top job and even, worst of all, how Carol Coolidge, his former protégé, was now one of his two bosses. But it was far too early to reveal anything about their history together. He tried to accentuate the lunacy of it all, more than the pain.

Rachel laughed. And listened. And her look of incredulity, holding her fingers to her mouth like a wide-eyed schoolchild, was particularly endearing. The awkwardness evaporated. While he was telling her about the return to the Grimley's office, she turned away for a moment, head inclined over the frying pan. He wanted to kiss her shoulder.

She cleared the magazines off the table and spread a red-and-white check tablecloth over it. Then she placed two red candles in the centre, lit them, and switched off the main light.

The food tasted delicious, warm and comforting. And as she poured him a small second glass of wine, she encouraged him to keep talking. He told her about the office transformation, including how the bar was to be replaced by a gym.

'You won't recognise me next time you see me, Rachel. I will have the body of a Greek god.'

'OK, that sounds more promising,' she said, taking another glug of smoothie.

He told her about the card reader, leaving out that he'd named it Laura. But as he moved on to describe Hardman and his demands, her smile of fascination changed to a look of sympathy. There was no amusing spin he could put on this bit.

'So there you have it. I no longer have my job title or in fact any official managerial status whatsoever as far as I can make out, but he still wants me to choose fifteen people to make redundant.'

Her face was cupped in her hands, lit by the candlelight.

'What are you going to do?'

Something about those eyes compelled honesty.

'You'll probably think this is mad, Rachel. But I've told him I'll do it.'

She continued looking at him, unblinking.

'You do think I'm mad, don't you? I think I might be going mad.'

'It's not my world, Stephen. I wouldn't think that for a moment. But why do you think you said yes?'

'I dunno,' he sighed. 'I've asked myself since and of course I can rationalise it. First off, I can't afford to go without work for any length of time, and marketing jobs around here aren't exactly two a penny. Never seen myself as a FastGro Fertilisers man, even if there was a job there, and that's about the only other option within fifty miles of here. That or Burton's Boilers.'

'Well, my dad likes to say where there's muck there's brass, when he's trying to reclaim his Yorkshire roots, but I can see what you mean. More fun in chocolate I'd have thought.'

'I used to think so. Not so sure now, mind.'

'And I assume you want to stay close by for the children,' she said. He hadn't talked this through with anyone before. But she'd got it, straight away.

'Yes, the thought had crossed my mind to look elsewhere, and come back here for weekends with the kids, but I can't afford to live two hundred miles away and keep my house here as well. If I move, I'm just terrified I'd lose touch with Kate and Jake.'

'I can see that.' She squeezed his arm tenderly. He couldn't remember anyone doing that before.

'And he's cutting my salary as well, of course,' he added.

She removed her hand, as if with this statement he had lost her sympathy. Probably not appropriate to complain about the alimony.

'Hey, look at me, bringing you sweetness and light on a Friday evening,' he said with a thin smile.

'Oh, that's all right. You bring what you bring,' she replied, more sadly. 'I guess I've had a fairly tough week too, though maybe not as dramatic as yours.'

'I'm sorry, Rachel, I'm so self-absorbed at the moment. I'm not normally like this, honest. I haven't asked anything about your week.' In truth, he knew that he had been this self-absorbed for too long now.

'It's just that I think we're in danger of running out of money at work by the end of this year. We've been having crisis meetings with the trustees, but unless something turns up, we can't continue long term.' Her expression had turned gloomy.

'That's terrible. Have you come up with any plans for what you're going to do about it?'

'The three of us who take a salary have decided to take a cut to keep us going for a few more months. But that's just delaying the inevitable. And we'll keep submitting funding applications, of course. Beyond that, I expect there'll be a lot of prayer meetings. That sometimes works.'

'Oh, maybe I should try that. Shit, sorry, there I go turning it back to my problem again. Oh, sorry, there I go saying "shit" when you never seem to swear.'

'Oh, stop it, Stephen,' she said, laughing again affectionately.

He felt relieved to have eased the mood.

Then, hesitantly, she asked, 'But would you?'

'Would I what?'

'Pray with me?'

God, this was an unfortunate turn of events. Up to now, he'd been able to forget about the Christian thing.

'I wouldn't even know how.' He gave an embarrassed little laugh.

'Well, I would. It's not rocket science. Just need to choose your method.'

Bugger it, she was serious.

'Er, are there different methods, then?' he asked, suddenly feeling uncomfortable.

'Yeah. So first there's what I call the 'ask and it shall be given' approach. There are people in my church who reckon if they're desperately trying to find a parking place at Tesco, and ask fervently enough, God will make sure that the bloke in the Audi will vacate his space at just the right moment.'

'I can see how that might be useful. That car park is a mare.' He tried to sound insouciantly breezy.

'What do I know? They swear it works. But I suppose I've always felt God has enough on his or her plate without needing to find me a parking spot. Anyway, I don't have a car. As I get older, I tend more to the contemplative. More like the monks, I suppose. Sort of pray and just see what turns up – or what it does to me.' She was resting her chin on her hand, gazing at him. 'So if you fancy giving it a lash, I'm your woman.'

'Well, that's quite a come-on line.'

'The Beatitudes, that's what we need,' she said, apparently ignoring this remark, although he was sure there was a glimmer in her eye. She sprang to her feet and went to the cluttered bookshelf.

'Are you sure about this?' he asked.

'Absolutely.' She picked out a dog-eared Bible and hopped up onto the sofa, tucking her legs beneath her.

'It's important to be comfortable then, is it?'

'It is. Care to join me?'

This was seriously weird. But placing his wine glass and the bottle on a coffee table, he settled in next to her, feeling her thigh brushing against his.

'So, the basic idea is, I'm going to read them – the Beatitudes, that is – and you're going to close your eyes.'

'I am?'

She gave him a stern look, a teacher who feels the fun needs to stop. 'It's an Ignatian technique,' she said, like this settled the matter. 'I'm going to read this passage slowly, and the idea is that you sort of imagine yourself into the scene, like you were there, as one of the disciples, I suppose.'

He could see it was important to her that he had a go. He closed his eyes.

She started by imitating a stuffy old priest. 'Dearly beloved, I take as my text today Matthew Chapter Five, beginning at the third verse.' But then she returned to her own voice, soft and calm, as she began to read.

'Blessed are the poor in spirit…'

What would it be like, curled up in bed with her, his face against her bare back? Her bedroom would probably have her clothes strewn all over the place, but her bed would smell of sweet vanilla sheets, with lovely soft pillows. Maybe he could just stay here all weekend, pretend that Schmaltz Europe was a dream.

'Blessed are those who are persecuted because of righteousness, for theirs is the kingdom of Heaven.'

He heard the faintest sound of her closing the book and opened his eyes. But hers were now shut tight.

God, he wanted to kiss her even more.

She opened her eyes and turned towards him. 'So, any thoughts, Mr Carreras?'

He was on the spot.

'Er, blessed are the poor? That rang some bells.'

'D'oh,' she wailed in frustration and gave him a playful thwack on the knee with the Bible. 'That bit was about being poor in *spirit*, not poor financially.'

'Ouch. Well that's me put in my place,' he said sharply. It was easy for her; she didn't have a grasping ex and two kids to support. Although he couldn't imagine how little she was living on.

'Well, how about blessed are the persecuted?' he proffered. 'I do think I might lay claim to be a bit persecuted.'

'OK, I'll give you that,' she said. 'You do sound very persecuted at the moment.' She paused, those brown eyes fixed on him. 'And as if you might need a friend or two.'

It was a warm, soft thought, having her as his friend, or maybe more.

He sipped from his almost empty glass, eyeing the bottle. He could risk another glass; he didn't think he'd be over the limit.

Rachel leapt up. 'I make a cappuccino to die for,' she said.

Over coffee, she told him more about her work, and in particular a boy who had been taken into care, and who hadn't talked to anyone for six months when he had first come to Action Stations. Until one day Rachel and a colleague had taken him and some other boys to watch football. She had seen the look in his eye and knew they'd found a way to connect with him. At the end of the story, she wiped her eyes. He slipped an arm around her, and her shoulder softened, relaxed into him.

'You are a very good woman, Rachel,' he said.

'Oh, piss off,' she snapped, although laughing at the same time. It was the first time he'd heard her swear.

'Language, please.'

'Mm, fine coming from you. Sorry, it's just that people often assume that I'm a good woman, but I have plenty of vices. I just like to keep them hidden.'

'That sounds like an interesting challenge,' he said with a smile.

Then she got to her feet, and the moment of intimacy had passed.

'Well, I've got to organise a party for a bunch of hyper teenagers tomorrow,' she sighed. 'And by the sound of it you'll be in the office with seventy hysterical adults. So we've both got a working Saturday.'

It didn't look like he'd be experiencing those vanilla-scented sheets for some time yet.

She walked downstairs with him. He needed to seal the evening somehow. They stopped on the path in the small garden.

'Can I call you?' he asked.

She hesitated for a moment, then smiled. 'Yes. I'd like that.' He leant to kiss her and was met by her lips, sweet and welcoming, before she eased gently from his embrace. She looked thoughtful.

'Stephen, I owe you an apology. I sort of implied that I didn't think the bit about "blessed are the poor" really applied to you. I mean, what do I know? I've not got your responsibilities. But I was thinking about the people you're going to have to get rid of, who I suspect don't have your talent and resilience. I just thought they might be genuinely in dire straits, and what's going to happen to them? I know this madman is calling you an operative, but it seems clear he still needs you as a leader. I was just wondering if, somehow or other, you could find a way to do some good among the carnage, if that doesn't sound too pompous.' Her eyes were searching his.

'No apology required,' he said, and touched her arm in reassurance.

Back in his car, he turned off the late-night radio phone-in and drove home in silence. She had him praying, for God's sake. She might still be after his soul more than his body. What was the devout Christian view on sex these days anyway? And specifically with a forty-year-old divorcé rather too fond of the grape? He laughed at himself. Just his luck to fall for a chaste woman. If he was falling. If she was chaste. Her warmth, the way she looked at him, the pulse of her throat, that kiss.

And that phrase, 'do good among the carnage'. It was probably just a throwaway line. And as she admitted, it was easy for her to say. But it seemed to be what she was trying to do, out there, every day. And unfortunately, it was not Rachel but her words that followed him all the way home and nestled into bed with him.

Chapter Ten

'OK, people, now let's switch into… star jumps!' screeched Madison, as 'Gonna Make You Sweat' went on and on. Her powerful arms and legs formed two perfectly synchronised V-shapes above and below her toned torso as she demonstrated. Her glossy white leotard had the words FIT FOR SCHMALTZ disturbingly stamped in brown letters across her impressive chest.

What a way to start the week. Stephen gave it a go. It wasn't easy, having all your limbs wide apart at the same time. To his right, Danny's grunting and puffing grew louder, as he formed a straggly Y-shape, feet glued together and arms above his head waving half-heartedly. He had opted for a pair of baggy tracksuit bottoms and a green-and-yellow striped West Bromwich Albion away shirt with ALLSOP printed on the back.

'Yes, Team Schmaltz, yes,' Madison roared. The fluorescent light reflecting from the floor imbued her ebony thighs with a tangerine glow. Did Hardman really want his male managers arriving for work in a state of arousal? Maybe that was the secret of Pet's Paradise's success: profitability pumped by testosterone.

A late arrival strode confidently onto the mat just in front of him, slipped off her white cotton top to reveal a perfectly coordinated black vest and yoga pants, and tied her long blonde hair into a ponytail. Carol was in the building. Why the hell wasn't she in Paris? Within moments she had picked up Madison's rhythm and was gliding seamlessly through the exercises, ponytail bobbing in perfect time as they segued into salsa.

If he focused straight ahead in order to follow Madison, he was staring at Carol's bottom.

He had tried so hard to be professional, to treat her like just another member of the team. And they had always agreed nobody else needed to know about what had happened between them. But here she was, his new boss, still bloody here. Waggling her bottom at him.

'OK, Stevie, stay focused,' yelled Madison. It was already evident the woman had eyes in the back of her head. She was on you like a ton of bricks if you lost the rhythm. And she was calling him Stevie.

'Right, people, now we're going to stretch those muscles with one of my favourite yoga positions, the downward-facing dog. And don't forget, later today I'm going to allocate you to future classes based on ability,' Madison warned them.

He was on all fours now, pushing his bum high into the air to impress her. But would he rather be in the Premier League with Carol, or spend his Monday mornings with Allsop's belly flop, destined for relegation?

Madison finished them on a high note, her gyrating thighs leading the way in a last heart-racing exercise.

'OK, y'all, as you leave, just give me your name, so I can make a note of your personal rating.'

Stephen approached her, trying not to appear out of breath.

'Good job, Stevie. When I'm finished, you'll have a great body.' She gave him an affirming pat on the bottom as he passed. Was this how she talked to all the boys?

He heard the familiar Brummie tones behind him.

'My name's Danny Allsop, love, and you don't need to tell me, you've never seen a body like this before, have you?'

'Thank you, Mr Allsop, plenty to work on, hey?' she said curtly.

As he left the gym, he felt a tap on the shoulder. Carol was still exuding orange blossom. He could smell his own sweat.

'What are you doing here, Carol?' He got in first.

'We need to talk. I'll see you in my office in fifteen minutes.' She strolled off to the changing room.

Stephen worked out that the posse of half-naked bodies in the men's changing room were gathered exactly where the bar used to be. Allsop was trudging back from the shower already, towel wrapped around his waist.

'Fuck this for a game of soldiers, sunshine, I'm outta here.'

'So you keep saying, Danny. OK, you go for it. If you are first over the wall, we'll see what's lying for you on the other side.'

'Are you seriously going to stick this out? It's a crime against humanity, that's what it is.'

'Well, it certainly seems to be mounting up to a crock of shit, but you might be slightly exaggerating there, Daniel, old son.'

Allsop grunted. 'Suit yourself. Anyway, I'll see you in the torture chamber a bit later.'

*

Her office door was open, so he could see her leaning back in her chair as she took a call. She had changed into a pin-striped suit, like the one she'd worn at the conference. But knowing her, it would be a different one. Maureen Birtles' desk was positioned so she could attend to both Hardman and Carol in their adjacent offices.

'You'll have to knock,' she smirked, without raising her head from her keyboard.

Carol gestured him in with a cursory wave of the hand. As in Hardman's office, there was nowhere for him to sit. She carried on the call while he stood, hands in pockets, his hard stare an attempt to intimidate her.

'That's what Mr Hardman wants from you, Vassos, and I'll expect to get your action plan when I fly into Athens next week. Anyway, I must go, I'm about to have a similar conversation with my man in the UK.'

Only now did she look at him.

'So, here we are,' she said. If there was any embarrassment at the reversal of roles, she was doing a good job of hiding it. If anything, her eyes betrayed amusement. She took a swig from her bottle of water. 'The gym's a great way to start the week, isn't it? There are more than a few people here who need toning up.' She gave him the once-over. 'And how are we finding the new structure?'

It was a bastard thing to say, her way of proclaiming victory.

'A little early to say, Carol, wouldn't you think?'

She grinned mischievously. 'I'm afraid you'd have to call me Miss Coolidge if Brad was here. I won't insist myself, but he does seem to be a stickler for hierarchy…'

'Let's just get on with it, Carol, shall we? I had assumed you would be operating from Paris, not back here.'

'Oh, I will of course, but I need to get around all the markets on a regular basis, so I might do the UK on a Monday some time, if I need to come back here to see my guy some weekends. And the company is actually subbing my mortgage here, as well as paying for the apartment over there. So I might as well make the most of it.'

'Yes, I imagine you must. And you get this office too, to share with Oscar. Congratulations.'

'Yes, we might need to share it odd days. But I think he plans to spend most of his weekends in Paris. Not sure what Mrs Newte thinks about that,' she laughed.

'Relief, I would imagine,' Stephen said. 'But I wouldn't vacate this office too often. We peasants in the workhouse will be squatting here if you aren't careful.'

She was checking a message on her phone. Was she even listening?

'Anyway, I've been thinking about what needs to be done here, so let's cut to the chase,' she said. She pressed a button on her desk and Maureen appeared promptly with two Schmaltz-branded carrier bags which she handed to her. From one of them, Carol slowly and deliberately took out packs of Bingo Bars, Munchy Moments, Grimley's Mint Regals and, lastly, Little Monkeys. She laid them out on the desk in front of her, as if to perform a conjuring trick she'd been rehearsing.

'I'm going through this exercise with each of the countries, as in each one Brad has given me a marketing operative whose job will be to help me deliver Project Harmony. You've heard of that, I assume?'

'Means nothing to me, Carol.'

She looked disappointed in him. 'It's very simple. Your job in the UK is to replace these...' she swept her hand across the packs '...with these.' She reached into the other carrier bag and put the two American brands on the table: a Schmaltzy Bar in a small dark brown wrapper and a yellow packet of Nutters.

Did she really believe it was that simple?

'So how exactly do you think that four brands can be replaced by two? Do you and Brad have a point of view on that?'

'We have more than a point of view, we've got a clear strategy, and your job as an operative is simply to carry it out,' she said sharply. She brushed a hand dismissively against the

Bingo Bar to send it sliding across the table onto the floor and put the Schmaltzy Bar in its place. 'Step One. Bingo out, Schmaltzy Bar in. Let me give you the rationale for that one, as you appear to be struggling. In the UK we've always talked up Bingo because it's the only one that makes even a small amount of money. But it's chicken feed.' She picked up the Schmaltzy Bar again. 'Whereas this baby netted a cool 2.6 billion dollars in the US last year. If you'd like to explain to Brad why we can't swap one with the other, please feel free.'

'OK, let me try this out on you, just for starters. Have you considered that American chocolate is much sweeter? Not only will Brits not like the taste, there's also the anti-sugar brigade to contend with.'

She frowned. 'Are you seriously suggesting that if we get rid of Bingo and replace it with Schmaltzy Bars, we might actually lose sales?' Her tone was incredulous.

'I'm saying it's a possibility, yes. I could quote you a few precedents in confectionery where an imported brand has bombed. If you want my advice, it would be a good idea to at least start with some market research, to check it out.'

Carol shook her head. 'I'm sure Brad Hardman didn't get where he is today by bothering with market research. If Henry Ford had just listened to customers, he would just have built a faster horse. No, Brad is all about driving through change, based on his instinct. We'll just fucking do it and the punters will follow.'

She was so obviously parroting Hardman. And if only he had a pound for every time he'd heard that Henry Ford line. But she clearly didn't want a debate.

'Now, moving on, as I don't have much more time this morning. Step Two is to replace Munchy Moments with Nutters.' Once again, the British incumbent was sent crashing to the floor by Carol's right hand, to be replaced by the American brand.

'So that's it for Munchy Moments, is it?' he asked. 'The brand you have personally been championing for the last two years and persuaded me to go on TV with last year?'

Carol gave a sigh of exasperation. He wouldn't let her off the hook yet.

'Pray explain the rationale for this one too,' he said.

'I think you'll find that it's about replacing one chocolate-covered nut with another. It's not complicated. Except I think you'll also find that Munchy Moments is a chocolate-covered peanut that's worth peanuts. Whereas Nutters is worth 1.4 billion.' She was obviously pleased with her little play on words. It sounded like the sort of smart-arse thing Oscar Newte would say.

'But hang on, it's not as simple as that, is it? You've been telling me for the last two years that Munchy Moments is unique. Have you forgotten your own advertising? A combination of crunchy peanut and succulent raisin wrapped in deliciously smooth chocolate. Remember? Whereas the nut in Nutters is a yolanda nut, and there's no raisin. And has it occurred to you that Nutters might just sell more because it's sold in America, which in case you haven't noticed is rather a big place? Oh, and finally, might I humbly suggest that the name Nutters leaves a little to be desired over here?'

This was more like it. The first opportunity to let off steam since he'd come back from Paris. But now Carol looked seriously vexed.

'Have you quite finished? You really are very insular, aren't you? You were marketing director here for how long? Six years, wasn't it? Did the brand share grow? No, it didn't. And yet you are so very resistant to change.' She stood up, as if to draw the meeting to a close. 'Right then, is that clear?'

'Actually, the brand share *has* grown on some brands, and would have done by more if we'd invested in them. And I have another issue, Carol. Unless you're thinking we can ship thousands of these things over from Chicago to East Midlands airport every day, we'll need to work out how to make them over here.'

'I am well aware of that,' she replied scornfully. 'Which is why you'd better get yourself up to Dumfries to discuss it with the manufacturing team as soon as possible, hadn't you?'

'Would you like to accompany me to explain the logic to Jim Jeffries and the technical boys? I'm sure they'll be very understanding.'

She slammed her fist on the desk. 'Jim Jeffries and his dinosaurs will simply do what they're told. And no, I haven't got time to come with you. That's below my pay grade now. Remember, I'm strategy and you are operations. Let me explain again how this is going to work—'

Maureen knocked, and Carol waved her in.

'I've got Mr Newte on the line for you, Miss Coolidge.'

'OK, put him through.' She held her palm up to Stephen to indicate she wanted him to wait as she picked up the call.

'Hi, Oscar, how are you? How was your weekend?' She swung round to gaze out of the window, leaving Stephen fuming for a second time. There was that twinge in his hamstring again. He'd probably overdone it with Madison.

'Yeah, that's a great restaurant, isn't it?' she said. 'I went there last year. Did you go in the cocktail bar beforehand?' Stephen imagined Newte's smug face, gazing out from his office over a Parisian boulevard. He didn't know how yet, but he was going to nail the wanker.

'Yeah, the office here is great. You wouldn't recognise the place. The gym's opened this morning, so that will sort out the men from the boys,' she laughed, walking past Stephen to look out onto the Hive. 'And I'm looking out on a floor full of eager beavers, standing at their workstations and cracking on with it.

It feels more like a factory, much more energy.' She looked at Stephen. 'I'm just making it clear what needs to happen to the brands over here.'

Phone crooked in her neck, she checked her appearance in her compact mirror and applied lipstick as Newte blathered on. She didn't look like a woman worried about reporting into Hardman. But then, why should she? If Stephen did her bidding and delivered the brand demolition plan Brad wanted, she would get all the credit. He would make her look good, the golden girl. If it all went pear-shaped, she had European Vice President at age twenty-eight on her CV, and that job on the board of the ad agency still waiting for her. It would just be him left scrabbling around for another job.

Finally she came off the phone. 'So, as I was saying, I am going to deliver the plan for Harmony by the end of March and the whole project will be completed by September. Therefore I'll need weekly updates from you on how we'll switch the brands. And it needs to be watertight, because I'll be presenting it to Brad. If you don't feel up to it, I can let Brad know. Now, I must get on.'

Why, in the heart of his outrage, did he see her for a moment in that black gym outfit, the two of them entangled in an advanced yoga position in the men's changing room?

'I still have one final question. You haven't told me what your plans for the other two brands are.'

'Those?' She considered with an air of mild distaste the box of Mint Regals and the packet of Little Monkeys still on the desk in front of her. Then she picked each one up with the tips of her fingers, and dropped them into the carrier bag. She held out the bag at arm's length. Her perfectly painted lips formed a grin.

'You can dispose of them for me.'

Chapter Eleven

His former team were all waiting for him in Sacrifice, the meeting room in which he had asked everyone to gather. The only rooms available were that or Ambition. Bit of a no-brainer in the circumstances.

Stephen assumed that they had an inkling he hadn't invited them to an afternoon tea party, but there did seem to be an inappropriately cheery mood, as they talked among themselves. It was the first time he had addressed them as a group since before Christmas. Technically they no longer answered to him, but to Carol Coolidge. He had simply been appointed by Hardman to destroy them.

He still needs you as a leader, Rachel had said. What was she doing right now, on a Friday afternoon?

He raised his voice above the buzz of conversation. 'If I can have your attention, please. Thanks for all being here.' The room quietened and thirty faces turned towards him. Now Sandra, standing at the front, looked anxious. Maybe his demeanour had betrayed him. 'You may have heard, as part of the plan to put the UK on a sound footing as partners in Schmaltz Europe, we need to identify significant savings in both staffing budgets and in our overall cost base.' The room was completely silent now. 'This review will be conducted across all departments, but Mr Hardman has asked me to explore how we can contribute within the UK marketing department.'

Textbook management speak was just flowing out of his mouth. Steve Carreras, safe pair of hands marketing director, had kicked in again. Hardman didn't deserve to have his barbaric methods conveyed so reasonably.

'When you say explore, Steve, what exactly do you mean?' asked Barry Evans, the grey-haired media manager, from the back of the room. Bazza had developed a finely tuned bullshit detector over the years. Might as well cut to the chase.

'Mr Hardman has informed me that fifteen of you will need to leave the company by the end of March.' There was a collective gasp. Sandra started to sniff, her eyes saying, 'how could you?' He would try not to look at her again.

'Naturally this will be very difficult for some of you, and I am truly sorry to have to be the bearer of this news, as I know many of you have been working here for a long time...'

'You could just refuse to carry out his orders.' Surprisingly it was Tony Perkins who interrupted with a surly expression. Normally he didn't say boo to a goose. Maybe telling him to 'man up' at his last appraisal hadn't been such a good idea after all.

Someone else said, 'That's right, Tony.' There was an outbreak of chuntering and a whiff of mutiny in the ranks.

'Tell me, Tony. What do you think would happen if I refused to take on Mr Hardman's instructions?' Stephen asked.

'Maybe he would have to sack *you*.' Perkins was retracting into his shell, but still just audible.

A couple of others tittered. God, Perkins was a slimeball. Stephen was furious now. He tried to picture Rachel in the lamplight, by her garden gate. *Do good among the carnage.*

'Actually, Tony, I think you're wrong. I think he would just lay waste to the whole department, with no regard for who could cope best with this. But I'm going to make a pledge to you all here and now to help you in whatever way I can. First, you should know that there will be a voluntary redundancy package for those who want to take it. I'm not going to pretend it's massively generous, but I can explore the details with you whenever you want. Unfortunately, however, I have to make final recommendations to Mr Hardman in a week's time.'

He paused to let the words sink in.

'For those of you who don't take the voluntary option, and who regrettably I have to recommend for redundancy, I am going to do everything I can in the next three months to personally help you find another job.'

'How, exactly?' muttered Perkins, head now bowed. In his particular case, Stephen had no idea – any offers for his toxic blend of bungling incompetence?

'By trying to write you good references, Tony, and by using my contacts in the recruitment world.' Contacts plural was pushing it a bit. There was only one recruitment consultant he really knew who would take this on. But it worked. The room was stilled.

'I suggest that nobody makes an immediate decision. I'm telling you on a Friday so you can discuss things with your loved ones over the weekend. I was about to say that my door is always open if anyone wants to talk about this – but as you may have noticed, I no longer have a door.'

There was a murmuring of sympathetic laughter, and then they filed out. Stephen re-entered the Hive with no option of retreating behind the sanctuary of an office wall. His team were standing around podiums in little clusters, obviously discussing the bombshell.

Well, he had done it. And he had done it as well as he could.

At the water cooler, Barry Evans approached him, munching an apple. 'Not easy, that, for you, Steve. Thank you for being straight with us. I can probably get the ball rolling for you. I'm happy to be out of here. Time for the allotment and the golf handicap, I think. I just need to chat to Beryl about it over the weekend, but you can probably put me down for voluntary redundancy by first thing Monday morning. Not exactly the swansong I was hoping for, but it will have to do. Good luck with it all, mate.'

'Thanks, Barry, I appreciate that.' Stephen shook his hand.

Barry turned away, paused, and then turned back. 'Oh, and if you need someone to push that snivelling little shit Perkins off the top of a high building, just give me the nod, won't you? That would be two down, thirteen to go.' He winked and munched off.

His phone rang – Laura. Almost certainly a problem over childcare.

'Hello, how are you?' Try to at least start on the right foot.

'You'll need to change your plans for the children over the weekend, assuming you have made some, that is.'

'Of course I've made plans, Laura. As soon as you confirmed you wanted me to have them, so you can go away again.'

'Well, Trist and I are not going away until tomorrow morning. But Kate is going to a sleep over at Megan's tonight. And Jake's said he doesn't want to come to you on his own, so I've had to find a sitter to come over here.'

'Hang on, I thought you said you weren't going away until tomorrow.'

'That's correct. We aren't going away until tomorrow, but we are going out tonight.'

She always unleashed this stuff like an avalanche.

'Why doesn't Jake want to come round here?' It would have been fun, a boys' night in on their own. They could have had fish and chips and watched something other than the diet of chick flicks that Kate fed on these days.

'I have no idea. He said last time you just ended up watching some girly film on a Friday evening. It's very inconvenient for us, but there it is. And then tomorrow morning he's playing football and won't be finished until twelve. So you'll need to pick him up from there. Oh, and Kate is going into town with Megan, so you'll need to text her and arrange where to meet her at lunchtime.'

'For God's sake, Laura, slow down. Does this mean Jake's finally got into the team?'

'Presumably,' she said with an edge of sarcasm.

'Where are they playing?'

'Oh, I don't know. I'll get him to text you.' She sounded impatient.

'Yes, you do that, Laura. Has it occurred to you that rather than pick him up at the end, I might want to go and watch him, give him some support? This is important for him.'

'Good, I think you should.'

'And how do we feel about Kate going into town on a Saturday morning?' he asked.

'Good grief, this is Middleton, hardly the mean streets of New York. And in case you hadn't noticed, she's fifteen. Better get used to it. She's about to get expensive.'

This was the future. More and more reasons why they wouldn't be around to spend time with him. If he was forced to move away in search of a job, it would be impossible. At least living close by, he could still provide a taxi service – and a bank.

He was still standing by the water cooler, gazing out at the car park. There might be one upside to the kids not being around this evening. Could he call Rachel, see if she was free tonight? It seemed a remote possibility. And what did she really think of him? Despite that parting kiss last week, he still wondered if he was just getting the sympathy vote from a good woman.

He was probably overanalysing the whole thing. Give her a call. What was there to lose? Well, his pride, of course; he couldn't cope with any more rejection at the moment.

She answered. That lovely warm greeting from somewhere outside Planet Schmaltz.

'I just wondered if you were around this evening?' he asked.

There was a moment's silence.

'I am. But I thought you had your children all weekend?'

'It turns out they're not around until tomorrow now, so I'm free if you are.'

'Sounds great.'

*

He managed to get a booking at La Belle Époque. Was it a bit over the top? Hell, no point failing for lack of effort.

Ducks were lining up in a row. Supper with Rachel, Jakey playing footy. And on his way back from a pee, Laura Card Reader informed him that the time remaining to achieve his fifty hours for the week was a mere one hour and forty-four minutes.

'Thanks Laura,' he said. 'Anything planned for the weekend? No, I thought not. You need to get out more, you know.' He patted the scanner before realising that Maureen Birtles was standing behind him, giving him a pitying look.

'Just the man I need to see,' she said. 'You've saved me an email. Mr Hardman needs to do a conference call with you at seven thirty this evening, in Winning.' She couldn't resist her now customary thin-lipped smile of triumph.

Hardman's perfect impression of a heartless bastard was hitting new heights. The timing was no doubt deliberate – a clear reminder that although he was back in Chicago for the weekend again, he was still pulling the strings, and that Stephen would go home only when he had done with him.

The restaurant couldn't take a booking for later in the evening. There was nowhere else in Middleton to compare. He just couldn't face the Old Ship, so soon after that party. And instantly Rachel felt out of reach again, out there in another, kinder world, with the unfeeling bulk of Hardman blocking out the light.

He called her to explain Hardman's alternative plan for his evening, apologetic but trying to mask his sense of quiet desperation.

'Ah well, never mind about the restaurant,' she said, sounding disappointed. Did she have any idea how impossible it would be to tell Hardman where to go? There was an awkward silence. Could he invite himself round to hers again?

'So then, your turn to cook?' she said. 'I'm not fussy. Well, I'm vegetarian but apart from that I'm not fussy.'

'Oh, OK. Well, I'll call as soon as the meeting is over. I'll probably need to go and buy some food.'

'That's all right. Just let me know when you leave your office. I'll wait outside if you're not back. I'll try not to scare the neighbours.'

He hadn't cooked a meal for a woman since the early years of being married to Laura. Before they had slipped into their roles. He felt a bit ashamed – and a sense of panic.

*

He felt that end of week tension in his neck again, as he stared at the screen perched high on the wall in Winning, awaiting Hardman's arrival. Naturally, the ogre kept him waiting for ages. He was probably still having lunch somewhere – or eating someone else. It was nearly eight o'clock when he appeared, sitting in front of a window so that a skyscraper seemed to rise from the top of his head. He glowered at Stephen as he held up a sheet of paper.

'I got a list of all the bozos in the UK who didn't do their fifty hours last week. There are a helluva lot of them.' His eyes narrowed on Stephen as if he was responsible for every one of them, in every department. Laura Card Reader had obviously snitched on them.

'You better tell 'em that if I see their names appear on this list again, they are outta here.' He pointed accusingly at the screen.

Was this a threat or a promise?

'I will, Mr Hardman.'

'And this idiot Allsop, in purchasing. Do you know him?'

'I do indeed.'

'OK, you can ask him a personal question from me. He only missed the mark by twenty fucking hours last week, that's all. Is he taking the piss?'

'I don't know. I'll ask him, Mr Hardman.'

Hardman didn't look amused. There was of course no need to ask Danny. Taking the piss was exactly what he was doing. And he'd doubtless have extracted it once more with feeling when the figures for this week were totted up.

Hardman gave a phlegmy snort of derision. 'That's it. I'll be back in the UK sometime next week – maybe. But if not, I'll get hold of you if I need you.'

Small mercies. He wasn't spending all his time in the UK after all. Clearly he had discovered a few other psychiatric patients requiring his tender loving care.

It was gone eight o'clock now. The evening had gone pear-shaped. He had so wanted to see her, but now he felt wrung out. Not a good condition for a date. And he couldn't be expected to go to the supermarket now and cook for her. He could go home, order himself a Chinese takeaway and have a couple of beers on his own. There was a match on TV. But he couldn't just blow her off either. Maybe she would take the hint. He called her again.

'Hello, it's Stephen. I'm afraid we've only just finished. I wonder if it's all getting a bit late?'

'No, that's OK, I'm on my way. There's a bus in ten minutes. I'll be there in an hour.'

He found a recipe for vegetarian cheesy bake on his phone. Thank God she wasn't a vegan. But it took an age to shop in the supermarket, slaloming his way through badly parked trolleys to navigate the vegetable section. Finally back home again, he groaned at the pile of dirty crockery in his kitchen. Knackered and unwashed, with a whole load of vegetable chopping facing him, he poured himself a glass of wine. He needed a few this evening – his house, his drinking rules. God, he was cross with her for not understanding, and even more so with Hardman. He should have been eating steak au poivre with a decent bottle of Malbec in La Belle Époque by now. He rolled up his shirtsleeves and brought his knife down hard on an innocent onion, just as the doorbell rang.

'Bonsoir, chef. What's cooking?' She thrust a bouquet of daffodils into one hand and a bottle of sparkling water into the other. She had cut her hair short and it looked great. And she had swapped her parka for a long black coat. As he cleared a space on the hall table to put the flowers down, she slipped it off to reveal a scarlet off-the-shoulder number. Red, in its many varieties, was definitely her colour. She held out her coat for him to take, and he led her through into his sitting room.

'You look busy,' she said. 'Anything I can do to help?'

'You could pour us both a glass of wine from that bottle over there.'

'Personally, I'm happy with water, thanks, but let me pour you another. Although I did wonder if you'd be OK to drive me home later. I know it's a bit cheeky, but otherwise I think the last bus from here into town is about ten thirty...'

His empty wine glass was by the chopping board. Maybe

he could order her a taxi. But if he drove her home, she might ask him in. The flatmate might be away again – or at least have gone to bed.

She stood before him, bottle of water in one hand, bottle of wine in the other, with a questioning look.

'So what will it be? Water or wine?'

Chapter Twelve

'You Do Something To Me' by Paul Weller. An old favourite. That was what Stephen needed. Loud.

He tapped out the piano intro on the steering wheel and launched into a soulful rendition. The boy racer poised next to him at the lights was smiling at him. Derision for a middle-aged rocker, or empathy? On green, the young gun roared off with a hoot and a wave. It was a crisp, sunny Saturday morning, and everyone seemed in a good mood.

Laura would have made him turn the volume down, as he started on his falsetto accompaniment to the chorus. Rachel's perfume was still detectable, and he could picture her next to him in the passenger seat, where they had kissed last night like two teenagers.

When she had asked him in, what were her intentions? Was she as fed up as he was to see the flatmate still up, watching a late-night chat show, her brooding presence kicking any chance of further intimacy firmly into the long grass? Next time he would ask her to stay the night at his place.

Still, he felt good this morning – at least drinking water all night meant a clear head, and he had a weekend with the kids ahead of him. He wasn't going to think about work today either – there was nothing he could do anyway until he knew how many would opt for redundancy. And Hardman was three thousand miles away.

His phone rang. It was her.

'Good morning. How are you this sunny day?' he asked.

'I am very well, Mr Carreras. I really enjoyed last night. Must admit I didn't have you down as a *Mean Girls* fan. And I'm not buying that story about it being Kate's DVD.'

He laughed. 'That's up to you, of course. But let's just say I hope I can share more of her chick flick collection with you in the very near future.'

'Yes, I'd like that too. Now, I do have one small problem this morning. You haven't stumbled upon my bus pass, have you? I used it to come round to you last night, but I haven't seen it since.'

There it was – on the floor of the passenger seat. It must have fallen out while they were snogging.

'Oh yes, it's here – just spotted it. I guess you'll be needing that sharpish.'

Returning it would be an excuse just to see her face again for a few minutes. But he was already running late for Jake's match.

'Phew, that's a relief. Well, I don't want you to come out of your way. I know you're going to watch Jake this morning. Maybe I can come to you there? I won't stop.'

She was throwing down the gauntlet. Cook me dinner even though you're exhausted. And bring me into your weekend.

He explained where Latham Road Recreation Ground was.

'OK, I think I'll run there, as it's such a lovely day – and I don't have a bus pass.'

*

There were several matches going on, gaggles of boys and girls creating a kaleidoscope of different team colours. The sharp morning air was punctuated by the shouts of players and spectators and the referees' whistles. But there was only one team in green, playing at the far end of the rec. That must be Jake's team, the Latham Emeralds. Stephen paced across, straining to pick out his frame, until he spotted the springy hair and that shuffly style of running – still like the little boy on Perranporth beach. He felt a pang of nervous excitement – Jake's first full match in the team, at last. But as he approached the pitch, the ball sailed over the Emerald goalie's head, and he heard a cheer from the supporters of the opposing team. Not a propitious start.

Jake hadn't noticed him yet, and his head was down. Moreover, he was lining up at right back. He'd always been very left-footed, just used his right foot to stand on, like his dad. It didn't make any sense to play him in this position.

A bloke acting as linesman officiously asked Stephen to stand back a yard so he could see the touchline properly.

'Sorry, of course. What's the score?'

'Uh, two-nil to Cropton already. Only about ten gone. Looks like it's going to be a long morning.'

Blimey, were all this Cropton team honestly the same age as Jake? Several of them were already pushing six foot and the centre forward was a hulk with an unreasonable amount of facial hair. When the Cropton lads shouted for the ball, they did so with the full-throated roar of Neanderthals. The Emeralds, by contrast, appeared to have taken a vow of silence. Jake glanced up and Stephen gave him a thumbs up. But he had a hangdog look about him.

Another wave of yellow opposition shirts came forward and the ball was played out to their left winger. He at least wasn't tall. If anything, he was smaller than Jake, a slimly built black lad. He showed the ball to Jake, sped past him as if he wasn't there, whipped in a cross, and the hulk scored, unchallenged by the green shirts. Three-nil.

Stephen tried to engage the linesman. 'Oh dear, looks like a bit of a mismatch.'

'It shouldn't be,' he replied gruffly. 'They're only two places above us in the league, but we're missing a couple of key defenders today. I haven't seen this right back before, but he looks way out of his depth.'

Why didn't he say, 'That's my son'? The linesman was off, panting down the touchline to keep up as the yellows surged forward again.

He hadn't anticipated just how primeval it all was. He realised there were a group of Cropton supporters next to him, and as the fast winger advanced on Jake again, they bellowed their encouragement.

'Go on, Jordan, skin him, skin him. He's useless.' The bloke shouting loudest was shaven headed with a beer gut, his face contorted with pure aggression.

Jordan didn't need a second invitation. He pushed the ball round one side of the hapless Jake and nipped round the other. Jake stuck out a flailing leg, and Jordan came crashing to the ground. He was just too quick.

'Fucking hell, referee, did you see that? He could have broken his fucking leg!' The throbbing-veined head was screaming at the referee and shaking a fist at Jake. Jordan just picked himself up, wiped his nose on his sleeve, and was ready to take the free kick.

The referee had lumbered over. 'OK, cut that out, number two, or you'll be off.'

Jake looked like he wanted the earth to swallow him whole.

'Stick at it, Jake,' Stephen shouted, drawing an angry look from the Cropton dads.

The veined head shouted down the touchline at him. 'Is that your son, mate?'

'It is.'

'You want to sort his fucking tackling out, mate. He's fucking dangerous.'

'And you want to watch your language.'

'You fucking what?' he snarled and took a few steps towards Stephen, ready for action, until a woman's raucous voice intervened.

'Leave it, Mitchell, leave it.' She didn't look the peacemaker type, but it did the trick.

God, this was supposed to be fun, but it was already turning into a nightmare. Jake was now a frightened rabbit, scared to even attempt a tackle after the referee's warning, and Jordan was having a field day. By half-time, it was five-nil and all the trouble was coming from the same source. Jordan either vanished past a static Jake and crossed for the hulk to create mayhem, or on one occasion scored himself with an audacious chip over the keeper, after which he did a little somersault of celebration.

'Serves the bastards right,' baited vein-head. Stephen suffered in silence.

At half-time the dispirited Emeralds trudged over to where their parents were gathered, several with offers of water and one even supplying orange segments, which felt like a bit of a throwback. Energy drinks might have been a better bet.

'We need to stop that left winger,' one of the bigger lads, wearing the captain's armband, moaned. 'Why isn't Abel playing today? He would have nailed him early on.' None of the team looked at Jake, head down on the edge of the group.

Stephen walked over and put an arm around Jake's shoulder. 'Never mind, mate, you're doing your best. It's ridiculous. This coach of yours, he's playing you out of position.'

'Just leave it, Dad.'

'But you could switch wings.'

'No, Dad, leave it.'

The linesman walked past. 'We haven't even got any subs today, so we can't take anyone off.'

Very sensitive.

It was painful to see his son so miserable, but he was clearly going to be embarrassed if Stephen said anything. If only he weren't an occasional dad. If he were a regular and knew the coach it would be easier to intervene, but right now it would just look like meddling.

As the coach gathered the team together for a pep talk, which would need to be Churchillian in its inspiration, a woman in a fluorescent yellow cagoule was jogging round behind the goal. It was Rachel. She spotted him and waved, and he waved back self-consciously. She was panting as she approached him on the touchline.

'Hello,' she smiled. 'Bit further than I thought.' She was perspiring slightly. 'How's it going?'

'Not exactly to plan. Jake's team are losing five-nil, and it's only half-time.'

'Oh no. Still time for a comeback, maybe?' Her pink cheeks glowed positivity.

'Er, not really. If it were a boxing match, the referee would have stopped it to save further punishment.'

She looked a bit disappointed by Stephen's lack of faith.

'Ah well, never mind. Can I stay for a while? Just to recover.'

He wasn't sure about this. It felt awkward. But she had a look of expectation.

'Yes, of course, as long as you don't wince.'

'Great. So which one is Jake?'

'He's over there, the green number two.'

Jake was still hanging off the back of the group as they were addressed by an animated coach. Just for a moment, Stephen felt ashamed. He wanted a son who was centre stage, clapping encouragement to his teammates.

Rachel was undeterred. 'Where will you be able to see him best in the second half?'

Stephen had been planning on staying put, on the opposite side to where Jake would now be playing, as he sensed his son would prefer to be left alone. But now she was here, it would seem odd to do that. So they walked round behind the goal and took a position on Jake's wing again. Only then did he see what was printed on the back of her jacket.

What Would Jesus Do?
St Anselm's Fun Day

He checked around to see if anyone else had noticed.

As they kicked off again, Rachel became even more enthusiastic. 'I know this boy, the one called Jordan. He's the one I told you about, who was taken into care and we didn't know how to get through to him, until we took him to football and he loved it so much.'

'He certainly seems to have learnt a thing or two,' Stephen remarked begrudgingly.

'Yes, it's great to see,' she added. Then she shouted, 'Well done, Jordan!' without any sense of disloyalty as he swept past Jake again.

The Cropton Fan Club had swapped sides too, including foul-mouthed Mitchell.

'Fuck me, their full back's still on. He's toast, Jordan.'

Stephen decided to just not look at him. But Mitchell, naturally, had noticed Rachel.

'Fucking hell, she's bright. You directing the fucking traffic, love?' he shouted down the touchline.

Stephen felt embarrassed for her. But Rachel was fixated

on the game, now shouting encouragement to Jake. Either she hadn't heard the tosspot or she was choosing to ignore him.

'What would Jesus do? He'd substitute the effing right back, that's what he'd do.'

'Stop it, Mitchell,' said his female companion, sniggering along with his mates.

The gruff linesman jogged over. 'Sorry, love, you'll have to cover that top. The Cropton coach has complained that it's the same colour as his team and it's distracting them.'

It occurred to Stephen that a bit of distraction for the yellows when they were winning five-nil, no, make that six, might be quite useful, but Rachel was looking to him for guidance.

'Sorry, I just grabbed this as my normal tracky top's in the wash. Any bright ideas?' she asked hopefully.

He took off his tweed coat and draped it round her shoulders.

Just before the end Jordan completed his personal hat-trick, and finally, thank God, it was over. Nine-nil.

'I suppose we restricted them to four in the second half,' the linesman said. 'Mind you, only because they got bored.'

Stephen and Rachel stood at a distance while the forlorn group of green shirts were going through the post-mortem with their coach.

'Well, I'd better get going,' Rachel said. 'I've got a stack of things to buy in town for a church lunch tomorrow. Thanks for letting me stay. I hope the rest of weekend is good. You're probably thinking things can only get better.' She gave him a consoling smile, and in that instant, he didn't want her to leave.

'We can give you a lift into town. We're going to meet Kate in Donny's Diner, so why not join us?'

Rachel hesitated. 'Oh, I don't know. I don't want to outstay my welcome, and you should have some time alone with your children.'

'I'll have all weekend with them, Rachel. You won't outstay your welcome. Anyway, you can help me counselling my son. Looks like he's going to need it.'

She still looked a little uncertain, but then she smiled. 'OK then, that would be nice. Sorry, I've realised I know Jake's coach as well. He's a really good man. He does some volunteering with us from time to time, teaching the kids table tennis and stuff like that. I'll just go and say hello while you're waiting for Jake.'

*

Maybe lunch had not been such a good idea. Jake slumped in the front passenger seat, managing only a disinterested grunt when Stephen introduced his friend Rachel, and then stuck on his headphones. Stephen asked Rachel, sat in the back, about what she needed to do for the church lunch, for the sake of filling the void. But he couldn't help feeling annoyed with Jake's slovenly manner.

Kate and her friend Megan were already in Donny's Diner when they arrived. Kate gave Rachel the once-over as Stephen introduced her, but as the café was crowded, they were obliged to sit apart, Stephen and Rachel saddled with the still morose Jake. He broke his silence just long enough to order a ham and cheese croissant and a large piece of chocolate cake, before disappearing behind his headphones again.

Stephen nudged him. 'OK, Jacob Carreras, you need to talk to us.'

His son took off his headphones with an affected sigh of irritation.

'Rachel was telling me she knows your coach. Chris, is it?'
'Oh.'
'Did he have any pearls of wisdom to offer on today's

performance, Rachel?' Stephen continued. 'Like why he played Jake out of position, for example?'

'Dad,' Jake whined with a long-suffering look.

Rachel jumped in. 'Actually, he has a very high regard for you, Jake.'

Jake was busy looking at his phone.

'Yes, he said he was going to have a chat with you during the week as straight after the match wasn't the best time. But he said you shouldn't get too downhearted about today, as he knew it wasn't your best position, and he called Jordan a wizard. He said you would definitely get another chance.'

'Why didn't he play Jake somewhere else?' Stephen grunted.

'He said something about that too. Nobody else wanted to play in that right back place, and he wanted to give Jake a try because he'd been training so hard.'

Jake looked up at her – and Stephen caught the slightest flicker of satisfaction on his face – before going back to his phone.

Why had he not known that Jake was training so hard? But he wanted to kiss Rachel.

She finished her coffee and stood up to leave.

'It's been lovely to meet you, Jake. I hope you all have a good weekend.'

'Thanks, you too,' said Jake, without looking her in the eye.

Stephen walked her to the door.

'Have fun,' she said again.

'Yes, hopefully we will. I'm sorry they've been so incommunicative. You barely got to meet Kate, and Jake wasn't very chatty. He'll probably come round a bit later. He normally does.'

'Stephen, I do work with dysfunctional teenagers for a living. So your two seem perfectly nice to me. One of them is a bit fed up because he lost at football, and the other one is out having a nice time with a friend.'

'Really? Well, I'll take your word for it.' He checked to see if either of the kids were watching, and then put his arm around her waist.

'And can I just say, what you just said to Jake, thank you. Believe me, Rachel, that was remarkable progress, getting him to wish you a nice weekend too. I think you might be a saint.'

Her smile vanished. 'I'm definitely not. Oh, I must give you this back.' She nodded down at his coat, which she hadn't taken off even in the café.

Stephen laughed. 'OK, so would I be right in thinking you haven't totally thought this one through?'

'Oh, haven't I?'

'You can't spend all afternoon just in that light cagoule. You'll catch your death. Plus you'll probably get asked what *would* Jesus do on a Saturday afternoon in Middleton?'

She laughed again too. 'It's true, I did set out this morning thinking I'd just run to the playing fields and straight back.'

'Why not hang onto the coat until we next meet? Which I hope will be soon. Anyway, it suits you. Car coat chic. Goes well with the sort of sophisto-punk haircut.'

She nodded, as if assessing the compliment. 'Car coat chic and sophisto-punk. That's good, as it is in fact exactly the combination I was aiming for.'

'Well, it works. So, can we try and do dinner again next Friday? I could re-book La Belle Époque. I'll find a way to work round Hardman.'

'I can't make that I'm afraid, although it would have been great. We've got a youth club at work next Friday.'

'Oh, right,' he said. More youth work. Was this going to put a kybosh on every Friday evening?

'But Sunday evenings are always good for me – next week, after evensong?' She looked at him hopefully.

Was that all she could offer? If so, it would have to do – for now.

'OK. I'll call you during the week,' he said. 'And hopefully see you next Sunday.'

She touched his arm lightly and said a quiet goodbye. He really wanted to kiss her again. But Jake was definitely looking at them now, mouth full of chocolate cake.

As he returned to the table, Kate hugged Megan, who was also leaving, and came over.

'Who was that, Dad?'

'Oh, just someone I met.' He hadn't worked out how to introduce Rachel to them yet. But he was still hoping for a seal of approval.

'OK,' Kate said, and started biting her nails. 'So can we get going?'

Chapter Thirteen

As nobody else was hanging out by the Eat Schmaltz counter, Stephen wandered over there for a moment's reflection, trying to look nonchalant. He fished out from his pocket a folded sheet of A4 on which he had typed fourteen names and went over them again while sipping an orange juice. He had drawn a line under the first six names: the ones who had followed Barry Evans' lead to say they would take voluntary redundancy. It was the eight below he focused on – his recommendations for the chop. This was the fourth time he had printed it out, each time marginally different.

It was a horrible, lonely job being a hatchet man. Was it harsh on young Ryan Milner? He had dropped a right clanger over that Mint Regals promotional stunt last year. They'd even had a letter from Buckingham Palace. And he was a self-confident young lad, maybe a confidence not entirely supported by ability, who would talk his way into a half-decent job somewhere.

Enough. He'd come at this from every angle. No more analysis on these fourteen. Already the last two nights he had lain awake at three in the morning, mentally selecting his worst ever Grimley's UK team. Fifteen was enough for a rugby union team, but he'd settled for football – eleven with three subs and one tbc. He even had the formation worked out. It didn't induce sleep. And he still needed one more name. A terrace chant popped into his head. *One more, we only need one more.*

There was, of course, one obvious candidate whose name wasn't on the list yet. In fact, this candidate could be captain of his worst ever eleven. If only he hadn't announced in the last week that his wife was expecting their first child. What were the chances? Talk of the devil, he was coming over.

'All right?' Stephen said cheerily, stuffing the paper back in his pocket as Tony Perkins inspected the fruit bowl with his normal gloom-laden expression. Stephen left him there and returned to his perch to issue a final reminder email. If anyone else wanted to take voluntary redundancy, they needed to tell him today. After that, the carnage would begin. Hardman would have his fifteen pounds of flesh, recommendations on his desk tomorrow morning as agreed.

In the afternoon, Sandra asked to see him. They met in Ambition, the only room that was free. She had a resigned look on her face.

'Well, Steve, I've decided I want to leave. At least it will mean you have one less to sack among those who want to stay.'

Bless her. But it didn't help. She was on his list anyway. He could swap her from 'let go' to 'volunteer' but it didn't change his overall numbers.

'That's very decent of you, Sandra. I know the announcement has affected you badly. But if it's any consolation, I think you're making the right decision. I'm sure there are other businesses in Middleton which can use your skills better than we can in the circumstances.'

In a land where he and everyone else were now just operatives, Sandra's skills as a PA were about as much use as a chocolate teapot.

She smiled. 'Maybe. But I've talked to my old man about it and he thinks we can manage on his salary. The world always needs a plumber. So I might go off and do something completely different. I'm thinking of opening a little tea shop with the redundancy money.'

Had she worked out the package? A tea hut maybe.

'That's a great idea. Maybe you can set it up around the corner. We'll all sneak out mid-afternoon for tea and scones – if we can give Laura the slip.'

'Laura? Your ex?'

'Er, no, sorry, I meant someone, something else. Anyway, it doesn't matter. The point is, well done you. I'll miss you, though.'

'Aah, come here.' She gave him a big hug. 'You look after yourself, Steve, and those children of yours.'

He would miss her. But his overriding emotion was envy – she was going off to follow a dream. If only he could find a rich wife and escape. Currently he was trying to go out with someone who earned a pittance and took the bus to work. Talk of scones had seen Sandra digress cheerily to a review of yet another TV cookery show, but Stephen had moved into a designer kitchen in Paris, taking off his apron to welcome Carol home from a hard day at the office with a gin and tonic and supper in the oven, as she slung her briefcase onto the sofa. He ripped off her suit and they were making love on the slate grey work surface, surrounded by chopped vegetables.

'Are you all right, Steve?' Sandra asked with concern.

'What? Oh yes, fine, thanks.' Hell, Carol Coolidge was still messing up his head, four years on.

Sandra walked back into the Hive with him, a relieved smile on her face. Another happy customer. The whole thing had been fairly civilised so far this week. Nobody taking the voluntary package had slagged him off, all seeming to appreciate he had no option. Several had even thanked him for his handling of the whole sorry business, told him what a good boss he had been. But with Sandra the only one to come forward at the last minute, opting for the departure he was going to force upon her anyway, his last hope of an easy win on Victim Fifteen was over. And he overheard Perkins telling Jerry that he was calculating how expensive parenthood would be.

'Can I get you anything from the juice bar, Steve?' Ryan Milner interrupted his thoughts.

'No, you're all right, Ryan, thanks. I've just come back.'

'You sure?'

More people had offered him a drink in the last week then he could ever remember. But he was incorruptible. Ryan was still on the list. And anyway, he was only offering orange juice.

*

It was pouring down when he left the office, and there was a long tailback to the ring road. Still fretting over tomorrow's meeting with Hardman and the names on his list, he reflected again on his promise, made a week ago, to help them find new jobs. It was not a bad time of day to call Phoebe Huntley-Parsons, the world's most voracious headhunter. If anyone could find homes for this lot, it was her.

Phoebe's plummy tones greeted him like the prodigal son.

'Ah, how lovely. Don't tell me you've seen sense at last? You must have read my mind. You were on my list to call. I've got rather an unusual position just come up, in leafy Devon, strangely enough. Let's be realistic, darling, you might have more chance moving from one, shall we say outpost, to another, rather than getting into the London scene at your stage in life. And believe me, sweety, Devon is considerably more scenic than where you are. Let me tell you about it—'

'I'm going to stop you right there, Phoebe. Your enthusiasm is infectious as ever, but as I've told you before, for personal reasons I just need to hang in here for the moment.'

Phoebe gave a thespian sigh down the phone, clearly thinking that this particular favourite son was a little unhinged.

'In fact, it wasn't me I was ringing about,' he continued. 'I told you I might be asking your help for a colleague or two?'

'Ah, yes,' she said, sounding as if she had lost interest if she couldn't help Stephen personally. But then she was a good actor.

'So, rather than helping one or two, can we make that nine?'

'Nine? Lord, what's happening up there? It sounds like the night of the long knives, darling.'

'Yeah, something like that. Anyway, I wondered if I could ask a few of them to send you their CVs, and then maybe I could talk them through with you? One or two bright prospects.'

'Of course, of course, although the "one or two" thing is worrying me. What about the other seven or eight?'

'I'll leave them to your unparalleled selling skills, Phoebe. The words sand and desert come to mind.'

'Aah, darling boy.'

'Great, so I'll be in touch properly next week, and then maybe if I can find an excuse one day, we can have lunch. Harder to find an excuse these days, mind you, now I'm Minister without Portfolio.'

'Any time, darling, that would be lovely. It sounds perfectly ghastly up there. And are you sure I can't tempt you to think about—'

'No, thanks all the same.'

As soon as the call ended, his mind flipped back to name number fifteen and the windscreen wipers joined in.

Per-kins, Per-kins, they swished.

Col-lins, Col-lins, they replied.

Jerry Collins was still liked by everyone. And after the shock of that first day back in the office, he was embracing life at Schmaltz. His positivity would be nauseating if it wasn't so endearing. The juice bar was great, the gym was great, it was all great. Stephen had no doubt that Jerry would have climbed the ladder quickly – if Schmaltz hadn't kicked it away. Good job Jerry was only on the second rung. Whereas he was stuck on the bloody roof.

The rain turned less torrential, and he flicked the wipers to intermittent. Drizzle, that's what Perkins should have been called. He'd only got the job as deputy because some better prospects had escaped, and Stephen had decided Carol wasn't quite ready. Look how that turned out. Perkins never made a decision. *What should I do about this, Steve? What are you going to do about that, Steve?* And he'd been going around with a long face since the takeover, moaning incessantly about the unfairness of it all. It would be a relief to get rid, but Perkins would struggle to get another job to feed that baby unless he improved his interpersonal skills. Whereas Jerry would walk into one. He'd be doing Jerry a favour, releasing him from this zoo back into the wild.

He eased into the driveway and stared hypnotically from the car at the rainwater dripping down the side of the house, where the downpipe had got dislodged from the guttering. He would sleep on the decision and give Hardman his list first thing in the morning, as agreed – or rather he probably wouldn't sleep on it. Sometimes doing the right thing was bloody difficult. Sometimes it was hard to even know what it meant.

He wanted Rachel here now, not just throwing him that line about doing good among the carnage and then leaving him to it. He called her, wanting to hear her voice, not just her voicemail – which was what he got, for the third time this week.

'Can I tempt you?' Phoebe had said. The truth was, she

could tempt him very easily. He tried to think about what he might do with the kids this weekend, to remind himself why living in leafy Devon was a daft idea.

*

Jennie Jacobs had been summoned to join Stephen for the meeting with Hardman the following day. Maureen Birtles told them to wait outside the office until he was ready for them, then continued with her work. The triumphant smirk was more emphatic than ever. She was fast becoming the second most feared person in Hardman's English kingdom, his appointed messenger.

Through the open door, Stephen could see that Hardman was hard at it on his exercise bike, in a tight-fitting black tracksuit, with a headset on so he could dictate orders to someone at the same time. Whoever it was, they were getting a right bollocking over the Greek company's annual profits. It was probably that guy Vassos who was fast becoming Carol's punchbag of choice.

'Yep,' he barked, which was the signal for Stephen and Jennie to enter. The normal smell of leather had given way to pungent sweat. He showed no sign of stopping his workout. Stephen glanced at Jennie, dressed in tweed and pearls, still the consummate HR professional. He felt for her. She was in the same bind as him: another director now reduced to the title of operative, but still with the responsibilities of office lying heavy on her shoulders. A muscle in her face was twitching as they waited.

'OK, what we got, Carreras?' Hardman was still pedalling away. Had he forgotten the reason for the meeting?

'Good morning, Mr Hardman. I'm hoping you have received my list of suggested redundancies which I sent through this morning?' Stephen said firmly. Why couldn't he stop bloody cycling for a moment and concentrate on the matter in hand?

Hardman grunted and, without stopping, turned sideways to look at a computer screen arranged at eye level next to his bike.

'Yeah, I got it.'

'As you will see there are seven who have volunteered for the redundancy package, and I have recommended—'

'Yep, I said I got it,' he snarled, eyes still focused on his screen as he started to pedal even more furiously.

'So you got fifteen of the fuckers. That's good.'

Stephen saw Jennie wince. 'Esteemed colleagues' was so last year.

'I have,' Stephen replied curtly. No point elaborating on how tough it had been.

'You seen this list, Missy?'

It was a safe bet that in twenty years at the heart of Human Resources, nobody had ever called Jennie Jacobs 'Missy' before.

'No, I haven't shared it with Mrs Jacobs yet, as you requested complete confidentiality,' Stephen reminded him.

'She better see it now, cos there's always some legal crap about getting HR involved in firing people.'

Stephen had come prepared and handed a copy of the list to Jennie. Hardman continued, panting more heavily.

'How... fast... can you... get them... outta here, Missy?'

She was still taking in the names, so Stephen intervened.

'Those who have volunteered are all happy to go now. The rest, as we agreed, will have their contracts terminated at the end of March, which gives them time to search for another job.'

Hardman grunted. It seemed like Stephen's efficient carrying out of his orders had taken the wind out of the American's sails. But then he turned to look at Jennie and finally stopped pedalling.

'I was asking the lady here how she's going to manage this. I'd say it's an HR job, wouldn't you, Missy?'

Jennie gathered herself. 'Of course—'

Stephen jumped in again. 'But with respect Mr Hardman, while I know Mrs Jacobs would do this particularly well, I would like to be involved too. Some of my team, my old team, will be very hurt by this. I think they deserve an explanation from me, and I don't want to hide behind my decisions. It's a self-respect thing. I'm sure you'll understand.'

Hardman glared at him for a moment. 'You better do it together then. As long as you get 'em out, I don't care who does it.' And with a resounding sniffing back of phlegm, he resumed pedalling.

They stood there waiting for more, but it became apparent by his silence that Hardman was done with them. Stephen nodded to the door to suggest they left the room.

They waited until they had reached Laura Card Reader, well out of earshot, before speaking. Jennie looked battered.

'Phew, can I just say, Steve, you were very impressive in there, while I froze in the headlights.'

'You were probably overcome by the stink, more like.' Stephen smiled to reassure her. 'And I've had a bit of practice now. I have regular close encounters with the fascist. In fact, I noticed this morning he's even started to pronounce my name correctly. Haven't you had the pleasure?'

'Indeed not. I think he regards HR as an unnecessary evil. He's a force of nature, isn't he?'

'That's one way of putting it. You were always diplomatic, Jennie.'

'But are you sure about sharing the dirty work? I mean, addressing them together?'

'Absolutely. As I said, I think I owe them it straight. You can owe me one if you like. We could sneak out for lunch one day and you can buy.' He nodded at Laura. 'Give *her* the slip.' It got more of a smile from Jennie than it had from Sandra yesterday.

'Anyway, what about you, Jennie? What are you going to do? There are only three of us ex-directors still in this building.'

'Er, and soon there will be two. Kevin Keeling is going,' Jennie said.

'Blimey. I had no idea. Did he jump or was he pushed?'

'Pushed. Well, ejected might be a more appropriate word. Still, it's not taken him any time to land another sales director role,' Jennie said. 'So I'm sure there is life after Schmaltz for you too.'

'Oh, interesting. Where is he going?'

'A sex toy business in Wolverhampton.' This announcement being made by a woman in tweed jacket and pearls seemed particularly bizarre.

'Mm, Kevin moving into the sex industry doesn't really surprise me,' Stephen said. 'The fact that Wolverhampton has a sex toy business, on the other hand—'

'It's an online business,' she said. 'I don't think it tells us anything particular about the citizens of Wolverhampton.' She sniggered in a most un-Jennie-like way.

He could always lighten her up. She was a likeable person, at least when she spoke human in the corridor and left the HR spin behind.

'So, Jennie, it's just thee, me and old Jim Jeffries ploughing on in Dumfries. But he's not really in the eye of the storm up there, is he? Can't imagine he's thinking of himself as a mere operative.'

Jennie sighed. 'I don't know what I'm going to do, Stephen. I'm in a dilemma. A bit like you, I imagine. I feel a loyalty to my brood here, but I don't think I can put up with it. But then where am I going to go?'

'You're kidding, aren't you? You'd get another HR director's job tomorrow. And your kids are away at uni now, aren't they?

So you can move away from Middleton.' He felt resentful momentarily.

'No, I can't. James has just been promoted to partner in his firm, so he doesn't want to move. Maybe I should open a tea shop or something.'

'You'd better be quick, as Sandra Smith just told me she's planning one. At this rate Middleton is going to have more tea shops than the Cotswolds. And I'm really not sure there's the market.'

They stood surveying the Hive. Jerry Collins and Tony Perkins were at podiums next to each other, unaware that they were being observed. Jerry turned to his left to say something to Cheryl from HR, which made her laugh and give him a playful jab on the shoulder. On his right, Perkins remained fixed on his computer screen, shoulders stooped, gently muttering beneath his breath at some injustice or other.

'Actually, Jennie, there is one favour you can do me. There's one person I'd like us to tell straight away. I'll feel better when I've got it out of the way.'

'Yes, I think I can guess who you mean.'

Was this how Hardman felt all the time, with the power to give the thumbs up or the thumb down? Where did the pulse of pleasure spring from, that he felt right now? Was it the ability to put the wounded animal out of its misery? Or something darker: the freedom to inflict pain, a final revenge to end the whingeing once and for all?

Perkins looked over his shoulder, the fox trapped in the corner of the garden.

Stephen wouldn't think about babies.

'Tony, can we speak to you for a few minutes, in Discipline?'

Chapter Fourteen

The smell of fresh paint in the cream, pristine hallway was unmistakable. Tristran had obviously been busy again. The children dumped their bags, and Kate disappeared straight up to her room, while Jake managed to mumble 'thanks, Dad' before he went through to put the TV on.

'Why did you say you had to return them early again?' Laura demanded, brushing out her long dark hair in front of him, with a long-suffering expression.

'Because I'm going out with a friend this evening. If that's quite all right with you, Laura?' Kate had given him the same inquisition this morning. He had told her he was seeing the friend she'd briefly met in Donny's Diner after Jake's football. Her face had clouded over.

'Couldn't you arrange to see this friend later? This is the second Sunday in a row you've done this. I thought the deal was not returning them before eight,' Laura said.

'Yes, and I thought the real deal was that I bail you out and fit in with your changing plans pretty much on a weekly basis, Laura. I wouldn't even have had the kids this weekend if you hadn't wanted to swap again. So if I need to bring them back an hour or so earlier from time to time, that isn't a big issue, is it? But it's nice to know you're so pleased to see them.'

At it hammer and tongs within two minutes. Situation normal. He heard Kate's door slam shut.

'I'm a bit worried about Kate,' he said more quietly.

'Oh, good, nice of you to catch up on that one. Anything in particular happen this weekend?'

'She's been very quiet. I thought I'd better take them to see their grandmother yesterday afternoon and Kate was barely civil.'

'Was your mother lecturing them as normal?'

'Don't try to make this an issue about my mother,' Stephen snapped. 'Then for most of today she just stayed in her room. Said she had homework. I don't know, I just felt there was more to it.' He hesitated, unsure whether to share more. 'She's been a bit tearful, in fact.'

Laura knotted her brow. At least this was the one common cause they could still connect on occasionally, stripping away the posturing to share worries about their children and how they were affected by the divorce.

'I know they're stepping it up a bit at school,' she said, the tone of her voice suggesting she wasn't convinced this was the full explanation. 'Anyway, I expect I'll have to get to the bottom of it,' she added. A little self-righteously, Stephen thought.

'I need to go, Laura, but let me know if you want to talk more. Otherwise, I'll see them both in three weeks' time I gather, but I assume that if I want to watch Jake play football again next Saturday that's not a problem. Unless of course Tristran wants to give him some moral support and be a taxi service.'

That wasn't a clever barb. What if the wanker did want to go and watch? But it wasn't very likely. He didn't do ball games. Too busy doing more bloody home improvement or organising their next holiday.

'Yes, I suppose that's fine. If it's what Jake wants.' Laura looked away, starting to brush out her hair again. He had her on the defensive for once. 'But make sure he doesn't get injured and he'll need to be back promptly, as our flight is on the Saturday afternoon. We've spent a lot of money on this skiing holiday and I don't want to waste it.'

*

It was going to be tight getting to church in time. Too much stress for a Sunday evening when there would be enough flying around in the week ahead. He could have relaxed, taken the kids back at seven as Laura had suggested, and just turned up after the service to take Rachel for a drink. But he'd told himself that if church was a big part of Rachel Pearson's life, he needed to give it a go – at least for a month. And this was week three. The first time he'd gone willingly, desperate for the oxygen of seeing her again. When she had met him afterwards in the foyer, he had kissed her openly in front of the parishioners. She had blushed, but he didn't care. They had stayed for coffee, and he had been charming and effusive as she introduced him to people – *what a lovely church, what an interesting sermon, everyone is so friendly*. He'd even shared a bit of banter with Terry as they put away the hymn books. He had wanted to be the person she wanted him to be.

But tonight, as he drew up outside just in time, he just didn't feel like it – the novelty was wearing thin, and yet he still didn't seem able to find an opportunity to get it together with Rachel anywhere else. On the rare occasions midweek when he wasn't working late into the evening, she always seemed to be busy with her choir practice or her good works. Wasn't he a good work?

And then there was the children issue. When he'd tentatively suggested he might ask 'a friend' to come round and watch a movie with them, Kate had said, 'I like it with just the three of us, Dad', in a way that brooked no argument. But next weekend, the kids were heading off on this ski trip. And it was Valentine's Day next Saturday. He should send her flowers, try to organise something.

The choir weren't assembled outside this evening, so he couldn't see her. And it felt all wrong from the moment he walked in. The noticeboard announced this was an 'Alternative Service', and it had certainly attracted a different crowd. Terry had been usurped on steward duties by a couple of twenty-somethings, whose badges proclaimed them to be Seb and Keira and who were intent on hugging most people as they entered, from which he was grateful to be excluded. He felt invisible.

He sat in the same place as previous weeks, expecting to have a good view of Rachel. But the robed choir had been replaced by an informal music group, sitting in chairs facing the congregation. Rachel was in the second row, partly obscured by a tall guy with a beard and a guitar. It was that Conrad who she'd been talking to at the Advent Carol Service back in December.

Like Terry, David the vicar was nowhere to be seen tonight, replaced by a younger, flame-haired man with rather too much exuberance, and instead of traditional hymns there were a series of songs whose words were shown on a screen high up at the front of the church. He had to strain his neck to see them and certainly had no intention of breaking his duck for singing with this stuff. Most of those around him looked about half his age. They raised their arms in the air when exhorted to join in a rousing chorus of 'I'm So Into Jesus'. About twenty times in a row. The group's drummer thumped away, blotting out all thought, and every time it showed the slightest sign of drawing to a close, the beard with the guitar raised his arm and exhorted them to 'sing it one more time!'

When Rachel stood up for a special a capella number, he

could see her clearly enough. She was still wearing the red headband she always seemed to wear in church, even though she still had that short, punky hairstyle. But the choral robes had been divested for a tight-fitting red jersey. And she was obviously really into it, her hips swaying back and forth as she clapped and sang, 'Ain't Nothing In My Life But The Lord'.

When flame-hair invited them all to 'share the peace with your brothers and sisters in Jesus,' Stephen stuck to a swift handshake with his neighbour, while everyone else embarked on a hug-athon, wandering from pew to pew. Rachel disappeared under a sea of embraces amidst the music group. When order was at last restored, some bright spark in the congregation started a sort of communal pray-in, with people shouting out how much they just wanted to thank God for everything from getting pregnant to finding that parking place. He tried to catch Rachel's eye at the mention of this, but she appeared to be deep in prayer.

He zoned out. The previous times, although she was the main attraction, he had got something out of it. He liked some of the hymns, and the whole ritual had become quite calming, a counterpoint before the next bout of Schmaltz madness. But this was just like *being* in Schmaltz. All that was missing was a woman in a chocolate leotard, twirling a sash.

It went on for an hour and a half. Then everyone adjourned to the foyer so the love-in could continue. Rachel was surrounded by a cluster of friends, all late teens or early twenties, except for Conrad, who Stephen reckoned must be about the same age as her. Hadn't she said they had known each other some time ago, before he'd moved away? Stephen hovered in the background, eyeing the exit. Then she spotted him and approached with her usual welcoming smile. He gave her a kiss on the cheek, determined to affect as much enthusiasm as he could muster.

'Well, you were clearly enjoying that,' he said.

'Yeah, sorry, I should have warned you that we're experimenting with this service once a month. It's Conrad's initiative.' She inclined her head towards the bearded one, who was keeping an eye on them, strategically positioned on the edge of the noisy youth group. 'What did you think of it?'

Why did she have to ask?

'It was certainly... different.'

Her smile froze for a moment, only to return as Conrad sidled up to them.

'Oh, hi. Conrad, Stephen. Stephen, Conrad. I was just telling Stephen this is all your fault,' she laughed. She turned back to Stephen. 'I did promise I would help with washing up this evening after coffee, so are you OK to stick around for a while and then we can go to the pub?'

'I'll come and help you.'

'No, you're all right. Stay here and chat. I won't be long.'

She seemed keen to leave him there, marooned with Conrad, whose deep-set blue eyes followed her as she walked off to the kitchen.

'So, I gather you grew up here but then moved away?' Stephen asked.

The beard turned towards him, but with a faraway look in his eye.

'Sorry? Oh, yes, but then I moved back,' he said, glancing back towards the kitchen door through which Rachel had now disappeared.

'What brought you back here?'

He stared intensely at Stephen now. 'The Lord, my friend.'

That was a turn-up for the books.

'I see. Where had he put you before then?'

'I was a youth worker in Lewisham, southeast London. But I've just been appointed as Chief Executive for an exciting young charity called Altogether Now, who are actually based in Middleton, so the Lord has truly brought me home. He told me I was needed here.' He was looking towards the kitchen again.

'That's convenient. And what does Altogether Now get up to, then?'

'We run a youth project in Malawi, sending passionate young people from the UK over there on aid projects. But my vision is to also set up an exchange programme where we'd arrange for young ministers and youth workers from there to come and work over here, bringing their faith into our communities. It's important to be humble – we have so much to learn from Africa in serving the Lord.' Humility didn't come across as Conrad's strong suit.

There was a moment's silence. This was the point where a normal person would ask what he did, in return. But evidently the beard didn't do small talk.

'Did you come to this church when you lived here before?' Stephen continued, knowing that he had but unable to think of anything else to ask him.

'I did. And I'm certain that's what the Lord is calling me back to as well. This church needs to experience the transforming love of Jesus.' He tapped the left of his chest. 'It needs more church like tonight. Look how much everyone was into it this evening. I've been invited onto the leadership team, so there'll be much more of this, and much less 1662 Evensong, I can tell you.' He was staring at Stephen with steely-eyed fervour now.

'Do you think that's what everyone wants?' Stephen had a feeling the vicar might regret inviting Conrad onto anything – there was the whiff of a coup in the air.

'The church will only grow through its young people and that's definitely what they want,' he said emphatically.

'Mm, I'm obviously not the target market,' Stephen observed.

'What brought you here, then?' he finally asked.

Was it those warm brown eyes or the smooth nape of her neck which had first attracted him? It was difficult to say.

'I'm a friend of Rachel's. She invited me to the Advent service before Christmas. I saw you there.'

'Oh, yeah, probably. She's a good woman, Rachel. She and I go back a long way. I want her to come and work for me. I'm sure she will be called to it.'

Before Stephen could respond to this, Rachel reappeared with several of her young entourage in tow. 'Anyone for the pub?'

'Why not?' Conrad said.

'Stephen?' She gave him that big smile, as if it was all perfectly lovely.

The pub was packed but Rachel spotted someone leaving in the corner and all nine of them crammed around one table. Conrad inevitably slipped in next to her, while Stephen found himself at the opposite end, squeezed between huggy Seb and two young women checking their text messages. And nobody had done anything about drinks yet.

He stood up. 'Right, what's everyone having?'

He wrote down the list of assorted soft drinks on a beer mat. He was definitely going to have a pint. Rachel accompanied him to the bar.

'This is lovely of you, Stephen,' she enthused.

'Someone needed to do something. That lot all seemed to think it was waitress service. I have to say your circle of friends makes me feel a bit old, Rachel.'

'This gang?' she said airily. 'They make me feel old too. They're basically the church youth group from about five years ago, when I ran it.'

'I assume Conrad doesn't come into that category?'

'No, I told you, didn't I? I first met him about ten years ago.'

He wanted to draw her further on Conrad, but he had lost her attention, as she waved at someone. 'Oh, I've just seen Lila from choir come in with her new man. I wonder if we can squeeze them in too?'

Why not? Maybe he could buy a round for the whole pub.

'Yes, of course, do you want to go and see what they're having, quickly, and I'll add them to the order.'

By time they had shuttled back and forth with a round of drinks, Lila and her man had wedged themselves into the group and added another small table on the end for Stephen and the texting girls.

He was done with this Sunday routine. This wasn't what he'd signed up for. It was hopeless trying to build a relationship around these meetings where he was just part of her audience, and now with Conrad as an appendage. And always that Sunday evening feeling hanging over him.

Seb and co. were now posing for team selfies. Stephen downed his pint in double-quick time and removed his coat from the back of his chair. He would leave her here with her tribe. In the corner of his eye, he caught sight of her standing up and coming towards him.

'Hello, are you all right?' she asked. 'I was going to organise a kitty to get another round in.'

'Yes, I'm fine. Just got the normal early start tomorrow and another tough week ahead. Heading up to Scotland tomorrow afternoon for a difficult conversation with the factory.' It would have been nice to share that with someone, but it clearly wasn't going to happen here. 'So, I'd better be off.' It was true it would be a tough week ahead. They always were. But it hadn't deterred him the previous Sundays.

'Yes, I'm sorry, of course. I do hope it goes OK,' she said. 'I'll walk with you to the car.'

'You don't need to.'

'Oh.' Her eyes widened in surprise. 'Well, I'd like to.'

They walked across the car park in silence, rain spitting at them from the cold black sky. Standing by his car, she was shivering as she stuck her hands in her pockets.

'Conrad is certainly on the fervent side, isn't he?' he said.

'Yes, as I think I told you before, he's definitely from the evangelical wing of the party.'

'You approve of his zeal for reform of the church, do you? You were swaying your hips with the best of them.'

She frowned. 'I like a change every now and then.' Her voice turned sharper. 'But I suspect this isn't either the time or place to discuss diverse forms of worship in the modern Church of England.' She looked down at her feet.

Now they both had their hands glued in their pockets. But he couldn't leave it.

'He seems to have great plans for you too. He obviously thinks a lot about you.'

'Oh, was he talking about this Malawi mission thing?'

So they were having conversations about it. She hadn't mentioned it before.

'He was. I should go,' Stephen said. 'Any chance of seeing you next weekend, maybe somewhere other than here?'

She avoided his gaze still. 'Sorry, that isn't going to work. We're leading a weekend away for the young people in the church – that lot in the pub.'

'Oh, right. Another Conrad initiative, I assume?'

She sighed, clearly exasperated with him now, but she didn't deny it. 'You could come too, if you wanted to?' It sounded more like a dare than an invite.

'No, you're all right. I think we both know it's not really me, is it? I don't want to cramp your style.'

'OK then.' She shivered again.

'You'd better go and get the kitty together.'

'Yes, you're right, I should. There is one other thing, though.

I've also got an early start tomorrow – and a tough week ahead. You don't have the monopoly on that, you know.'

He watched her walk back into the pub, arms wrapped around herself to shield against the cold. Then he opened the car door, sat down and headbutted the steering wheel.

Chapter Fifteen

Satnav Alice predicted only ten more minutes until he got there. Her ETAs were usually a triumph of hope over experience, but surely there wouldn't be any traffic jams to upset her forecasts out here. The sleet was turning to snow as a herd of bedraggled sheep trundled across a whitened field towards a farmer tossing bales of hay from the back of a tractor. It felt a million miles from head office – and from the car crash with Rachel last night. The phone could stay off, at least until he reached the hotel.

He normally enjoyed these trips across the border to meet Jim Jeffries and his team who actually made the chocolate. All right, maybe implementing a change to the emulsifiers in Little Monkeys wasn't at the cutting edge of scientific endeavour, but they all knew their chemistry – you even still saw the odd test tube in the lab. It wasn't going to be much fun this time, however, negotiating with them to ditch production of the old Grimley's brands and start making Schmaltz ones instead. That was his mission tomorrow. Project Harmony.

The Fraser Arms in Kirkcudbright felt about as far removed from the Hotel Splendid at Charles de Gaulle airport as it was possible to be. Morag greeted him warmly in reception, as always.

'Good evening, Mr Carreras, nice to see you again. It's been a while, mind.'

Indeed it had. This was his first trip to Scotland since Hardman had arrived. Here in the wilds of Galloway, he was still a VIP, not a marketing minion. Morag assured him that he had his usual lovely room with a view over the water. Not that this would be particularly advantageous at seven o'clock on a *dreich* February evening, but it was the thought that counted. Yes, a nice hot shower, then down for a spot of her home cooking in the bar, and maybe a wee dram for a nightcap. But not late to bed.

'And your colleague arrived about half an hour ago, Mr Carreras. I've booked her in the room next to yours.'

'Colleague?'

'Aye. In fact, she's just over there in the bar ordering food. She seemed a bit anxious – was asking when you were arriving.'

Carol, in a sharp black suit and looking distinctly grumpy, was sitting in the corner of the inviting but empty bar, perusing a tartan-clad menu through dark-framed reading glasses. He had never seen her in glasses before. Her hair was up in a bun.

'Carol. What are you doing here?'

'Obviously, I am joining your meeting with Jim Jeffries in the morning.'

'And how did you know I was here?'

'Tony Perkins told me. He was even more miserable than normal. I assume he was on your list for the chop?'

'Might have been.'

She cast the menu aside. 'God, this food is like something from the eighties. No wonder the Scots are so unhealthy.'

'What, no falafel burger or smashed avocado? I'll have a word with Morag about it.'

'Who's Morag?'

'The very nice woman who runs this place, along with Alexander. Personally, Carol, I like it here – good home cooking and a comfortable bed – but it's probably not up to your new standards. Anyway, the point is, a month back you kindly explained that coming up here to sort out the old dinosaurs, as you called them, was my job, way below your pay grade. And while I appreciate the concern and all that, I still don't know why you bothered coming.'

She looked up at him from behind her glasses. 'Brad has raised the stakes.'

It seemed like the hot shower would have to wait. Instead he went to the bar and ordered a large glass of white wine. When he returned to Carol's table, she launched in before he could even sit down.

'He's told me now that he wants them to be making Schmaltzy Bars and Nutters here by July.'

'And you, needless to say, told him that's out of the question.'

She gave him a stern look. 'Of course I didn't, I told him I'd get on it. Which means you need to get on it. As you point out, I told you about this a month ago. I would have expected a plan by now. I don't know what you've been doing. So I decided to get on a plane and help you apply some pressure.'

'Well, of course, I've just been sitting on my backside doing sweet FA since we last spoke. There was something else I had to do – oh, I remember, I had to make half the marketing department redundant. That was it. And then, as we're getting rid of so many people, I had to step back into being brand manager for Munchy Moments. You might have heard of it? The previous incumbent seems to have left things in a hurry.' His challenging look didn't get a reaction. 'And anyway, you didn't tell me about this ridiculous timescale when we talked before.'

'Brad's timelines are subject to change, as you might have anticipated. So now he's booked a meeting with us this Friday for a full run-through of how it's going to be achieved. Which means we need to tell Jeffries tomorrow – no ifs, no buts.'

Her phone rang and she stood up to take the call, pacing around the bar, leaving him to check out Morag's specials. He'd been trying to get the ball rolling on the changes, but Jim Jeffries was not a man to be hurried. A couple of weeks ago he'd tried calling the old rogue to warn him that they needed to discuss 'factory capacity', only to discover that Jim was on holiday. So he hadn't managed a conversation since the Schmaltz coup, as Jim had also somehow avoided the conference in Paris – probably still recovering from Hogmanay. Had he worked in January at all?

Carol was still agitated when the food arrived. She picked at her sea bream, declaring it barely edible, while Stephen tucked into the venison stew and a glass of robust red. He hadn't seen her like this before. She was normally so assured, but Hardman's deadline had clearly put her off her stride. Whereas he was definitely developing an existential *sang froid*. He might be facing a bollocking from Hardman if they couldn't deliver what he wanted, and Jim Jeffries would be a tough old nut to persuade tomorrow. But just for the moment, he was sitting next to a log fire, away from the orange Hive and his empty, untidy house, in a little bubble of warmth. And for all his irritation, having dinner with her stirred up again those feelings he had been trying to suppress in the office for the last four years. A middle-aged couple came into the bar for a drink, the man nodding a good evening to them. He and Carol must look like a successful business couple catching up after a day at work.

What she wasn't going to tell Jim Jeffries wasn't worth telling. She was working herself up into a real lather, like a thoroughbred in the starting stalls at Ascot. The fossil would just have to get his arse in gear and get the factory turning out Schmaltzy Bars and Nutters by the lorryload in five months, or he would be replaced by someone who could. She would see to that.

'Mm, I suspect Jim Jeffries will be happy to be replaced within the next couple of years,' Stephen said. 'He's easing towards retirement. But at a time of his own choosing, and on decent terms. And Jim will give you a whole load of reasons why it's difficult, because he's emotionally attached to these brands. You need to be much cleverer than just slamming your fist on the table. The crosser you get, the happier he will be. I guarantee he'll have the factory manager Archie Macleod with him too. Have you met him before?'

'I've no idea,' Carol said dismissively.

'Oh, believe me, you'd remember if you had. Archie's all right too, if you stroke his belly. But if you upset him, he turns into an attack dog. Jim once explained to me that while he came from the respectable end of Glasgow, Archie was from the dodgy end. Think about that for a moment – the dodgy end of Glasgow.'

The more he considered it, the more he thought her presence in the meeting would be like a bull in a china shop. He talked it through with her. Of course she was right: Jim was a dinosaur. But he wasn't extinct yet, and his unreconstituted male chauvinism would have to be factored into the conversation if they wanted to get anywhere. Jim being told what he had to do by a woman thirty years his junior was not a recipe for instant success.

Eventually, like a demented Catherine wheel, her fizz of belligerence got slower and slower, until finally it burnt out. Stephen persuaded her to leave the negotiating to him. She reverted to fidgeting with her phone while he tucked into Morag's raspberry oatcake surprise.

'Right, I'm going to my room,' Carol said. 'Still got emails to catch up on. How long will it take us to get to the factory in the morning? I assume you can drive us there. I got the cab here from the airport – couldn't understand a word the guy was saying.'

'About thirty minutes. Maybe thirty-five to allow for the rush hour – those sheep on the road can slow you down. Yeah, I'll drive us there. If we leave just gone nine that's fine – they aren't expecting us until ten. It normally takes Jim a while to clear his tubes in the morning.'

She looked totally revolted as Morag arrived to clear the table.

'So, are you two off to bed now?'

'Yes, I think we are, Morag. Not together, obviously.' Shit, why had he said that?

Morag had a distinct twinkle in the eye. He had spent one winter evening a year ago telling her and Alexander about his divorce over a bottle of Talisker, so she was appraised of the situation. Well, not totally appraised. She didn't know that the woman standing next to him now was a primary accomplice.

Alexander came over. 'Good evening Mr Carreras. Madam. Can I interest you both in a wee dram on the house before you retire?'

'Yes, that would be very nice,' Stephen jumped in.

As Alexander returned to the bar, Carol frowned at Stephen. 'I didn't want another drink,' she protested.

'I know, but think of it as medicinal. You'll sleep well, nice and relaxed. Just a quick one,' he said.

She sighed, but sat down again, and at last he got her off the subject of the factory and onto what it was like living in Paris. He was so envious; it was so unfair. But she didn't seem entirely happy there. Brad was piling on the pressure, and had so many European issues to deal with that he was spending as much time in Paris as in the UK. He was breathing down her neck just as much as Stephen's. Hard to be sympathetic, of course, when she had clawed the job from nowhere before she was ready for it, was earning megabucks and based in such an amazing place. She assured Stephen that she could handle Hardman, but it clearly wasn't a barrel of laughs. And reading between the lines, her boyfriend, the cool-looking individual who had picked her up from the pub before Christmas, was already fed up with how little he was seeing of her since the move.

For once she was looking at Stephen, not at her phone.

'And how is dear Oscar Newte faring?' Why had he asked that?

'I think Brad is keeping him particularly busy. He's all over the profit targets is Brad. Why do you ask?'

'Oh, you know me, Carol, always been so fond of Oscar.'

For the first time that evening, she laughed. It was cynical laughter, but it made her eyes shine a little brighter.

They walked upstairs to their rooms, arranging to meet for breakfast. At the door she said good night with the flicker of a smile. Then, as she turned away, she undid her bun and with a shake of her head let her long blonde hair fall over her shoulders.

In his room, Stephen checked his phone. Rachel had called, but not left a message. He would ring back tomorrow – maybe.

On the other side of a locked adjoining door, Carol was running a bath. He heard her climbing into it. Probably immersed in bubbles, reading a feisty thriller, twiddling the hot water tap with her toes.

*

The distinct aroma of roasting cocoa beans seeped through the air vents into the car. If he lived here, he'd never eat the stuff. Unlike in Middleton, the neon green sign was still there on the façade of the grey brick building, piercing the morning rain.

GRIM Y'S IN D FRIES SIN 1906.

Definitely more letters missing since his last visit.

Jim's PA Arlene showed them into the chilly boardroom, with its strong smell of furniture polish from the long wooden table, which had no doubt seen many a curmudgeonly board meeting in its day. At one time this would have been the heart of the Grimley's empire, when the whole operation ran from here, before marketing became all the rage and head office moved to England. The original Mr Hamish Grimley, his portrait staring down at them stern and moustachioed from the nicotine-stained walls, had no doubt sat here, plotting with his fellow dour Scottish Presbyterians to feed chocolate to the working-class poor. On the wall alongside him hung sepia-tinted photos of the factory before the war, with ragtag bunches of men in cloth caps staring at the camera. There were colour photos of the current brands too, all now faded, and with pack designs that had been replaced at least ten years ago. Even one of Grimley's Cheesy Wurlitzers, long extinct. Whose desperate idea had that been, trying to branch out into savoury snacks? He could just see Oscar Newte rolling his eyes in disbelief.

Arlene brought him a coffee from the machine, which made him feel quite nostalgic. The coffee here had a synthetic sugary taste all of its own, nothing like real stuff. Carol declined the offer, requesting water, which was also brought from the machine in a small plastic cup. She inspected it, then took out her own bottle from her bag. She was in a different suit this morning, dark blue – did she ever wear the same clothes twice? Stephen sat down to wait, choosing one of the less stained old chairs, but Carol was pacing around with her headset on, one hand on her hip, the other making firm chopping movements as she gave another tongue-lashing to poor Vassos in Greece, evidently still struggling with the concept of Project Harmony.

She continued to speak on the phone as Jim's arrival was heralded by a bout of coughing and spluttering. His tweed jacket had seen better days, and his loosely knotted red tie clashed cheerfully with a blue check shirt. Archie was by his side as normal, still in his factory overalls on which his name was partially obscured by a blob of something – it had the look of a Munchy Moment.

Jim greeted Stephen like a long-lost younger brother, clasping him by the hand and slapping him on the back. Archie gave him a taciturn nod, which Stephen interpreted as positive. As long as he wasn't already snarling at you when he entered the room, you were in with a chance.

'We'll just wait for Carol to finish,' said Stephen loudly, staring at her. 'Well, nothing much seems to have changed up here, Jim. It's rather reassuring. You feel like the last outpost.'

Jim appeared nonplussed. 'What do ya mean, laddie?'

'You won't have been down to Middleton since last year, but you wouldn't recognise the place. Open plan, standing room only, even a gym. You'd love that. Oh, and we get to check in every day with a card scanner which kindly tells us how many hours we have to do before we get time off for good behaviour.'

Jim shook his head. 'Nay, lad, we haven't got any of that nonsense up here. There was a rumour last month about reintroducing clocking on, but I don't think anyone has been up from HR to discuss it with Robbie McFadden and the union yet.' He cackled. 'Robbie was schooled in the miner's strike, remember, in the court of King Arthur Scargill. No, I don't think a few American gobshites will get far with that one.'

Stephen wanted to hug him.

Archie was sitting with arms folded, an impenetrable wall of resistance. 'Aye, of course my men are used to being on their feet all day anyway,' he growled. He always appeared to regard anyone from Middleton head office as a lily-livered Sassenach. Stephen always told his brand managers that the factory head's bark was worse than his bite, but then he'd never been a postman delivering such bad news as he was doing today.

Carol was *still* on the phone, grinding Vassos into the dust, and the two Scotsmen exchanged a distinctly unimpressed look.

'Anyway, just before we start, how are you both? How's your golf, Jim? How was the holiday in Marbella?' Stephen asked.

'Not bad, not bad. My short game was awful all week, mind. And now I've got this pain in the arm.' He bent his arm up and down, pointing to the painful spot. 'Have you ever had it, Steve? My doctor reckons it's tennis elbow but I told him I never play bloody tennis.'

They discussed chip shots and muscle pains for several minutes, until Carol finally finished her call and sat down. She rooted around in her bag and pulled out a leather-bound notebook, still without making eye contact. But now Jim was in full flow, unveiling a selection of other muscular issues which were affecting his golf.

Stephen was aware of Carol as an impatient presence by his side. He knew what she was thinking – men's talk, all about golf. Why didn't they just cut to the chase? But he was in charge today and he would play it his way. Now she would have to wait for him.

'And how about your game, Archie?' he continued, feeling Carol's stare.

Archie didn't warm to the theme immediately. Like any good attack dog, he clearly smelt a rat. But eventually Stephen elicited that Archie's game was in good working order for the time of year, particularly his driving off the tee, and after a few minutes he appeared to be ready for tummy tickling. He even reciprocated.

'How about yourself, lad? Why did you nae come on a Friday? We could have arranged a game out at Castle Douglas.' He stared accusingly at Carol, who he clearly saw as responsible for spoiling all the fun.

'I last played about four years ago, Archie, back when I had a life.'

There was a moment of silence and further head shaking. Jim and Archie were only now appreciating the paucity of his situation.

Archie continued. 'Aye, well, you're welcome anyway. Just so long as you don't bring that arsehole Newte with you. Didn't I see he's been moved somewhere?'

'Yes, Archie, he's now Finance Vice President for the whole of Europe.' Clearly the exciting news of Schmaltz senior appointments hadn't made a big impact north of the border. He could quite fancy living here.

'Ach, good riddance to bad rubbish, eh, laddie?'

Stephen saw Carol's eyes roll heavenward.

'So anyway, Jim, you've met Carol before,' Stephen said cheerily. He couldn't bring himself to clarify that she was his boss now, although Jim must surely know. 'But Archie, I don't believe you have?'

'No,' said Archie, arms folded a little tighter.

It was probably time to go over the top.

'Now, gentlemen, we do need to discuss why we are here. As you know, our new VP Mr Hardman is very committed to delivering a growth strategy—'

'Aye, he sounds like a lunatic, Steve. Have you met him?' Archie grunted.

'Er, I work for him now, Archie. As, in a sense, we all do.'

'Aye, well, you need to talk some sense into him,' Archie observed, as if growth strategy was just a whimsical notion of Hardman's that could easily be averted over a glass of Scotch.

'I'll certainly try, Archie, but we do at least need to work through the practicalities of how this growth is going to happen. I'm kind of between a rock and a hard place on this one, guys.' Hell, where had he picked up that Americanism?

'Shit creek and no paddle, eh, laddie?' Archie chuckled for the first time. 'OK, I'll give you a hearing.' He paused. 'And then I'll tell you why it's a crap idea.'

It soon became apparent that Stephen's buttering-up strategy had got him nowhere. Jim and Archie were a formidable team. They listened in silence while Stephen outlined the business projections on how sales of Schmaltzy Bars would far outstrip Bingo. But then they whistled through their teeth in perfect unison, like a couple of plumbers being asked to replace a dodgy old boiler with a spanking new one.

Jim patted Stephen on the arm paternally. 'I'm sorry, but it's just not that simple, lad. The A line in number-one plant is already at maximum throughput. We couldn't increase the capacity there, even if we wanted to.'

'What do you mean, even if you wanted to?' Carol looked at him in disgust. 'Don't you want to increase productivity?'

Jim shook his head in a pitying fashion and screwed up his wrinkled face even more. 'It's not a question of whether we want or don't want. You'll have a major safety issue on your hands if you try to speed up the DY belt on the A line, and it will have a direct impact on the flux capacity on B line.' He might well be spouting complete gobbledygook, but it was enough to see off Carol. She let out an exasperated sigh and fell silent.

Stephen remained emollient. 'To start with, Jim, you might not need to increase capacity – even if we can just maintain capacity, but with Schmaltzy Bars coming in, that would be a good start. That way we buy some time to think about how to build capacity—'

'And there's another thing too. Those American bars contain far more sugar than Bingo Bars. Processing that bar, with all the ingredient changes, you're looking at starting again with completely new kit – I'd say you're looking at two years minimum. And anyway, given the nanny state we live in these days, I wouldn't want to be the person who had to defend adding more sugar. It looks like bad PR to me.'

He turned deliberately to give Carol an icy stare as he stirred another lump of sugar into his coffee. It was hard to see Jim as a guardian of the nation's healthy eating, but he seemed particularly chuffed over erecting this last roadblock. Archie still had his arms folded.

Stephen had experienced enough conversations like this with the factory over the years to know a dead horse when he saw one. Stop flogging and move on.

'OK, OK, let's come back to that one. Now, replacing Munchy Moments with Nutters. That's just replacing one nut with another, isn't it, Carol?' He turned to her, keeping a straight face. He couldn't resist it. That's what she had suggested in the security of her comfy office a month ago.

'Yes, and there's no raisin, so it should be a lot easier to make,' she added sulkily.

Archie was chuckling again, shaking his head.

'Tell me, lassie. What about storing these yolanda nuts? What temperature should they be stored at?'

'I don't know, that's your job.'

'Aye, indeed. That's my job. And I'm telling you it can't be done.' He was bristling now, baring his teeth. 'They will require an entirely different storage facility and they're a completely different shape. You cannae process them through this plant.'

Soon it was Dinosaurs 3, Schmaltz Europe 0. The formidable duo had shown equally strong resistance to stopping production of Little Monkeys, as Jim explained that they weren't doing too badly in Scotland – his grandchildren were big fans. Stephen knew there was an element of truth in this. Sales in this part of Scotland had held up relatively well, probably due to everyone having a relative who worked in the factory. But Hardman was hardly likely to change his pan-European strategy on the basis that Little Monkeys still went down a storm in Mrs Beattie's sweet shop. Unless he had Scottish roots. Was there a McHardman clan somewhere from which the man was descended? Or maybe he played golf – could they negotiate over a round at Muirfield? Beyond that, it felt hopeless.

The only concession granted was a willingness to consider phasing out production of Mint Regals, but only over a period of time.

'Aye, they've always been a bugger to make and I've never liked the name,' snarled Archie. He wasn't likely to be a fan of the royals.

Within the space of an hour and a half, Stephen and Carol had been effortlessly chewed up and spat out.

'Well, clearly we will report back to Mr Hardman that this is not an easy fix. I'm sure we'll talk further,' Stephen concluded, while Carol fumed silently by his side.

Magnanimous in their overwhelming victory, Jim suggested an early lunch, although only in the works canteen rather than the pub down the road as normal. They sat at a long table with a bunch of men from the factory eyeing them suspiciously from the other end. Jim was keen to talk more about golf. It was as if now that they'd had a bit of a chat about work, and made clear that what Stephen and this woman were suggesting was obviously ridiculous, that was an end to it. They could go back to being friends again.

Stephen did his best to join in, although he wasn't feeling so sociable as at the start of the morning. Carol got the hygienic wipes out to clear a smear of tomato sauce from the table, delicately unwrapped the cling film from a tired-looking chicken salad sandwich and then sat stiffly, swigging water and checking her messages while the rest of them tucked into fish and chips.

When Jim and Archie had said their goodbyes, Stephen and Carol were deposited back in reception.

'That was a disaster.' She glared at him accusingly.

'Yes, thanks for your support. I felt you really made a big effort to communicate with them. It made all the difference.'

'Sorry, but you suggested I leave it to you. Look where that got us. All that crap about the golf, and then they resisted every single demand.'

She did have a point.

'Yes, but there's leaving it to me, and there's fiddling with your phone all morning like a prima donna. You've got to learn to engage with these people, Carol, if you want to survive in your newly elevated position. But then why the hell you need to survive here I don't understand. I imagine if the going gets tough, you'll just piss off.'

It felt cathartic, having a go at each other, but she didn't respond to this. They sat in silence while she consulted her phone again.

'There's a flight back from Glasgow to Charles de Gaulle at half three,' she said. 'I might just make it if I order a taxi and it comes quickly. Mind you, fat chance of that round here.' Removing her glasses, the belligerence was replaced by a more worried look. 'Seriously, we are in deep shit with Brad on Friday. I have no idea what we're going to tell him.'

'I'll drive you to the airport.' It was a sudden impulse. A good hour in the wrong direction for him.

'Good idea. We need to talk.'

Was there just a spark of gratitude in those eyes?

They didn't talk. Or not for at least twenty minutes, as Carol embarked on a further series of phone calls. Why had he offered to do this? Eventually, after more rapid-fire texting, she turned to him.

'So, what do you suggest we do?'

'Who is being paid the fat salary here, Carol? Why don't you sort it out?' he retorted sharply. But glancing at her, he could now see a look of quiet desperation, which made him go easy. 'I mean, if I knew that, I'd have suggested something, wouldn't I? Of course, it's possible there might have been a bit of posturing from them today. They do normally concede a bit more than that on a first meeting, but normally I'm only asking them to consider making a minor change to an ingredient or something equally trivial. It took me about a year to get them to accept a new raisin supplier for Munchy Moments. And today we have just asked them to change the whole lot. I can call Jim tomorrow, talk to him without Archie there, see if I can make some progress. But we do need to stall for time. Can't you postpone Hardman, at least for a couple of weeks?'

She put her hands to her head and made a lowing sound, like a cow about to calf.

'OK, I'll take that as a no, then.'

As they drove in silence on the motorway, he could see them both standing naked in Brad Hardman's office, Adam and Eve, with hands in the fig leaf position.

'You do realise he's irresistible, don't you?' she burst out. 'He'll close down Jurassic Park here if he needs to.'

'That's hardly a solution, is it? Closing it down is not going to help solve his sourcing—'

Her phone rang again and she answered it. That was another thing that irritated him. The caller on the phone was always more important than the person next to her, at least when that person was him. She was arranging her next trip, to Hamburg. She slipped straight back into assertive mode, calling the shots on when she wanted the meeting, who she expected to be there. When she'd told them, she slipped her phone back in her bag, and pulled down the passenger mirror to reapply her lipstick.

'There you are, no problems with the Germans. Brand new plant, custom built to produce Schmaltzy Bars and anything else we want, and on time.'

'Hang on, are you telling me the Germans are being allowed to invest in a new plant to make Schmaltzy Bars?'

'Absolutely. State of the art German efficiency. You should know these things.'

'Thanks. You might discuss these things in board meetings, but we operatives are fed scraps these days. Clearly if I had known about this before, I would have mentioned it.'

'Why?'

'Because this might be your answer. If the Germans are building a plant anyway to make Schmaltzy Bars for Germany—'

'And most of Italy.'

'Well, hell, even more so. If they're designing a plant to deliver for two markets, maybe the incremental cost for them to feed the UK on top is minimal. At least compared with knocking down Jurassic Park, as you call it, and starting again.'

The fire was back in her eyes.

'Right, the man you need to talk to is Helmut Wimmer in Hamburg. He's very keen to please. Just let him know I told you to call him.'

'Helmut − he's not built like a brick shithouse, wire-brush hair and jowly chops, by any chance?'

'That's Helmut.'

'I've met him − at the Paris conference. He looked particularly keen to please you.'

A smile played around her lips. 'OK, looks like we're going to be busy between now and Paris on Friday afternoon,' she said.

'Whoa, you didn't tell me the meeting with Hardman is in Paris.'

'Oh, well it is. He's there all week. Four o'clock.'

'Huh, so nice friendly time on a Friday, then.'

'Yeah, you'd better get someone to book your flight pronto.'

'Fat chance of that. I'll have to do it myself. Sandra's already left the building, dreaming of her tea room empire. Anyway, I'll sort it. I always bloody do, don't I? And I guess it's got to be worth a try with these Germans. At least if your friend Helmut says they might be able to supply it from there, that will concentrate the minds of Jim and Archie to be a bit more cooperative.'

'Oh, you'll find the Germans' attitude will be vastly different. Might is not an option – they will do it. And your pals up here should have concentrated their minds today. They just signed their own death warrant. Thank God we won't have to come to this hole ever again. Hamburg's a cool city. I should have been born German.'

'I thought most women felt they should have been born Italian.'

'I'm not most women.'

And with that she pushed her seat back into the recline position, kicked off her shoes and closed her eyes.

He drove in silence, glancing back occasionally to see her chest gently rising and falling, and a lock of hair brushing her face. She was a different person when she was asleep. Maybe they could just disappear together – he wouldn't turn off for the airport, but keep going. Find another cosy hotel in a little fishing village somewhere along the Ayrshire coast. Just leave everything behind. He brought his concentration back to the road and hit the brakes as the tail lights of the car in front rushed towards him.

Only as he drew to a halt outside departures did she wake up, flexing her neck.

'Thanks for the lift. Keep me up to speed by email tomorrow, and we're going to need an action plan to make this happen by Thursday lunchtime so I'm ready for him.'

'Don't you mean, *we* are ready for him?'

'Of course,' she said, stepping out of the car. Her face broke into a satisfied smile. 'It's turned out to be a very good day after all.'

As he drove away from the airport, he thought of Jim Jeffries and Archie Macleod, going home for their tea, unaware of the guided missile he had just launched, already heading their way. What had he done? Only gone into partnership with Lady Macbeth.

Chapter Sixteen

Sat outside her office with laptop perched on his knee, he scrolled through his presentation one more time, sipping black coffee from a plastic cup. He needed the caffeine to kick in. After a late drive back from Glasgow on Tuesday, an early flight to Hamburg on Wednesday morning and forty-eight hours there hammering out the detail with horny Helmut Wimmer, he was running on empty. As predicted by Carol, the German certainly had a can-do attitude on how his spanking new factory could supply all the Schmaltzy Bars and Nutters that the unsuspecting British public could possibly scoff. And with each 'yes, surely it's possible' from Helmut, Stephen had realised they were cooking Jim Jeffries' goose to perfection.

She opened her office door and ushered him in. White dress with a high neckline and red slingbacks today. The hair was up and the glasses on. Fresh as a daisy, while he was wilting.

'You look ready for action,' Stephen said.

There was the faintest of smiles. 'Armani, darling. I always turn to Giorgio for the big occasion. Let's just go through it again before we see Brad.'

Most people would have found an afternoon facing up to Hardman far more daunting than a meeting with Archie

Macleod – like playing Barcelona after you'd been away to Partick Thistle. But not Carol. She was clearly back in her element, swimming with the big fish. And the vulnerability briefly on show as they had sat in Alexander and Morag's snug bar earlier that week was well under wraps again.

'Leave me to lead,' she said. 'I'll bring you in when I need you.'

'OK, so you're going to take all the credit then.'

'That's not what I meant.'

Hardman had not made quite the same effort over his appearance as Carol. He was in a blue tracksuit, and while on this occasion not actively engaged in a gym session during the meeting, it was obvious from the beads of sweat on his forehead and the aroma of his office that he had just completed one. Pearls before swine, Stephen thought. His office here in the Paris HQ was pretty much a replica of his office in the UK, except there was even more gym paraphernalia. And chairs, round a meeting table. So Stephen actually got to sit down, as Carol took control of the laptop and walked Hardman through the plan. It was, Stephen had to admit, a masterclass. She gave Hardman the 'great news' that they could supply the UK market with the American brands from Hamburg, without a hitch.

Hardman was normally a man on the shortest of fuses, but today he seemed perfectly calm and he was right there, focused on her every step. The white dress was a great move. It made her seem softer, less confrontational. It was like when Stephen first encountered her. He was sure nobody had ever come for an interview at Grimley's in a white dress before. When the interview panel met to discuss her afterwards, Jennie Jacobs joked that she'd be either marketing director or prime minister in five years, and that Stephen had better watch out. How they'd laughed.

Having listened respectfully for once, Hardman sniffed phlegm back into his throat.

'OK, you've clearly thought outside the box on this one, which I like,' he drawled. His face took on a lecherous smile. 'I like a woman who brings me solutions, not problems.' Stephen detected a twitch of revulsion on Carol's face. 'But I need more detail on the numbers. I still don't get why the fuck those trolls in Scotland can't produce it for the UK. Didn't they just vote to stick with England?

She turned to Stephen and he caught a hint of panic in her eyes.

'If you'd allow me, Carol.' He gestured towards the laptop, and she nudged it in his direction. He instantly located the key chart which compared the high costs of installing new equipment in Dumfries with the more efficient alternative of sourcing in Hamburg. It had taken him most of yesterday to put this one slide together, to make the case watertight.

'So let me explain, Mr—'

Hardman raised a hand. 'Just leave it up there.' His eyes scurried up and down the screen.

Carol was sitting on the edge of her seat, and Stephen gave her a slight smile of reassurance. For some reason he still wanted to protect her.

Eventually Hardman leant back in his chair with a sinister grin on his face.

'Excellent. Let's just fucking do this.'

'Thank you,' Carol said, smiling back at him in obvious relief. 'And beyond the immediate saving, there is a huge longer-term benefit as the Dumfries plant can be closed as soon as Hamburg is fully operational. Oscar Newte's been running the numbers on that and he's coming up with some sensational figures on how much we're going to save by closing Scotland.'

She really didn't need any protection. And yes, this must be right up Oscar's alley. He was exactly the sort of man who would like to close Scotland.

Hardman was stroking his chin, looking at her thoughtfully. Was even he momentarily shocked by her rampaging zeal?

'Even better,' he sniffed and turned to Stephen. 'This all make sense to you, Carreras?'

Patronising wanker.

'Yes, Mr Hardman, I've been working on the numbers,' Stephen said, glancing pointedly at Carol. 'However, I still think we can avoid the collateral damage. Dumfries isn't a big town, and this will have a huge impact there. Maybe now we have this Plan B on the table to source through Hamburg, we can go back to the team in Scotland and knock some heads together. It should concentrate their minds.' He avoided eye contact with her now. This wasn't in the script.

'Nah, if they can't make the fucking product, they can't make the fucking product,' Hardman said, relaxing back in his chair, hands clasped behind his head. 'Hamburg just became Plan A. But maybe we could leave this Dumfries open as a theme park.' He laughed, before his expression turned stern again. 'So look, we need to keep those fuckers up there completely in the dark about this. I don't want anybody to know about this except you two, Nudey, and this Wammer guy in Germany. And I want this in place by mid-June, not mid-July. Then four weeks after we switch on Hamburg, we switch off Dumfries.'

In Hardman's world, poor Jim Jeffries was on life support.

'It'll be like a summer holiday for 'em,' he chuckled, 'but just an extended one. Of course, there'll be some squealing when we do it, but I've done this kinda crapshoot many times before. We give them minimum notice, so we avoid protracted negotiation with the fucking unions.' He smiled cynically again. 'We just present it as a done deal. Product can be manufactured more efficiently elsewhere, regrettable closures, modern progress, all that shit.'

He pointed at Carol. 'I'll need you to help me with the PR strategy and we'll need to hire some legal eagle to make sure they can't slip out of it. And you might want to use this fella too,' he thumbed at Stephen. 'He's been practising by getting rid of the time-wasters in Middleton for me already.'

He turned to address Stephen directly. 'Carreras, you done good so far on getting rid of the bodies, but nice and discreet on this one, huh? No squealing. Don't wanna end up in the theme park too, do ya?'

Stephen and Carol retreated to her office after the meeting. She called Newte immediately, ecstatically conveying the glad news and indulging in a bout of mutual telephonic back slapping.

Finally she turned back to Stephen with a triumphant smile on her face.

'What a great way that was to end Friday. Roll on the weekend.'

'I blame the teachers,' Stephen said.

'What?'

'They should have taken him in hand when he was about eight, given him a good clip round the ear for taking sweets off the other kids, and it would all be different.'

She frowned at him. 'I have no idea what you're talking about.'

'Yes, you do. I mean, how the hell does he think we can just jump and find him another four weeks in a plan that's patently ridiculous anyway? But that's what people have always done for Brad Hardman, isn't it? Jumped. He just always gets his way. His teachers should have cut that bully boy down years ago. Or maybe it's his parents' fault. I wonder what they're like.'

'Have you finished?' she asked.

'No, I haven't. There's another thing. You're both still assuming the great British public will accept sweet American chocolate.

That anti-sugar pressure group I told you about, they're called LISA. Life Is Sweet Already. And they're gaining momentum. There's a piece about them on the BBC website today.'

'I'm sure there is.' She sounded disinterested and started looking at her phone again. 'But you don't need to worry about LISA, just concentrate on Marlene. That's the project name for this operation.'

'Given up pretending it's Project Harmony, have we?'

'No.' She looked disappointed by him. 'Harmony covers the whole brand replacement strategy across Europe. Marlene is specifically for the diversion of manufacturing to Hamburg. Marlene Dietrich – something dramatic coming out of Germany. It was my idea – good, don't you think?' she said.

'Should have been Project Mushroom really.'

'What?'

'We're treating Dumfries like mushrooms, aren't we? Keeping them in the dark and piling them in shit.'

'Are you on side or not? If not, I can find someone else who will be.'

He hesitated for a moment. 'Yeah, Carol, I'm on side. Like I have an alternative.'

He glanced at his watch. 'Right, I'd better get the taxi back to Charles de Gaulle. It'll take forever at this time of day.'

Amidst all his anger, he realised, that he didn't want to leave. She had become his focus, for better or worse, all week, ever since she'd turned up at the hotel in Kirkcudbright on Monday evening. Only four days ago.

'What flight are you on?' she asked.

'Oh, I think it's the eight-fifteen BA one,' he said, reaching for his coat from the peg on her door.

'I'm going back this weekend as well,' she said, without looking at him. 'Same flight. I've got a car booked to take me to the airport in ten minutes. You can come with me if you like.'

She spent the whole of the Friday night slog out to the airport on the phone to her team of runners around Europe – Sven in Stockholm, Hipólito in Madrid and, last but not least, Vassos. The poor lad had probably been settling down for a well-deserved glass of wine before Friday night moussaka with his extended family when she tracked him down to deliver her regular lambasting.

Ultimately Vassos was saved further punishment by a grumpy man at airport security telling *mademoiselle* she needed to turn off her phone to go through the security scanner. Stephen waited on the other side as she slowly and deliberately refastened the belt round that tight-waisted white dress, still looking like she had stepped off the catwalk.

'Well, I'll probably see you at the other end. Back of the plane for me,' Stephen said.

Carol glanced at her gold bracelet watch. 'There's still half an hour until they'll call the flight. You can come and join me in the business lounge if you like. I'll sign you in. We can talk next steps.'

He sorted two glasses of champagne and a bowl of nibbles while she went off to find a seat. When he found her, she had draped her coat across two seats and was thumbing a copy of *Vogue*. Maybe she had decided next steps could wait; that she was at last through with the week. She moved the coat to allow him to sit down next to her. A group of loud businessmen drinking beers on the other side of the table cast what looked like admiring glances in their direction.

His phone vibrated a text alert in his jacket pocket.

'Hope you have a good weekend. R x'

She was probably on her way to that church weekend with Jesus of Middleton by now. Well, doing good among the carnage had taken a backward step this week. In fact, it was in full-on retreat.

'So, good work this week.' Carol raised her glass. They clinked. 'Here's to Project Mushroom,' she laughed. And then, more softly, added, 'Thanks for your help. We're a good team, you and I.'

This was his world, celebrating the end of the week, exhausted and light-headed, with Carol. Not spending Valentine's night away with some evangelical do-gooders in a draughty Outward Bound centre. There'd been no point in sending a card, after that conversation in the car park. Just stay on the treadmill. Project Mushroom was going to close a factory in Dumfries and put one hundred and fifty people on the dole. It was going to mean an end to the brands he and generations before him had spent their working lives trying to create and preserve. But he couldn't do anything about that. All he could do, and do faultlessly, was plan it all. He could just live in the moment, and the moment was sitting with Carol Coolidge sipping champagne in the business lounge at Charles de Gaulle, making her laugh as he impersonated horny Helmut.

His phone rang, a number rather than a name showing on the screen – not one of his contacts.

'Hello there, Steve, it's Jim Jeffries here.'

Shit, what was Jim doing, ringing him at this time on a Friday? He should have put him into contacts so he could have avoided this, let it go to voicemail.

'Hi, Jim. How are you? I don't often get a call from you. Particularly not late on a Friday. I thought you'd be in the golf club bar by this time,' he laughed nervously.

'Aye, well, I realised we hadn't spoken since you came up here, laddie. Archie had the bit between his teeth that day. I think it was that Coolidge woman, Steve. You should never have brought her. She was like a red rag to a bull.'

Stephen was aware of her looking at him.

'I'm sorry you felt that way, Jim, but we needed the conversation.'

'Anyway, I've not heard from you since, so I assume we talked some sense into you.'

Stephen hesitated. Did Jim suspect anything?

'As I said, it was a useful discussion, Jim.'

'Good. Oh, and congratulations laddie. I noticed the Bingo brand share is starting to go up. I knew you had it in you.'

'I guess that's the power of Schmaltz, Jim.'

Carol winked at him.

'Bullshit, laddie. That's down to you, not those idiots. Anyway, after our wee chat and what with the brand share going up, it's obviously business as usual?'

'Of course, Jim, business as usual.'

Carol gave him the thumbs up.

He diverted Jim onto his weekend golfing plans before he ended the call and tried to put him out of his mind and focus on her again. Her eyes had closed for a moment, a picture of beautiful serenity.

'So, what plans for a weekend in Middleton? It must be pretty dull compared with a weekend in Paris,' he said.

'Oh, I've just got to get a few things in order in the house. I'm putting it on the market, aiming for something bigger,' she said casually, resuming her perusal of the magazine. 'So at least if I do have to spend the odd night in Middleton, I'll have somewhere half-decent to come back to. Might as well, with the company subbing my mortgage.' As if he'd forgotten that. 'And I might catch up with a few friends. Now I'm a free agent.'

His heart skipped. It was mad, but his heart skipped. Wasn't it only Monday when she had confided in him that the relationship with Mr Cool Boyfriend was in trouble? Had she ditched him?

'Oh, really? I'm sorry about that.'

She sipped her champagne and flicked over another page. 'I'm not. I told him if he couldn't fit in with my lifestyle and me living in Paris, he wasn't the man for me.'

Chapter Seventeen

Kate was still staring out of the car window, sticking to her apparent vow of silence.

'OK, Kate, I don't exactly make a habit of going out on a Saturday evening when you two are staying for the weekend. It's just a one-off, for an old friend's birthday party.'

Still no response.

'Look, Jake had this invitation to a sleepover with one of his new pals in the football team, and your mother and I thought it would be nice for him,' he said, increasingly exasperated. 'And you might have a good time at Emily's. Just consider that as a possibility,' Stephen said.

'I won't.'

He had no idea it would be so difficult to fix her up with a friend for the evening.

'Remind me again why you didn't want to stay with Megan?'

'Because I'm not talking to her.'

It was difficult keeping up with who was in or out, in a teenager's world. Emily had been Laura's suggestion when Stephen was forced to admit he was drawing a blank, and Laura had stressed she wouldn't countenance Kate being left on her own given she was still in a bit of a state. He remembered Emily as a best friend at primary school, but she had gone to the private school at eleven and was now, in Kate's eyes, seriously uncool.

'All I can say, Kate, is that Emily's mum was very friendly on the phone and said it would be nice to see you again. I'm sure she'll make you very welcome.'

'Why do I need to stay the night there? Why can't you just pick me up later?'

'Because it might be late. I don't want Emily's parents having to wait up for me.'

The silence returned.

'Are you taking your friend?' she asked eventually.

'Which friend?'

'That one in the café. Rachel.' The name was uttered with a certain amount of venom, he thought.

'No, she's not going.'

They pulled into a driveway bigger than his house. Emily's mother opened the door with a welcoming smile.

'Hello, Kate, come on in. Nice to see you again. Wow, you're growing into a tall girl. Emily has just got a couple of friends round from school. They're about to start a board game, I think. Do you want to head up and I'll bring you a soft drink in a minute?'

Stephen could see that Kate was holding back the tears as she dragged her body up the stairs. He watched her go, trying to quell the rising guilt. But he needed to get out of here. He grovelled appropriately to Emily's mother, whose initial enthusiasm as hostess appeared to have diminished already.

By the time he had driven home, the taxi was already waiting outside. He jumped in straight away but as the driver started to burble on about the weather, his thoughts returned to his daughter with a mixture of anxiety and anger. How was she getting on? She wasn't making life easy for him at the moment with this teenage angst. But he really shouldn't feel guilty about it. Under normal circumstances, he genuinely did turn down any invitation when the kids were staying. Not that there were many. And he might even have turned down this one as well. If Carol hadn't happened to mention that she was going to be in Middleton again this weekend to get started on the house-hunting.

'What number did you say it was?' said the driver.

'Fourteen. I think it's here.'

He'd never been to her house before, but he knew this development of neat town houses with their perfect open-plan gardens. Quite nice by Middleton standards, especially for someone still not thirty. But evidently not nice enough – a 'For Sale' sign was already outside.

His stomach was making little rumbling noises as he rang the bell.

She looked fabulous, in a silver jacket and flowing black trousers. But the greeting was perfunctory and she instantly turned to walk back upstairs, saying she wouldn't be long. Her perfume lingering in the hallway was headier than usual. Photos on the pure white walls showed her on a skiing trip with a group of friends, all perfect smiling teeth and Ray-Bans.

When she came down again, she was clutching a classy leather handbag and a black coat, which she asked him to hold while she slipped into a pair of heels – it felt soft and luxurious. The taxi driver hooted.

'You look great, Carol.' He leant towards her cheek, catching her by surprise, before she moved away.

'Remind me where this party is again?'

'Middleton rugby club. You should meet a few familiar faces from the UK office. Well, any who are left. Let's see how it goes. We don't have to stay long.'

Now he was here, it felt excruciating. He'd said he could pick her up and take her to the party, but was it a 'date'? It was to him – sort of.

'And whose fortieth is it again?'

'Danny Allsop. Works in purchasing?'

'Can't say I remember him.'

He could well believe that Carol wouldn't remember Danny. He was sure that Danny would remember Carol.

*

'Bloody hell, you're not giving her one, are you?' Danny nudged him in the ribs. Carol had gone to the cloakroom almost immediately after they'd arrived, and Danny's face was a picture of envy. His green T-shirt, emblazoned with 40 YEAR OLD VINTAGE. PLEASE HANDLE WITH CARE, was clinging round his beer belly.

'Er, none of your business, Daniel.' It was nice to leave him wondering, at least.

'She's way out of your league, mate.'

'Well, thanks for the vote of confidence.' She hadn't been out of his league in that hotel bedroom four years ago.

Hopefully there would be something more interesting on offer for Carol. Maybe he hadn't thought this one through. Danny had been banging on all week about how there would be a free bar, but he should have guessed that Mr Allsop wasn't the sort of man to serve champagne on arrival.

Carol returned, already looking like a woman who had stepped into the wrong evening.

'OK, let me get you a drink,' Stephen said, and went to queue at the bar, leaving her with Danny and a couple of other old lags from purchasing who appeared out of the woodwork. Her eyes were flicking round the room, probably in search of an escape route.

'What do you want, mate?' the barman asked him gruffly.

'Do you have a bottle of champagne?'

'No mate, we've got white or red.'

Danny and his pals were still standing next to Carol when Stephen returned, but they were evidently not finding areas of common interest.

'Sorry, no bubbly.' He handed her the white wine, which she examined distrustfully.

'So, Happy Birthday, Danny.' Stephen raised his pint in Danny's direction. 'How does it feel to be forty?'

'You tell me, mate.'

He needed to get her to a different place, not one that would remind her of the age gap.

'Anyway,' Danny continued, 'I have bigger news than turning forty.' He was not a man prone to lightness but right now he was almost radiant. 'I'm out of here.'

'What do you mean?' asked Stephen.

'I've got another job. Handed in my notice yesterday. No more house of bloody fun for me.'

Danny's other mates didn't seem entirely delighted for him, so someone had to congratulate him.

'Well done, mate. I'm very pleased for you. Anywhere good?'

'FastGro.' He looked rather sheepish.

'Oh, nice one. And you won't have to move house. How did you find it?'

'I called that woman you mentioned. Phoebe double-barrel something. Mad as a March hare I thought, but then she said there was this job coming up there, so I applied, and I got it.' He looked around as if wanting to share a secret. 'Looks like a piece of piss actually.'

Of course it was FastGro, now becoming the escape tunnel of choice. Phoebe had already placed a couple of his lesser lights there. It was hard not to feel envious of anyone jumping ship, although it was so old-school that it made even pre-Schmaltz Grimley's look cutting-edge. And Stephen was still to be convinced of the fun to be had in flogging fertiliser. Given it was his old mate's birthday, it felt important not to rain on his parade.

'Well, good luck. I'll miss you, old son,' he said, raising his glass again.

Danny gave a toothy smile. 'Anyway, the best bloody thing of all is that I won't have to put up with that wanker Hardman any longer. Right, enjoy yourselves, the bar is free until we run out of money, which at the rate you bastards drink won't be long. And there's a band coming on later.'

'Oh, anybody we know?' Stephen asked.

'I doubt it. One of my neighbours saw them at the King's Head last month and said they were good. Apparently the lead singer is a bit of all right. See you later. Good luck – you'll need it.' Danny nodded in the direction of Carol who was standing apart, checking her phone. And then he wandered off with his purchasing pals.

'Are you all right? How's the wine?' Stephen asked Carol.

She pulled a disgusted face at the drink and apparently Danny too. 'It's people like that who've been dragging the company down. No room for dead weight like him in the new world. Thank God he's going.'

'OK, OK, I know this isn't your scene. It's not mine either. To be honest, I thought there would be more of the old marketing team here. Seems like it's mainly his mates from other departments, or the rugby club, and his family.'

He spotted Sheila, Danny's wife, who always seemed to withstand her spouse's lugubrious sexism with remarkable good humour. The disco had started, and she was already on the dance floor with two other women, laughing and shuffling along to 'You Sexy Thing' by Hot Chocolate.

The music was loud, making conversation difficult. Carol's face was now that of a woman suffering from acute constipation.

'Shall we go somewhere else?' Stephen shouted. 'I only wanted to put in an appearance. How about dinner?'

Her face lit up.

'I've just spotted someone,' she yelled, and gyrated across the dance floor – accompanied by wolf whistles from Danny's cronies – to reach a tanned, well-groomed man in a bold pink shirt. He flashed a smile as he saw her coming. She threw her arms round him and kissed him on both cheeks.

'Hi, Steve, how are you?' Alan from accounts had sidled up next to Stephen, clasping a half pint. The music stopped for a moment. 'I see the January gross profits were reasonable, all things considered.'

An hour later Stephen was still propping up the bar, moaning about the office with Danny's mates. He had lost Carol.

Danny returned with a cheery grin. 'Pace yourself, mate,' he advised. 'The bar's open till one. I was joking about running out of money – I think.'

There was a whoop from the dance floor. Now she was out there with that self-satisfied smarm ball who now looked like he was auditioning for *Dirty Dancing*. He was flexing his groin in her direction to 'You're The One That I Want'.

Danny gave him a hard jab in the ribs this time.

'Ow, what was that for?'

'I did tell you she was out of your league.'

'Who is that she's dancing with?'

'Oh, I thought you'd recognise him. I must tell him he's not as well known as he thinks he is.'

'Danny, the fact I don't recognise him doesn't mean he isn't famous. You're mistaking me for someone who has a life.'

'He's Sheila's younger brother – well, half-brother. Which is probably why you can't see an immediate resemblance to my little goddess. Simon Perry. Owns Perry's Leisure Club. Generally thought to be the wealthiest man in Middleton. Oh, and also a complete wanker in my humble opinion. Although your date clearly doesn't think so.'

Carol was practically having sex with him now to 'Sisters Are Doin' It For Themselves'.

'Sorry this music is crap. I knew I shouldn't have let the missus choose it. The band will be on in a few minutes, though. Bit of punk. We can pogo around to that stuff, even with too many arms and legs.'

'I wonder how she knows him,' Stephen said, still fixated on Carol.

'People like that just know each other. Money attracts money, pal. She'll be a member at Perry's. They probably ski together. Get over it. Have another beer.'

It was all right for Danny, happy in his middle-aged mediocrity. But Stephen could still be a successful young professional. Or a middle-aged one, at any rate. Laura and he used to be members of Perry's. And he'd always fancied skiing.

Danny's wife Sheila came over, panting heavily. She gave Stephen a wide-eyed smile.

'Excuse me, Steve. Daniel, you old fart, we need to dance.'

To a chorus of cheers, she dragged her red-faced husband out onto the dance floor, where they performed a series of awkward but enthusiastic moves which at least drew Stephen's attention away briefly from Carol's leg, now wrapped around Simon Perry's thigh.

Pre-ordering the taxi for midnight had seemed like a good idea at the time. Better to have it all organised and avoid having to join the taxi rank outside Josie's Night Club with Middleton's binge drinkers. She would appreciate that. As they drew up outside her house, she would turn to him in the dark of the taxi and invite him in for a nightcap, just as he had invited her that night. When they entered her house, she would tell him to make himself comfortable. And when she reappeared…

'Hello.' Carol addressed him, her eyes expressionless. 'I'm heading off. Let's do a call on Monday to go through the next presentation for Brad.' She turned and walked away from him to Simon Perry, waiting by the exit with her coat tucked under his arm.

There was deafening high-pitched feedback from a microphone as Sheila shuffled onto the small stage beyond the dance floor.

'Ooh, sorry about that, ladies and gents. Right, I hope you're all having a great time. The night is young.' There was a chorus of cheers. 'The bar is open for another three hours. And to help old farts like my husband get through the night and remember when they were young, please put your hands together for the Clams!'

More whooping and clapping. Two hours to go before his taxi. To think he'd farmed Kate out for the evening as well. He'd have one more pint, and then call to see if it could pick him up earlier.

He stood near the bar at the back of the room, withdrawn slightly from most of the guests who were already bobbing up and down as the band launched into a driving rendition of 'London's Burning' by The Clash. Everyone else at the bar was focused on getting another drink, shouting to compete with the music. Accounts Alan came up to him again, his hand still wrapped round a half-pint jug, mouthing something. Stephen shook his head, touched his ear to indicate he couldn't hear and stared trance-like at the band, partially hidden by various blokes with dome-shaped heads.

He was a complete fool. He had even spent this afternoon tidying up the house, with the ridiculous notion that Carol might end up there this evening. But it hadn't been a date after all. More like he'd provided her with a taxi to a party where she got off with someone else. He was just her bloody accomplice, same as at work. How had he let himself believe she might be interested in him again? He'd allowed her to use him, to revive stirrings of something best forgotten, and now he was in deep, helping her to shine and providing Hardman with the ammunition to destroy a whole factory. And he was about to spend his Sunday trying to keep the kids entertained while getting her next presentation together.

It was 'A Town Called Malice' now, and the crowd were really getting going. Sheila was trying to teach Danny a move or two on the dance floor. Stephen felt ashamed of thinking them mediocre. The truth was that Danny knew he was onto a good thing with Sheila. He knew what he wanted from life – simple, no frills, the love of a good woman, an easy job, a few beers with his mates. Sorted.

There were three older shaven-headed blokes in the band, with T-shirts and beer bellies, sort of Danny lookalikes. They were undemonstrative, seasoned musicians who had no doubt been banging this stuff out for years – a tight sound. Some of the crowd in front of him were accepting the lead singer's exhortation to come on and pogo, by jumping up and down in some fashion. She looked the part – pink hair, a very short red leather skirt that matched her lipstick, fishnets and little black bootees. She was pacing the stage with both hands clutching her mic. Small and fragile next to the three burly men, but a real belter.

They moved seamlessly from song to song. There was a brilliant version of 'Teenage Kicks' where the singer even managed to capture Feargal Sharkey's Northern Irish warble. The crowd were really loving it now, several men playing their air guitars, and everyone else bouncing up and down, except for the few poor sods around him at the back, still drinking beer.

Danny was coerced onstage for a spot of karaoke on the final number. With his arm round the singer's waist, they launched into 'The Tide Is High' by Blondie. He was way out of tune but clearly enjoying himself. She had a great range, impersonating Debbie Harry just as well as Feargal Sharkey. She gave Danny a big kiss at the end and held his hand high in the air in triumph as they all sang 'Happy Birthday'. The Clams took their bow to wild applause, the crowd calling for more. They returned to the stage, with a special roar of adulation for the lady in pink.

The bass player stepped forward.

'Ey up, you lot all right?' he shouted in a South Yorkshire accent. 'We're gonna finish with another number from Blondie. Some awkward tosser earlier told me Blondie were new wave not punk. But she who must be obeyed likes this,' he nodded towards the singer, 'so Blondie it is.'

With hand on her hip in provocative pose, she went for it one more time. 'A Picture of You'. Stephen's mind flashed to another party, another woman. Her inheritance track. She would have embraced this evening with him and had fun. But no doubt she would be too busy doing good somewhere – again.

It was only half an hour to his taxi now. He might as well hang on, have one more for the road. But he definitely needed some fresh air first. He stepped out into the damp, cold evening. It felt like this winter would go on forever. A couple of the blokes from the band were leaning against the railings, having a smoke. A few yards apart from them, the lead singer stood alone, hunched in the drizzle, now wearing a parka with the hood up. She was an incongruous sight, the combination of that coat with fishnet tights and bootees, holding the pink wig in her hand now while managing to tap on her phone. She pulled down her hood to put the phone to her ear. She looked a bit like Rachel.

Stephen hovered behind her. He needed to see her face-on.

'You want something, mate?' the bass player shouted across to him. Hell, did he look like a stalker?

'No, I'm all right.'

She put the phone in her pocket and turned round. He was sure it was her. But she had not registered him yet.

'Rachel?'

She walked towards him until her face became clearer in the pool of orange street light. The face which normally broke into a smile at seeing him remained impassive, ghostly pale with streaks of dark mascara below both eyes.

'Oh, hi. I thought you might be here when they said it was a party for someone from Grimley's.'

'How are you? That was amazing. I mean, I had no idea.'

'No. Well, thanks.' She shrugged her shoulders and looked away.

'Er, will you come in and have a drink?'

'No, that's OK. I'm getting a lift home. I just need my bed.'

'Yes, of course, you must be knack— exhausted. I'm getting a taxi in a few minutes. I can give you a—'

'No, it's fine, thanks. My lift should be here in a minute.' Her eyes were straining across the car park.

'Are you around tomorrow by any chance?'

'Church stuff all day. Why do you ask?'

'Oh, just wondered. But no, of course.' There was an awkward silence. 'I can't imagine most punk rockers are going to church tomorrow morning.'

'No. I'm not most punk rockers.'

A car's headlights lit up the rain as it drove up alongside them.

'Here's my lift. Maybe I'll see you around. Look after yourself, Stephen. Nice jacket, by the way.'

The driver reached over to open the door for her. It was too dark to make the face out clearly, but it was a man – with a beard. And she leant towards him before she shut the door.

Part Three

_____

March to August 2015

Chapter Eighteen

'I just *know* I'm going to wear down your resistance eventually, darling boy.'

She chose her moments, Phoebe Huntley-Parsons. Dangling this job in leafy Devon again as his taxi circled the airport perimeter road at Charles de Gaulle.

'In many ways, I'd love to go down there, Phoebe, I really would. But as I've said before, moving far away from Middleton is… complicated.'

There was an exaggerated sigh. Complications weren't Phoebe's thing – particularly when she was homing in on a nice recruitment fee. He changed the subject.

'Anyway, I gather you lined a good friend of mine up with a job at FastGro? Not one of the young marketing blades this time, either.'

'Did I? Quite possibly.'

'Danny Allsop?'

'Ah, yes, Mr Allsop. Such a strange man, but they seemed to think he would fit their bill. *Entre nous*, sweety, those fertiliser people are somewhat strange too, although perhaps not in the same way as your Mr Allsop.'

'I'm sure it's a marriage made in heaven, Phoebe. And

you've got another one from my old team going to Burton's Boilers, I understand.'

'Indeed, that's six in a month I've sorted out from the list you sent me. Your glowing references are definitely helping. You can always find a career in creative writing if it gets any worse up there,' she said with a laugh.

Six in a month. He should be sharing her commission.

'*Voilà, monsieur. Hotel Splendid,*' the taxi driver grunted.

'Phoebe, I'll have to go. I've arrived at my exciting Parisian destination.'

'Ah, *tant pis*, sweety. Do give my love to Gay Paree.'

'Believe me, Phoebe, there's nothing to love about this bit of Paris.'

He stood for a moment in the now familiar wasteland of the hotel car park. God, she was tempting him. It was too cruel. Now she'd told him the Devon job was with a small artisanal chocolate company, in a slow reveal of details designed to suck him in. He'd blown it with Rachel, been made a fool of by Carol, and was currently combining his role as Phoebe's recruitment assistant with facilitating a nuclear holocaust in Dumfries. It would be lovely to run away. He tried to focus very hard for a moment on Kate's and Jake's faces, picture the three of them when they were all laughing and having fun together. And that wasn't happening much these days – particularly not with Kate.

As normal, Solène on reception wore the look of a woman who should have been smoking *Gitanes* and reading poetry in a small café on the Boulevard St-Michel, but who, through some tragic twist of fate, found herself dealing with idiots like him at a fourth-rate airport hotel. It was his eighth visit in two months, but still she gave the impression she'd never seen him before. He filled out his address, next of kin and passport number yet again, and as per usual she intoned some incomprehensible fire instructions. The bar remained closed.

In his room, he opened a small plastic bottle of wine that he'd bought on the plane and a packet of prawn sandwiches purchased at East Midlands airport. There was a knock at the door. Odd – had he left something in reception?

He was faced by a smiling man wearing stylish dark-framed glasses.

'Stephen, how are you? I hope I am not disturbing?'

Stephen ran his eyes over the dark jacket, the casual but crisply ironed open-collared shirt. Where had he seen him before?

'I am Salvatore Carnevale. From Milano? We met briefly at the mad conference.'

Of course. The one person there who'd felt like a kindred spirit. Originally marketing director in Italy, but presumably he'd been demoted too since they met.

'Salvatore, I'm so sorry it's taken me a moment to place you. You're definitely not disturbing anything. And I'm sorry I've not been in touch as well. I still have your business card in my wallet.'

'No problem. I think you've had plenty to think about. But I saw you arrive, and I am just down the corridor.'

'Poor you. But nice of you to give me some company in Europe's most glamorous hotel. Are you over here with some colleagues?' Stephen beckoned him into the room.

'No, on my own. Here for my regular fight with Carol Coolidge.' He raised his eyes heavenward.

'Oh, really? Me too.'

'Yes, I have the eight o'clock meeting in the morning, so I'll warm the ice-woman up for you.'

'Good luck with that. Sounds like we're partners in adversity, Salvatore.'

The Italian seemed pleased by this idiom. 'Yes, partners in adversity,' he repeated, trying it out for size. 'Yes, very good.' He cast an eye around the room. 'So, clearly you are not planning a feast this evening?'

'On the contrary, Salvatore. Welcome to my home from home. I can offer you half a miniature bottle of warm white wine in a small plastic cup. Never let it be said we English aren't hospitable.'

Salvatore held up his hand. 'No, no, don't even think of it. I came to ask if you would like to get out of your room. Of course, you may want to be alone and do some work, but I'm leaving tonight at seven, if you like to join me? And *informale*, no tie required.' He patted Stephen on the shoulder.

*

Salvatore was waiting in the soulless turquoise foyer, talking animatedly on his phone. But on seeing Stephen, he slipped it into his top pocket and smiled warmly.

'OK, *andiamo*, the car's here.'

Stephen felt like a naughty boy slipping out of dorm after lights out. Would they have to shin their way up a drainpipe to get back in and avoid Solène later?

Salvatore immediately struck up a lively conversation in French with the driver, but after a few minutes turned to him.

'I am sorry, Stephen, that was rude of me. Pierre-Louis likes to talk politics. He complains about his government and I complain about mine.' He smiled mischievously. 'And then we both complain about yours.'

'No problem, Salvatore. It was very impressive. Now, just to embarrass me further, how many languages do you speak?'

Salvatore looked like he was mentally totting them up. 'Five, maybe six. I am learning Mandarin but it's slow. Oh, and I suppose I could count Italian.'

Why the hell was someone of his intellect taking orders from Carol Coolidge?

They drove along a straight, tree-lined country road into the open, flat French countryside.

'Wow, Salvatore, you realise we Brits never venture out, even though there's nowhere to eat in the hotel? Apart from smuggling in the odd bottle of cheap wine, we don't bother.'

'I know.' Salvatore looked at him sympathetically. 'It's odd because I always thought you English resist a dictator. Where is the spirit of Winston Churchill? I thought you would dig an escape hole by now. I could not meet your Miss Coolidge on an empty stomach.'

'Please don't think of her as my Miss Coolidge,' Stephen grunted. 'Anyway, where exactly are we going in Paris?'

'Oh, we're not going into Paris. Too difficult to get there in an evening. No, I always go for "home from home" as you called it earlier. I use a little *trattoria* in Auvois, a small town only twenty minutes away. It's simple but, what is it you say, fit for purpose?'

Stephen laughed at the sheer joy of escaping the Splendid, with a man who clearly had his priorities sorted.

The car trundled over a pretty cobbled square, where the shuttered houses announced that work was done for the day. The lights from one little restaurant pierced the gloomy twilight, and they drew up outside it. Under its cheerful green, white and red awning, Trattoria del Pietro was defiantly open for business.

Stephen got out and sniffed the slightly smoky air, while Salvatore thrust a note into Pierre-Louis' hand, bringing a grin to the driver's previously curmudgeonly face. He waved as he drove off.

'Wow, Salvatore, this is amazing.'

'Oh, Stephen, it's just a simple little place.' He put an arm around Stephen's shoulder. 'But it is definitely better than your hotel room.'

A clock struck the half hour, and Salvatore nodded in the direction of a church across the square, beyond a little fountain and war memorial.

'The *église* is worth a look some time. One of the best examples of Gothic architecture in the Île de France. But maybe not tonight. Let's eat.'

Salvatore led the way into the restaurant and a bell rang to announce their arrival. Only one of the small cluster of tables, bedecked in red and white tablecloths, was occupied, by a couple in muted conversation. A grey-haired man with a bushy moustache waddled out from the kitchen, with a mournful air. But at the sight of his new customers, his face transformed into a wide smile, he threw open his arms and kissed Salvatore on both cheeks. There was back slapping and friendly poking of each other in the stomach. A woman of similar age to Pietro appeared and Salvatore opened his arms even wider to wrap them around her comfortable girth. It was a scene from *The Godfather*.

Pietro beckoned them to a cosy little table in the corner where *Signora* lit the candle. Then he returned with large leather-bound menus. But Salvatore already appeared to be conveying orders. Pietro listened attentively, interspersing only with the occasional '*Si, signore.*'

'*E bere, signore?*' Pietro addressed Stephen, with a hopeful manner.

Salvatore smiled at him. 'You like red wine, Stephen?'

'Definitely yes, but maybe not too much on a school night.' Lord, he sounded like his mother.

'A school night,' chuckled Salvatore, clearly delighted at this further addition to his repertoire. 'No, of course not. But I think we can enjoy one bottle of something good, yes?' He ordered without consulting the wine list and Pietro scuttled off.

Salvatore relaxed back into his chair. 'I hope this is good for you, Stephen. Pietro does the best *risotto al Barolo* this side of

Milano. You must try it. I ordered us that and a decent bottle of Chianti. And some calamari to start, with just a glass of Pinot Grigio. We can't eat Pietro's calamari without a little white wine.'

It was a bit presumptuous. Stephen hadn't even had the chance to look at the menu. But very charming.

Salvatore peered at Stephen from above his dark frames.

'Now, please, tell me how things are in the UK since the bomb dropped.' His kind face invited confession.

'How long have you got, Salvatore?'

'All night my friend, all night,' he laughed.

Stephen poured it all out. And Salvatore listened attentively, expressing indignation at the gym, the size of Hardman's office, the orange Hive and everyone having to stand up all day. But it didn't seem to be the reaction of a man going through the same ordeal.

The calamari were delicious, transporting Stephen for a moment to Sardinia with Laura, that great restaurant on the bay. And the Pinot Grigio didn't taste anything like the stuff he bought from the off-licence at home.

'So, enough about me, Salvatore,' he said as Pietro cleared away the starters. 'Given the chance I could whinge for England at the moment. What about you? I have the sense you aren't quite going through the same pain?'

Salvatore shrugged. 'There is pain, yes, being run by lunatics, but we don't feel it so much.'

'How come?'

'Well, I think maybe the Americans are using you as the, what do you say, *porcellini*?'

'Guinea pigs?'

'Yes. I mean, the gym, the lack of chairs, it's not civilised.'

'You mean you don't have any of that?'

'No, no, of course not. And also, we have several cards in our sleeve.'

'*Up* your sleeve.'

Salvatore laughed. 'Oh, yes, *up* our sleeve. It's very good you correct me. We have several cards *up* our sleeve. Remember, they bought us a year ago. We have got used to Schmaltz, even if Signor Hardman is new. You British haven't maybe learnt our boxes of tricks yet.' He winked.

Now Stephen was chuckling. 'OK, Salvatore, I want to know more about both the cards up your sleeve and your box of tricks.'

'Well, for sure, language is our first great weapon. I do not think Hardman had to talk to any Italians when he was selling that dog food,' he said with an air of distaste, as if the very thought of meaty chunks put him off his dinner. 'So naturally he hasn't thought about appointing anyone to manage us who can speak our language. When Schmaltz bought us, before Hardman arrived, they already made another American the president of the Italian company. And this man is definitely an idiot, Stephen, no question. He can't speak a word of Italian either. So it's easy to frustrate them both when they speak to me in English by not understanding a few things.' He chuckled again. 'And of course, Hardman thinks if he just shouts louder, I'll understand perfectly the next time.'

'But, Salvatore, you're fluent.'

'Yes, yes,' he waved, acknowledging the compliment without demur, 'but these two Americans do not know this. And most of my colleagues are not as fluent as me. So with them really not understanding, and me pretending, we slow down their mad plans.'

'But, with respect, if you're frustrating him, isn't he trying to get rid of you personally?'

'Not at the moment. He needs me, Stephen – like he needs you.'

Pietro hovered over him solicitously, as he sniffed the Chianti and let it roll round his mouth, before giving it his benediction.

'The only thing Hardman seems to need me for is to be chief hatchet man,' Stephen said.

'Hatchet – what is a hatchet?'

'Erm, axeman. Chief axeman.' Stephen made a chopping motion with his hand.

'Hatchet man, I see.' Salvatore pulled a face.

'Don't you have to do that too?'

'We have paid a few people to go in the last two years. They are all delighted. Giuseppe Baresi, the old president, bought himself a beautiful place on Capri. My wife Silvia and I spent a great weekend there just last week – some winter sunshine. And now they want to lose a few more, maybe me at some stage, but let's see. It's not easy to lose Italians. Lots of, what is it you say, red ribbon. That is our second card up the sleeve. Or second box,' he smiled. 'It's impossible to get anything changed in Italy. Good luck, Brad.' He raised a glass. 'What do you think of the Chianti? I hope it's to your taste?'

'It's great, Salvatore, this is all great. Your perspective is great.'

Salvatore looked reflective, as if wanting to impress something further upon him.

'Think of your wonderful Shakespeare, Stephen, *gather ye rosebuds while ye may*. Brad Hardman might make life a little difficult at the moment, so I think less about work and more about the good things. This, for example.' He gestured at the risotto which had now arrived. 'I predict that Schmaltz will all go peach-shape and Brad Hardman will not be here in two years' time. But then maybe neither will I.'

It seemed unnecessarily pedantic to point out it was pear-shaped when the sentiment was so liberating. And was it really Shakespeare who wrote that? He vaguely remembered it from English 'A' level. But churlish to argue that one either. He wasn't about to quote any Dante in return.

For a few mouthfuls they were silent, Stephen savouring the taste of the risotto, slowly releasing its subtle cherry flavours.

'You like football, Stephen?'

'I do. Well, I like Middleton Dynamos.' This little joke was lost on Salvatore. 'They're my local team – non-league,' he added weakly.

'I love football. When I was a boy, my father used to tell me about Internazionale in the sixties. Inter Milano. They had a manager, Helenio Herrera, who used this tactic called *catenaccio*.'

'I know about *catenaccio*. They won the European Cup with that system, didn't they?'

Salvatore was clearly impressed. 'Yes, yes. *Catenaccio* means the chain. They used to play the defensive waiting game, they would lock up the opposing team forwards in the chain, and then when they strangle them, they strike.' He slapped his hand against the table. 'One-nil to Inter. The great Italian teams, they all know how to defend, to be patient, and then when the opposition is tired, we score. It's like that with Schmaltz. They will run out of patience, and then we score.'

They talked football for a while. Stephen couldn't remember when he'd last been even to watch Middleton. Certainly not since his dad died. Whereas Salvatore went to see Inter Milan at the San Siro several times a season. The Italian company had a number of complimentary seats that Salvatore felt Schmaltz didn't need to know about.

Despite the fact he liked him so much, Stephen felt a compulsion to try and find a chink in the man's armour.

'So, tell me Salvatore, I get the idea of your long game, but what will you do if he does get rid of you personally?'

'First I will try to get Schmaltz to buy me a nice little vineyard in Toscana, and then I will get another job.'

Just for a moment, his confidence was annoying. It was

easy for him, not in the eye of the storm, nor in the bind that Stephen was.

'And wouldn't you do the same?' Those intelligent eyes challenged him.

'Not that simple, I'm afraid. Have you ever been to Middleton, where our office is? It's a bit stuck out on a limb. I'd struggle to find a comparable job within a hundred miles if I lose this one.'

'And you can't move?'

Stephen told him about his kids. About how good he felt when he picked them up on a Friday night and the feeling in his stomach when he dropped them off on Sunday evening. He focused on the positives, not the current difficulties with Kate. And he explained how if he moved away, he would barely see them. It was the first time he had talked about it to another man. Salvatore reached over and clasped him by the arm.

'Yes, I can see it's difficult for you. Family is very important.'

They sat in silence for a few minutes, with just the soundtrack of what sounded like Pavarotti in the background. It was the 'Just one Cornetto' song.

Stephen drained his glass, then said, 'How about you, Salvatore? I can't imagine you have these problems.'

With an apologetic shrug, Salvatore admitted his good fortune to be happily married with two children, a girl and a boy, who were a similar age to Kate and Jake. But somehow it made Stephen feel warm and mellow. He had been locked in his own problems, rehearsing his own story to himself for so long.

Pietro was hovering over them again, holding the empty bottle with a questioning look.

'You want another bottle, Stephen? The night is not too old,' Salvatore asked. Pietro suggested a little *formaggio* as well.

His meeting with Carol blotted the horizon – only twelve hours away. Her leg wrapped round Simon Perry's thigh threatened to thrust itself into his evening.

'Yes, let's have another bottle, Salvatore. This one is on me.'

As the second bottle arrived, Salvatore asked, 'So, is there another woman after Laura?'

God, he was inquisitive.

'Oh, I don't know, Salvatore.' The Italian's eyes searched his own. Did he do relationship counselling too? 'Well, there was this woman I met, not at work.'

Salvatore gave him the thumbs-up. 'Ah, so this is a good start. She is out of the cage looking in.' Again, a little smile played on his lips. 'And you like her, yes?'

'Yes, I really like her. I mean, she's very different to me, but… it's not straightforward.'

'Oh. How is it not straightforward?' He was like a dog with a bone.

'Well, for starters, I'm not sure I'm good enough for her.'

'This sounds interesting. Are you a bad man then, Stephen?'

'No, I suppose not. Well, maybe.' It was tempting for a moment, relaxing over the wine, to tell all, about why he and Laura split up. That would give Salvatore more background on Carol Coolidge than he was expecting. But he had never shared that with anyone. Confession didn't need to go that far.

There was silence but for Pavarotti, as Salvatore patiently waited for more.

'You are right, though, she did give me some perspective on it all, through being outside the cage as you put it. She has this saying: "do good among the carnage".'

'What does that mean? I don't know this saying.'

'It's not an idiom, just something she said. It sort of means, however bad the situation, there is something that we can do to try and retain our integrity – or maybe regain it, in my case.'

'She sounds interesting. What is her name?'

'Rachel.'

As the candle flickered and Salvatore nibbled at the gorgonzola, it felt so obvious. Of course there was another woman after Laura. Of course it was Rachel.

'If I were you, I would think about this woman, not about meeting Carol Coolidge tomorrow morning,' Salvatore said. But he had broken the spell.

'Indeed. But what do you think of Carol, Salvatore?'

'I try not to think of her, Stephen. She is not worth much thought.' He waved his hand dismissively.

'So how is her plan to introduce Schmaltzy Bars and the appropriately named Nutters going with you? Are you doing her bidding?'

'Let's just say that, like everything else, it's going slowly,' Salvatore sniggered. 'I have invited her to come and explain the plan to the Italian supermarket buyers, but so far she has declined. And at the moment, my own brands, *Magie* and *Duo*, are selling very well.' Clearly Salvatore still regarded himself as Italian marketing director in all but name. 'And Hardman has so many problems elsewhere. He might be a bastard, but surely he is not a stupid bastard when it comes to money. And after all, that is what counts to a man like him. Maybe we can change his mind about replacing our brands.' It sounded a ridiculously hopeful notion, and yet his optimism was strangely intoxicating.

There were still a couple of glasses left in the bottle. Stephen picked it up to refill them both, but Salvatore held a hand up.

'Not for me. We should think about going. I'll ask Pietro to order the taxi for fifteen minutes. But there's time for you to finish it if you want.'

Stephen did want, but instead Pietro turned up with the bill and a complimentary grappa that nearly took the back of his mouth off.

*

His head was still fuzzy the following morning as the Metro spewed its load of commuters blinking into the daylight outside the Rue du Bac station, just around the corner from head office. He took the lift to the tenth-floor reception, and there, to his surprise, sat Salvatore, a picture of tranquillity as he read *Le Figaro*.

'Salvatore, what happened to your eight o'clock?'

'It appears the ice-woman is unwell this week. Our meetings are cancelled.'

'What? She could have told us that yesterday, saved us a wasted trip.'

Salvatore looked slightly hurt. 'Ah, yes, but maybe it was meant to be, Stephen. After all, if she had cancelled yesterday, we would not have met last night.'

'You are so right, Salvatore.'

Suddenly the morning stretched in front of him. No other appointments and his flight back was not until gone three.

'So, Signor Carnevale. How about coffee? I need one after last night. I'm sure you know the best place in Paris for a decent cappuccino.'

Salvatore beamed. 'Great idea. Unfortunately, the Parisians cannot be trusted with cappuccino under any circumstances. But I do know the best place for a *grand crème* and a croissant.'

The sun had broken through, and it was just warm enough to sit outside at a café on the Boulevard St-Germain, whose chairs all faced the pavement for prime people-watching. There was a sprinkling of cherry blossom on the trees. Stephen turned his face to the sun. It felt wonderful. His new friend was sporting the coolest pair of shades, and they sat there in companionable silence, enjoying the coffee as the fashion parade passed before them.

Salvatore tapped him on the knee. 'I have been thinking about what Rachel said to you, Stephen. It's very wise.'

'You mean doing something good among the carnage?'

'Yes, it's a nice concept. I think we could have some fun with that.'

'Fun?'

'Yes, definitely. Here is to Rachel.' He raised his cup.

Stephen didn't know what Salvatore had in mind. He wasn't sure he wanted to. But it probably wasn't what Rachel had meant.

'I've been thinking too, Salvatore. I like your football analogies. In England, football managers always talk about a game of two halves. You've probably heard that cliché, but if not it's another one for your notebook. Well, I reckon the ref's blown the whistle for half-time. We are sucking the oranges. Inter Milan probably don't do that, but my boy's team the Latham Emeralds still do on a Saturday morning. I'd say we're a goal down, possibly even two, but we've hung in there – *catenaccio* style. We can still get an away win here.'

Salvatore took off his shades and offered his hand. He had a glint in his eye.

'Agreed. Time for the second half.'

Chapter Nineteen

The traffic was worse than usual on the ring road this morning. Probably because he was later than usual. At this rate, he wouldn't be in before nine. When had he last got to work so late? Certainly not since before Hardman. The alarm had gone off at six as normal, but after drifting in and out of sleep, dreaming about flapping up and down like a performing seal in front of Madison, his body had rebelled against the idea. Next thing he knew it was eight o'clock.

He shaved while waiting at the lights, the rear-view mirror mercilessly showing every little crease. At least the Great Dictator was at a board meeting in Paris today – so hopefully not on his case. He decided to have a day off from macrobiotic breakfast mush at Eat Schmaltz and grab a coffee and a pastry at the petrol station instead.

The Munchy Moments Easter display by the counter was pretty classy. They would get the first sales data for the pre-Easter push today. It'd better be good. Even though they'd now had four weeks of good sales figures, Hardman had still given them all a haranguing about the need to make him a 'happy Easter Bunny'. Pretty ironic when he planned to ditch all these brands anyway.

Back in the car, sipping his coffee, he inched slowly forward in the jam. Political point-scoring was in full swing on Radio Four, so he flicked through pre-set music stations in search of something more uplifting.

Instead he found 'Babylon' by David Gray. He'd told Rachel it was his favourite song, back in that hallway before Christmas. Only three months ago. He recalled that moment when her eyes had connected with his for the first time. Her scent as she turned away from him to join her friends.

This radio station's God slot had some cheery old Bishop explaining to the DJ that we were now well into the season of Lent.

'Now tell me, Bish, why do some folk traditionally like to give something up at Lent?'

'Well, Dave, Lent is a time when we remember Jesus spending forty days in the wilderness denying himself before his return to Jerusalem. That old Devil, he had three goes at tempting Jesus. Stuff like, "Hey, if you're so cool, why don't you turn these stones into bread?" And that was just for starters.'

It was cringeworthy, hearing the old guy trying to sound right on.

'What did Jesus do then, Bish?'

'Well, he wasn't having it. He said, "Get thee behind me, Satan." You know, sort of, "On yer bike, mate." And many Christians like to try and deny themselves as well for forty days. It's also become a time of repentance for our sins. I know that's rather an old-fashioned idea these days, but—'

'So how about you, Bish, anything naughty but nice you're giving up?'

'I know it may seem trivial, but I always give up chocolate.'

'Oh great, thanks for the plug, mate,' Stephen groaned as he turned into the car park.

Laura Card Reader told him he had twenty-nine hours and

fifteen minutes still to work this week. Although he regularly fell short now as he was spending so much time travelling to Paris and Hamburg, where there was nothing to compare with Laura. Hardman seemed to have stopped checking up on him.

'Morning, Laura. Not even remotely curious as to why I'm late this morning? Well, to tell you the truth, I couldn't be arsed to get here any earlier. Take a chill pill.'

Cheryl from HR was following him in, smiling. Most people humoured his little eccentricity now. Several others had even started a dialogue with Laura recently.

He found a podium in a corner of the Hive and logged in, but he couldn't concentrate. His head was full of Lent, bishops and Babylon. And repentance. There was one woman he knew would definitely be observing Lent.

He didn't have that much to repent about with regard to Rachel, did he? He'd gone to church three weeks in a row, even bought them all a round of drinks the last time after that youth service which had felt so alien to him. And it wasn't really like they'd had a major fall out that last time. Plus it took two to tango. She could try harder to fit him into her life.

And yet, he did feel sorry. She had been like a light in the darkness of the first few weeks in Schmaltz. And somehow, he hadn't quite been able to follow the light. Maybe he hadn't completely fallen out with her – but he hadn't completely fallen in either. And he had a feeling she might be entering into ever closer communion with a fellow traveller, beyond the point of no return, if he didn't do something – soon. Tonight he had to go to Hamburg again, and then later in the week on to Paris again. So he needed to do it now. Not soon, but now.

'Steve, have you seen the sales data this morning? Pretty impressive, eh?' Jerry was stood next to him, looking very chuffed.

'I haven't seen them yet but that's great, Jerry. I'll take a look a bit later. I'm just going to nip out to check how the Munchy Moment eggs look at the Tesco by the ring road.'

'Oh, don't worry, I can look on the way home if you want. It's still a nightmare parking there, you know?'

Typical Jerry, trying to be helpful.

'No, that's OK. I'd really like to see for myself. The one small mercy of not being marketing director is that I get to do some of the fun stuff like when I was a brand manager. I feel quite proud of that display.'

'Yes, so you should. I'd love to see it as well. Mind if I come too?'

Sometimes his enthusiasm could be a bloody nuisance.

'Would you mind sticking around here, just to cover me? I know Hardman's in an all-day, but just in case he needs something when they break. Shan't be more than an hour.'

Soon he had driven past Tesco, which had never been his intended destination, and was staring into the window of Blooming Good, 'Middleton's Premier Florist'. It was Middleton's only florist to his knowledge. 'Say it with flowers', exhorted the sign in the window, not entirely original. But say what exactly? And with what flowers? He stepped inside, relieved that the florist was dealing with another customer so that he wouldn't be accosted immediately.

Of course they offered delivery. But he felt compelled to go round there himself with flowers and a handwritten card. To make the effort, rather than hit the send button on his laptop, and to stand again on that garden path where they'd kissed under the lamplight. A dozen roses? A strong statement, but maybe a bit of a cliché for a woman who defied convention. He didn't know what she liked. But tulips, the cherry red of her lips when she was belting it out with the Clams, felt right.

As he flipped through the card rack, a young shop assistant came over to ask if he was looking for anything in particular but he had to admit he didn't know what. Everything was too floral or too flirty, with sentiments inside which didn't come close to what he wanted to say. Until he noticed, tucked away behind another design, a single copy of a plain square card with 'Sorry' embossed in red letters on a white background. No message inside.

*

She wouldn't be at home during working hours, so he would have to just post the card through the letterbox and leave the flowers on the step. In the grey light of day, the garden was revealed to be even more unkempt than his own, with a sodden crisp packet flattened on the path, and an empty beer can rammed into the hedge.

Still in the car, he removed the card from the envelope. Should he read what he'd written one more time, just to check it still felt right?

> *Dear Rachel,*
> *You might choose to ignore this*
> *and I will not blame you if you do.*
> *But I told you when we first met*
> *that my favourite song was 'Babylon'.*
> *And I wondered if you would listen to it for me?*
> *I've never felt the words as much as I do now.*
>
> *I've been an idiot – and I'd really love to see you again.*
> *Stephen xx*

God, it felt cheesy all of a sudden. Maybe he should have done the whole thing from the office after all. To make sure she definitely got the flowers, and so that he could have altered the message before sending it online. To start crossing bits out now would look a bit crap, to say the least. And was the last line too pushy? Should he have just left her to decide whether she ever wanted to see *him* again?

He sighed and looked towards the letterbox. What he needed at this moment was not the romantic poetry of Salvatore Carnevale gathering rosebuds, but the more brutal abbreviated prose of Brad Hardman: J-F-D-I.

Chapter Twenty

Lois, on Schmaltz Europe reception, still looked to Stephen like the twin sister of Taylor on the Middleton front desk. Although she denied it, and still claimed she came from Milwaukee. The likeness of their empty smiles was uncanny.

'Miss Coolidge is running late this morning,' Lois said. 'She asked that you wait here, and she'll call you when she's ready.'

It was par for the course. Carol always thought her time was more important than his. At least it gave him time to send a few emails and check his messages. Still not a sausage from Rachel, forty-eight hours since he sent her that card. Whereas Jim Jeffries had been trying to reach him, leaving a voicemail that he wanted to catch up some time today. That sounded ominous. He resolved to call back later, after his meeting with Carol.

An hour and a half later, he was still waiting. If he'd known she would leave him here with only a glass of water, he could have flown from Germany this morning, still arrived in time, and saved himself a night in the bloody Hotel Splendid. The airport hotel in Hamburg was hardly the Ritz, but it was all relative. Having attended to business, he turned to Twitter, aiming to catch up with the Middleton Dynamos team news for the weekend. But another tweet caught his eye.

LISA @L-I-S-A

Life Is Sweet Already.

Join our Mums' campaign to cut sugar in UK chocolate.

They kept popping up, these people. And they might have started with sugary drinks, but now they were definitely turning the heat up on chocolate.

Finally Lois gave him the nod. He knocked on Carol's door and entered without waiting for her normal 'come'.

She looked great as usual, damn her. A navy silk top this morning, and her hair down. He felt his anger ebbing away again.

'So, how are you?' he asked. 'Feeling better?'

'I'm fine. What have you got for me? I've only got an hour now.'

A switch flicked in his brain. If that was how she wanted it, so be it.

'That's your problem, Carol, not mine.'

'Sorry?'

'I've been here since nine thirty, which was when we were supposed to meet. But anyway, it suits me to do this in an hour too. I must catch the plane at three today. I've got the kids coming this evening and I need to be back for them.'

'Oh, right. We'd better get on then.'

He sensed he had unsettled her, as intended. A not so subtle reminder that he was an estranged dad because of their affair.

'But before we get on, Carol, I want to sit down.'

As Carol sighed and summoned Lois to find a chair, he found the LISA tweet on his phone and slid it across the desk. 'And you need to look at this.'

'Why would I be interested in Dynamos' midfield worries for Wanderers clash?'

'No, the one below.' He waited for her reaction.

There was an audible sigh, but a show of defiance in her eyes.

'And your point is?'

'My point is, the pressure on this sugar thing is ramping up, and as you may have noticed, we are about to introduce a couple of brands whose sugar content will make Bingo Bars and Munchy Moments look like health foods by comparison.'

'Oh, per-lease, give me a break, Stephen. If we react each time a bunch of elitist earth mothers in Hampstead complain about their little Lucinda's sweetie consumption, we might as well give up.' She slid the phone back towards him disdainfully.

'You're wrong. I tell you, this could be bad news. They only need to get some celebrity mother on their side and this thing will rise up like a tsunami. Or they'll get a national treasure. Joanna Lumley – it'll be Joanna Lumley. Always is. Brad aware of this pressure group stuff, is he?'

'I'm sure he is, and I'm sure he thinks the same as me.'

'Have you discussed it with him?'

'He's got far bigger issues than this to worry about. The French factory are threatening to go on strike over some ridiculous EU directive we're supposed to have breached. And you're doing it again: undermining things. These brands are going to come in and they're going to be successful. What we need right now is to rally behind Brad's strong leadership. You can either help me make them a success or leave me to find someone else who'll cooperate.'

'OK, I'll take that to mean you haven't discussed it with him. You're all too frightened of him. That's what happens when you surround yourself with yes men and women.'

She knotted her brow. 'Are you going to show me the latest plan for how we make this happen, or aren't you?'

If he said no, what would she do? She was up shit creek, as Archie would say.

'Yeah, don't worry, I'll show you *my* plan for you to share with him.'

Lois eventually appeared with a chair, and he pulled it alongside Carol's, so they could share his laptop.

He knew the plan was rock solid. The Germans would do a trial run of Schmaltzy Bars at the new factory at the end of May. All the relevant quality controls were in place. Nutters would follow a week later. By the middle of June, they could be supplying every supermarket in Britain. And production of all the old brands in Dumfries would grind to a halt. He had found a way to accelerate things even further, as Brad had demanded. Which meant the window of opportunity to find a way of scuppering his own plan was narrowing to a slit.

Normally Carol found something to quibble over. Not today.

'Any questions?' he asked.

'No, that looks pretty good. We can walk Brad through it next week. I'll book a time with him.'

'We? Can't you do it yourself? I thought you'd prefer to take the glory as usual.'

He expected some retort to this. But instead she closed her eyes and started taking long deep breaths.

'Are you all right, Carol?' he asked.

'Yes, of course.' She opened her eyes but avoided looking at him. 'But I need you in there too, with the detail.'

'Oh, OK then. But when are we going to start talking to Dumfries? I think the Project Mushroom tactics have gone on long enough. It's outrageous keeping them in the dark. I've got another message to call Jim. I think they might be suspicious.'

'I'll let you know, OK? Just not yet. Brad will make that decision. Anything else?' She picked up her phone to indicate she was moving on.

Stephen shook his head in disbelief that they were still

keeping it a secret. 'Yes, one other thing. I understand that in Greece, the one market where we've introduced the American brands so far, our brand shares have fallen through the floor.'

She looked up with a start. 'Who told you that? It's confidential information.'

'I think I saw it in the *FT*. You should keep in touch with the media more.'

It was Salvatore who had started to drip-feed him market share data from around Europe. Heaven knows how he got hold of it. He pressed on, enjoying her discomfort.

'Anyway, if we're to avoid a similar fiasco in the UK, we need to get going on the launch marketing. I'm beginning to think we'll have product but nothing else. How's your launch advertising campaign coming along? Have Zachary Beavis and his pals come up with anything yet?'

'That's none of your business.'

'I'm afraid it is. If I'm going to sell this into the UK market for you, I need an idea of the marketing plans.'

Suddenly she threw her hands in the air and screeched, 'I don't bloody know what the marketing plans are yet! OK? Are you satisfied now?' She stood up and began pacing round the office, like a caged tiger.

'Would you like some input, Carol?'

'No, I would not like some input. If I do, I'll call you, OK?'

'All right, all right, keep your hair on. I'll look forward to seeing the advertising in due course.'

'Yes, I'm sure you will,' she said. And then, almost as an aside, 'Just don't hold your breath.' She turned away from him to gaze out of the window, and he could hear those deep breaths again. He sensed she wanted to cry for help. But that wasn't Carol.

*

Back at Charles de Gaulle, he went to buy himself an overpriced beer at the bar to while away the time waiting for his flight. He got another text alert. Maybe this time it would be Rachel. But it was Jim Jeffries again, still wanting to talk to him today. He couldn't put off calling him any longer.

'Hi Jim, sorry it's taken me this long to get back to you. Another busy one, I'm afraid. You said you needed to talk to me urgently.'

'Aye, that's right, Steve. We're having a factory invitation golf day at Troon in the summer. I wondered if you'd like to come as my guest. It's normally a good crack. And it's a great course.'

Was that all? He'd been worrying all day that Jim had rumbled him – for nothing. He didn't know whether to be relieved or angry.

'That's very nice of you, Jim. Can I let you know?'

'I'm sorry to push you, lad, but we need to confirm the guest list by Monday. That's why I wanted to get hold of you today.'

This probably wasn't the time to be accepting any favours from Jim Jeffries.

'What's the actual date, Jim?'

'May 29.'

The week of the German trial, just before Jim's life support would be switched off. Definitely not the time to be accepting any favours.

'Jim, you know what? It's a nice thought, but I'm just checking my diary as we speak,' he lied, 'and I'm already booked in for a meeting with Hardman that day.'

He expected Jim to tell him to grow some balls.

'Ah well, never mind, laddie. Another time.' There was a pause. 'Oh, and one other thing. I know you wouldn't pull the wool over my eyes on this one, Steve, but there hasn't been any change of plan, has there? The Yank and your lady friend aren't

235

still thinking of bringing in those bloody American bars, are they?'

'Er, no, I don't think there's any change there, Jim.' The lies were popping out with alacrity now. 'Why do you ask?'

'It's just that normally by this time in the year, you're asking me for product so you can set up the market research test against the competition. I just want to check why you've not done so this year.'

Blimey, he'd slipped in a dagger beneath the cloak of all that golf day stuff.

'Er, we might do it later in the year, Jim. No hurry at present.'

'Mm.' Jim paused for a moment. 'It's just that I'm not totally isolated up here, laddie. I was talking to someone in the Italian factory in Genoa. He seemed a bit worried that they might still be introducing those bloody Nutters over there. Just a rumour, I know, but I thought I'd check nothing was happening over here.'

'There's nothing I can report on that, Jim,' he said firmly, inwardly cringing at his own weasel words. Saying there was nothing he could report to Jim was true. But only because Hardman had gagged him.

'Good, I assumed not.' It looked like Jim had swallowed it. But his tone took on a more sinister edge. 'Because that would be ridiculous, wouldn't it, as the brands are doing so well at the moment? The way things are going, we'll have to consider bringing the C line back into operation for the first time in five years. That bite-size Bingo Bar is flying off the lines, laddie.'

'That's great. Thanks again, Jim. Now I'd better go, I'm in Paris and I think my flight is about to be called. Let's keep in touch.'

Keeping in touch with Jim was the last thing he needed. Avoiding him like the plague was the better strategy.

He checked the departure board.

EAST MIDLANDS FLIGHT DELAYED UNTIL 18:15.

PLEASE WAIT IN LOUNGE.

A three-hour delay? It was karma – he had lied again to Jim when he said the flight was being called, just to avoid further interrogation. Now, even allowing for the hour's time difference, he wouldn't land until at least half six – the time he normally aimed to pick up Kate and Jake. It was a situation he'd been dreading for a while: being stuck in Paris on a Friday and not able to get back for them in time.

He would have to call Laura. He knew what she would say, harrumphing, accusing him of being unreliable. Did he really want to see the children these days? All the normal garbage.

'Hello, it's me.'

'I can't talk. Please don't ring me at work.'

'I didn't think you worked Fridays.'

'I've gone back to working full-time. I'm sure I told you.'

He didn't think she had.

'OK, I won't take up much of your precious time, but there's a slight problem. I might be just a tiny bit late this evening. I'm in Paris and the flight's been delayed. Beyond my control, I'm afraid.'

She was the champion of the disapproving silence, Laura.

'You still there?' he asked.

'Yes, I'm still here.'

'I don't think this needs to be too difficult. I just wondered if you could drop them round for once? Kate has a key so she can let you all in.'

'What, and leave them in an empty house?'

'It won't be empty for long. Or maybe you could stay? I should be home by half past seven.'

'Trist and I are due out at seven. So you need to be back by then. You know the rules for a Friday evening.'

'Oh, yes, thanks, I'll remind the pilot of the rules as well, Laura – I'm sure he'll put his foot down.' Damn it, he didn't want her in his house anyway, surveying the mess. He pictured the pile of dirty washing in the hallway which hadn't quite made it into the machine as he'd rushed out for the plane on Wednesday. And as for the kitchen...

'Actually, Laura, come to think of it, I wouldn't want you to put yourself out. I have another idea. Would you arrange a taxi for them? I'll pay you back. If you arranged for them to get picked up when you have to go out, they'll arrive at mine for about seven thirty. I'm sure I can be home by then – or shortly after.'

Another silence. 'I've explained to you that your daughter is quite insecure at the moment. She doesn't like being left on her own. This is not going to help.'

He felt defenceless and stuck for words. He was staring at the departure board as it changed again. Delayed by a further half hour.

'Are you still there?'

'Yes, I'm still here. She's fifteen, Laura. I'm sure she'll be OK for a... few minutes.'

'Just how late do you think you're going to be?'

'I don't know.'

'And it's not just about her. It's making her responsible for Jake as well. Don't you know your neighbours? Isn't there someone else you can call in?'

'I'll have a think.' There was nobody that he knew well enough in the road. He had barely exchanged more than a minute's chat with anyone since that party before Christmas. How crap was that?

'And I can call Kate, if she needs to talk to me.' That wasn't strictly true. He couldn't call her at thirty thousand feet. He closed his eyes. If she didn't agree to this, he was in a mess. But it was convenient for her, so he was hopeful she'd buy it.

'OK, as a one-off. I'll order the taxi for seven. You owe us for this.'

Owe *us*? Since when had he owed Tristran anything?

'I'm sure you'll remind me of that, Laura. By the way, how is the altitude sickness?'

'What?'

'Up there on the moral high ground. It must get pretty rarefied.'

They were done.

He leant over his beer, staring mesmerised at the little bubbles floating to the surface, wrists firmly pressed against his temples. Of all the low points he had plummeted to in the last few months, this felt like the worst of all. He pictured his children, being passed from pillar to post, thinking he was a bad dad. When he was really trying to be a good dad, and his determination to hang on to this job and be close by for them was making him do lots of other bad stuff. Bringing in brands with more sugar, and still firmly on course to close a factory in Dumfries, but not having the courage to even warn them because he was afraid of being sacked as a whistle-blower. Which would force him to look elsewhere. It was a vicious, hellish circle.

It had been fun deciding in the Parisian sunshine with Salvatore that it was time for the second half, but who was he kidding?

John Motson, who hadn't appeared in Stephen's head for some time, came and sat on the bar stool next to him in his sheepskin coat, to pass comment over his sunken form.

'And we're into the second half here, but things seem to be going from bad to worse for Stephen Carreras. The crowd are beginning to doubt whether he can make an impact and turn this one round.'

*

The pilot twisted the knife further as they approached East Midlands by jauntily announcing that there was a bit of a Friday evening tailback, so he would have to run them round the block a couple of times before they made their final descent. But they would get a good view of Birmingham on the left-hand side – and then on the right-hand side.

By the time Stephen was able to call Kate again to tell them he had landed, it was approaching eight o'clock. He pictured her sobbing hysterically as she picked up the phone.

'Oh, hi Dad. Where are you?'

She *sounded* OK.

'I'm so sorry, my girl. The plane got delayed again. I've just landed. Are you all right?

'Yes.'

He sensed she was a bit distracted, and there were noises off.

'You must be starving. Why don't you order the Friday night takeaway if you want? I know we normally go round there but they'll deliver. There's some spare cash tucked away in the kitchen drawer, the one under the microwave.'

'It's OK, we're in the Chinese now, just ordering. With Rachel. Do you want chicken and cashew nuts as normal?'

*

Virtually every light in the house was on as he finally pulled into the driveway. He let himself in and went into the sitting room. The floor was scattered with plastic containers. Just how many dishes had they ordered? Kate was sitting on the sofa, laughing at whatever she was watching. He hadn't seen Kate laugh for a while. Jake was less interested in the TV but was managing to shovel in the noodles while he checked his phone.

Stephen's presence remained unacknowledged.

'Er, hello everyone. Hello, dear Father, how nice to see you,' he said to the room. 'Tell me, has Rachel been and gone?'

Jake mumbled something unintelligible through a mouthful of food and thumbed towards the kitchen.

Rachel was facing him, with her back against his sink, the detritus of his week surrounding her. His heart melted.

'Hello, my saviour,' he said.

'Hello, I was just calling round to drop something off for you, but when I rang the bell Jake answered and told me you weren't back yet. I was just going to stop for five minutes, see they were OK. But then he asked if I could go with them to the Chinese.' She smiled for the first time. 'Jake said you're boring and always choose chicken and cashew nuts. It's in the microwave.'

He laughed. 'I need a word with that boy. I'll also tell him there's no need to answer the doorbell if I'm not here.' He smiled at her. 'Thank God he did.'

He pushed the kitchen door closed behind them. There were so many things he wanted to say. But hell, it really was a mess in here. On the work surface amidst the unwashed dishes was a houseplant with delicate white flowers springing from bushy green leaves. Presumably this was what she had come to drop off.

'It's so good to see you, Rachel.' He moved towards her, but she bent down to start loading his dishwasher, still business-like. He didn't feel he could touch her, unsure what degree of intimacy she would allow.

'Then I was just planning to come back from the Chinese with them and leave them to it, but they asked if I would stay – just until you got back.'

'I'm so pleased you did stay. You did get my card, didn't you?' he asked. 'And the flowers? I realised I didn't know what your favourite flowers are.'

She stopped loading his dishwasher and looked at him. 'I've been away on a work retreat since Wednesday. Bit of a crisis meeting. Like one of your away days, I suppose, with probably just as much swearing.' She paused. 'So I didn't see them until I got home this afternoon. Beatrice had brought them in and arranged them for me.' She smiled at the recollection. 'I love tulips in spring – a sign of hope.' She nodded towards the houseplant. 'I brought you a peace lily. They're pretty hard to kill but not impossible.'

'Thank you. I'll do my best – I mean not to kill it. You must have noticed this house was a plant-free zone.'

'I had,' she said, as her eyes turned more serious. 'And the card. That was brave of you, Stephen.'

'I don't know about that.'

'No, it was. And it would be good to talk. But for tonight, I should leave you with your children.'

'I can't persuade you to join us? For Friday night movie and chocolate? It's only the Little Monkeys consignment from work, but a bit of a tradition here after the Chinese takeaway. And I'm sure Jake can be persuaded that what he really wants to watch is *Legally Blonde*, after you got his tea for him. And I'll drive you home afterwards.' He would forget about that wine in the fridge.

There was the trace of a smile. 'Afraid I've given up chocolate for Lent. Not a very good customer, I'm afraid.' But then her eyes lowered. 'Anyway, I don't think you should leave the kids on their own again. And it's all a bit complicated.'

'I'm sure they'll be fine, just for half an hour—'

'I meant other things are complicated.' She stuck her hands in her pockets. She wanted away, he could see that. 'But I'll see you around, I'm sure,' she said.

He gave her a light kiss on the cheek and let her go, as she insisted she didn't want to interrupt the kids' TV watching.

At least he had a foothold in her life again. Well, maybe a toehold. There was plenty of climbing to be done.

Within a few seconds, Kate appeared in the kitchen.

'Anything sweet in here?' she said, as she opened the freezer door.

'Probably not, but I've got some chocolate. Anyway, how was it with Rachel?'

Kate continued rummaging in the freezer. 'Yeah, it was OK. She was telling me about her work. It sounded kind of cool.'

As she gave up on her search and was about to return to the TV, he touched her lightly and opened his arms wide.

'I could do with a hug, Katie Carreras.'

She nestled against his chest. He had her for the weekend, his anticipation these days mixed with a tinge of apprehension. How would she be?

'Yeah, she seemed nice,' she said as he let her go. 'Maybe a bit young for you?'

Chapter Twenty-One

'You all right, Laura? Do we need to talk?' he asked.

Laura Card Reader remained impassive.

Jennie Jacobs was standing behind him, waiting to clock off.

'You're wasting your time with her today, Steve, she's been quiet and frosty all afternoon,' she said with a laugh.

'I hope she's still noting our hours, Jennie, even if she isn't talking to us.' He tried swiping again. Although Laura remained mute, at least her digits responded this time.

CARRERAS, S.
HOURS WORKED 27:59
HOURS REMAINING 22:01

Stephen shook his head. 'Look at this, Jennie. I mean that's very generous of her, but even I can't complete twenty-seven hours of a working week by seven o'clock on a Monday evening.'

Jerry Collins joined the group of bemused onlookers. On Stephen's third swipe, Laura changed her mind again.

CARRERAS, S.
HOURS WORKED 35:12
HOURS REMAINING 6:18

'Now she's just firing numbers at random,' he said.

'Yep, reckon she's lost it completely,' Jerry said. 'Still, could be helpful. Swipe in again and she'll probably say you've done your fifty hours for the week already.'

'She's clearly having a meltdown,' Stephen said. 'I knew Hardman was driving her too hard.'

The following morning, Stephen arrived to find an engineer operating on Laura. She was suffering the indignity of having her smart silver head removed and her inner workings exposed, a tangle of wires. The man waved Stephen through.

'You'll have to try again later, mate. I might be here a while.'

When Stephen ventured out of the Hive mid-morning, Laura's head had ostensibly been restored but her mental maths was still all over the place. At lunchtime, she responded to the swish of his card by displaying the fateful words SYSTEM FAILURE. By late afternoon, an email from the IT department had informed them that Laura was out of commission until further notice, as she was harbouring a major bug which threatened to bring down the whole network.

'Fancy that, Laura being a bug smuggler,' was Jerry's chirpy response to this news.

With Hardman tied up in an industrial dispute in Spain, and Laura indisposed, Stephen was in his car by five that evening, for the first time in living memory. He was about to drive off when Salvatore called.

'Signor Carnivale, how's it going?'

'*Bene, bene*, Stephen. You know Carol Coolidge is holding her Friday morning fun in the UK this week? I am coming over on Thursday, so I thought maybe we could have dinner together, if you are not doing anything?'

'That's a great idea, Salvatore. And definitely my treat after that great meal in Auvois. We could do something typically English – maybe a curry and a few beers at the local Indian.'

There was a moment's pause.

'I see,' said Salvatore, who clearly didn't.

'OK, on balance, you're probably more of a Belle Époque man. I can't promise you hugs from the waiter, or even the waiter's wife, and we might need to order from the menu, which I know will feel a bit conventional to you, but it's the best I can do around here.'

'OK, I promise not to demand too much,' Salvatore said with a laugh.

'Great. And can I help you with booking a hotel for the Thursday night? We normally put visitors in the Hamilton. It's not the Ritz, but compared with the Hotel Splendid, it might feel like it.'

'Thank you, Stephen, that's very kind. Dinner sounds wonderful, but I have already booked a room for the night. Let me see, I have the details here. Yes, a booking in the Oakley Park Castle. Is that right?'

Knowing Salvatore, it probably was right. It was ten miles out of town, with grounds which ran down to a lake. Stephen had only been there once, to a very top-notch wedding reception.

'Wow, Salvatore, you might have trouble justifying that one on expenses.'

'I never have to justify my expenses,' the Italian replied emphatically.

Although there had been a couple of long phone calls since the meal in Auvois a fortnight ago, this would still be only their second face-to-face meeting. But as Stephen drove home, he decided he'd come clean with Salvatore – he needed to talk to *someone* about Project Marlene, weighing on his soul. Although he wasn't expecting to gain anything by confiding in his new friend, other than unburdening himself. Somehow, he still needed to do something more concrete. Hardman had made it patently clear that if he told Jim Jeffries anything, he risked his own dismissal, but he knew deep down that even if he *did* find a way to win over Rachel, failure to save Dumfries would scar him, no matter how many times he told himself he had no alternative.

*

When they met for dinner on the Thursday evening, it took only a matter of minutes for Stephen to be lifted by Salvatore's relaxed air and easy charm. He complimented Stephen on the choice of restaurant and the wine selection, a St-Émilion which Stephen thought was wincingly expensive but necessary to reciprocate for the amazing Chianti they'd drunk at Pietro's. But before Stephen could shift the conversation onto work, Salvatore had his own worry that he needed to share. Would Inter Milan qualify for the Champions League at the end of the season?

Inevitably this led to a more discursive conversation about the relative merits of English versus Italian football, which for some reason morphed into an explanation of why Italian men preferred ice cream to beer after work, and then how Salvatore thought the English could still despite everything be saved as a nation if only they went to the opera. It was only when the cheese course arrived that work got a look-in, and even then, not in the way that Stephen had intended.

'So, tell me, Stephen, how is that hours-checking machine in your office?' Salvatore asked, as he placed a neat slice of Roquefort atop an oatcake.

'The card reader? Well, funny you should mention that, because it's all gone peach-shaped, as you like to say.'

'Surely you mean pear-shaped?'

'Salvatore, I know it's... never mind. Anyway, it's been suspended, as of yesterday. Turns out it was buggering up the whole IT system. But tell me, why are you interested in our card reader?'

'Oh, it's just that I heard last week they were considering to introduce it in Italy, as it was a success with you English, er, guinea pigs. But what a shame. I imagine they will not introduce it now.'

A little smile played around his mouth, which he patted delicately with his napkin before laying it on the table with a satisfied air.

Before they deviated away from work again, Stephen needed to make his move and tell Salvatore about Project Marlene. But first he wanted to tease out if Salvatore already knew anything.

'Anyway, Salvatore, last time we met you suggested we might still be able to change Hardman's mind about surrendering our brands to the American invasion. Can't say I see any signs of progress on that notion. How about you?'

Salvatore shrugged. 'It's still possible,' he said, without embellishing. 'The *formaggio* is good, Stephen,' he smiled, 'considering it's French.'

'Yes, good, but have you heard anything about plans on how they might source the American stuff?'

'Of course I know Hardman thinks that if he introduces these brands in Italy, he will do so from Germany,' he said, as if this was common knowledge but not particularly concerning. He raised an eyebrow. 'So I suppose they might think they could supply you from Germany too?'

He had heard the whole plan, Stephen could tell. Was there anything this man didn't know?

'You think so?' Stephen said, feigning innocence and cutting a last tranche of camembert to allow himself a pause for thought. Was this the time for a full confession, which had after all been his original intention? Admit that he was personally masterminding such a plan with Carol but was fretting over the implications for Jim and co in Dumfries? But before he could do so, Salvatore leant over and gripped him by the hand.

'You look very anxious, Stephen, but don't worry too much yet. Hardman and the ice-woman still have big problems on their hands before they can launch in your country or mine, I can tell you.'

'You mean the sweetness thing? Do you think that will be a problem in Italy too?'

Salvatore hesitated. 'Sweetness? Er, no, well maybe that.'

'OK, what sort of other problems might there be? What are your sources telling you?'

Salvatore brushed off Stephen's slight tone of mockery. 'I think you'll see. Now I just noticed the time. My man should be outside to take me back to the Oakley Park Castle.' He made it sound like he had a personal chauffeur. 'It's not bad. You should go there sometime. Which reminds me. We have been here all evening and I am very rude because I haven't asked you the most important thing. How is it with Rachel?'

'It's nice of you to ask, Salvatore, but… it's complicated.'

'How so? And of course I ask. I think she is important to you. I have not forgotten the saying, "Do good among the carnage".'

'I think she maybe just wants to be a friend. An occasional friend.'

'And this is what you want?' Salvatore asked, with that searching look again.

'Of course not, but we still don't seem able to quite get it together. And I think there might be some competition.'

'Is she attractive?'

'I certainly think so,' Stephen said as the waiter slipped him the bill. Blimey, entertaining Signor Carnevale was a pricey affair.

'Well, thank you for a lovely evening, Stephen,' Salvatore smiled, but then his expression turned sterner. 'Of course there's competition. This is Champions League, yes, not a pre-season friendly?'

He thought about Rachel, probably fast asleep in bed after a hard day's night at Action Stations. He thought about her integrity and commitment. About how much he wanted to bring her here. And he resolved not to even try to claim expenses for this evening. It would just feel wrong somehow.

'You're right, Salvatore, she is Champions League,' he said, as they stood up to leave. 'Better make sure I qualify, even if Inter Milan don't make it.'

*

The following morning, the Italian found Stephen as he was catching up with emails.

'This is mad, my friend, you cannot work like this.'

'Ah, good morning, *signore*. Are you done with the ice-woman's morning surgery?'

'Yes, yes, Stephen, she asked me to send you in… But my friend, these conditions, it is crazy.' He threw his arms wide to indicate the other ants all tapping away at their workstations.

'What did you expect, Salvatore? I told you what it's like here. You should have seen it before we started to get rid of people. At least now there are more podiums than humans.'

'Yes, yes, I know you told me, but I was thinking maybe you have been exaggerating, Stephen, gliding the lily.'

'You mean gilding the lily, and no I wasn't,' he said irritably.

'No, I see this now. You stand all day? I would not allow this.'

'Truth is, Salvatore, I've got used to it. There must be some law of behavioural psychology that says if you treat people like shit, eventually they think shit is normal.'

Salvatore shook his head in incredulity. 'Well, I suppose you should go and see Carol Coolidge now. Where can I get an espresso?'

'Good luck with that. You could try Bob's café on the edge

of the industrial estate. That will be an interesting cultural experience for you. But your best bet is to get the hell out of here and hope you find one at the airport. Bet you're relieved you were born Italian.'

Salvatore nodded a little too readily.

'How is she this morning?' Stephen asked, gathering the papers he needed for the encounter.

'She is not a happy woman, Stephen. I think she has a problem with Nutters.'

'Don't we all. What sort of problem?'

'She wouldn't tell me, but I know,' Salvatore said, clearly pleased with himself at this little riddle. 'But maybe she will tell you – her special friend.'

Stephen gave him a rap on the arm with his rolled-up meeting papers, and the Italian chuckled.

'Oh, and by the way, her little office friend Oscar Newte is here today as well. He kept going in and out during our meeting, disturbing us. It must be hard sharing an office with that idiot, I think, even an office that size.'

'Oh great, thanks. Not just the ice-woman, but smug-features too.'

*

Carol was staring at her mobile on the desk in front of her, hands clasped behind her neck, when Stephen entered the office. Oscar wasn't in the room.

'Have you seen this in today's *FT*?' she asked abruptly, sliding the phone across her desk in his direction. Still nowhere for him to sit down in her office here.

'So was I right? Is it Joanna Lumley? Or Judi Dench?' He picked up the phone, expecting more news about the women of LISA. It wasn't.

PROBLEMS MOUNT FOR SCHMALTZ IN EUROPE

Schmaltz Europe, the newly formed division of the US chocolate giant, is facing increasing difficulties as it plans to introduce its American brands Schmaltzy Bar and Nutters into European markets.

Media sources indicate that sales data for the Greek test market is not encouraging for either brand, while workers at the company's factories in France and Spain are threatening strike action over new working directives. Now there are rumours of an unusual additional problem with the Nutters product. A leaked report from the company's R&D labs in Genoa indicates that the yolanda nut used in the original US product may contribute to flatulence.

A Schmaltz spokesman denied any evidence of this effect in the US, where the brand has been marketed successfully for over 50 years, but news of Schmaltz troubles in Europe appear to be affecting its S&P 500 performance, with the share price dropping by a quarter in the last week.

Carol had still not moved.

'Mm. Maybe it'll blow over.' Stephen couldn't resist a snigger.

She growled.

'Sorry, there was genuinely no pun intended there. I mean, I think I read some stuff once before that nuts can give you gas,' he imitated an American accent, 'but it's probably not a big deal.'

'You think not, do you? You'd better be right.'

'Somehow you manage to make it sound like my fault. Well, you'd better get the R&D people to check it out properly, hadn't you, Carol? I'm sure your friend Helmut Herr Can Do in Hamburg will be more than happy to test it out for you.'

Newte burst into the room, waving a printed copy of the offending article.

'Good grief, have you seen this, Carreras?' he screeched.

A flapping Newte only increased Stephen's determination to remain calm. 'We're in a meeting at the moment, Oscar. You might have noticed?' he said caustically. 'In fact, we are just discussing the article to which I assume you are referring. Who'd have thought it, eh? Nutters makes you fart. That's an interesting strapline.'

'What little shit in the Italian lab is leaking this crap? We need Carnevale to get his ass in gear and fire some people.'

'Given the problem we're discussing, Oscar, you might want to go easy on the defecation and posterior references,' Stephen said.

Newte sat down and put his feet up on his desk. He stared at Carol, her head now bowed in despair again.

'So, presumably the first thing we do is to put the switch from Munchy Moments to Nutters on hold, while we check it out?' Stephen suggested airily.

'*Au contraire*, we crack on. Get the thing launched. We're not going to let a few flatulent Italians divert us,' snorted Newte. 'And Carol, you need to get your PR agency lining up a press conference so we can ram home the message that our first quarter profits will be better than the bloody media are predicting. Get on the front foot.'

She looked up and nodded blankly at him, but said nothing. Stephen could see her chest rising and falling. Was she trying that deep breathing thing again?

'OK, Carreras, I'm sure you've got stuff to do.' Newte dismissed Stephen with a wave. 'Carol and I need to talk.'

Stephen looked towards Carol but she was holding her head in her hands, eyes closed. If only she would let him help her. But Newte seemed to have some Svengali-like grip on her. Probably because she owed her promotion to this idiot in the first place.

'Close the door on your way out,' Newte sneered.

Salvatore hadn't left yet after all, but was standing by the juice bar, in conversation with Cheryl from HR, who was clearly smitten.

'Salvatore, you're still here. Can I have a word when you're done?'

'Of course.' He gave Cheryl a winning smile. 'Very nice to meet you, *signora*.'

Turning to Stephen, he explained, 'My flight is not for two hours. I wanted to hear if you found out anything.'

Stephen waited until Cheryl was out of earshot, then glanced around the Hive. 'Tell you what, *signore*, why don't we find somewhere a little more discreet?'

Salvatore shrugged. 'If you wish.'

Stephen didn't say anything more until they were safely ensconced in Sacrifice.

'OK, I did find out why she was in a sour mood. As I suspect you know, there's some report in the media that our own R&D people are suggesting Nutters give you wind.'

'Wind?'

'Gas – you know.'

Salvatore beamed. 'Ah, *flatulenza*.'

'You heard anything about this?'

'No, why should I?' Salvatore furrowed his brow.

'Well, you intimated last night that there were problems and then this morning, before I went in to see her, you said she wouldn't tell you what the problem was, but you knew. And it appears the research lab from which the report was leaked is yours, in Genoa. So I just wondered.'

Salvatore looked indignant. 'Stephen, what are you suggesting?'

Stephen's phone rang before he could press the point. It was Jim Jeffries – again. His immediate instinct was to ignore it, but Jim would catch up with him eventually.

'Sorry, I need to take this,' he said to Salvatore. 'Morning, Jim.' He tried to sound perky.

'Good morning, laddie. All good?' Jim sounded pleased with life.

In the corner of his eye, Stephen caught Salvatore putting on his expensive coat and scarf and clearly heading to the airport to escape further interrogation.

'Yes, I think all's good,' Stephen said guardedly. 'What can I do for you?'

'Ach, nothing, laddie. I just wondered if you'd seen this piece in the press this morning about Nutters?' His rasping laugh rattled down the phone.

'Yes, I'm not sure it's a big deal—'

'Makes buggers fart. You couldnae make it up. The Italians must be shitting themselves.'

'I imagine so, Jim.' It seemed Jim didn't want anything other than to crow.

'I mean if they're testing it, they must be thinking of launching it in Italy. We had a narrow escape there when we decided not to progress it over here. And I see the Munchy share has gone up again. Well done, you. So I assume I can continue to reassure everyone here that the Nutters problems don't affect us here, because we're—'

'Sorry, Jim, can you just give me a moment?'

The meeting room door had burst open and Carol was giving him a demanding look. He muffled the phone so Jim wouldn't hear them. 'What is it?' he asked, not trying to hide his irritation.

'Just to confirm. Oscar and I are agreed. We push on with the UK launch. I'm in meetings rest of the day but we need to talk on Monday.' She announced it like a robot, and then she was gone. He returned to Jim.

'Sorry about that, Jim, I'm back now.'

The Scot's tone sharpened. 'I was just saying, laddie, that I'm assuming that Nutters farting crap doesn't affect us in Dumfries, because we're committed to the future of Bingo, Munchy Moments and Little Monkeys.'

'Our position on that is unchanged, Jim.'

He could sense Jim weighing up this response.

'OK. Well, you have a good weekend, Steve, and keep in touch, now.'

Stephen walked back into the Hive, lost in thought. It really was time to make an impact on the second half – on several fronts. After all, he was pretty sure a certain Italian had already got started.

Chapter Twenty-Two

This time, Phoebe had tracked him down as he waited in the church car park.

'I know you said you weren't interested in a move, darling, but I still can't believe it. All this bad PR for your brands in the last week. You must want to leave, sweetness. Look, I didn't know this before and I shouldn't really tell you this, but I'm down here in Devon and this position at Homefair chocolates, it turns out the non-exec chairman there is a chap called Geoffrey Palmerston, one of my oldest friends, darling. What are the chances? I could just shoe you in there so easily. In fact, he's heard about you and he's simply gagging to meet you.'

'Is he now, Phoebe?' You had to laugh. It was a fair bet Geoffrey Palmerston didn't know him from Adam. But Phoebe was weaving her spell. 'Well I'm still flattered that you want to put me forward—'

'Stephen, darling, never be flattered. Always believe you're worth it.'

'OK, I'm massively flattered to be worth it, but as I've said before, it's just not the right time.'

There was a silence. He could imagine Phoebe shaking her head.

'Well, and I say this as a friend, just be careful, darling. You want to leave there before your reputation is tarnished. I've tried to reassure Geoffrey that this flatulence frenzy is nothing to do with you.'

'Thanks very much for that, Phoebe. I'm glad you told him that because it really isn't anything to do with me. There's an unsubstantiated rumour about one of the American brands, that's all. And I hope to get to the bottom of it very soon.'

'Oh, very good, darling – bottom of it.' She emitted a theatrical sigh. 'You haven't even asked me about the package,' she added forlornly. 'My first little suggestion to Geoffrey didn't even raise a *frisson*. I'm sure we could be talking six figures here, and some simply gorgeous perks on top.'

He looked through the windscreen at the steps leading up to the church, as the rain started to fall. Six figures. Bloody hell. What did that cheesy radio bishop say? Get thee behind me, Phoebe.

Then there she was. His hunch had paid off. She was wearing her long black coat, and she had cut her hair again, the sophisto-punk look. She entered the church alone, without noticing him.

'Are you reconsidering, darling?'

'Phoebe, I'd prefer not to know about the salary because I'm not moving. I've got my reasons for staying here. It's not just the money. And you might not understand this, given how crap it's been here for the past few months, but I've come to the conclusion I'm not finished with Grim—, sorry, Schmaltz yet.'

Her tone became more resigned. 'Well, such a shame. *Such* a shame. And it would have been an easy job for you, they're small fry really.' So she'd wanted him to leave for small fry after all. 'I'm not often flabbergasted, sweety, but on this occasion I truly am.' There was a further silence.

'Ah, well,' Stephen said. 'Right, Phoebe, I need to go.'

'Can you suggest anyone else, darling? I'm desperate to throw Geoffrey a titbit.'

Good old Phoebe, her state of flabbergastedness at his decision had lasted all of thirty seconds. Back to business.

The church bell was tolling. Here he was, on Good Friday, still wanting to be where she was, still trying to be good. And risking Hardman's wrath if the bastard found out, since the public holiday hadn't registered with him.

'Are you still there, Stephen?'

'Yes, Phoebe, I was just thinking. If you really don't think it's that difficult, I know someone else with years of chocolate marketing experience under his belt. I'll even prep him for you, if you send me the brief. And your pal Geoffrey could get him for much less than six figures.'

'Lord, it's Tony Perkins, isn't it?'

*

It was clearly going to be a reflective affair today. Even Terry on the door, handing out the books, forsook his usual cheery welcome for a solemn nod. And there were only about twenty in, scattered around the pews, quite different from the normally full church. Clearly this was one for the committed.

He'd known she would be there. Something she'd said in the pub after church one evening about Easter Sunday not making any sense without Good Friday. They'd agreed it would be good to talk when she had reappeared in his life that evening with the Chinese takeaway – but they still hadn't. Yet another week of trips to Hamburg and Paris, making plans with Helmut and Carol despite the farting scare, had seen to that.

She was in a pew on her own, on her knees, waiting for the service to begin. She had taken off her coat but was still sombrely dressed, in a charcoal grey jacket and skirt. He slipped in beside her. Her eyes expressed surprise but also, he thought, pleasure. But before he could say anything, she put her finger to her lips, and the vicar started to explain what was going to happen. There would be a hymn, then he would read a Bible passage and reflect on it, and then the cycle would be repeated three more times. At least it was David, the top man, running the show today, not that twelve-year-old who'd been in charge on the Sunday evening that went peach-shaped.

Rachel sank to her knees again. Was she genuinely just thinking about God? She did know he was only here for her, didn't she? And could he really have been so magnanimous to Perkins if it wasn't to rise to Rachel's challenge to help those less resilient than he was? His conscience was clear on that, at least – not so much good among the carnage as a bloody miracle if that halfwit landed a job. But please God, not at six figures. That would be too much to bear.

As before in this place, his mind wandered on long, unexplored pathways. Hadn't Mum and Dad dragged him to church on Good Friday once? They always insisted on eating fish to commemorate it – boring grilled white fish with boiled potatoes, not fish and chips. And his dad wearing a jacket and tie. What had they made of it all, religion? He'd never talked to them about it. Before Dad's funeral the vicar had asked if he had any favourite hymns. Nobody knew. He would ask his mother next time he went to see her: what she believed in, if anything. Although she would probably try to sweep it under the table.

David's resonant voice as he commented on the Bible passage he had just read called Stephen back to the present. He was describing how the disciple Peter got the Spanish inquisition over whether he knew Jesus and kept denying it. As Stephen glanced up, David was looking straight at him.

'And then Peter remembered what Jesus had said to him.

Before the rooster crows today, you will disown me three times. And he went outside and wept bitterly.'

He closed the Bible, and silence descended again over the church. Stephen found himself wondering what Peter had done next. And about Jim Jeffries, asking him to confirm there was no plan to replace Bingo Bars and Munchy Moments.

Halfway through the service, just when he'd got down on his knees next to her, he became aware of another person settling in on her opposite side. Conrad. It was a distraction he could have done without, glancing at Rachel to see if she was glancing at Conrad, but she appeared to remain eyes front throughout.

The final hymn was another tune he recognised from way back. He still didn't join in the singing. Rachel had heard him once in the car, accompanying some song on the radio, and told him he actually had a nice voice. But this stuff in a church was far too difficult. They were good words, though, not one wasted.

'They rise, and needs will have
My dear Lord made away;
A murderer they save,
The Prince of Life they slay.
Yet cheerful he to suff'ring goes,
That he his foes from thence might free.'

It was powerful stuff, especially compared with those 'Jesus Wants Me For a Sunbeam' numbers that Conrad wanted to introduce.

Finally, David's last reading described the crucifixion itself, and Christ saying 'it is finished'. And then the church clock struck three.

It was, he had to admit, beautifully stage-managed.

Rachel was back praying. Slowly the rest of the congregation filed out in silence. Small talk obviously wasn't the done thing today. But Conrad was also still kneeling next to her. Trying to outlast her in reverence perhaps, prove he was up to the job? If it came down to a pray-off between him and Conrad for Rachel, he had no chance.

Eventually she opened her eyes and turned to Stephen. Conrad was still down there. She motioned Stephen outside.

'Well, I wasn't expecting you. Thank you so much for coming,' she said, on the church steps. 'As you can see, this one is not for the faint-hearted.' She pulled out a hanky from her sleeve and pierced the silence by blowing her nose. 'Sorry, I always get a bit emotional on Good Friday.'

Conrad, inevitably, joined them.

'Good to see you, brother,' he said, his blue eyes piercing deep into Stephen's soul.

'And you, Conrad.' He didn't trust himself not to think bad things about Conrad. Best to just go.

'I'll see you at the prayer meeting in five?' Conrad said to her. There was an easy familiarity, an expectation.

'Sure, I'll be there,' she replied. 'I just need to discuss something with Stephen.'

'Great. I'll see you in there.' Conrad eyed Stephen suspiciously before heading back into the hall adjoining the church.

When he'd gone, Rachel looked uncomfortable. 'So, how are the children?' she asked.

'They're fine, thanks. Any plans for the weekend?' he said, rather too hurriedly.

'Rehearsing first thing in the morning for the Easter Sunday extravaganza, obviously. As ever, last-minute panics.'

He wasn't going to take no for an answer this time.

'OK, but what about later? Fancy joining the Carreras family for a fun-filled Saturday afternoon?'

Her eyes shifted towards the church hall.

'I don't know... I'm not sure it's fair to get in the way of your time with Kate and Jake.'

'My children like you, Rachel,' he blurted out. 'Well, Kate thinks your job is cool, and Jake thinks you're all right for a female, which is practically love on Jake's empathy scale.'

She blushed, the way she did when paid a compliment.

'And you'd be doing us a favour. We'll be at each other's throats by Saturday night otherwise. Good among the carnage and all that.'

*

Kate was mopey and monosyllabic again the following morning, and not very forthcoming when Stephen asked what was wrong. It sounded like her continued impasse with Megan and the fact she'd been given a load of homework for the Easter holidays might be contributory factors, but he remained unconvinced that this was the sum of her problems. And he worried now that he might have overplayed things by telling them that Rachel was going to spend the afternoon with them. OK, Kate *had* said her job sounded 'cool' when she took them to the Chinese, but her admiration might not stretch to wanting to share a Saturday with her. He had to try.

He bought them all tickets for a Bond movie, being shown at the local Odeon as part of an Easter Saturday Film Fest. Happily, he got the last four seats together in the cinema. Kate sat at one end of the foursome and Jake at the other, with Rachel and Stephen between them. He glanced around regularly to catch a glimpse of their faces. On this occasion it was Kate's attention that was split between the film and her phone, on silent but not turned off. Whereas Jake was mindlessly and repetitively putting popcorn-filled hand to mouth without taking his eyes from the screen. And Rachel was as expressive as ever, her eyes widening at moments of excitement. Whether she was at the Good Friday church service, watching Jake play football or with James Bond in a high-stakes poker game, she was always right there – in the moment. She didn't do anything by halves.

When it had finished, they all stood outside, discussing their favourite bits. As they talked, Stephen was very aware that he hadn't been clear to Rachel about the rest of the Saturday routine and that he hadn't established either how the children would feel about her continued presence.

'I'm starving,' Jake said. 'Is Rachel coming to San Remo with us?'

His son was playing a blinder, possibly without knowing it.

'I hope so. Will you join us for pizza, Rachel?' He looked at her hopefully and avoided looking at Kate. He was half-expecting another choir practice to have emerged in advance of tomorrow.

'I'd like that very much,' she said.

The San Remo Pizzeria was buzzing with lots of other families who had poured out of the cinema. But their favourite friendly young waitress gave Stephen a conspiratorial wink and said she would find them a table. Rachel asked which pizza they recommended. Kate said she always had margherita, and Jake and Dad always had the Spicy Special. Rachel ordered something called a Vesuvio and said yes, they could both have a try. She sparkled. The elegant black of Good Friday had given way to a crimson blouse which he recognised from their first meeting, open at the throat to reveal a small silver cross on a pendant. And she was wearing hooped silver earrings which glinted in the light. He couldn't take his eyes off her, admiring too the emotional intelligence with which she interacted with the children. Clearly trying hard, but not too hard, and sharing a moment of complicit eye contact with Stephen that seemed to say *I'm doing this for you*. Kate, guarded at first, began to open up like a sunflower when Rachel asked if her dad was as consistently boring in his choice of pizza as he was in his choice of Chinese takeaway. And then she asked them to name their favourite movie of all time.

'Reckon it's got to be *Pirates of the Caribbean*,' Jake jumped in. 'Dad, you remember when we used to play that "Best thing of the weekend" game with Mum?' he asked, before displaying hitherto latent sensitivity. 'Ooh, sorry, Rachel.'

Rachel laughed, seemingly a little embarrassed, but Stephen said, 'Jake, old son, I think it's all right – Rachel does know you have a mother.'

Stephen drank cola like the rest of them. He wanted a glass of wine, but he wanted even more to show her that he didn't need wine to have a good time with her and his children. Besides, he would have to drive her home later. For the first time he could remember in years, an afternoon with the children felt complete, and he had an idea for squeezing the pips out of it a little more, extending it into the evening.

'I'm going to suggest we go back home for chocolate and *The X Factor*. I've even got some of the American stuff this week. You can see what you think of it.' He had pushed Jim Jeffries to the recesses of his mind all afternoon – but thoughts of Schmaltzy Bars brought his craggy face to the forefront again.

'Cool,' said Jake, as he mopped up the remains of Rachel's pizza. 'You got any of that one that makes you fart?'

'Jake!' Stephen gave him a hard stare. 'Sorry, Rachel.'

'Oh, yeah, I read that too,' Rachel laughed. 'One of the volunteers at work told me about it.' She gave Stephen an amused look.

He teased her back. 'So, Rachel, I really hope you'll come back although I've just remembered you've given up chocolate, haven't you? I mean, theology's never been my strong point, but aren't you supposed to hold out until tomorrow? Perhaps I can find you some fresh fruit instead.'

'Don't worry yourself. Officially Saturdays don't count. Forty days excluding Saturdays. And anyway, I'll say it was important research if they threaten to chuck me out of the choir – just let them try.'

The children both went to the toilet while Stephen sorted the bill. He had a moment alone with her.

'It's been great that you could come today. There's a Van Morrison song, I don't know if you know it, called "Days Like This". Well, I'd almost forgotten days like today were possible.'

She was rendered speechless for the first time all afternoon.

'And I haven't thought about work at all,' he said. 'Well, not much – at least not until I thought about the chocolate.'

'That's probably a good thing. How's it going? I feel I've lost touch a bit.'

'Mm, much the same.' He didn't want to talk about it now. He'd not had the chance to tell her about the likely bloodshed in Dumfries. She probably still thought he was just doing a great job heading up the Middleton escape committee. Maybe best to leave it that way for the moment. But once again, with those questioning brown eyes holding him to account, he knew he had to do something about Dumfries. He still didn't know what.

'And how about you?' he asked.

She pulled a face, the first time she had looked unhappy all afternoon. 'You know I told you we were running out of money?'

'I do.'

'Well, we're still running out of money. I still can't see—'

Before she could say more the kids returned, and she switched back to full beam, laughing in the back seat with Kate as Stephen drove them home.

'Any more drinks for anyone?' Stephen asked as they settled in front of the TV. 'Tea, maybe, Rachel?'

'I do not want tea, when I've been promised chocolate.'

'OK, relax. I'm afraid I can't offer you any Nutters, which

is the one that's rumoured to make you fart, Jake, although it's not proven obviously. But I've got some Schmaltzy Bars, so you could try them.'

'Great,' Rachel said. 'But have you got any Bingo Bars too, so we can compare them?' She was clearly fully engaged by this opportunity to end her Lenten denial.

'That's an idea,' Stephen said. 'I've always got a stash of those. In fact I could get you to do a blind taste test.'

He unwrapped the Bingo Bar, and broke it into pieces for everyone, sworn to keep their eyes closed. His hand trembled a little as he slid a piece into Rachel's mouth.

'This is definitely Bingo,' Kate declared. 'Isn't it?'

'It's certainly tasty,' Rachel said. 'Firm texture, but melts in the mouth.'

Jake was chomping away but keeping his views to himself.

'OK, and here is product B.' Stephen broke off some pieces of Schmaltzy.

Rachel started chewing, and a look of distaste broke across her face.

'Now this one is sweet – very sweet. I mean, you're in the presence of a woman who hasn't had a sugar boost for forty days, but this is going some.'

'Yeah, you're right, Rachel, this is too much,' Kate concurred.

Jake had demolished his sample in double-quick time, without any apparent qualms.

'Jake, what do you reckon?' Stephen tried to bring him into the conversation.

'S'alright, I suppose.' He sniffed. '*X Factor* starts in five minutes.'

'So what do other people think?' Rachel asked.

'Sorry?' Stephen said, sticking a piece in his own mouth. Rachel and Kate had confirmed what he already knew. In truth, it was not only too sweet, but a bit stale. Salvatore had supplied him with it, so it might have been festering in Casa Carnevale for a while.

'What do other people think?' Rachel repeated. 'I remember doing one of those market research group thingies once, where I got paid fifty quid to sit with a bunch of other women and tell some bloke what I thought of cheese and chive crisps. Don't you do that sort of thing?' she asked innocently.

For the first time in front of his children, he gave Rachel a kiss. Only on the cheek, though.

Chapter Twenty-Three

Whenever Carol turned up here, she was always five minutes late, and still always found a place in front of him, so he had to make a conscious effort to avoid looking at her backside. Today she had chosen a fluorescent pink crop top with matching leggings, and her ponytail swung from side to side as she stepped out to Gloria Gaynor and 'I Will Survive'. It was one of Madison's favourites for putting her aerobics disciples through their paces. Felt like the Schmaltz theme tune.

Why did Carol have to be here again today? She must have spent the long weekend here with Simon Perry. Trying to keep in step behind her, Stephen railed inwardly against the unfairness of it all. Come on, God, if you're there, give me a break. I've just spent Good Friday and Easter Saturday with one of your top fans. I'm really trying, and you do this to me.

She was still so bloody omnipresent in his life. Meetings or lengthy video conferences at least twice a week. Whereas Rachel still felt pretty elusive. After their blissfully happy Saturday she had, sheepishly, explained that she wouldn't be around next weekend as she was helping Conrad run a church youth jamboree.

He looked around to reflect on who *had* survived. Only

eight of them this morning. Numbers had definitely dropped off since January. There was plenty of space, so by time Gloria had drawn to a close and Madison was into the next exercise, he had niftily side-stepped to his left. He wasn't going to be distracted by Carol's bottom any more.

'OK, last five everyone, and we're gonna burn some fat for Schmaltz right now!' Madison drove them on. How did she retain this level of energy? And how did Carol do it when work was piling up around her? Presumably she hadn't seen *The Sun*'s headline this morning yet. That would have got her hopping out of Perry's bed.

No doubt she'd collar him at the end of the session, breathing 'we need to talk' as usual. Well, he didn't need to talk to her. Not at the moment. Hugging Rachel goodbye on Saturday evening, he'd decided what needed to be done today – and it didn't involve talking to Carol. At least not until he'd talked to Hardman. He mouthed 'sorry, got to go' at Madison as he wove through the sweating bodies to sneak out for an early shower.

Maureen Birtles wasn't on duty yet. But Hardman's door was half open, and Stephen heard the tell-tale snorting of phlegm. He was facing the window, so all Stephen could see was the back of his bullet-shaped head and two outstretched arms holding a newspaper.

Don't you do that sort of thing? That's what Rachel had asked him, as they ate their way through the chocolate.

This was as good a chance as he would get.

'Fucking wankers,' Hardman growled at the paper.

Stephen knocked.

Hardman spun round, his face a mix of anger and surprise. 'What the fuck do you want, Carreras? I haven't called for you. Maureen!' He yelled at the open door. The guard dog would be in big trouble for not being on duty.

'No, Mr Hardman, but I needed to discuss something with you urgently.'

'I'm busy, Carreras. I'm always fucking busy. You seen this?' He waved the paper accusingly in Stephen's direction.

'*WHAT A STINKER!*' screamed the headline from *The Sun*.

'Your newspapers are a fucking disgrace,' he snarled, looking ready to burst a blood vessel.

'That was what I wanted to discuss with you, Mr Hardman.' Stephen swallowed hard. 'I think we should delay the launch of Nutters.'

He expected apoplexy. But Hardman just stared back at him. OK, in for a penny… 'In fact, I think we should delay the launch of Schmaltzy Bars as well.'

'Oh you fucking do, do you? And why might that be?'

'Because although they might be unfounded, all these rumours about Nutters and, er, wind – they're not going to go away. And I'm increasingly convinced the sweetness of both brands could be a problem in Europe too.'

Hardman's eyes narrowed. 'So how the fuck is delaying going to help?'

'I think it would just make sense to actually test the products with European consumers. I mean, if there's no problem with the – er – wind, and they like the extra sweetness, we've got a great PR story to take back to the press. It will put a stop to all of that.' Stephen nodded towards the offending newspaper, now lying on the desk.

Hardman sniffed loudly. 'And if the fuckers don't like the product, what then?'

'Well, logically, if they don't like it, we would have to cancel the launch – or maybe just delay it until we've changed the formulation to work in Europe.'

He was aware of his own breathing, as Hardman looked at him. What had Salvatore said? Hardman might be a bastard but surely he wasn't a stupid bastard? He was about to find out. He knew the Americans wouldn't want to change the formulation of their precious bar just for Europe. That would make the whole process more difficult. If that was their only option, they might forget about the whole crappy project.

'Is this Coolidge's idea?'

'No, Mr Hardman, entirely mine.'

'Thought as much. What does she think? You've discussed it with her, right?'

The truth was he'd suggested it to her back in January, and she'd told him Hardman wouldn't be interested.

'In principle,' he said.

'How'd you plan to do it, your fucking market research?' Hardman spat out the words dismissively.

'We would set up a taste test. Ask people to compare Schmaltzy Bars with Bingo, and Nutters with Munchy Moments. But we'd do it blind, so they can't see the pack and don't know what the brand is.' Surely the man knew about this stuff? Then again, he'd worked in pet food – maybe they never asked poodles for an opinion. 'As long as they don't prefer the UK products, you're OK. I mean, we're OK. You could – we could – cope with a draw.' He tried to offer Hardman a reassuring smile.

'A draw?' Hardman snorted. It occurred to Stephen that US sport didn't do draws.

The American lowered his head and rubbed his eyes. It made him look even more weary.

'How long would it take?'

Stephen's mind whirred, with no time to work it out exactly. 'To do it properly, we'd give people the products to try at home for a week. I think given we need to get the product together, run the test and get the results, probably eight weeks?' That sounded tight but manageable.

'Eight fucking weeks? You're kidding me, right?' Hardman

was fired up again. 'Tell you what Carreras, you got four. And how much is this going to fucking cost?'

His brain was in overdrive now. What could they possibly do in four weeks? They had to get the products over from Chicago first.

'I'll need to talk to the market research agency. I would think about thirty thousand?' The research guys were going to love him for this – not.

'Thirty? Again, you're kidding me, right?'

Maybe Hardman *was* a stupid bastard. How much would it cost to launch a product that bombed? Compared with spending a measly 30K on a test?

'Well, Mr Hardman, if you give me the go-ahead to set up the test, I'm sure I can work on the cost. Although I also think we should test in Italy.' God, he was pushing his luck here.

'Italy? What the fuck has Italy got to do with you?'

'I gather that's the other country in Europe where the existing brands are doing pretty well. So, like here, there is more to lose.' It was a risky line. He wasn't even supposed to know how things were going in Italy.

Hardman stood up and paced around, clearly thinking about it. Then he bent over his desk, with a pained expression, eyeing the front-page headline again.

'OK, Carreras. Here's the deal. You got four weeks, and 30K to do UK and Italy. Two for the price of fucking one. And you better fucking make sure America wins, OK? I'm not interested in any draw.'

'Thanks Mr Hardman. I'll get onto it. Do you want me to tell Miss Coolidge?'

'Nope, send her in on your way out.'

Stephen allowed himself a discreet fist pump as he headed for the door. He had no idea what he could do for that money or in that time. But it was a shaft of light.

As he came out, Carol was stalking back towards her office with an orange juice and a face like thunder. Evidently she had caught up with the newspapers now.

'There you are,' she said. 'That headline is a disaster. We need to talk.'

'Ah, Carol, I've just been talking to Brad. He wants to see you. Maybe we can talk later?' He smiled at her benignly. She glared back.

Returning to the Hive, he called Salvatore, his mind already racing with thoughts of how to do the testing. There were other voices and laughter in the background.

'Ciao, Salvatore. There's something I need to discuss with you urgently. But where are you? It doesn't sound like you're in the office.'

'No, no. I told you I was planning a long Easter weekend. I'm still in Toscana. Just having coffee.' More laughter in the background. '*Si, grazie.*'

'Put your cappuccino down for a moment, *signore*. I've just persuaded Hardman to do some market research – Bingo and Munchy against Schmaltzy Bars and Nutters. And he's prepared to do it in Italy as well. So I guess in your case that'll be Magie taking on Schmaltzy Bars and Duo versus Nutters.'

He could hear Salvatore ordering something else.

'Did you hear me, Salvatore?'

'Yes, of course, a product test. Good idea. We are doing the same.'

'What do you mean?'

'I have already talked to the people in the lab here about setting up a test.'

'And when exactly were you planning to say anything about that?'

'Maybe I wait until I get the results,' Salvatore said. 'See what happens before I decide whether to share them with anyone.'

'Then I'm afraid I've just blown your cover. I've persuaded Hardman to do this test in both countries simultaneously, but we've got four weeks. Oh, and thirty thousand pounds. I'll go halves with you – might even let you pay in Euros.'

'Pah, *impossibile*.'

'If we don't do it, I think he'll just launch anyway. How long were you anticipating for your own testing?'

'Oh, I don't know. Three months maybe? It's complicated, Stephen. You have to prepare the test product. And finding the right sample of consumers to test it, that's not easy—'

'Salvatore, I've done more product tests than you've had hot dinners. OK, in your case, that's probably not true. Anyway, I do know how long it normally takes... although three months, blimey, you take a laid-back approach in Italy, don't you? But I'm telling you, we've got four weeks, that's all. I assume you can just divert some Magie and Duo from your normal production line and use that for the test. But I admit I have no idea yet how we're going to get hold of the American product. That's what I'm about to spend the day exploring – it could be a long one.'

'I have some, Stephen,' Salvatore said matter-of-factly.

'What? Have some what?'

'I have some Schmaltzy Bars and some Nutters.'

'Yeah, I know you've got your own little stash of Schmaltzy. We tried it over the weekend. That's where we – I – got the idea. But we're going to need a lot. I mean, even if we're only going to let people try one bar, we're probably talking three hundred people per bar per country—'

'It's fine, Stephen, relax. I've got plenty for both of us.'

'How many?'

'Oh, about ten thousand of each I think.'

'Ten thousand? How?'

'I told you, I was planning a test anyway. So I got hold of some.'

'But how? Where? I mean, where did you get ten thousand?'

'Stephen, you have a saying, I think, that is for me to know and you not to know?'

'That's not quite what we say, Salvatore, but let's just go with that. Anyway, assuming you're back in the office, I'll call you again later in the week. There's another call I need to make urgently. Hope your cappuccino didn't get cold.'

As Stephen had suspected, Jim Jeffries was up to date with current media speculation.

'Morning, laddie. Seen the headline this morning. What a stinker, eh? It gets worse.' Jim's throaty cackle implied that on the contrary it seemed to be getting better and better.

'I have indeed, Jim, but I need to tell you something urgently. Despite all this stuff about Nutters making you fart and the anti-sugar brigade preparing to take on Schmaltzy Bars, I think Hardman still has a notion to launch them in the UK.' He paused to allow time for Jim's response. Did he really sound as if he had just found out about Hardman's scheme, rather than having planned it personally for the past month?

'You cannot be serious, Steve. Why would he want to do that? You told me there were no plans.'

'I know, it's hard to credit, isn't it? But anyway, I've just persuaded him that he needs to do some research to test consumer reaction, so hopefully that gives us a chance to persuade him it's a bad idea.'

'But you did tell me several times there were no plans. Have you just found out?'

'Absolutely.' The lie just popped out – again. 'Anyway, I need to discuss with you how quickly you can deliver Bingo Bars and Munchy Moments for this test. He's only giving us four weeks.'

And as Jim first expressed his own disbelief at the timescale, but then started to think aloud about the logistics of supplying the product, Stephen realised that he had now lied to him four times. Three denials in the past that they were planning to launch the products and then just now a lie about knowing anything before today. But at least, now, he'd done the right thing, and Bingo Bars, Munchy Moments, maybe even Little Monkeys had one last chance. If the UK products won the test, hopefully a hundred and fifty people in Dumfries might not be spending more time with their families after all. Then again, for him personally, given that Hardman seemed to be banking on him to deliver an American victory, success might leave him with no option but to follow Danny Allsop into the fertiliser after all.

Chapter Twenty-Four

Bjorn, a hairy man from Malmö who looked like his namesake from ABBA, had been droning on about trends in Swedish internet habits for half an hour now. Hardman had been tapping the table with barely disguised impatience for at least as long. At last, the imperturbable Swede turned away from his screen of figures and faced the audience. He appeared to be done.

Piers Poynton, hovering at the side of the boardroom, clapped his hands together and moved centre-stage. A trim, tanned figure, but in tight-fitting jeans that were too young for him, he gave Bjorn a patronising smile. 'OK, great, thanks for that, Bjorn. Let's call it a wrap.'

He addressed the rest of the room. 'Right guys, let's take five and then the advertising show will begin.'

Hardman had stomped out before he could finish the sentence.

Stephen thought he noted just a hint of anxiety on Piers' face, on his debut in Paris. It was the first time Stephen had seen him since last year, before the inception of Schmaltz Europe. But he was still trying to sound like a Hollywood film director rather than a marketing consultant from Basingstoke. The consistency of his pretentiousness was almost reassuring in a world of change.

The rest of the audience gathered at the back of the room, which was laid out with coffee jugs, and cups and saucers.

As Stephen poured himself a cup, he was joined by Salvatore.

'Well, Signor Carnevale, this is the first time anybody has offered me coffee in anything other than a plastic cup this year. Can I pour you one?'

Salvatore eyed the sludgy grey liquid and held his hand up to decline the offer. 'I am not that desperate. Tell me, do you know this fool, Stephen?' He motioned with a disdainful tilt of the head towards Piers.

Stephen laughed. 'Piers Poynton? Or Piers Pointless, as I like to call him. Yeah, I know him. We used to get him in to facilitate some of our Grimley's away days. Especially towards the end when they were increasingly dysfunctional. He heads up his own consultancy, called the Breakdown Truck. It's all about helping to rescue companies from difficult situations, apparently. Mind you, I think he might be better suited to a minor prang on a country road than the motorway pile-up we've got in this place.'

'What is he supposed to do exactly?' Salvatore asked.

'Ah, so you've noticed. Sweet FA, in my humble opinion. That means nothing much,' he added. 'Actually, he's incredibly good at standing there and telling us we're exactly on track at this point in the day, and that we should "take five". And he's very keen that we build on other people's ideas. Mainly because he never has any of his own.'

'Huh,' sniffed Salvatore. 'The company should not waste money on this.'

Stephen laughed. 'Possibly a little rich coming from the man who reserved the bridal suite at Oakley Park Castle on his last trip to Middleton. But yeah, he's a complete waste of money. And I must say I was surprised to see him here. I wouldn't have thought he was Hardman's cup of tea at all. And nothing that's happened so far today has changed my mind.'

'I think it's the ice-woman's fault that the pointless man is here,' Salvatore said.

'You do?'

'Yes, when I saw her last week she told me she is very worried about today. She is nervous about what the advertising agency is going to present.'

'She told you this? So you're still Carol Coolidge's confidant, are you, despite the disparaging things you say about her?'

'I'm always very trusted by younger women, Stephen. I am very calm. They like that in me.' He had that infuriating superior look again.

'OK, she's nervous. But that still doesn't explain Piers Pointless.'

'She is worried that Hardman is going to hate the launch advertising idea for Schmaltzy Bars. In fact, she doesn't think the agency is ready to present it. But Hardman has told her he can't wait any longer. So she thinks that if the agency's idea could be presented as part of a bigger meeting, a nice discussion about European advertising trends, this sort of thing, it might not feel like such a big deal.'

'Which explains the last half hour with the riveting Bjorn, I suppose,' Stephen observed.

'What? Ah yes, that idiot. And she also thought if she could get a few other people invited, like you and me, and get this pointless man to run the meeting, there might be more discussion, and less Hardman.'

'She really thought that?' Stephen was incredulous.

'Yes, really,' Salvatore chuckled. 'But tell me, Stephen, how are you? And how is Rachel?'

Stephen grimaced. 'It's one step forward and two steps back there, I think. She was away last weekend, but not with me.'

'Oh, I see. Care to tell me more?' Salvatore turned inquisitor as usual.

'I did tell you there was competition. And it's got God on its side.'

'Pah,' the Italian snorted, as if he'd never let divine intervention get in his way.

Before Stephen could say more, loud greetings were heard at the door as Carol's friends from her pet advertising agency, Oyster Inc, entered the room.

'I'll tell you more over a proper coffee another time,' Stephen said. 'Looks like the fun is about to begin.'

Zachary Beavis led the way, followed by three men and three women, all younger than him and exuding manic keenness. Like Piers Poynton, Zachary was the epitome of smart casual in his coordinated blue jacket and shirt, cream chinos and shiny brogues, and he set the tone for the rest of his team. None of the agency men had put on a tie, which Hardman still insisted on for the Schmaltz employees.

'Talk about hunting in packs,' Stephen said in an aside to Salvatore. Or maybe it was strength in numbers, in anticipation of a Hardman hammering. But Brad would have made a note – seven of them? How much was that costing him in air fares?

Zachary was working the room, pressing the flesh. Stephen had never entirely trusted him. He was the one who had tried to recruit Carol for Oyster Inc. Before Newte stuck his oar in.

'Is this agency any good?' Salvatore asked Stephen, as Zachary loudly greeted Carol as 'darling' and embraced her enthusiastically.

'Not bad. Probably mid-table rather than title-winning material. It's a gamble asking them to do a European launch campaign.'

Piers Poynton summoned them back to their seats, the board members sitting around the table while Stephen, Salvatore and a small band of other marketing operatives from around Europe perched on a row of stools at the back, like first years allowed to sit in on big school assembly.

Stephen could detect tension in the faces of the board. A few months in, they seemed more fearful of Hardman than he was. In one way at least the man was a true democrat: he treated them with just as much contempt as he did the minions.

Carol had gone for the white dress, like when she and Stephen had presented Hardman with the plan to close Dumfries. Did she double up even on Armani outfits? Probably, on her salary. But this morning it accentuated her pallid features and even her perfectly applied make-up couldn't mask an air of fatigue. She also appeared less keen to take the situation by the scruff of the neck than normal. She gave a very short, breathless introduction to Zachary, who would present the proposed advertising. Stephen knew how Hardman worked. He liked his own people to be in the driving seat, not shifting responsibility to expensive third parties.

When Zachary stood up, he hid Carol from view. He declared himself supremely confident that the agency had come up with a compelling idea for the launch advertising, which would generate a 'wave of passion' around Schmaltzy Bars throughout Europe. It sounded like he hadn't been told about the test now being planned to decide if the thing could be launched at all. But then Hardman and Carol were still acting as if the launch was nailed on.

'OK, let's see what ya got.' Hardman gave a particularly aggressive, phlegm-infused snort and leant back in his chair: Nero waiting to be amused by the gladiators. Stephen had never before felt sorry for Zachary Beavis.

The reason for the gang of six lackeys soon became apparent. Stephen had assumed that they would be seeing a video, a polished first cut of a TV commercial. Instead, what Oyster Inc were serving up was simply a written script, to be acted out in front of them, with each member of the team taking a role.

'We have set out to create the sense of excitement as people of all ages try Schmaltzy Bars for the first time,' Zachary enthused further.

'OK, let's just see it, for fuck's sake,' Hardman snapped.

Any hope of a pacy rendition was well and truly scotched by Zachary helpfully intervening to explain which part everyone was playing. Two of the youngsters stepped forward. The young man, described by Zachary as 'an old guy in his mid-fifties', tasted a Schmaltzy Bar and then offered it to the female colleague playing his wife, with the question 'Are you naughty enough to nibble, dear?' The next pair, who Zachary explained represented primary school kids in the playground, enacted exactly the same scene, this time with the girl posing the same nibbling question. Finally, the last couple, rather more convincingly in role as a couple of hipsters at a party, performed the scenario again, the man whipping a bar from his pocket with some elan.

Zachary stood before his troupe. 'And we end with the strapline: *Schmaltzy Bars – are you naughty enough to nibble?*'

There was complete silence.

It was extremely hard to credit, Stephen thought, that three months of highly paid navel contemplation had produced this.

They seemed frozen in time: Zachary's pathetically expectant smile towards his audience; the stunned looks of the board members as they realised this was all there was; Carol, now deathly white as she looked at Hardman, whose eyes were like long dark tunnels.

And still the silence.

Stephen felt a nudge as Salvatore slipped him a sheet of paper which he unfolded to reveal the Italian's scrawl: *This is bad. Very bad.*

Piers Poynton finally seized the moment.

'OK everyone, I'm sure Carol and Zachary and the team are excited to hear your feedback. And can I remind you again that we are nugget-mining here? I want you to find me the gold in this idea before we examine the whole rock.'

Oh, God, no. Not that nugget-mining idea again. Piers' naivety was touching. A certain someone would definitely be seizing the whole rock and hurling it at Zachary's head.

Hardman snorted again. 'What else you got?' he asked with quiet venom.

'Sorry, Brad?' Zachary's sunny disposition remained intact.

'I said, what else you got?'

Only now did a small cloud of panic cast its shadow across Zachary's face.

'Er, it's our philosophy to focus all our energies into expressing one big idea with confidence, rather than present a series of options. We sense you're the kind of guy, Brad, who doesn't like to hedge your bets.'

The car crash was still unfolding in slow motion. Never try to flatter him, never try to second guess him. And, when he was in this mood, don't try to be chummy.

Stephen could see that Hardman was simmering. He had seen this look many times over the last few weeks. Whereas Piers evidently decided yet another intervention might help.

'Great, as Zachary says, I think we need to focus on the big idea on the table here, people,' he said, but his voice was wavering.

Stephen turned to Salvatore and winced.

'Oh, you fucking do, do you?' The lava flow erupted, turning Piers to stone in an instant. 'OK, I'll fucking focus on the idea on the fucking table. It's crap.' Hardman stood up and marched to Zachary at the front of the room. 'Do you need me to tell you why it's crap?' His head jutted into Zachary's face, until the adman's neck lurched back, like a distressed chicken. Hardman picked up a Schmaltzy Bar lying on the table and thrust it in front of the chicken's beak.

'Have you even tasted the fucking bar?'

'Of course, Brad, we have—'

'You telling me you *nibbled* the fucker?'

'Well—'

'You don't nibble this fucker, you bite off a fucking mouthful.'

'Of course—'

'And who the hell shares one? You just chomp the fat bastard on your own.' His stare circulated the room. 'Don't you?' he bawled.

There were bleats of agreement.

'Indeed, Brad, indeed. Point well made,' said Newte.

Hardman scowled at him. Then his eyes fixed on Carol, who had shrunk into her chair.

'You. What the fuck did you think of this when they showed it to you?' He shouted across the table at her.

Carol squirmed on the hook. 'Well, Brad, I thought there was a big idea in there, but maybe the execution—'

'You thought there was a big idea, did you? Fuck me. And didn't I tell you I don't wanna target this at kids? People like Carreras here keep telling me we got a shitting sugar problem. Why've we got kids in the ad?'

Carol said nothing.

'Is it worth opening it up to get other views, Brad?' Piers suggested, more timidly this time. Hardman was shaking his head, anger having apparently turned to despair, while Piers directed his gaze around the inner sanctum of the board, not encompassing those in the back seats.

'I think essentially Brad is right,' offered Newte.

'Frankly, Nudey, I don't give a flying fuck what you think about this,' Hardman raged, oblivious to the fact that Newte was agreeing with him. 'You're supposed to be a bean counter, not a fucking advertising guru.' He took on Newte's Etonian accent. 'So if you wouldn't mind sticking to the day job and sorting out the fucking profits, old boy?'

He jabbed a finger towards the back of the room, his glare fixed on Stephen. 'Tell you what, why don't we ask these guys what they think? Otherwise, why the hell are they here? Carreras?'

He was so hoping not to be asked.

'Great idea, Brad.' Piers smiled encouragingly. 'Steve, can you find us the nuggets here?'

The whole idea was clearly a pig's breakfast. And in truth Carol Coolidge deserved everything she was getting. But she was a small, huddled, miserable figure now. What could he say?

'Er, I like the idea of the word spreading about Schmaltzy Bars – one person inviting another to try it, across the generations. I think there's some social media potential here.'

Hardman threw up his hands in exasperation. 'Hell, I thought you had some judgement, Carreras. You better stick to firing people – you're shit hot at that.'

Suddenly Carol intervened, with a more determined tone.

'Brad, I'm sure we can have a rethink and come up with a new idea in a couple of weeks.' She looked expectantly towards Zachary, who stared back at her like a man betrayed.

'You're seriously joking, right?' said Hardman. 'It's taken you and these time-wasters three months to come up with this crap, and now you expect me to give you more time? No way, Missy, you better just make sure we get the result we need from this fucking market research Carreras has persuaded me to run. I've seen more than enough of your advertising expertise. I got an agency in Chicago who will sort this shit out for me in two weeks. And that's where I'm fucking off to now.'

And with that, muttering under his breath, he stalked out.

'Thanks, Brad,' Piers chirruped.

There was a collective exhalation, but nobody spoke, as if worried that Hardman would bound back in for a final tirade. When the coast eventually seemed clear, the shuffling of papers began, and several of the board members stood up to leave.

Piers tried to rally the troops. 'Guys, guys, we've got the cream of Schmaltz Europe in this room, right here, right now. And we're due to go through until two. It's only twelve. We can go off-piste here and cover some other big meaty issues.'

But the shuffling continued, and the exodus began.

'Or, if you prefer, I guess we can call it a wrap.' Piers' voice faded away.

Stephen nudged Salvatore. 'I think they already have, Piers,' he whispered.

The only person still seated was Carol, hunched over the table, head down and hands clasped behind her neck. It was fast becoming her customary pose.

Zachary was having an animated discussion with Newte which didn't sound entirely cordial.

'Are you going to say anything to the ice-woman?' Salvatore enquired.

'I thought you were the one who's good with younger women. What do you suggest?'

'Pah, I think leave her. She got what she deserved, choosing that agency – hopeless, hopeless. I am out of here because I can get an earlier plane if I go now. I will be popular with my family. See you next week for more fun.' He winked and slipped out.

Stephen walked over to Carol, still sitting alone and motionless.

'Ah well, you win some, you lose some,' he said.

She looked up at him mournfully. 'God, that was excruciating. I've never been so humiliated.'

'Do you want to catch up on anything else?' he asked. 'I need to get the plane at four but I've got a couple of hours.'

'No, I do not want to talk about anything else. I need a drink,' she said, wearily. And then more softly, 'How about it?'

*

Stephen hailed a taxi on the street, while Carol, make-up slightly smudged, consulted her phone. The driver wound down the window with a questioning look.

'Where do you fancy? Maybe we could grab a quick lunch?' Stephen suggested.

She stopped texting for a moment. 'The first thing I'd like to do is go home and take these shoes off. They're killing me.'

He had never been in her apartment before, except in his imagination. It was on the fourth floor, at the top of a beautifully ornate building. The interior was all tastefully but sparingly furnished. The walls of her sitting room were pure white, except for a huge modern art canvas of yellow, blue and black squares which dominated one side. A jade coloured divan was angled precisely across the middle of the wooden floor, with a soft white rug and a long glass-topped coffee table in front of it, on which stood a single empty wine glass. Her fruity scent marked the territory.

Carol threw open French doors which led onto a balcony, but didn't go onto it herself, choosing instead to slip off her shoes and slump onto the divan to check her messages. Stephen stepped out and took in the panoramic view of Sacré-Coeur, its dome shimmering in the distance on a perfect, warm spring afternoon. The sounds of the traffic down below rose into the room.

'Wow, Carol, this place is even more amazing than I expected,' he said, still gazing out. It was so unfair. Presumably Newte's place was equally swanky, but probably didn't smell so good. How much crap would it be worth putting up with, to have a place like this?

When he turned round, Carol was now curled up, cat-like,

on the divan. But she was still scrolling through messages and still visibly tense.

'It can probably wait until Monday, Carol. With a bit of luck, Hardman's on his way back to Chicago by now,' he said.

She breathed out, and then put her phone down on the table.

'You're right. In fact, it can probably wait forever, the way I'm feeling right now.'

She undid the knot in her hair and shook it out. Stephen perched on the divan arm.

'Don't let the bastard grind you down. You don't need him. You could walk out tomorrow and get a good job somewhere. Although maybe not with an apartment like this, I grant you that.'

'You think so?' It was the look he elicited from her just occasionally, wanting his reassurance. She gave a dry little laugh. 'I think we can safely say that Oyster Inc will not be offering me a place on their board after today's little episode.'

'Really?'

'Didn't you hear Beavis talking to Oscar at the end? Telling him they'd been sold down the river?'

'Maybe they didn't mean you.'

'Oh, come on. I think the words "bloody Carol" were a clue.'

'But it wasn't your fault their advertising was so crap. Well, not entirely your fault anyway.'

'Oh, thanks.'

'I was being sarcastic.'

'Yeah, so was I,' she said. 'God, it really was crap though, wasn't it?' She shook her head. 'Naughty enough to nibble.'

If only she had realised that before they presented it. Perhaps not the moment to mention that.

'Yeah, I will admit I did enjoy seeing Zachary get knocked off his perch. And as for Pointless—'

'Who?'

'Piers Pointless. That's what I always used to call him at our Grimley's away days.'

She laughed again. 'Piers Pointless. I like that.'

'But Carol, don't tell me that was your idea, getting him involved?'

'Oscar suggested it.'

'Enough said.'

'I shouldn't have listened to him.'

'No, you shouldn't. Now, how about that drink?'

'Oh yeah, I'm sure I've got something in the fridge. Just give me a moment.' She sprang up and left the room, but not in the direction of the kitchen, which he could see through an open door.

He stood by the balcony doors again to admire the view. A passing ambulance wailed at him from below.

Carol reappeared from the kitchen door. She had shed the Armani dress and stockings for a loosely tied, silver silk dressing gown. Her hair was now piled high on top of her head, held by a clip. And in each hand she was holding a large glass of white wine, which she set down on the coffee table.

She rolled her right shoulder up and down. 'God, I feel so tense in the shoulder. Right up into the neck.' She smiled at him. 'I seem to remember you do a good massage.'

Not now he didn't.

From the pocket of his jacket, flung over a chair, his phone was buzzing. He fumbled to find it, but the call had gone to voicemail already.

'Don't forget, it can wait until Monday,' Carol said, lying the length of the divan, eyes closed, a relaxed smile on her face.

The caller ID was Rachel.

'Sorry, Carol, this can't wait.'

Chapter Twenty-Five

'We're going to be far too early, Dad,' Jake whined from the passenger seat, deigning to remove his headphones for a moment to register his complaint.

'No, we're not. By time we've got to the ground it will be ten thirty. Which is the time the coach asked you to be there.'

'What time is it now, then?'

'Ten.'

'It doesn't take that long to get there. We *will* be early,' Jake reasserted.

'Jake, I told you, but I expect you weren't listening, that we are going to pick Rachel up, so by the time we've driven to her flat and then to the ground, it will be just right.'

Jake considered this for a moment, munching on a piece of jammy toast.

'Does Rachel like football then?'

'I think she enjoys the fresh air, being able to have a good shout. You don't get too many chances to have a good shout as an adult.'

Jake wiped a buttery hand on the car seat, and apparently satisfied with this explanation, returned to his own little world.

Did Rachel like football? Well, it might not be her preferred

Saturday morning activity, but needs must. Her words from the phone call yesterday played over in his mind. The initial apology for disturbing him during working hours, still more like the politeness of a friend than the informality of a girlfriend. And then her wondering if they might talk over the weekend. Tentative on the surface, but he had sensed the approach of something significant. Enough to make him wonder what the hell he was even doing in Carol Coolidge's apartment, and to tell Carol that actually he needed to leave, and he needed to leave now. 'Thanks for nothing,' she'd shouted, as he shut the door behind him and escaped into the Parisian afternoon.

But talking over the weekend was not going to be simple. He had the kids, for one thing. And he sensed that what Rachel wanted to talk about might not be stuff to share over a family pizza margherita. So football it was. Far from ideal, but with Jake occupied on the pitch, and having ultimately persuaded a sullen Kate that staying at home on Saturday morning would be a good time to get her weekend homework out of the way, it might be their only chance.

She was waiting at her door, in a yellow vest and black leggings. The front of her vest posed the same question as the back of the cagoule she had worn in January, when Jake first got into the team.

What Would Jesus Do?

St Anselm's Fun Day

She looked great in this gear. This particular Fun Day top was certainly racier than the previous one he'd seen, although it might not have looked so good on all of the congregation. She was holding a bottle of water in one hand, while pulling her left foot up behind her with the other, doing a quad stretch.

'Hi, Jake. Ready for the big game?' she asked enthusiastically as she clambered into the back seat. No evidence here of the anxious Rachel he'd sensed in their phone call yesterday, but then she was good at this 'not in front of the children' routine – same as him.

'Jake, Rachel asked you a question. Will you just take those headphones off?' He rapped his son firmly on the knee.

'What?' Jake blinked at him.

'Rachel asked if you're ready for the big game.'

'It's not a big game. Last game of the season and we're both just mid-table.'

'Jake!' Stephen groaned at him. 'How many years do you think I'd get for infanticide, Rachel? Just roughly.'

She laughed. 'Oh well, never mind. I hope you enjoy it. That's the main thing.'

Stephen gave his son another stern look. 'Jake, here's an idea, why don't you get in the back and let Rachel come in the front.'

Jake gave a long-suffering sigh.

'No, honestly, don't worry. It's nice and comfy in the back,' Rachel said. 'You two are probably talking tactics.'

Stephen tried to catch her eye in his rear-view mirror to express his admiration, but her head was turned as she adjusted the seat belt.

'How's the running going, Rachel?' he asked. He needed to get beyond pleasantries this morning. But there was no point attempting anything more until he could tip Jake out.

'Mm. Well, later this morning I'm going to attempt 5K, which will probably feel like a half-marathon. Not massively encouraging when I've just signed up to do a 10K. Not till end of the year, but still.'

'Wow, a 10K is impressive. I'm sure you'll get there. Are you going to try and get sponsored for anyone?'

'Yes, Action Stations,' she said, and then more quietly, 'if we last that long. I'll explain later.'

A cluster of Jake's teammates were gathered in the car park, hands in pockets but still kicking a football around.

'Here we are, Jake, bang on time,' Stephen observed pointedly. 'I'll leave you here. I need to have a catch-up with Rachel.'

They wandered round to the other side of the pitch, away from where the team were being sent on a pre-match jog by the coach. But even here, they had to ward off a friendly linesman, who introduced himself as Harry's dad and insisted on taking them through the details of last week's two-all draw, which Stephen had seen anyway, in infinitesimal detail. Only when the match started, and Harry's dad had to attend to his linesman duties, did they fully shake him off.

'I'm sorry to drag you here, Rachel, but I really want to know what you wanted to talk about.'

She took a deep breath. 'Well, we had another meeting on the financial situation at work this week. The chairman of the trustees came in. And basically he confirmed that there's definitely no money as things stand to pay anyone beyond the end of this year, even though we've taken a cut in salary.' Her voice faltered. 'Which means, unless something significant turns up in the next few months, we'll have to close, or just run the whole thing voluntarily.'

He had never seen her look so disconsolate.

'I can't do that, Stephen, I can't do it for nothing. But I've no idea what's going to happen to those kids. It's the best thing in their lives, coming along to us. Heaven knows they haven't had a lot else. They're going to feel so let down. I just keep hearing Jordan, you know that boy who was playing football against Jake the first time I came? I keep hearing him say, "How could you do this, Rache?" ' She imitated his cheeky Cockney accent, still looking miserable. 'And I don't think people realise how lucky we are in Middleton. I mean, for a town of this size, we have remarkably little youth crime. I just don't know what's going to happen if places like ours close and these kids are on the street all the time.'

'It's not luck, Rachel. It's what you do. I'm so sorry. It must feel awful for you. Even though you do know it's not your fault, don't you?' Different woman, same conversation. But whereas Carol Coolidge deserved everything she got, Rachel Pearson didn't.

'Oh, I don't know. I'm not sure whose fault it is. It's just a mess.'

He comforted her, face nestled against his chest, just at the moment when Jake slipped effortlessly past his marker and crossed for the Emeralds' striker to score. He was a different young man from the dejected figure on his first appearance. In fact, he was a different young man from the slumped teenager in the passenger seat an hour ago.

'We should watch the match,' Rachel said, recovering herself. 'Did I just miss a goal?'

'No, it's OK. Well, sorry, yes, one-nil to us, but it's not important. I mean, what do you think you'll do? Sorry, you probably haven't had time to think about it yet.'

'Er, this is kind of what I wanted to talk to you about.' She paused. 'Something's come up, for me personally, but not for Action Stations.'

'OK, go on.'

'Just after I'd come out of the trustees meeting, Conrad called me.' Her eyes were checking him for a reaction.

'Go on,' he repeated firmly.

'He's working for this organisation called Altogether Now. Their head office is in Middleton.'

'Yes, I know all that.' Stephen recalled Conrad telling him about it that night after happy-clappy church. It sounded like a party political slogan.

'Oh. Well, he's had this idea for a project to get youth

workers from Malawi to come and evangelise here, while we provide aid and advice for youth projects over there.'

'Yes, I know about that too.' He tried to curb his impatience.

'OK. Anyway, he called me to say the funding for that project has now been confirmed. So, he's heading off to Malawi for a year in September to get it up and running.'

Conrad disappearing off to the middle of Africa was at least a positive turn of events. Stephen thought he remembered Conrad saying the Lord had brought him back to Middleton, but personally he was very pleased that the Lord now appeared to be sending him away again.

'Good for him.'

'Yes, he's really happy. He wants it so much.' She paused for a moment. 'And he thinks that's opened up a role for me too.'

Of course he did. Even from deepest Africa, he was obviously planning to recruit her and would no doubt be Skyping her back in head office for regular pep talks, keeping an eye on her. But it wasn't going to help if he expressed how he felt about Conrad right now.

'That could be interesting. I suppose at least it offers you another job in Middleton – there can't be many charities around here. But if you're asking my advice, I wouldn't rush into anything.'

'No, sorry, Stephen, I don't think you've quite understood. He wants me to join him there in Malawi for a year, to help establish the project.'

A chill ran down his body.

'Oh. Wow. What did you say?' He tried to sound calm and reasonable.

'Well, I told him I was a bit shocked, that it was now so concrete, and also because I was only just coming to terms with exactly how dire things are for Action Stations.'

'And what did he say to that?'

'He said maybe it was meant to be,' she said weakly.

'What?' Stephen raised his voice.

'He said that the fact my job was probably going to disappear, it was a sign of where God wanted me to be.'

'He works in mysterious ways, your God, doesn't he? What with the parking spaces in Tesco and now this.'

'Stephen, please don't.' She looked away, her shoulders slumped.

The ball thudded against his shin.

'Here, Dad, what are you doing? Give us the ball. It's our throw-in,' Jake shouted. The ball had rebounded ten yards behind him, onto the adjacent pitch. Was he the ball boy? He trotted off to pick it up and kicked it back hard, past Jake.

Dad, what are you doing? Son, that's a fair question.

'Rachel. I don't want you to go. I know I haven't quite made this – us – work yet. But, just, please don't go.'

Rachel fished a hanky from her pocket and blew her nose loudly.

He put an arm around her. 'I really want us to try going out again, on a conventional date. Sorry, I don't mean conventional, I know you're not conventional. But, I don't know, just go to the cinema again or something – without the kids this time. I mean, those first trips to the pub after church on a Sunday were great – but I'd love to do something else.'

She sighed. 'It's just so difficult, isn't it, when you're just getting on with your life, finding time for something, somebody new? The thing is, though, I really like you, Stephen.' She was quite loud. For a moment he felt all twenty-two players and the ref were listening to the conversation, watching him.

'Dad, come on,' Jake wailed in exasperation.

They *were* watching him. Because the ball had rolled up against his foot again.

He threw it back, rather self-consciously this time.

'I love that you feel things so deeply – that card you sent me about "Babylon". I admire what you're trying to do at work, helping people. And I see how much you love your kids. Oh, and Lila in choir informs me that you're a bit of a hunk as well.' She paused for a second. 'Which I happen to agree with.'

'Oh, so have you discussed me with lots of your friends, then?' he said, trying to hide his embarrassment.

'Oh, one or two. Jane, who you met at your neighbour's party, likes you. I think Greg's still dubious – probably because you can't remember his name and puked on his car. It's funny how that colours a person's judgement.'

A couple of other dads were in earshot now, he was sure of it. But Rachel was in full flow.

'Anyway, the point is, I thought you really liked me too. That night round at your house when you cooked me dinner, I loved that. It just felt funny and relaxed, and I didn't think you were worrying about work.'

'I do like you, Rachel. I like you very much.' How could he prove it, here and now?

'I thought you did. I mean, you were calling me and texting me and everything. And then you suddenly stopped. After that last time in the pub when we had a row in the car park about church worship, for heaven's sake. So I assumed something went wrong. Or there's someone else. Actually, I didn't know what to think.' Her eyes were searching him. There was a cheer. She glanced at the pitch and suddenly her face broke into an unexpected teary smile. 'Er, I think Jake might have scored.'

They were trotting back to the centre spot, and a couple of the players were running over to Jake. They exchanged high fives. 'Nice goal, JC,' the captain shouted across.

He'd missed it. Jake had scored, and he'd missed it. JC. His son had a nickname in the team. Jake looked across and Stephen gave him a fist pump. And with that, the referee blew for half time. On the pitch, the Emeralds were well in control. Off it, not so good. But maybe he hadn't lost to Conrad – yet.

'Excuse me, Jake's dad.' Harry's dad approached him, offering the linesman's orange flag. 'I told the coach I could only stay to do the first half today. Any chance you could take over? We like to share out the linesman duties,' he said with the air of a man who didn't expect no for an answer.

There must be someone else who could do it. Here he was, picking his way through this conversation which might just change the rest of his life, and this bloke wanted him to be a bloody linesman.

'Oh, I don't know, mate,' Stephen said. 'I'm not sure I can stay until the end either.' He looked at Rachel for support.

'It looks like it's you or the guy over there on crutches,' she said cheerfully.

Harry's dad handed over his flag with a look of relief. 'Nice one, mate. You just need to be linesman for the end we're defending. I assume you know the offside rule? But if in doubt, get that flag up pronto. Mind you, this lot we're playing are useless. You should have a quiet half.'

'I should go, leave you to it,' Rachel said.

'God, no, Rachel, please don't go now. We can still talk.'

The ref blew the whistle for the second half.

'There's nobody else, Rachel,' Stephen said. It was absolutely true now, he knew it. He sighed. 'I think I've been a bit confused.'

'What are you confused about?'

Might as well say it. 'That evening at church when all your friends came to the pub after. I found it – difficult.'

She looked at him thoughtfully. 'I know you did.'

'It just all seemed so – I don't know – cut and dried. You'd been singing all those cheery choruses and you all appeared so sure of yourselves. And then you were pouring sweetness and light on your young friends. I was jealous, Rachel, and then I just felt – old and bad.'

'Oh, no, I can see that. I mean, not that you're old – or bad. Well, hopefully a little bit bad. But I can see how it all felt a bit cliquey, even though I did try to explain they aren't really my friends, just a group of young people I've tried to help a bit. But church is crap for cliques sometimes.' She smiled. 'That's partly why I like singing in the Clams, you know. It's an escape from the clique. I can be someone else completely.'

'Yes, I can see that too. By the way, I've never told you properly – you were incredible. It's such a cool thing to do. I've been meaning to ask why you didn't tell me about that – when we first met and we were both waxing lyrical about Blondie.'

She looked away, as if recalling something painful. 'There's a reason for that. I met someone a while back and told him I was an occasional punk singer. In fact, he came to see me perform, after we'd only been going out a couple of weeks. He thought it was cool too, loved it, seemed to like me as well. Then, when I told him I also loved singing in a church choir, he ran a mile.' She turned towards him again. 'So I decided that, in future, I would get the church-going out there straight away. I mean, if anyone's going to run a mile because of that, I'd rather they did it immediately – save us both the disappointment.' She paused. 'You were my first experiment.'

Stephen checked that the Emeralds were safely entrenched in the orange team's half, as Harry's dad had predicted, before he replied.

'And I did OK, didn't I? I turned up, and I was beginning to enjoy it – until that youth service at least. And I really want you to know that I'm not antagonistic towards church. I haven't told you this, but things keep popping up, either from David your vicar or from this old bishop I hear on the radio, that seem to have these odd connections with what's happening to me.'

'What do you mean?'

'There's this woman who keeps trying to offer *me* another job, at the other end of the country. She's like a sort of posh Satan, tempting me in the desert, which I heard the radio bishop talking about. And then, there's never been an occasion to tell you this properly, but there's a situation brewing up at our factory in Scotland which could make the carnage in Middleton look like a children's tea party. And I seem to have found myself evading the truth with an old colleague up there more often than Peter when he's being asked if Jesus is a mate of his.'

She looked at him intently. 'There's something important you need to know about me, Stephen. I often don't know what I believe. I mean, do I believe in God? Yes, most of the time. Do I think of myself as a Christian and could I explain what that means to me? Yes, I think so. But I spend far more time fumbling around in the dark than I do gazing up at the light. So I'm hardly likely to try and convert you, whatever that means, when I'm not even sure myself. I've sometimes worried that you think I do want to convert you. Besides, it would be so arrogant. But it matters to me, that's the thing, it matters a lot. And I sometimes need someone to talk to about this stuff too.' She shivered a little.

He wanted to hug her now, right here on the touchline. But he didn't. Somehow it felt right to remain silent, not to fill the void, to wait for her to continue. The boys' voices were sharp and clear in the cold morning air.

'Oy, linesman!' The dad on crutches was shouting at him because suddenly the opposition's orange shirts were surging forward. That centre forward was definitely nippy. Was he offside there? Better get the flag up.

'You're having a laugh, lino. That was never offside,' one of the opposition dads shouted along the touchline.

'It's harder than it looks, this malarkey, isn't it?' Rachel said. 'I think you'd better concentrate.' The oranges were coming forward in waves now, and Stephen had to sprint along the touchline again to keep up. 'They must have had a bit of a talking-to at half time,' she observed.

How come when Rachel turned up there always seemed to be some incident with an opposition dad? He really did not want to be doing this, not just now. And although she had told him to concentrate, she wasn't letting up.

'Frankly, Stephen, you and Conrad, you've been like London buses. I hadn't met an interesting new man since – well, the one who liked punk but wasn't so sure about "Make Me a Channel of Your Peace". And then you both turn up at the same time. I know you don't like him, but there's something very attractive about his conviction. I've been feeling quite lost and Conrad is so reassuringly certain about God, certain about what direction the church should go, certain about this mission – and certain I should be with him.'

'So... have you been going out with him?'

She hesitated for a moment. 'Yes. Not for long. When you seemed to have lost interest, I needed someone. I mean, he's talked to me about this job a lot, kept saying what a great team we would make together. He's sort of been selling me the job and selling me himself at the same time.'

'He's offside, linesman,' shrieked one of Jake's teammates, hand held high in the air.

'Oh, shit,' Stephen cried. The oranges had hoofed the ball upfield and the nifty striker was running at pace towards the Emeralds' goal.

Was he offside? Stephen wasn't sure. He hadn't been paying attention. Hopefully the lad would miss anyway, then it wouldn't matter.

He didn't miss. Two-one. This second half was threatening to go peach-shaped on the field as well as off it.

'Dad, what are you doing? He was yards off.' Jake was holding his hands out in apparent disbelief at his father's ineptitude.

'All right, son, calm down, play to the whistle.' Stephen tried to sound authoritative, despite the lump in his throat.

'Sorry, that was definitely my fault,' Rachel said. 'I really do need to go and try that run and leave you to focus, or you'll be in Jake's bad books for the weekend.'

He checked the pitch. The ball was up at the far end again. He had a moment. He put down the flag and held her by the shoulders.

'Rachel. I have to know. Have you decided – on Malawi?'

'No, I haven't decided.'

He felt the most powerful wave of relief break over him.

'I've told Conrad I need more time – just to think it through and see how things work out.' She didn't elaborate.

'So please can I see you again soon, to talk to you about it?' he said. 'I'll find a time during the week – anytime, anywhere.'

'Well, it's tricky again this week.' He knew this apologetic face. 'I'm going on retreat for a few days – back to see my monks.'

Here we go again, he thought. 'What about next weekend?'

She shook her head. 'I'm just so busy, Stephen. I'm always so busy. We're taking the kids to Alton Towers on Saturday. I'm dreading it. Looking at their happy little faces, not able to tell them yet that they won't be doing this any more after this year. And then on Sunday I've got choir, in the morning and the evening.'

'I'll come to church on Sunday morning. I'd like to hear you sing in the choir again.'

'It's even more complicated than that. Straight after I have to run the church lunch. I'm on the organising committee. Cooking for about eighty people. I don't suppose we'll tip out until about half past three.'

'And will Conrad be there?'

'Expect so,' she said.

The ball was still at the far end. He had a good look around to check if anyone was looking. And went down on his knees.

'Rachel, I'll come and peel vegetables, wash up, anything. Just give me an hour, when it's all over, on my own, please.'

Now he was down here, it felt squirmingly over the top. But she was looking down at him with eyes full of compassion.

'Of course. Of course I'll give you an hour. But I think you should get off your knees. I'm not sure you can do this linesman thing from that position.' She smiled. 'In honour of Ms. Harry and a certain song we both like, I'll try to make it one of my best hours, although after four hours in the kitchen at the church lunch, I think we all know that might be a big lie.' Her eyes widened. 'Ooh, look out.'

'Oy, linesman, what the fuck...' came a gruff voice from along the touchline, as Stephen struggled to his feet.

The bloody oranges were coming again.

Chapter Twenty-Six

He had never been to a morning service before, so wasn't prepared for the church car park being full. Eventually he squeezed the car onto the end of a side road, but his plan to arrive early, so Rachel would see he was present and correct, was scuppered. In fact, he would need to leg it to make it for the start.

He walked briskly back towards the church, with John Motson keeping step.

'It's a return to St Anselm's for Stephen Carreras today, and you suspect he will have just an hour to save his season later this afternoon. You'd have to say the odds are stacked against him. He's very much playing away from home here, on Beardy Conrad's home patch. So can the boy Carreras dig deep and pull off an unlikely victory here?'

'Thanks, John, I do know what's at stake, mate,' he said. Not only was he still hearing Motty's voice in his head, now he was answering back.

The eight days since seeing her at Jake's football had felt interminable, working all hours on combating a further raft of farting enquiries from assorted journalists. And while he had been sorting out this shit, she was consulting a bunch of monks about her future. And the trouble was, she was likely to do the right thing. The sacrificial thing. Maybe it wasn't even sacrificial. After all, Conrad offered certainty – not just in a job, but apparently in the life hereafter too. And even though she said she wasn't trying to convert him, she must deep down want a Christian, with all the fringe benefits. He couldn't compete with that. And if there was a God, chances were he'd prefer Rachel to be a missionary saving souls of the deserving poor in Africa, rather than struggling on with a sceptical, swearing divorcé who flogged sugar for a living.

He could hear the organ as he got closer to the church. And when he entered there was no friendly steward awaiting him. Until Terry, sat on his own at the back, approached him with a hymn book in his hand.

'We begin fifteen minutes earlier on the fourth Sunday, Stephen,' he whispered. 'Just starting the second hymn already. "All My Hope on God Is Founded",' he added with a wink.

Fortunately, there was a near empty pew towards the back and Stephen slipped into it, quietly seething. How the hell was he supposed to know some quirky fourth Sunday rule, for God's sake? Once again he was being invited to play some complex game without having the rules explained. He opened his hymn book to number 336 and realised that Terry had been giving him the first line rather than making a personal statement. Or maybe both.

She was in the middle of the choir, red headband in place. He kept his eyes focused on her throughout the hymn, wanting to signify he was here, better late than never, but he suspected her smiling face was simply reflecting the joy of singing rather than any recognition of his arrival. Had she noticed him? He still didn't know what more he could do. At work he was always very well prepared for presentations. But this afternoon he would have to give the most important one of his life to Rachel

Pearson: the case to stay in England with him. And he still didn't have a clue how to do it.

Conrad, naturally, had positioned himself in the front pew, the chairman of her fan club. What was the betting he had smuggled himself into her theme park trip with the youth group yesterday too – just to seal the deal? Why hadn't he thought about joining that? Because it wasn't his thing, that was why.

Mercifully, David the main man was in charge again this morning, and once again he read the bit from the Bible himself. It was about Christ washing the disciples' smelly feet. God, that was a challenging one. David was always very deliberate in his movements, imbuing small acts with significance. He closed the Bible, held the silence for a few seconds and then walked slowly across to the other side of the church, from where he climbed up into the pulpit and looked out at the congregation.

'I hope I can never be accused of being a fire and brimstone preacher,' he said, to sympathetic laughter. 'But just for once, I want to talk about sin. Remember those words we say so often in that old pre-communion prayer? *We have done those things which we ought not to have done. And we have left undone those things which we ought to have done...*'

Not for the first time, he appeared to be focussing directly on Stephen. And Stephen knew what he ought not to have done – four years ago.

The whole Grimley's marketing team had been camped out at that conference hotel in the centre of Birmingham – yet another two-day planning session. He had left Sandra to arrange the seating plan for dinner at the end of the first day. If only she'd not taken it upon herself to mix things up a little. That's how the marketing director came to be sat next to a bright new marketing recruit.

Carol Coolidge, tall, blonde and by far the most glamorous being to enter Grimley's marketing department in many a year.

She could only have been twenty-two or twenty-three then, but with self-confidence already oozing from every pore. He had kept his distance since recruiting her a few weeks previously – deliberately so. He knew instantly he was attracted to her. And knew at some level he was vulnerable. Laura had just started working again at the estate agents, a change which had proved more stressful than they had anticipated. While he was increasingly under the cosh at Grimley's – so their time together was ever more squeezed, stressed and accusatory over chores not done and childcare responsibilities. Enter Carol Coolidge stage right – young, gifted and free of all inhibitions.

He had been a bloody fool at that dinner – tired, a little drunk, but basically just a bloody fool. Flattered by the fact that she was mildly flirtatious, seemingly interested in a man just beginning to feel his age. They hadn't talked about work, only about holidays. She had just spent a couple of weeks on some Greek island learning massage and yoga, which at the time made the holiday he'd recently spent on Perranporth beach with the kids seem pretty run of the mill. Later, when they'd all retired to the bar, she had pursued him still, asking him where he would really like to go on holiday. At one in the morning, when he was back in his room, undressing and about to slump into bed, she had knocked on his door. She had lost her key, and there was nobody on reception.

'I think we all know there are moments in life when we could have tried a bit harder,' David said, still looking at him.

Surely other options would have occurred to him if he had been thinking straight. Telling her to go and share with one of the other women was an obvious example. Instead of asking her in for a nightcap from the minibar. And offering her his bed while he would sleep on the floor. He could have said no when she stepped out of a late-night shower and offered to demonstrate her new massage skills as a thank you. He didn't.

And he could have said no when she slipped the hotel bath robe off her gossamer shoulders and asked him to return the favour.

The sex had been wild. Dangerous, forbidden, away from home. And then she found her key.

He remembered waking up the following morning, the smell of the shower gel on his sheets. Wanting to pretend it had never happened. Carol was in a different working team from him that day, he made sure of that, and they never exchanged a word. He got home late, embraced Laura, and looked in on the children, already asleep in bed. Just a normal evening after a long day at work.

Left undone those things which we ought to have done. Yep, that was him too.

The days that followed had been filled with more lengthy planning meetings and even longer working hours than normal. Most evenings, by the time he got home, Laura was on her way out to meet a girlfriend or go to book club or something, leaving him with hurried instructions about supper and what he ought to know about his children's day at school. At the weekends, she pointed out correctly that he should be spending more time with them, ferrying them to the round of kids' parties, ballet and karate club. And every Saturday evening there seemed to be a dinner with neighbours, at their house or in a local restaurant. He had often thought since that it was what most married couples aspired to: the happy, well-adjusted kids, the dinner parties with other couples, a nice four-bedroom detached house. But where on that conveyor belt should he have found the moment to tell her? *Darling, I'm just nipping out to the DIY store for that new spade. Oh, by the way, did I mention I slept with the new trainee?*

'So, in conclusion, I have to say that I'm sometimes envious of the Catholic sacrament of confession,' David said. 'It seems to me that confession to another person, knowing that person will listen and not judge you, is one of the most liberating experiences of human existence.'

He should have told her. Told her how stressful work was at the time, how he knew he was not being a good father, or even a good husband, but that he would sort it out. How he loved her still, if only he could find that love somewhere in the clutter of their lives. But there was to be no such moment, no such time spent away from the glare of the office or the excusing distraction of two demanding little souls. And in truth, would she have been able to forgive him, when it was so raw?

And so, he realised, the lack of the right moment had made a coward out of him. A week of saying nothing became a fortnight, a fortnight became a month, and then two months, and he convinced himself it was better to leave it that way. It wasn't going to happen again; their marriage would survive; the night with Carol would be a minor footnote in his life story; and somewhere down the line, when the children had left home, he naively thought that he and Laura would be walking arm in arm on a golden beach somewhere, and maybe he would find the words. *Laura, I've never told you this before, but once many years ago, I had one, just one, very foolish moment of weakness...*

And then it happened again.

'The offertory hymn, "Great Is Thy Faithfulness",' David announced.

He stood up, staring blankly at the words in the hymn book.

Returning from the ad agency on a Friday afternoon together, in his car. Managing to discuss the meeting like normal work colleagues, but still so intoxicated by her presence, that only when they got back to Middleton did he remember that Laura had taken the children away to her parents, as he'd said he would be working all weekend. He was on his own. He asked her in for a drink, could still remember the moment of ecstatic surprise when she said yes. The thought that she wanted this too.

When Laura returned without the children the following morning, Carol was sitting in her conservatory: barefoot, wrapped in the fluffy pink towel normally reserved for Kate, and awaiting the coffee and croissant he was about to serve her.

Terry was holding the offertory plate in front of him expectantly. He rustled in his back pocket and found a fifty-pence coin. Terry avoided further eye contact.

Laura's face showed no anger, just a pathetic, childlike puzzlement, as he entered like some bit player in a French farce with the silver tray. He still recalled Carol walking past them both without a word, her head held high, slipping out of the room, and then the front door closing a short while later. And then, quite calmly, Laura telling him she was going back to her parents, and by the time she returned with his children on the Sunday evening, she wanted him out. She would find a way to tell them, make an excuse for him.

'Blimey, you're very reverent today.' Rachel was standing above him, bright eyes questioning. The pews around them were now empty, but there was the general hubbub from the back of church as people filed out into the foyer. 'Pretty impressive, Mr C, remaining on your knees as we processed out. I'll choose not to see it as a comment on the choir.' She smiled, then noticed that he wasn't laughing. 'Sorry, Stephen, you've probably realised by now I make stupid jokes when I'm nervous. Are you OK?'

'Yes, a lot to think about.' He got to his feet.

'Hello everyone,' David called out. 'Just a reminder to those of you staying for lunch that it will be served at one o'clock.'

Her expression changed. 'Agh! I should have put the oven on ten minutes ago.'

'I'm coming to help. I don't suppose those spuds will peel themselves.'

'You don't have to.' She touched him on the arm.

'I think I do,' Stephen said.

*

He emptied another bowl of dirty water, full of potato peels, and refreshed it for the fifth time. How had he ended up here? If anyone had asked his marketing colleagues what Steve Carreras would be doing on a Sunday morning, he was willing to wager that no one would have placed him in a church hall kitchen wearing a bright red apron emblazoned with the words,

Let's get cooking with St Anselm.

'Praise the Lord – a man in an apron. About time too. Come on there. Chop, chop.' Mavis Constable, the grey-haired, matronly head of the church catering team unloaded a bag full of unwashed leeks on the draining board next to him. 'Beware of the dragon,' Rachel had warned him.

'We have our uses, Mavis,' he joked. Silly old cow.

It was endless, like feeding the five thousand. But he was resolved to maintain a cheerful exterior and put up with the ribbing. All for one person. He tried to catch Rachel's eye, hoping for a reassuring smile, but she was full on, working the kitchen, her red headband still intact but her robe replaced today by an amber roll-neck top and smart black cropped trousers. Mavis might be the nominal CEO, but it was clear who was running the show. It was classic management by wandering about, an encouraging word here, a firm direction there, while exuding a calm poise, even though he knew that she would be paddling like a duck under the surface. He owned that secret.

Conrad was conspicuous by his absence in the kitchen. Like all the other men. Through the serving hatch, Stephen saw Rachel directing the laying out of tables, and there he was, the bearded wonder, engaged in conversation with David, a glass of wine in one hand and gesticulating with the other. He had his prey pinned to the door, no doubt telling him how he would have run the service. At least when he went to Africa, David would be free to get on with it. The temptation to shout, 'Oy, Conrad, never mind discussing the sermon, get your arse through here and start peeling,' was almost irresistible. Then Rachel paused from her work to say something to them both, and David escaped, leaving her and Conrad talking together. She was smiling at him while he gave her that look, up and down.

There was no rest for the wicked. About a hundred hungry parishioners were now taking their places round the tables, with a bunch of Sunday school kids running around pretending to shoot each other. Finally, they were ready. Still aproned, Stephen took bowls of steaming vegetables out to the tables, and then the chicken portions which were being plated up back in the kitchen. Barely anyone acknowledged him; they were all chatting away in their little groups.

Conrad was talking to Seb the football player when Stephen plonked a plate of chicken in front of him with as much grace as he could muster. He didn't even look up until Stephen had moved down the table, serving the assorted youth sitting at the court of the bearded king. Only then did he call across.

'Hi, Stephen, is there a vegan option?'

Who on earth was vegan? 'There's vegetable lasagne, Conrad – that's the best we can do,' he said, trying very hard not to swear at him.

'Mm,' Conrad mused, at this seemingly unsatisfactory quandary. 'OK, can I have that then, please. Sorry, I should probably have said.'

'Of course,' Stephen replied with a forced smile, removing

the offending poultry from under Conrad's nose and marching back to the kitchen.

'Can I have another veggie option, please, Mavis?'

'Who's that for?' she barked.

'Conrad.'

'He should have ordered in advance. He's not on my list.'

No doubt Conrad had higher things on his mind than ordering in advance. Maybe he just expected the Lord would provide.

'It's all right, Mavis, there's plenty to go around,' soothed Rachel, touching her arm. 'He must have forgotten, naughty boy.'

Mavis dolloped out another portion of vegetable lasagne with an extravagant harrumph.

Eventually, as most people were finishing their meal and the Sunday school shootout recommenced, the kitchen staff got to sit down and eat too. It was a case of finding a seat where you could, taking a space vacated by an errant child. No chance of two together.

Stephen sat next to a couple about his age that he'd never met before and reached for the one remaining wine bottle on the table, only to discover it was completely empty. Rachel was sat at the next table with two of the elderly parishioners, chuckling at something they were saying. But now at least he caught her eye, if only just for a moment, and she smiled appreciatively at him. Encouraged, he threw himself into answering the couple's queries about local state schools. They had some penetrating questions about the curriculum at Kate and Jake's academy, which left him feeling he didn't have his finger sufficiently on the pulse of his children's education. Why did every avenue lead to guilt?

Finally the vicar stood up to thank Mavis and Rachel and their team.

'And I'm sure if anyone would like to help the catering

team with the washing up, they will be more than welcome,' he concluded.

'Right.' Mavis gave Stephen a playful prod in the shoulder blade. 'This is where the real work begins.'

It was nearly half past three as he loaded another pile of greasy plates into another bowl of warm soapy water. Rachel had been buzzing about, putting stuff away, thanking various helpers as they apologised that they couldn't stay any longer. But for the last fifteen minutes she'd been nowhere to be seen.

And then on the other side of the hall, where a small cluster of people lingered while the tables were folded up around them, there she was, coming out of the church office with Conrad; the two of them laughing, exchanging a joke.

'Here, Stephen, the work surfaces need to be wiped down.' Mavis tossed a J-Cloth in his direction. When he had finished, Conrad had gone and Rachel was back in the kitchen, reaching up on tiptoe to put cups on the top shelf.

'Can I drive you home?' he asked. Had she forgotten that she'd promised him an hour this afternoon?

She turned towards him, a weary smile on her face.

'No, you're all right, I've got my bike here.' She paused for a second, and then rummaged in her shoulder bag. She threw him a set of keys. 'Beatrice is away. So let yourself in. And put the kettle on.'

*

He was waiting at the window as her small figure appeared at the corner of the street, cycling towards him. By now he knew what he needed to do. But how?

When he opened the door, she was removing her headband, revealing beads of perspiration on her forehead. The sophisto-punk look was more punk than sophisto.

'Phew, I think that went well,' she exhaled. 'You poor thing. You must be exhausted.'

'No, I'm fine,' he lied. 'Thanks for the top tip on Mavis, mind. You were brilliant, holding it all together. The kettle's on.'

'I'd better come in then.'

He didn't know how to start. If only he knew what she'd said to Conrad. That joke looked conspiratorial to him, intimate even.

Rachel slumped onto the sofa. 'Ooh, my feet are killing me,' she groaned, slipping off her shoes.

He knew now how he had to do it.

'Rachel, there's something I want to tell you... need to tell you. And something I'd like to do, while I'm telling you.'

She looked at him with an intrigued smile. 'Well, I did promise you an hour. In fact, I think I might have rashly promised to make it a good one – so it's up to you how you use it.'

'OK. So you need to sit back, close your eyes and relax, if that's possible. Try not to think about Mavis. And I'll be back in a minute.'

He returned from the kitchen with a mug of tea for her, and then with a washing up bowl full of hot water, and told her not to open her eyes yet.

He went into the bathroom and returned with a flannel and her vanilla bath mousse.

'OK, you'll think I'm mad... but I'm going to wash your feet, if you'll let me, and I need to tell you something. A confession, I suppose.'

Even with eyes closed, Rachel looked dubious. 'That's brave. They might be on the fresh side after the last few hours.' But then she opened her eyes, and as if recognising the significance of the moment for him, she added, 'But I don't get men offering to wash my feet every day.' Her face relaxed into a smile, she pulled her cropped trousers up tight at the top of her calves, and laid her head back.

And so he knelt down, a towel draped over his shoulder, bathing and kneading her feet, and recounted to her the story as he had remembered it yet again in church that morning. The circumstances in which he had sex with Carol Coolidge, the woman who, as he had explained, was now his marketing boss. How to his lasting regret he'd never found a way to tell Laura. How, even more shamefully, it had happened again. And how, by the end of that weekend, he was staying in a damp-smelling room in the Ship Hotel, wailing at all he had lost.

He didn't look up at Rachel, not daring to see her reaction, in case this was the final curtain. And she didn't say a word.

Eventually, when he had finished, he lightly lifted her feet one by one out of the bowl, folded the towel around them and gently dried them.

'So, there you have it.' Only now did he look up. Her eyes were closed again.

He focused again on drying the little crevices between her toes.

'How do you feel?' she asked gently.

'What do you mean?'

'How do you feel, now that you've told me?'

He breathed out. 'Well, guilty I suppose. Yes, definitely very guilty. Fearful of what you'll think of me. But sort of... clean?'

There was silence for what seemed a long time. He kept drying her toes.

'Er, I think they're dry, Stephen. Do you do the full pedicure?'

He breathed a small laugh of relief. It was done. He was about to stand up, but Rachel held her hand out to stop him.

'I have two questions,' she said.

'Only two?'

'Yep, only two. Question one, and I realise this might seem incidental, but what did Laura come back for that morning, when you thought she was spending the weekend at her parents' with the children?'

'She said she'd told me in advance that if the children were happy, she was going to leave them with her parents for a few hours, have a bit of time to herself, back in the house. I'm sure she had told me. I think I'd just stopped listening. So she came back. She came back because the children were happy.' He'd never seen the irony before.

'And question two. How do you feel about Carol Coolidge now?'

Her voice was soft and reassuring, but it was the sharpest question. And one he knew he had to answer.

'We never had any intimacy from that moment on. At first, I thought that as my marriage was in tatters, we might as well keep going, that I had lost everything else anyway. But she didn't want to keep going. Too bright to get involved. And I didn't press it, because very soon I didn't want to either. Even though I'd lost my wife and children, trying to build a relationship out of the events which had caused that loss came to feel like just one more act of betrayal.'

'And how do you feel about her now?' She was demanding a full answer to her question.

He looked up at her. 'When I didn't think it was working out with you, and Carol and I have been forced to spend so much time in each other's company at work again recently, I did have a moment of madness when I wondered if we might get together. Whether somehow this was the only world available to me. But we really have nothing in common.' He wanted to convey just how much he meant this.

'You both work in marketing for the same company.'

'We have nothing in common that matters. I know I've moved on.' He was still looking up at her, like a supplicant. 'I know who I want. I want you. All I can do is ask you to trust me.'

'You do know you're amazing, don't you?'

'What do you mean?

'Nobody has ever spent as long on their knees in my presence, and nobody has ever told me something as intimate as that.'

Stephen breathed in her words and then exhaled. And with that long exhalation, he felt as if he was releasing some long pent up toxin. But it meant her answer to his next question was even more important. He couldn't put it off any longer.

'Can I ask if you've thought any more? About your future?'

'I did a lot of thinking on my retreat and praying in church this morning, although not as much as you, obviously.'

'So, what have you decided?' His stomach was fluttering.

'I haven't. I did say I need time.'

Relief and frustration mingled in his head. And, rather surprisingly, John Motson popped up again.

'So it's still everything to play for at the moment between Stephen Carreras and the beardy evangelist. I think Carreras might take that at this stage. But who's going to get the winner here?'

'Wow, well, I guess Conrad and I could go pistols at dawn, best man wins?'

Rachel twirled a scented foot in front of him. 'I don't think that will help, although I do find the thought of you two fighting over me interesting. Bare-chested wrestling would be more erotic, and nobody would get hurt.' She raised the foot to anoint his shoulder. 'But the thing is, Stephen, this isn't just about you two. It's about me.'

Chapter Twenty-Seven

The enormous Schmaltz sign still offended him, screaming across the car park, a reminder of that nightmare start to January. As he drove past the office entrance, he noticed Salvatore stepping out of a taxi, and by the time he had parked the Italian was sitting in reception, a picture of calm. In a light grey suit, he folded one knee across the other to reveal red diamonds on a calf-length sock, as he casually flicked across his tablet screen.

'Signor Carnevale, you're very early.'

'Ah, Stephen, there you are. I was just catching up on my team.' He smirked. 'I'm sorry, but strangely there doesn't seem to be any update on your Middleton Dynamos in *La Gazetta dello Sport*.'

'Maybe just as well,' Stephen said. 'So, are you going to apply for the Inter Milan job when it comes up again then? Sure it won't be long. Mind you, the job security's about on a par with here.'

'This is true,' Salvatore said. 'Although I think the money is rather better.'

'Just a tad. Anyway, I assume from this that you didn't catch the red-eye flight from Milan this morning. Don't tell me, another night in the Oakley Park Castle?'

'I told you, it's not bad there. Even the restaurant. To fly this morning, I would have to get up at four o'clock.' He looked at Stephen as if he hadn't understood this problem. 'And with the fog in Milano, if the flight was delayed this morning, I would have missed all the fun.'

'Fog? In May?'

'It can happen,' Salvatore said, not entirely with conviction. 'Now, as we don't get the results of the market research until ten, maybe we have time to talk about next steps?'

'No, I've got an eight thirty with someone, which won't finish until the research agency arrives at about quarter to ten. Anyway, what's the point discussing next steps until we know the results?' He gave Salvatore a quizzical look.

'OK, OK, I suppose you're right.' Did he suddenly look a little shifty? 'But tell me, Stephen, how are things with *la bella donna*?' That was a deft change of direction.

'Everything to play for. It could go either way. Bit like this market research. Care to make a prediction?'

'I told you, Stephen, it's up to you. But I'm sure you will defeat this man eventually. What do you call him? The bearded wonder?'

'I meant the market research.'

'Oh, that?' Yes, he definitely looked shifty. 'I never predict market research results. Anything can happen.'

'Can it now? Bit like Inter Milan, eh? Unpredictable.'

'Too cruel, Stephen,' Salvatore said, looking hurt.

*

The ashen figure of Colin Weekes, the director of Useful Numbers market research agency, arrived in reception just before ten, in an ill-fitting suit. He was keen to explain that he had worked through the night before driving up from Potters Bar this morning – and it looked like it.

Stephen ushered him hastily into the Winning meeting room where Salvatore was already waiting. Maybe there was just time for Colin to divulge the results to them while he was setting up, before the others arrived.

'OK, Colin, so quickly, tell me how it's looking?' he whispered, but the door burst open and Hardman marched in, with Oscar Newte and Carol Coolidge following. The American was scowling, not a good start, while Newte and Coolidge were heads down, suggesting they'd already had their first encouraging pep talk of the day. Newte took off his glasses to wipe them, revealing dark shadows under his eyes.

'Mr Hardman, can I introduce you to Colin Weekes from Useful Numbers, our long-standing market research partners?' Stephen said.

'Useful Numbers? They better be fucking useful. OK, Weak, you are gonna bring me some good news.' It was a command, not a question. He eyed the researcher maliciously, sat down at the opposite end of the table, and folded his arms in an expectant pose. Stephen hadn't seen him much recently and thought he had definitely put on a few pounds. In fact, he had a look of Henry VIII this morning, with his fawning courtier Sir Oscar Newte on one side and Lady Carol Coolidge on the other, both looking ready for the tower.

Colin Weekes tittered nervously. 'Well, the results are interesting, Mr Hardman.'

'OK, let's go. I got thirty minutes.'

Weekes launched into a long explanation of how they had selected the guinea pigs in both the UK and Italy to test the products. The chart on the screen behind him contained far more numbers than was good for it. Stephen was kicking himself. He should have warned him – if you didn't go straight for the jugular with Brad, you were dead meat.

'OK, you did your goddam job. Just give me the results,' Hardman said, already coming nicely to the boil.

Stephen intervened. 'I suggest, Colin, given Mr Hardman is pushed for time, that you move straight to showing how our respondents compared Schmaltzy Bars with Bingo and Nutters with Munchy Moments?'

'Yes, of course,' Weekes squeaked. Like every other poor soul that Stephen had seen present to Hardman in the last six months, he was a rabbit in the headlights. A state he avoided for a short while by turning his back on his audience while he scuttled through a series of slides in search of something a little less dense. Finally he settled on one, turned towards them again, and was just about to speak when a phone rang.

Hardman's eyes flicked round the room in search of the culprit.

'Ah, sorry, Brad,' Newte said, red-faced. 'I think I'd better take this.'

Hardman's face would have made it apparent to anyone with half a brain that this was not a decision he entirely agreed with. But Newte shuffled furtively to the back of the room, talking to his caller in hushed tones.

All other eyes turned back to Weekes's chosen chart.

'OK, I, er, think if we compare Bingo Bars with Schmaltzy Bars this is the crux of the matter,' he mumbled.

Even on this summary slide there were still too many figures, with the results of the Bingo versus Schmaltzy Bars test analysed by every possible group – men, women, young, old, Brits, Italians – you name it, Weekes had covered it. But Stephen, accustomed to his little presentation peccadillos, had grasped it in a moment. Whichever way you looked at it, the guinea pig jury had delivered their verdict.

'Fuck off.' Hardman's eyes had swept across the sea of data too and reached their own pithy conclusion.

Bingo Bars had given Schmaltzy Bars the mother of all shellackings.

Weekes cleared his throat nervously. 'So, as you can see, the results are fascinating in that—'

'Fascinating, huh. You call these fucking fascinating, do you?' Hardman raised his voice, eyes still firmly on the screen. 'Do you think they're fascinating, Nudey?'

Oscar Newte had finished his call, but was peering owlishly through his red-framed glasses at the screen and had clearly not caught up yet.

'I said, do you think they're fucking fascinating, Nudey?' Hardman shouted this time, but still focused on the screen, not Newte.

'Sorry, Brad, I'm just struggling to—'

'What the hell were you doing there, Nudey? Confirming your fucking Pinot noir order?' Newte had now turned the colour of a Pinot noir, maybe even a Bordeaux. And his mouth dropped open as he finally seemed to clock what he was being shown.

'Brad, I just find these results unacceptable,' he blustered and turned on the presenter. 'Are you seriously expecting us to believe that Bingo has beaten the world's most successful chocolate bar? *C'est incroyable.*' He shook his head, uncomprehendingly.

Stephen felt a surge of pleasure. He had always told Newte that Bingo was a cracking product, if only he had been given the money to support it.

Newte was still indignant. 'In fact, are you sure you've got these results the right way round? I remember a market research presentation once where they'd got the bloody products mixed up. Can't remember if it was your agency,' he sneered.

Weekes may have appeared on the edge of collapse in front of Hardman, but there was clearly something about Oscar Newte that stiffened his backbone.

'Yes, I am absolutely sure we've got the products the right way round, and the next chart will confirm it.' He stared at Newte. 'It shows *why* people didn't like Schmaltzy Bars. They are far too sweet for most people. They couldn't have claimed Bingo is sweeter, because it contains half as much sugar.'

'Well, it seems very odd to me,' Newte harrumphed. 'I think we need to—'

'OK, leave it, Nudey,' Hardman barked, arms still folded. 'What about Nutters?'

'Ah, yes,' Weekes said hesitantly, as if reluctant to convey more bad news. You couldn't blame him. On his next comparison, this time between Munchy Moments and Nutters, the news for Team USA went from bad to calamitous. Ninety-five percent of people preferred Munchy. Not so much a victory, more a walkover. As Weekes laboriously waded through extraneous detail, Newte was frowning at the screen like a man again struggling to make sense of it all. But Hardman, suddenly and unexpectedly, burst out laughing, shaking his head. It was more disarming than his usual anger.

'Fuck me, can we have the names and addresses of the people who prefer Nutters? There are so few of 'em, we could give 'em a lifetime supply. Cos fuck knows what we're gonna do with the rest of it.'

Carol, who hadn't said a word, gave a nervous, sycophantic laugh. Judging from Hardman's glare, he wasn't fishing for appreciation of his jokes.

Still Newte was shaking his head, coming back for more. 'I don't get this, Brad, really I don't. Are these guys telling us that only five percent, that's one in twenty, liked Nutters more?'

'That's what it says on the chart, Oscar,' Stephen said emphatically. Turning back to Weekes, he asked, 'Can you tell us why there was such a strong preference for Munchy?'

'Yes, of course. Well, once again, as with Schmaltzy Bars, a lot of people thought Nutters tasted too sweet, but there were also a lot of comments about it being, how can I say this, rather dull – just containing a nut, whereas Munchy contains a raisin and, er, a different type of nut.'

Stephen looked at Carol, pale and sullen. So it wasn't quite as simple as just replacing one nut with another after all.

Weekes continued. 'And, er, we should report one other thing, mentioned by quite a lot of people but only in Italy, strangely enough.'

'And what is that?' Salvatore had kept his head down so far but seized upon this.

'Erm, to put it delicately, it seems that some of the press reports might be right. Is it possible that Nutters could, er, create a lot of gas?' enquired Weekes tentatively.

'Fuck me. You couldn't make it up.' Hardman laughed even louder.

'Just to clarify, you're saying this problem of gas only occurred in Italy?' Stephen asked.

'Yes, no mentions at all in the UK,' Weekes confirmed.

'Hey, get that, Carnival. You Italians seem to trump a lot more than the Brits. What's that about?' Hardman was reaching a state of high-pitched hysteria.

Salvatore shrugged. 'I don't know, maybe there is an interaction with our healthy diet.'

Stephen tried to share a secret smile just with Salvatore, but the Italian's face was impassive. You couldn't make it up, Hardman had said. But you had to wonder.

As Weekes found yet more data to show exactly the same thing, Hardman sprang to his feet. 'OK, fella, enough. I don't need to see the results cross-analysed by their fucking leg measurement to know we're in deep shit here.'

Newte interjected. 'Brad, I still think—'

'Nudey, you know what? I don't give a flying fuck what you think. You in particular are knee-high in the shit, goddamn it. And I suggest you stop fucking digging.' At the door, he turned back towards them. 'There's one fucking thing you do need to do, Nudey, if it's not too much trouble,' he said, his voice thick with sarcasm. 'You need to get your ass over to Hamburg and make sure we don't waste any more money with that Wammer guy working out how to ship those fucking products to the UK. Because that ain't going to happen any time soon.' And with that he stomped out, leaving the room in silence.

'Anyone care to see any more detail?' Weekes asked, with a relieved smile on his face.

'No, Colin, I think we're done.' Stephen winked at him.

Newte walked out, still shaking his head and muttering. Then Carol picked up her phone, gave Stephen the frostiest of stares and followed him. Stephen saw a perspiring Colin Weekes off the premises with a pat on his clammy back and returned to the Hive, where Salvatore greeted him, beaming triumphantly.

'So, my friend, that's it. The end of the American invasion.'

'You reckon?' Stephen still felt numb, unable to fully take it in, especially the magnitude of the victory. His instinctive reaction had been delight, his convictions about the products vindicated. But the farting Italians had the distinct whiff of foul play. And how would Hardman react?

'Of course it's the end. They'll never recover from this. They can't possibly launch two products that the consumers hate, and one of them causes *flatulenza*,' Salvatore chortled. 'You heard what Hardman said to that idiot Newte at the end. Congratulations, my friend. If you hadn't persuaded them to test, just think what might have happened. Now... time for coffee? Surely there must be a decent coffee somewhere in Middleton – I don't mean that nasty snack bar you sent me to last time.'

'No, let's celebrate properly at Pietro's next time we're staying at the Splendid,' Stephen said pensively. 'Assuming we ever get summoned to Paris again. Now, there's a certain canny Scot I should definitely call before I do anything else. And I have a feeling I might need to pick up the pieces with our favourite ice-woman.' He looked Salvatore straight in the eye. 'But just before I do that, Salvatore, how did you do it?'

'How did I do what?' Salvatore looked perplexed.

'What did your lot in Genoa put into the Nutters to make your fellow countrymen and women fart?'

'I have no idea what you are talking about.'

'And why didn't you put it in the Nutters you sent over for the test here as well? Was there some strange sense of fair play going on? Happy to nobble the jury on your own patch but not in mine?'

'Nobble? What is nobble?'

'Actually, I tell you what, Salvatore. Just at the moment, I'd rather not know. I'll wheedle it out of you over a bottle of Barolo or two at Pietro's.'

'I still don't know what you are saying. What is wheedle?'

'Carreras!' Hardman shouted across the Hive, as Salvatore suddenly became fascinated by his phone. The moment of triumph had indeed been fleeting. *Better make sure America wins*, the boss had said. So was he now about to shoot the messenger for bringing him the wrong result? He would be the sacrificial lamb, saving the Scottish factory but losing his own job as a result.

Hardman was on his laptop as Stephen entered his office, and kept him waiting as usual.

'So, Carreras,' he said eventually, 'you got the result you fucking wanted.'

'Not at all, Mr Hardman. I would have loved the new brands to win,' he lied.

Hardman fixed him with a hard stare, then issued his trademark snorting of phlegm – always a precursor to a pronouncement of some sort.

'Look, Carreras, there's something about Nutters making the Italians fart that stinks. I got my suspicions on Carnival.'

Best to remain silent at this point.

'But this fucking sweetness data…' He hesitated, and then gave Stephen a look he had never seen from Hardman before. The look of a man taking him into his confidence. 'I gotta tell you, Carreras, those pesky women at LISA are clogging up my darned Twitter feed with their anti-sugar crap.' He ran his hands over his head and sighed. 'So looks like you're gonna be spending a lot of time in Scotland over the next six months, making sure those bastards up there are churning out crateloads of Bingo Bars and the rest of 'em. And make sure you keep that fucking market share up.'

Stephen walked slowly back to his perch in the Hive, grinning and shaking his head at the same time. Because of course what Brad Hardman had been trying to say, in his own sweet way, was 'Your job's safe for now – and so is Dumfries'. Salvatore, not surprisingly, appeared to have slipped away.

When he switched his phone back on, there was a text waiting from Rachel.

Thinking of you. How did it go? The little emoji had a furrowed brow.

Do good among the carnage, that's what she had challenged him to do, back in the depths of January. He had truly done so now.

Grimley's 2, Schmaltz 0. Celebration dinner, sometime soon? x

He called Jim Jeffries.

'Jim, I have some news that I think will make you a very happy bunny. We got the test results.'

Jim sounded as if he was in a wind tunnel.

'Oh, aye, laddie. Sorry, it's not a very clear line. Archie and I are at Turnberry, just about to tee off. It's blowing a gale up here this morning – going to be a fair test of golf.'

So while the fate of one hundred and fifty men and women in the Dumfries factory hung in the balance, their esteemed leader was exercising his four-wood.

'Do you *want* to know the results, Jim?' Stephen hoped he sounded irritated.

'I see from the papers we thrashed the bastards.'

'The papers?'

'Aye, we made it onto page three of the *Daily Record*.'

'Already? That's certainly an interesting development, Jim, and I can't quite understand that, but we did indeed thrash the bastards. Bingo wiped the floor with Schmaltzy Bars and Munchy annihilated Nutters. So the factory is safe – at least for the moment.'

'Aye, of course. I hope Madame Sin was there to see it?'

'Indeed, Jim. She was.'

'That's good news. Well done, laddie. Although to be honest, Archie and I were never in any doubt. Archie, I've got Steve on the phone…' His voice became muffled for a moment. Then he was back.

'Archie sends his compliments to Mr Hardman, Steve,' he cackled. 'We both agree, it couldn't have happened to a nicer guy. And he sends a big kiss for you.'

That seemed very unlikely – and wasn't an image he wanted to linger over.

'I'd better be going, laddie. Need a couple of practice swings to get the wheels oiled these days, you know?' His smoke-filled laugh rattled down the phone. 'But keep in touch, there. And you definitely need to come up here for a game soon.'

Stephen walked over to Eat Schmaltz and took a celebratory quinoa smoothie (this week's special) back to his podium. 'Ah well, job done,' he said to nobody in particular.

Never in any doubt, was it, Jim? It was hard not to be exasperated with the old rogue. Did he genuinely have no idea how close the Exocet had come to landing in his back garden? Hopefully there would be a few men and women up there who would sleep more easily in their beds tonight – or maybe they too didn't realise what had been averted. At least John Motson recognised the achievement.

'This is incredible! The boy Carreras has done it here, saving the Scottish factory from the grasp of Brad Hardman. They'll surely be singing his name in the bars of Dumfries tonight.'

Actually, today he sounded more like that old Scottish rugby commentator.

It felt weird. A bit like he remembered feeling after finishing A levels. You worked your socks off, building up for the big push, and suddenly it was all over and you were left with a curiously empty feeling. Just for a moment, Stephen wondered if he too had bought the hype. There had been something quite intoxicating about the vision of Schmaltzy Bars and Nutters marching across Europe, sweeping all before them. Nothing for it now but to keep nudging Bingo and Munchy Moments along the road, even Little Monkeys too. And he would have to get his mind around promotions plans for next Christmas after all, now that they would have a Christmas. But first he'd check out the Scottish papers.

He clicked on the *Daily Record* website.

What a Chocker!
US sweet invaders blown away

The future of old favourites Bingo Bars and Munchy Moments at the Grimley's factory in Dumfries is safe after Britain's chocoholics gave the thumbs down to replacing them with American imports. Consumer tests showed the local heroes are clearly preferred to the 'windy duo' of Schmaltzy Bars and Nutters, which the company's new owners Schmaltz had planned to introduce. The research confirmed earlier lab evidence that the American invaders cause flatulence, and they were firmly rejected in favour of the local brands which have been made at Dumfries for over a century.

How on earth had the papers got hold of this? The research agency had only finished working on the results this morning. There must be a mole somewhere – and a bloody fast-tunnelling one at that.

Stephen could hear Salvatore chatting up one of his female admirers – he was still in the building after all. He never missed an opportunity to bring a little Italian style into their humdrum lives. From across the floor he gave Stephen the thumbs up, put an imaginary phone to his ear to indicate they should talk, and then he was out of the building.

Stephen idly clicked on Google Translate – what was the Italian for 'mole'? But then he smiled to himself again over the crushing defeat he had just inflicted on Nutters in particular, and the look on Newte's face. What was the Italian for 'let sleeping dogs lie'? Salvatore would like that one.

Chapter Twenty-Eight

A glance around the bar confirmed, to his relief, that she hadn't arrived yet. It was right that he should get here first. He ordered a gin and tonic and chose a seat in the corner, at a table for two.

A bunch of raucous young office workers next to him were finding it necessary to celebrate the end of the week by laughing and shouting at each other, as if they were spread round the whole pub rather than crammed round one table. But, as he had hoped, there was nobody here from Schmaltz. He didn't bother with the depleted Friday evening drinking contingent these days. Since Danny had left, the community whingeing had lost its appeal – and most of its members. But he had double-checked that the few who upheld the tradition didn't frequent the Old Ship. In other respects, maybe it wasn't the best choice. Echoes of that drunken Christmas party, and also the place he had ended up when Laura threw him out. He'd forgotten just how down at heel it was now. Maybe he should have chosen somewhere more elegant – the lounge bar of the Hamilton Hotel perhaps, in the old marketplace. As he'd told Salvatore, that was hardly the Ritz but a bit classier than this. And if she was going to throw a drink over him, there would have been fewer to witness it in the Hamilton.

Quarter to six. With a bit of luck she wouldn't turn up. He should never have suggested this. After all, she had been pretty resistant last week when he had dropped off the kids and said he wanted to meet to discuss something with her. She had finally agreed, only on the understanding that it wouldn't take more than half an hour.

And then immediately after they had arranged it – sod's law. Rachel ringing to say she was free for the first Friday night in living memory. Could she cook him supper? Almost three weeks since he'd confessed all, over the feet washing, and still he didn't know which way she was going to turn. But he did know she was involved in some music group event organised by Conrad for most of this weekend – so tonight was the only opportunity to see her alone. In the event, it was just as well this first part of the evening wasn't going to take long. He could still get to Rachel's.

He had downed the G&T already. He'd give Laura another five minutes.

She came in, eyes searching around anxiously. Perfectly turned out as usual, in a navy-blue trouser suit, with her hair tied in a bun. Yes, the Hamilton's lounge would have been better.

He stood up and waved, and she came over, her face now devoid of emotion.

'Hi, how are you? Thanks for coming. How's it going now you're back full time?' He jabbered out the questions.

'The traffic was awful. I've got to be back home by six thirty. I don't understand why we couldn't just talk on the phone.'

'What I wanted to say wasn't really suitable material for a phone call, Laura.' He had raised his voice already. He must remember his plan. As soon as he was going to lose it, just visualise the rest of the evening, with Rachel. This would soon be over.

She didn't want a drink, but he persuaded her to have a still mineral water. He eyed his empty glass. Better make it two mineral waters.

When he returned from the bar, she had at least sat down, but was already checking her phone.

'I'm expecting a call from Tristran,' she said, placing it on the table between them. 'What did you want to talk about?' She laid her hands on her lap, her eyes once again flicking nervously around the pub. He felt a darting stab of pain. How different it had all been. But if she wanted to conduct this as a business meeting, he would cut the preamble.

'Laura, I've been doing a lot of thinking recently about the past, and, well, it's quite simple really. I wanted to say how sorry I am – for everything.'

A woman at the next table laughed loudly and shouted, 'I don't believe it!' to the cheery man next to her.

'What do you mean?' Only now did she look at him directly.

He could see it was a bit weird, just spitting it out after all this time.

'For what happened. For my... infidelity.' He'd never used the word before.

She took a sip of her drink, still avoiding eye contact.

'I was a stupid fool, Laura. You know I regretted that – those moments of weakness with – that woman, and I'll regret what it did to us for the rest of my life.'

'I don't want to do this.'

'I mean, work was tough, for both of us, and maybe we weren't getting on so well, but... I just wanted to say, that's no excuse. I shouldn't have done it. I was completely to blame. And I should have tried harder to save our marriage after it happened.' In truth, he didn't think she'd given him a look-in, but he was trying to be conciliatory.

Maybe it was just as well the crew at the next table were loud – imagine doing this in a hushed cocktail bar.

'What do you want?' she asked, suddenly. God, did she honestly think he was trying to strike a bargain here?

'I don't want anything. Actually, that's not true. I suppose I'd like your forgiveness, or maybe at least a truce, so we can get on with the rest of our lives without antagonising each other every time we meet.'

'In case you hadn't noticed, I have got on with the rest of my life.'

'Yes, you have, I agree. Maybe much better than I have. Well, I'm sorry anyway. I'm sorry for the pain I caused you, and I'm sorry, of course, for the pain I caused the kids. And I'm happy for you that you're happy again now, with Tristran.' The last bit was probably a lie.

'Well, good,' she said. There was an uneasy silence. She stood up. 'Look, I need to go. We're due out at seven.'

'Of course. Thank you for coming.' He stood up too, sensing a woman at the next table looking at them. The two glasses of water on the table were barely touched.

'I'll walk out with you,' Stephen offered.

'There's no need.'

'No, I know there isn't, but I'd like to.'

They stood opposite each other in the car park, Laura with her arms folded, looking away. Uncomfortable encounters with women in pub car parks were becoming his party piece.

'You hurt me so much,' she said quietly. Suddenly he thought she was going to cry.

'I know. I'm truly sorry.' He risked a gentle hand on her arm.

She took a handkerchief from her shoulder bag and wiped her eye.

'Have a good weekend,' he said, feigning cheerfulness but not knowing where else to go. 'And say hello to the kids for me. I'm going to miss seeing Jake every Saturday morning, now the football season's ended. Planning anything nice with them?' Even amid his contrition, he knew he was being passive aggressive – he was sure she was more interested in gadding about with good time Charlie than with the kids.

Laura raised her eyes heavenward. 'I don't know. I need to do something, to stop Kate moping about the house.' She looked more concerned now. 'You do realise she's still in a state, don't you?'

'She's been a bit mopey, as you say, for weeks now,' he agreed. 'But not all the time.' That Saturday eating pizza and then chocolate tasting with Rachel – Kate had seemed to be truly having fun then.

'If it's not all the time, she must be happier with you than she is with us.'

He felt a guilty pleasure at this thought, even if he wasn't totally convinced it was true.

'What do you think's the problem?' he asked.

'I think the worst thing is she's short of friends. They're so cliquey, those girls. Megan is going out with this boy who I think Kate liked a lot, so she and Megan have broken off diplomatic relations, and all the rest of her gang have sided with Megan. They seem to have formed a WhatsApp group without inviting her.'

'Oh, I hadn't realised.' He felt a moment of guilt that he'd not delved into Kate's moodiness enough, and awaited Laura's barb. But it didn't come.

'It's all made her feel terribly self-conscious. What's Megan got that I haven't, all that sort of thing. Now she wants a tattoo – thinks it would make her more edgy.'

'Oh God, no.'

'Exactly. You need to back me up on that. And then on top, she's feeling the pressure at school. Her form teacher said she hasn't progressed so well since Christmas and now Kate's obsessed that she's not bright enough – that she won't get good results in her GCSEs. And they're still a year away.'

'It's crazy, isn't it?' he said, very conscious that he hadn't made it to the last parents' evening. 'Remember all those parents' evenings when she was in the juniors? What her headmistress used to say about her? *She's bright as a button, that girl.*'

Laura managed a thin smile, as if recalling those happier days. 'I know that. And you know that. Just at the moment our darling daughter seems to have lost sight of it.' She looked at him. 'I guess we just need to be aware of it and think about what we can do.'

The 'we' word. It was the first time for an age he could remember Laura suggesting they were still a team when it came to parenting.

'It is good to talk about these things,' she said, looking him fully in the eye for once.

'I know. Thanks for telling me.'

He moved to hug her, and she didn't flinch. He felt her soften slightly, although without hugging him back. He couldn't remember when he had last touched her like that.

Now she seemed hesitant about leaving, as if she was considering saying more. But then she sighed. 'I need to go.' She rummaged in her bag for her car keys and from a distance flicked the alarm on a shiny white convertible that he'd never seen before.

*

Stephen drove home, changed, grabbed a bottle of white wine from his fridge that he knew Rachel wouldn't share with him and drove on to her place, still mulling over the brief encounter with Laura. What were they achieving, these acts of penitence which had started coming over him? First, he'd told Rachel he felt clean after telling her about Carol – and he did. But if he'd thought that with one afternoon of confession he had completely won her over, he had clearly been wrong. She was still deliberating. And he couldn't say he immediately felt much better after saying sorry to Laura. It seemed like this repentance thing didn't have any big payback. If anything he felt worse, thinking about his sweet innocent Kate, weighed down by the fickleness of friends and worries about her future.

The instant Rachel opened her door, he knew that something wasn't right. Her greeting was half-hearted, without her usual cheerful smile, and as he followed her up the stairs and into her kitchen, she didn't say anything more. He found himself talking about the traffic on the ring road. He'd never discussed the ring road with Rachel before. And she appeared to be focusing extra hard on frying the vegetables.

'I think we might need a window open,' he said, trying to lighten the mood. 'You're steaming up in here.'

'You're a bit earlier than I expected,' she said, still stirring. 'Nothing's ready yet.' As if it mattered.

Suddenly it hit him. Of course. He was an idiot. She was cooking him dinner to tell him she was heading to Malawi.

He started burbling, wanting to prevent her saying the words. 'This is so great,' he said encouragingly. 'How was your day? I don't suppose the trustees have come up with a rescue plan?'

'No, that's not going to happen. How about you? Not such a long day as normal, by the look of it.' This wasn't the understanding 'tell me all' tone that he'd come to expect from Rachel.

'No, I suppose not. I left the office a bit early. Actually, Rachel, I've been to see Laura.' He didn't quite know why he had to tell her this, as if reporting his latest bout of penitence would make any difference to her decision. But she had become the one now – the woman with whom he wanted to share everything. No secrets.

'Oh, really?' She was looking at the hob again, not at him. Maybe he shouldn't have told her. Maybe there was only so much confession the poor woman could take. But he couldn't stop.

'Yes, I arranged to see her in the Ship after work, just for half an hour.'

'Ah, I see,' she said, putting the pasta on to simmer.

'I'm not sure you do yet. I seem to have turned into Mr Fess-Up. I'll blame your vicar and that radio bishop. I saw her to apologise for being unfaithful, after all these years.'

'Oh, right,' she said. 'How was it?' She had turned to face him, hands thrust tightly into the pockets of her jeans.

He puffed out his cheeks. 'I'm not sure, to be honest. I suppose I hoped it would feel more, what's the word, cathartic? But I've been realising that forgiveness is a tricky thing, isn't it? If I'm honest, maybe I hadn't forgiven her. For not giving me another chance.'

'And will she give you one now?'

'What?'

'Another chance.'

This was unravelling at speed. He moved towards her and held her tightly, but her hands were still in her pockets, her body rigid in his embrace.

'Rachel, Rachel, Rachel, don't be crazy. I meant not giving me another chance at the time. Not now. I don't want another chance now. I just want you. Even though I know what you're going to tell me.'

'It's just that I saw you.'

'What?'

'I got home from work early for once, so I decided to do a training run. My route goes past the pub. And I saw you in the car park, hugging.'

'Rachel, tell me you didn't really think we were getting back together?'

'Well, I don't know.' Her wriggle indicated she wanted to be set free, and he let go. She turned away from him to switch off the hob and then stood with her back to the fridge door, concentrating hard on the floor. 'There *is* something I need to tell you.'

'Go on. It's OK, I'm sure.' He tried to sound reassuring. But this would be the announcement.

'It's just that, I've been holding back a bit with you.'

'Oh.' He heard the surprise in his own voice. It wasn't a surprise. Just not what he was expecting her to say right now.

'And it's been partly because you're a married man, or rather a previously married man.'

'OK, I get that. I mean it's not straightforward, with the children—'

'No, it's not that. I like your children. But when it comes to relationships with married men, I've, well, I've got previous, Stephen.'

'Oh,' he said again. This definitely wasn't what he was expecting. 'What does that mean exactly?'

'It means I had an affair with a married man.' She looked up at him for a moment, then lowered her eyes again.

So she wasn't entirely chaste after all. Why was relief his first sensation? Probably not one he should share right now.

'Oh. So, who was he?'

'Does it matter?'

'Er, no, I suppose not. I'm sure I'll come up with something more intelligent in a minute. It's something of a shock. When was this?

'About six years ago.' Her head remained bowed. 'You see, Stephen, I worry sometimes that you think I'm a very moral person. But I'm not. Or at least I wasn't. I know what you think. Bishop's daughter, all very straightforward. And I suppose it was, for about twenty-five years.' She snorted at a recollection.

341

'Even when I went off to university, I was more likely to spend Saturday nights in the Christian Union than in the bar.'

'So, what changed?'

'I became a charity worker.' She gave a sad little laugh.

'Ah, yes, the dark side.' He was still trying to make light of it.

'I've never told you this but after I left university, I dabbled with a couple of charity jobs, but I was drifting really, and my father encouraged me to apply for this really junior training position with a law firm in London. He used to joke it was a respectable profession, not like the church. It wasn't a graduate level job – basically I was the office assistant. Anyway, I was bored stiff there and I started doing some more volunteer charity work in the evenings, something that felt a bit more me, I suppose. Helping in a shelter for the homeless.'

'This doesn't sound exactly immoral. In fact, your morality index has just ratcheted up a level,' he said with an encouraging smile. But Rachel wasn't smiling.

'And that's where I met this guy.' She paused. 'Everyone there drank a lot.'

'I'm not surprised. Anything to numb the pain of being on the streets, I suppose.'

'No, I mean the volunteer team, not the clients. Then one night, we were all at some party together, and he was there. He was a trustee, one of the management team, so I'd never met him on my normal shifts. I'd had a few drinks and we got chatting. No mention of Debbie Harry as far as I recall. And then he said, it's obvious we're attracted to one another, so why don't we just do it now to get it out of the way?'

'How romantic.' He was shocked but didn't want to show it. And a small wave of irritation rose up as well. He'd been respecting their distance, not even pushed to have sex. Whereas this bloke had gone for it on the first night. 'Did you turn him down?' he asked hopefully, and then saw the look on her face. 'OK, you didn't turn him down.'

'And then it became a pattern,' she said. 'After work on a Friday, round about this time.'

'Hold on, slow down. Did you love this guy? What was he like?'

'I suppose he was quite charismatic. He was ten years older than me. I seem to be drawn to – er – more mature men.'

He wanted to remind her he was only eight years older, but it was probably nit-picking.

'And he knew the charity world,' she went on, 'so I think I was a bit in awe of him. He's probably Head of Social Services in some trendy London borough by now,' she said dismissively, shaking her head.

'So what happened then?'

'Well, this was the first time I'd had sex. I was so naive, I thought it was a big deal, the start of something. But after about six weeks I cottoned on that he never seemed to be around after Friday at weekends. I'd ask if we could do things, and there was always an excuse, even though he'd told me he was no longer with his wife. Then one night, when he was in the bathroom, his phone rang. I answered it, don't know why. Next thing she was asking me who I was and where was her husband.'

'Ah.'

'Ah indeed. Turned out I was his weekly bit on the side, while he had a wife and two kids back at home. When I confronted him, he said he was going to get divorced, that his marriage was dead, that he would work out a way to be with me, but it was complicated and would take time.' She laughed cynically, in a way that he'd not seen before.

'And was that it? The end?'

Rachel's shoulders slumped a little further. 'No, that's the thing. It wasn't. I suppose up to that point I hadn't done anything too awful. I hadn't known he was still married. But it didn't stop.'

'You kept seeing him?' He knew his face was expressing shock.

'Yep, Friday nights, the odd snatched hour over a weekend – the schemes and the fabrications became ever more intricate. Now, of course, I rationalised that he was going to leave his wife, so that was OK too. Even though I don't think I ever really believed he would. It's fair to say I had lost my moral compass. In fact, not so much lost it as chucked the thing overboard. I was completely screwed up. I was doing cold turkey on Christianity, and the reverse on vodka, just to get through it all. And then to try and get over it.'

She paused and looked up at him, as if awaiting his reaction.

'It's OK, Rachel. You can tell me.'

'Then after about another three months of sex and nothing much else, he told me he had decided he was going to stay with his wife. He wanted to leave her, but he couldn't, for the children. And that was it. So I didn't even break up with him. He broke up with me. He even won that particular victory.'

She looked crestfallen. And in that moment, Stephen recognised in himself something that felt overwhelmingly significant. He wanted with all his heart to comfort her, not to condemn her. But he knew too that he just had to see this conversation through, to hear everything, just as she had when he told her about his affair.

'What did you do then?'

'I left London straight after, packed in the law job. I moved back to Middleton, with my tail between my legs. My mum, who really is a saint by the way, fussed over me, but all I could feel at the time was my old man's disappointment. He pretended to be very forgiving, but I could tell he was ashamed. Was never sure whether it was abandoning the law career or the sex with a married man that bothered him most. I'm not sure our relationship has fully recovered even now, but we're working on it.'

'And this man, you've never seen him since?'

She bit her lip, her eyes seemingly lost in recall.

'I bumped into him once, about a year later, at a conference. I tried to avoid him but he came across the room to say hello. He told me they'd had another baby.' He had never heard her sound so bitter.

Finally, she looked at him again. 'So there you go. I thought I'd moved on, but falling for another married man – that's you, by the way – even one who told me he was divorced, brought it all back. And then when you made that amazing confession to me, I was awestruck. I've been struggling since then about how I could open up to you in return. But I also got it into my head that maybe your regret meant you really just wanted things to be back like they were, with Laura.'

'And then you saw me hugging her.'

'And then I saw you hugging her. It's all been to do with me, when you were just trying to do a good thing.'

They both fell silent. But it was an OK silence. Like the end of a storm.

'So, anyone for pasta, or are you off to watch some football on TV?' she said eventually.

'Is that everything?' he asked.

'You want more? I think that's it.' She paused. 'No, there is one more thing I need to explain. You see, the other problem for you, I suppose, apart from my past, is that I've now gone back to being good. Not as good as I'd like to be, but I am trying, and I'm happier this way. I haven't trusted myself to start drinking again and maybe never will. Drinking has somehow just become associated with all the crap things in life. I don't know how you feel about being with someone for whom trying to be good has become almost an obsession.'

One small tear trickled slowly down her cheek. He gently brushed it away.

'You know that day at football, when you told me that most of the time you were fumbling around in the dark?'

'Ah yes, the morning of your linesman triumph.' She managed a watery smile.

'Yes, that's the one. I've thought about this a lot, Rachel. If you're fumbling in the dark, I don't think I can seriously pretend to be a bright shining light to show you the way. I suspect there's another man who'd like to do that. And as you might have discovered by now, I've been pretty much in a state of blackout myself. But I'd like to, I don't know, maybe hold a candle for you, at least light up the ground right in front of you. I'm not sure I know yet how to find complete forgiveness when a marriage goes wrong. But I do know I'm over it. And I know there's absolutely nothing in your past that will make me love you any less. And for what it's worth, I'm trying bloody hard to be good too.'

She held his face gently and kissed him. She tasted of red summer berries.

'A bright light can be a bit dazzling sometimes,' she said, and he enfolded her. She looked searchingly into his eyes. 'There is one other question I have for you, before I return to the pasta.'

'OK, try me.'

'When exactly are you planning to invite me to La Belle Époque again?' She had a look of mock desperation.

Delicately he brushed a single strand of hair behind her ear.

'I don't know. When can you fit me into your schedule?'

'Oh, pretty much any time. Well, no, of course we both know that's not true. But there's no hurry. I'm not going anywhere.'

That night, he stayed with her for the first time. She folded into him, and he kissed her neck, warm and salty on his lips. Within minutes, he felt the gentle rise and fall of her back against his chest as she drifted into sleep. When she woke in the morning, she slipped out of bed, drew back the curtains, and the light flooded in. She had a small dark brown birthmark, just above her hip, that he had not seen before.

Chapter Twenty-Nine

'*Salaud!*' shouted the bald taxi driver, sweating profusely. The driver in front, having just cut him up so precisely, stuck a hand out of his window and offered a jaunty one-fingered salute in reply.

Ah, the joy of this journey back from the centre of Paris towards Charles de Gaulle on a Friday afternoon. Always the same crawl from the office, around the Périphérique and then nose to tail for about ten kilometres along the autoroute. And this driver, true to type, had perfected the art of waiting for the car in front to ease a hundred metres ahead, and then ramming his accelerator down to close the gap.

To take his mind off this nausea-inducing manoeuvre, Stephen tried to work out how many times he'd made this trip. He must have averaged three times a month since the start of the year. So well over twenty by now. Still, judging from this morning's meeting, there might not be too many more of them. Carol had been a picture of *ennui* as he walked her through the Bingo and Munchy Moments Christmas plans, although admittedly it always seemed a bit surreal to be discussing the contents of an Advent calendar on a hot day in August. It felt like the whole concept of Schmaltz Europe was fragmenting with every passing week, and now that the launch of Schmaltzy and Nutters was definitely off the agenda in the UK and Italy, she was a woman without a cause. Then she had looked cross when he reported on the success of his viral marketing campaign for Little Monkeys, as if their continued existence represented her ultimate failure.

Finally, the taxi driver had broken loose from the stranglehold of the traffic and was hurtling the last few kilometres to the airport. He rested his phone against the steering wheel and keyed in a number with remarkable dexterity, while maintaining the same frightening speed. Soon he was shouting at whoever he was on the phone to.

For once Stephen wasn't in a hurry, with no plane to catch. It would be the final bloody irony, being killed in a hideous motorway carve-up today of all days. He felt a huge wave of relief when the driver deposited him outside the Hotel Splendid, grunting at the paucity of the tip.

Only now could he believe this weekend was really going to happen. The heat was searing and the sun reflected dazzlingly in the hotel's glass frontage. He should have gone with his instincts and booked somewhere romantic in town for the whole weekend. But she'd talked him into one night here, and then he'd splashed out on another hotel for the Saturday. He had told her so much about this place, she had explained, that now she wanted to see it for herself. 'I feel it's a part of us,' she said, before giving him a lingering kiss. His pulse quickened again, from anticipation not anxiety this time. Her text an hour ago had confirmed her arrival and that the Splendid was 'everything I was hoping for!'

Naturally, there was no queue in reception at five on a Friday evening. It wouldn't be high on Tripadvisor's list of weekend getaways. And naturally Solène was on reception. At least these days she acknowledged him with a little nod of the head, if not a smile. But yet again, she needed him to fill in his details.

'I should get loyalty points, Solène.'

'*Comment*? Ah, we don't do loyalty points.'

She consulted her screen, behind her hair as always.

'There is a woman in your room.'

'Ah, *oui, merci*.' For some reason he felt embarrassed as she raised her head and looked him in the eye for once, like a disapproving guesthouse proprietor from a bygone age. He half expected a speech about no hanky-panky and lights out before ten.

He knocked on the door of room 213, then realised it was left on the latch. A large, well-used red travel bag was lying unzipped on his bed. Rather than the smell of bleach which normally filled his nostrils, the room was infused with her vanilla scent. The wastepaper bin had become an ice bucket on the small bedside table, with a bottle of champagne and a bottle of fizzy water peeping over the edge, and two plastic champagne glasses next to it. The small table beneath the television was laid out with nuts and olives in assorted plastic bowls. And the desk had red roses strewn across it. A gloriously sassy black and white striped jacket and black leather trousers were hung on a coat hanger hooked over the door of the wardrobe. He heard the bathroom door unlock, and Rachel stepped out.

*

Could the commuters on the metro tell that they had made love? They stood in the centre of the carriage, holding onto the small springy straps suspended from the roof, bodies lurching together as the train rattled along, their mouths touching in a kiss from time to time. In England, the other passengers would have been studiously examining their own shoes, but not in Paris. There were plenty of eyes focused on them.

'*La Fayette*. I love the names of these metro stations. They sound so much more romantic than the London ones,' Rachel said as they stopped again, one group of staring Parisians replaced by a fresh batch.

'Oh, I dunno, what about North Acton? Can't get much more romantic than that.'

She laughed. 'Where are we getting off?'

'Next stop. *Opéra*.'

She gave him another kiss. 'This sort of stuff never happens to me,' she said loudly, oblivious to the gaze of an accordion player who had just got on and was swaying drunkenly by the door.

As they emerged from the bowels of the underground into a still warm evening, he nodded across the boulevard to a restaurant façade decorated lavishly with red geraniums.

'This is it,' he said, trying not to sound too pleased with himself.

'Oh, wow,' Rachel's face was a picture of excitement. 'Ah, and so clever, Mr Carreras.' She squeezed him tight.

'Well, I did promise you La Belle Époque. You didn't specify which one.'

The ambience was formal enough to make its Middleton namesake feel like Donny's Diner. High narrow windows tempered the natural light. Chandeliers dripping with crystals hung from a white ceiling braided with gold leaf. And the waiter had a slightly superior air as he slid out the velvety maroon chairs for them to sit at a table in the centre of the dining room.

As Stephen perused the wine list, Rachel leant across to hold his arm.

'This is fantastic, and can I just say I'm happy with *vin de maison*,' she whispered.

'Wow, you're drinking then?'

'Thought I might. Care to make something of it?' She was deadpan, until her eyes betrayed her pleasure at surprising him.

'You don't have to, you know.'

She looked amused. 'Thanks. I know I don't have to.'

He wanted to spoil her. They would drink Chablis – but maybe not the most eye-wateringly expensive one on the list.

Their waiter returned with menus, opening Rachel's for her ceremoniously like some holy text.

'I did check they have vegetarian dishes,' Stephen said, suddenly anxious that it might be slim pickings.

'I'm sure they do far more exotic things with their aubergines than I can manage,' Rachel smiled, casting an eye down the menu. He felt her foot stroking his leg reassuringly. 'It's amazing, Stephen, really.'

'I hope so,' he said, glancing around the room. 'Blimey, it's a serious business, this fine dining.' The tables were spaced well apart and all occupied, except for the one directly behind Rachel, but there was just muted conversation and no background music. The generally mature clientele were smartly dressed, and he suspected, mainly Parisians, not tourists – maybe those who for reasons of age or wealth didn't need to take their annual leave with the rest of the country. While the diners were mainly couples, he was struck by the man at the table next to them, wearing a stylish linen suit and dining on his own. They nodded to each other, and the man continued to work his way through a large platter of seafood which Stephen wouldn't have attempted for love nor money. It was, Stephen thought, very continental behaviour. An English businessman on his own would have ordered room service in his hotel or contented himself with a snack at the bar while reading a paperback.

They'd finished their starters, and Stephen was contemplating whether to help themselves to another glass or attract the attention of a passing waiter when he heard an unmistakable English voice.

'Is this *vraiment* the only table? Nothing by *la vitrine*?'

He knew without looking, but he glanced anyway. Oscar Newte. And he was here with Brad Hardman. What were the chances – in this place, at this moment, and about to sit at the one free table in the whole place? The American was standing hand in pocket fiddling with his crotch, while barking at someone on his phone. The waiter was making it very clear to Newte that this was indeed the only table and muttering what was probably French for 'like it or lump it'.

'Are you OK? What's the matter?' Rachel asked.

Stephen lowered his voice while Newte continued grumbling to the waiter. 'I can't believe it but Newte and Hardman have just come in.'

'Ooh, really?' She was clearly fascinated.

Hardman was pacing around, still attached to his mobile.

'Has the guy come about the pool?' He raised his voice even more and adjusted his crotch again. 'Hell, honey, I can't do much about that from goddam Paris. I'll call him next week. I gotta go.' There was an audible murmuring of disapproval from other diners. This was not the Parisian way. But at least Stephen knew now there was a wife after all, or at least a woman – and that Hardman treated her with as little respect as everyone else in his life.

As Hardman finally took his seat, Stephen detected a momentary cloud of disappointment now cast over Rachel's face, as if she suddenly feared her lovely evening slipping away because he was distracted. He needed to do something, rather than sit there uncomfortably for the rest of the meal, awaiting the inevitable moment when they noticed him. He stood up. 'I'll introduce you,' he announced and approached the other table.

'Good evening Oscar, Mr Hardman. What a coincidence! Good to see you. Can I introduce you both to Rachel Pearson?'

'Ah, Carreras, er, Steve, didn't see you there,' bumbled Newte, a little red-faced and clearly surprised. He sprang up, took Rachel's proffered hand, and instead of shaking it, placed his lips against it, to her evident amusement. But then he was civility personified, asking her how well she knew Paris, what tourist sites she wanted to visit. Jennie Jacobs had once told Stephen that the Newtes were one of the oldest and most aristocratic families in England, and that Oscar was the black sheep who had ended up in the tawdry world of commerce rather than the law. Now that breeding showed and Stephen, despite himself, felt grateful. Hardman, on the other hand, was a graceless fish out of water. Although he had also stood up, he seemed incapable of making small talk or even raising a smile, fists clenched tightly by his side, and he clearly wanted to sit down again as soon as possible.

Formalities done, Stephen was ready to retreat, but Rachel was in full flow now. How amazing it must be living in Paris. Wasn't it a lovely restaurant? Eventually Stephen intervened. 'Anyway, I'm sure you gentlemen have a lot to discuss. *Bon appetit.*' And taking her by the hand, he ushered her back to their table.

'Blimey, you played a blinder.' He clinked her glass.

'We're so lucky,' she said softly, giving him a wink. 'Imagine being here with one of those two on a Friday evening.'

They absorbed themselves back into the dinner, anticipating the days ahead. Rachel had not visited since childhood, and there was a lot of Paris she wanted to explore. Stephen didn't care what they did. The weekend stretched out before him, to be as busy or as leisurely as she wanted. Secretly he quite liked the idea of making love all weekend. There was a lot of Rachel Pearson he wanted to explore. Particularly once they escaped Solène and the Hotel Splendid.

After the main course, which Rachel pronounced to be basically an upmarket ratatouille but very tasty nevertheless, she went to powder her nose. Suddenly Stephen became aware of the verbal barrage underway as Hardman, completely immune to embarrassment as usual, turned up the volume.

'I'm not fucking happy with this, Nudey.'

'Of course, Brad, I'll get onto it over the weekend,' came the feeble response.

'I don't know what the fuck made you think I'd approve this.'

'No, Brad, I can see that.'

'So you need to work out a damn solution I can take to Chicago…'

'La carte aux desserts, monsieur?' Stephen's attention was distracted from their conversation as the waiter reappeared. And Rachel was returning. Those leather trousers really were quite something. But Hardman was still boiling over, his fury now turned in another direction.

'Hey, I told you, I just want another damn Coke,' he shouted, waving his empty glass accusingly at the waiter. There was a bottle of red wine on the table and Newte had a full glass. But Hardman didn't seem to be entering into the spirit of things. The waiter stalked off, muttering under his breath.

'What was that all about?' Rachel whispered.

'I'm not totally sure, but I think the restaurant is a bit insulted that Hardman doesn't want to drink something more refined than cola with his châteaubriand. Although I suspect Oscar might be drinking for two.'

Another loud 'fuck' shattered the low murmurs of conversation from around the other tables. Newte had stood up and managed to knock over the bottle of wine, soaking not just the white tablecloth but also, it became apparent as Hardman stood up, his master's lap.

Hardman turned puce. 'You fucking idiot, Nudey. Can't you get anything right?'

The room had gone deathly quiet. Fifty pairs of eyes were tuned into this manifestation of Anglo-Saxon vulgarity.

The waiter came over at a leisurely pace to hover over Hardman with a cloth in his hand and an amused expression on his face.

'Don't just stand there, you idiot. Give me the fucking cloth,' Hardman bawled.

'*Oui, monsieur, bien sûr.*'

As Hardman started dabbing at the large dark splodge on his inside leg, the waiter turned, winked at Stephen and Rachel, and raised his eyes heavenward, before returning to the kitchen, still unhurried.

Another man came over, one who was clearly in charge.

'Good evening, gentlemen. I am the manager of the restaurant. I think maybe you gentlemen would like to leave?' he said, in perfect English and loudly enough for the surrounding tables to hear.

'What?' Hardman glowered at him, still wiping at the stain with a napkin.

'I think it is best if you both leave, gentlemen.' He gave a slight bow.

'What the fuck. You throwing me out?' Hardman looked incredulous.

'I think it is for the best, *monsieur.*'

'OK, you can fuck right off. I'm outta here.' And indeed he was, tucking his phone into his jacket pocket and striding towards the exit.

A flustered Newte was left on his own, in front of the manager. 'I'm terribly sorry. If I could just have *l'addition, s'il vous plaît.*'

'No need, *monsieur.* We do not need your payment,' the manager said. 'My colleagues will attend to your coats,' he added, before turning on his heel and walking away. There was a smattering of applause from the other diners.

'Blimey, I'm expecting at least a verse of the *Marseillaise,*'

Stephen sniggered. But Rachel was looking at the lonely figure of Newte, tottering towards the cloakroom.

'That poor man. Do something, Stephen,' she implored him.

Why should he?

'Please, Stephen.'

He walked over to where Newte was being handed his briefcase by the waiter.

'Oscar, you look like a man who needs a cognac,' he said, although in truth Oscar looked like a man who really didn't. 'Will you join us?'

Newte focused on him, wide-eyed. 'That's jolly decent of you, sir.' He looked back towards Rachel. 'But I don't want to rain on your parade, old boy. I hope you have a good weekend. I'm sure you will.'

Stephen felt a wave of relief.

'Thank you, Oscar. What are you going to do?'

'Oh, I'll just go home – or at least back to my apartment.'

'I meant what are you going to do, well, in the future?'

'Oh, that? I expect I'll do as I'm told.' He was a broken man, the ultimate victim of Hardman's tyranny.

'Oscar, I know this isn't my business, and we haven't always been allies, but why don't you just leave? You'd walk into another job.'

Newte gave him a sad smile.

'Would that it were so simple, old man, would that it were so simple.' He shook Stephen by the hand and made for the door.

As Stephen returned to Rachel, capturing her appreciation that he had tried, he recalled his rival, arms raised in triumph, as he strutted onto stage at the Méridien back in January.

Part Four

———

Late November to December 2015

Chapter Thirty

He gently pushed open his bedroom door.

A short mop of hair was just visible over the top of the duvet, the sleeping form turned away from him. But as he trod softly over to place a mug of tea on the bedside table, the body stirred.

'What time is it?' She sat up and yawned.

'Only seven o'clock. But I need to get in early. There's cereal, bread and jam. Even some blueberries.'

'I know. I bought them, remember?'

'Ah, yes, good point.' He bent down to kiss her. 'Thank you for being there last night. It meant a lot to me.'

Rachel cradled the mug, smiling. 'Sorry, I think I misjudged the dress code – again. I thought the East Midlands Marketing Association annual dinner might have been a little more edgy, with all those advertising people. I could have conformed to the standard little black number required if I'd known.'

He laughed. 'Edgy? We are talking East Midlands here, not Madison Avenue. Anyway, you looked great.' He sensed she hadn't misjudged it – she enjoyed not going with the flow and that skirt had raised a few eyebrows. 'You left the pink wig at home, that was all I asked.' Although she had looked great in that too, appearing last Saturday with the Clams at the Middleton Dynamos Winter Social. He could get into being her groupie.

'I did enjoy it, even if I was a little humbled to be in the presence of such marketing greatness. Mind you, two awards in one evening, Mr East Midlands Marketing Personality of the Year – snappy title, by the way. I do think you might have given the others a chance.'

'All right, all right, don't rub it in.'

'Remind me again what the other award was in aid of – the one you got for Little Monkeys?'

'I knew you weren't paying attention.'

'Definitely not by that point. Just watching that bloke from Burton's Boilers. He looked daggers when you went up for a second time.'

'Most improved brand. Although as Jerry Collins rather savagely pointed out, I suppose you could say it had plenty of room for improvement. Anyway, I'll see you this evening.'

'OK, I might be a bit late back. I'm going for a training run. Probably try and do my last long one and then rest up for the weekend. Care to join me?'

'I'll see,' he said. 'I don't know what time I'll be home either.'

'Mm,' Rachel sounded dubious. 'I'd say you're a tad complacent about this 10K.'

'I'm sure I'll be fine,' he said. 'It's Kate I'm worried about.'

'So exactly how many training runs have you managed with your daughter?'

'Er, OK.'

'And how many do you think I've done?'

'Well... several?'

Rachel looked amused. 'Let's just put it this way – don't you worry your pretty little head about Kate.'

For the first time this winter, he had to defrost the car windscreen, sharing a cheery good morning with Ron Fletcher from number fifty-six, without dwelling long enough for an update on the latest twist in the parking permit fiasco, which had turned into a saga. And as he drove into work, even the central reservation on the ring road looked oddly beautiful, with its dusting of frost in the first light of morning. The thought of Rachel padding around his house was a warm one. Three months together now. And an increasing number of nights when she stayed over. With each passing week, their lives felt more intertwined. And now there was all the time in the world to build on this, with Conrad safely ensconced in Malawi. It had been brave of her too, he recognised, throwing herself into this relationship while the rest of her life was up in the air. It still looked like Action Stations wasn't going to make it beyond Christmas. She had confided in him all along that the sponsorship she had raised for running Middleton's Winter 10K wasn't going to be anywhere near enough to save it. Typical Rachel, she actually felt guilty about asking people to support what was probably a lost cause. But it felt good to be doing something, even if only delaying the inevitable, and he knew she'd put the money to good use, even if it was just for a last Christmas party for all the kids.

Before he'd even switched on his laptop at work, his phone was ringing.

'Mr Hardman wants to see you – immediately,' Maureen Birtles told him.

Almost a year of this now, but those words could still strike terror into a man's heart. A summons from Hardman still normally meant trouble. Even though he'd stared the tyrant right between the eyes over his plan to replace the UK brands – and won. He shouldn't feel so nervous. And yet – you still never knew what was coming next. He could guarantee it wouldn't be hearty congratulations over being East Midlands Marketing Personality of the Year.

Maureen was tapping away, outside Hardman's office, as haughty as ever. He had to hand it to her – she was a survivor too. Almost a year as his PA when a betting man would have given her two weeks before being replaced by another transatlantic Schmaltz clone. What was her secret? He tried to suppress a mental picture of Hardman and Maureen wrestling passionately on his desk. Maureen removing her glasses and pressing him down with her considerable bosom.

She looked up at Stephen. That smirk had survived the year too.

He rapped confidently on the open door. Hardman was sitting in his customary position facing the window, on the phone. He beckoned Stephen in with a wave of the hand, without putting the phone down. But he wasn't speaking, evidently having to listen to someone else for once, whoever it was. The exercise bike was covered by a dust sheet. It was some time since he had endured a meeting where Hardman was carrying on his gym routine at the same time. Something else about the office was different too, but he couldn't immediately work out what.

Suddenly Hardman replied to his caller, sounding agitated. 'OK, honey, it must be two in the morning. You need to get a grip, pop a damn pill and get some sleep. And when you wake up, tell the idiot that the scum on the pool is his fucking problem, not ours. And if he ain't gonna sort it, I'll make sure he never sells another pool in the whole fucking state. I gotta go. I'll catch you later.'

He turned to face Stephen.

'You married, Carreras?'

It was the first time Hardman had ever asked about his personal life.

'Not any longer, Mr Hardman.'

'Huh,' the American grunted, as if considering this option. 'Anyway, sit down, Carreras.'

That was the difference. There was a black office chair on this side of the desk. And although Hardman was not smiling, his expression fell some way short of a full-on scowl.

'How's it going?'

'Sorry, Mr Hardman?'

'I'm asking you how you see the market at the moment, for fuck's sake.'

Hardman was asking his opinion? He took a moment to recover.

'Well, we're still on course to get the best market share in the UK we've had in fifteen years. We just need to make sure we keep up the momentum. On all the brands,' he added, just in case Little Monkeys were still in Hardman's sights.

There was no reaction, so Stephen continued. 'I've shared my plan for next year with Carol Coolidge, just waiting for her feedback.'

'Yup, no need to bother with that.'

'Sorry?'

'She's gone – resigned last week. I had her out the door before her ass touched the floor.'

Stephen felt a stab of shock. No wonder she hadn't seemed very interested in anything recently.

'Oh, wow, I'm so sorry to hear that.'

'Sorry? I ain't. I should never have taken a chance on the kid. Guess she just couldn't cut it.' He put his feet on the desk. 'If she hadn't quit, I'd have got rid anyway. I should have fired her after that crap advertising idea. Must be getting soft in my old age.'

Stephen had told her that she could escape all this, but now she had done, he felt momentarily betrayed.

'Why the hell I listened to Nudey – he recommended her.'

'Ah,' Stephen said. It was the only diplomatic thing that came to mind. 'Can I ask where she's moving to?'

Hardman looked irritated by this irrelevance. 'I've no idea. Not sure she's moving anywhere yet. But don't start feeling sorry for her, son.' He snorted back the phlegm as usual. 'No doubt she'll be polishing her résumé, reinventing a year of underachieving shit here as a life-enhancing experience.' He casually tossed a file to the other side of his desk, the remnants of Carol Coolidge's career perhaps. 'Anyway, I don't want to talk about her,' he continued, making a strangled attempt at a smile. 'You, Carreras, I guess you're feeling pretty pleased with yourself, huh?'

This felt like a trap.

'I'm just sorry it hasn't worked out for Carol. I'm sure she'll blossom again somewhere else.'

'What? Oh yeah, she'll probably fool someone for a while – like she did me. I meant you must still be feeling pleased that you were proved right on that fucking market research. I had to use it to explain to the big boss in Chicago why we're holding onto your brands – at least for next year.'

It was the first time Stephen had ever heard Hardman refer directly to a superior being. Was head office beginning to make his life a misery, like he did for everyone else?

'As I said at the time, Mr Hardman, I just wanted to do what I thought was best for the business,' Stephen said. 'But I'm afraid LISA and the rest of the anti-sugar brigade still aren't going away. I think they'll start having a go at Bingo Bars and Munchy Moments too, even though the sugar level is much lower than in Schmaltzy and Nutters. Now they've got the bit between their teeth, I think we might need to go further and reduce—'

'Don't get me wrong, though, Carreras,' Hardman interrupted. 'There are a whole load of crap local brands around the arse end of Europe that I *am* still gonna replace with Schmaltzy and Nutters. I'll find a way. And you're gonna help me.'

'Sorry?'

'Let's cut the crap here. I'm offering you her job, European Marketing Vice President for the biggest chocolate company this side of fucking Beijing.'

Stephen's mouth dropped open. He had won. Eleven months ago, he had stood here and accepted a humiliating demotion and a slashed salary. Now he was to be Champion of Europe.

'So you going to accept or stand there like a fucking guppy?' Hardman was impatient already.

He needed to focus, play it cool. 'Well, that's very good of you to offer it to me, Mr Hardman. I'm very flattered. Obviously I just need to understand the details a little more.'

Hardman looked puzzled. 'I'm not fucking around here, son, I'll pay you what I paid her. I always said I'd reward my top people – just turns out she wasn't one of them. I need you in Paris, of course, not here. I'm hoping to be there more next year too, once this shithole is fixed. When I started, Nudey told me you Brits were the basket case. Now it looks like the rest of Europe is more of a nut job. So, think of yourself as my advance party in kicking ass. You can probably have Coolidge's apartment if you want it. I gather it's pretty good.'

He was already kissing Rachel on that balcony, looking out over Paris.

'But I'll need you to get your butt on an airplane every week to go and flex some muscle – particularly with those idiots in Athens,' Hardman continued.

'Sorry? Yes, of course. It's obviously a fantastic offer.'

'It is. So what the fuck are you waiting for?'

'Well, my personal circumstances have changed a little in the last month or so. I'm in a new relationship.'

'Huh?' Hardman had the blank look of a man for whom personal circumstances were an alien concept. Clearly he hadn't clocked anything from seeing Stephen with Rachel in La Belle Époque back in August. He'd probably even forgotten they were there, on account of having a bottle of claret emptied into his lap.

'Take her with you. Or is she earning more than 200K a year plus bonus and a fucking apartment?'

Two hundred thousand. And Rachel. In Paris. In that apartment. Concentrate.

'I do have children as well.'

'Take them too, goddammit. Hold on, you told me a minute ago you were divorced. You got to keep the kids?'

'No, I just see them every fortnight – sometimes more often.' He didn't know why he was raising reservations. He couldn't let being Jake's football chauffeur get in the way of this, could he? There must be a solution.

'Shit, if it's only once a fortnight, you can probably get back... some time,' Hardman said. But Stephen suspected that picking his kids up at six every other Friday would be quite a challenge. Kicking ass around Europe would have to come first.

Hardman stood up and started to pace around the room, hands in pockets. Stephen wondered if he had pushed him too far. Was Paris slipping away already? He really wanted this triumph. But then Hardman turned to him again, looking almost benevolent.

'Look, Carreras, I want you to take this job, fella. I'm sure with the money I'm paying, you can work something out with your kids. How old are they anyway?'

'Sixteen and thirteen.'

'Shit, practically adults. They can come see you. Travel is good for kids – especially if they live here,' he said, staring out over the car park. 'I went weeks without seeing mine when I worked in LA and they were back in Texas. You miss this opportunity for your kids' sake, they ain't gonna thank you in ten years' time, I can tell you.' He paused for a moment, uncharacteristically thoughtful. 'Tell you what. I'll get HR to draw up the contract today, email it to you. Get yourself over to Paris this week if you want, go and look at Coolidge's apartment or anywhere else for that matter. Then come back a week from today and tell me you're going to do this for me. I don't normally give people a week to make a decision,' he added.

'Wow, OK, thank you.' Stephen offered his hand and Hardman gripped it firmly.

'Don't lose the big picture here, son. Back in January, I was offering you shit money to sort out the crap here. Now I'm offering you big money to live in Paris and sort out the rest of it for me. I know you won't turn it down.'

As Stephen turned to leave, he added, 'If you do, I'm sure there's a smooth-talking fucking Italian who will take it on for me.'

*

Stephen floated back through the Hive as John Motson filed his latest match report.

'So, there we are. It's been a long hard season, but what a turnaround we've seen over the last few weeks. Who'd have thought it? Stephen Carreras, who seemed to be very much on his way out back in January, has not just got his old job back but gone a lot further. He's poised to enjoy the riches of the European Champions League next season.'

He texted Rachel, with a smiley emoji.

Looking fwd to seeing you later. Have I got news for you? xx.

She had never been in a job that earned decent money. Now he was going to lavish gifts on her. He would spend as much time in Paris as he could, getting the European operatives to come and see him like Carol had, although it did sound like there'd be a fair amount of trouble-shooting to do around Europe. And then he and Rachel would meet after a day in the office, Rachel fabulous in a red dress he'd bought for her, turning heads as they strolled along the Left Bank. And the kids' faces when they saw the view from the apartment. Even Jake would look up from his phone for that one, surely. There *must* be a way he could get them over regularly.

On the way home from work, he stopped off for champagne at the off-licence around the corner, and then at Blooming Good – this time it would be red roses, seasonal or not. He burst into his house, where Rachel had let herself in and was standing in the kitchen, dipping a teabag into a mug. She was still in a fleece and tracky bottoms, back from the training run he had forgotten all about.

'Hello, you look pleased with yourself, Mr East Midlands Marketing Personality. Are these for me?'

'Er, just a bit pleased. And of course they are. Things just got a whole lot better. I need you to listen while I tell you this.' He was already popping the champagne cork. 'Where do you want to live – Middleton or Paris?'

'What?' Her laughter bubbled up.

While Rachel perched on a kitchen stool, he told her about the demise of Carol Coolidge, and Hardman's offer.

She gave him a hug. 'That's fantastic. I mean, when I think what that man did to you at the start of the year, and then how you've managed the redundancies and saved the brands. For him to be even offering you this job – it's incredible.'

He sensed her congratulations were slightly guarded. He needed to tell her more, when he'd poured them both a glass of champagne.

'What about Kate and Jake?' she asked, taking it from him.

'Of course, I've thought about that. I – we – could afford to fly back every fortnight. Or they could come out – to us. On the money he's paying me.'

'OK,' she said, without sounding totally convinced.

'The other incredible thing is they'll pay for an apartment. I've seen Carol Coolidge's place, and I – we – could have that. It's fantastic. You'd love it.'

'Oh. Wow.'

He embraced her again. 'I'm sorry, I'm going too fast, when I'd agreed to take it slowly. And it suddenly occurs to me you might be wondering when I was in Carol Coolidge's apartment, which I'm quite prepared to explain fully a bit later. But I was wondering if – and I know you'll want to think about it – it's just that I wondered if this might be the time when we sort of made this a bit more permanent, and you moved in with me – in Paris?'

He hadn't planned it like this. But he couldn't take it slowly any longer. It had just burst out of him.

Rachel eased herself from his grip and looked at him with an expression he couldn't work out.

'Whoo. It's amazing, Stephen, honestly. If you're really asking me, do I want to move in with you, that's... I mean, I've been kind of living in the moment, enjoying the last few weeks and not thinking about what happens next.'

'I understand. Of course. But there's a chance you'll say yes?'

She gave him a tantalisingly short kiss on the lips. 'There's a chance I'll say yes.' Her intonation made it sound some way short of a dead cert.

'How much chance? Give me a percentage.'

She laughed but didn't answer. Instead she walked over to where he had left the flowers on the table and started to unwrap them.

'I could definitely come over for weekends. That would be very romantic.'

'I was thinking more permanently.'

'I know you were,' she said, looking at him compassionately. 'But it's important to think it through and make sure it's really what will make you happy.'

'Of course. But being recognised for what I've done makes me happy. And what I've achieved here is bloody brilliant. I don't often blow my own trumpet, you said so yourself. But if I'd thought a year ago that I'd get to be the European Marketing VP for one of the world's biggest chocolate companies... It's incredible.'

'I know. I did say that.'

'And I can still do something good over there. I'm sure I can. And to live in Paris – with you. If I'm with you in Paris, I'll be ecstatically happy.' He pictured her lying on that divan again.

Rachel was now placing the flowers in a vase.

'What do you think I'd do in Paris, Stephen?'

'I'm sure you'd find some work, but there's no hurry. I can definitely keep you in the manner to which you'd like to be accustomed.'

She stopped arranging the flowers. She had a sadder expression now.

'I don't want keeping, Stephen. I really want to be with you, but I also want to keep helping my kids. I know it might seem mad, but I haven't given up hope – even now. You remember me telling you I didn't go in for petitional prayer – you know, asking for a parking spot and all that? Well, now I do find myself praying that something will turn up for Action Stations. And if I can't save it, I need to find something else meaningful to do with my life. So I'd have to think about where Paris might fit into all that, given until about thirty minutes ago it wasn't even on the list of possibilities.'

Somewhere deep in a part of him he didn't want to acknowledge, he was desperately hoping her prayer wouldn't be answered and there would be no last-minute reprieve for Action Stations. What had Conrad said, when she first said it was in big trouble? Maybe it was meant to be, Rachel's job disappearing. But he wasn't as daft as Conrad – he wasn't going to *say* that.

Now she held her arms wide open to embrace him.

'Now I sound like a self-absorbed cow. Mr C, it sounds as if you do really want this job, and it's amazing to have been offered it. If that's true, that you want it, I'm sure we'll make it work – one way or another.'

'Well, he has given me a week to make a decision,' he said. But what else was there for him? Turn it down, and Hardman would either sack him or promote someone else – probably both – and the someone else would be Salvatore, by the sound of it. However much he liked Salvatore, he was convinced that reporting to him would mark the end of a beautiful friendship.

'Can you take a day off to come to Paris with me on Friday, to look around?' That would give him a chance to convince her.

'Not at such short notice,' she said. 'I need to be in work, especially as I'm off for a few days next week. Remember I'm heading up to Northumberland on retreat?'

Oh, hell, he'd forgotten that. Another retreat?

She smiled encouragingly. 'I don't need to go to Paris with you on Friday to know that the apartment will be fantastic, do I? I trust you, on that and everything else.'

'But I'll need to decide while you're away,' he said.

'That's OK.'

'When are you back? You haven't forgotten about a week on Friday, have you?' He'd planned to take her away for the weekend, a surprise for the anniversary of their meeting.

'Of course not. I wouldn't miss it for the world, whatever it is. I'm coming back on the train that Friday afternoon and I've made sure I'm free for the weekend. No commitments.' She smiled. 'I always try to go on retreat at the start of Advent. Last year I went a couple of weeks later than normal because I was at a low ebb right at the beginning of December and didn't feel like being on my own.' She planted a kiss on his cheek. 'Which is why my friends invited me to a party.'

A year ago, he hadn't known of her existence. Now they were in touching distance of living together, in Paris.

Chapter Thirty-One

Paris looked more beautiful than ever at this time of year, on a bright day such as this. The few remaining leaves on the tree-lined avenues allowed a clear view of the elegant apartments. Those shutters always lent an air of secrecy. What was going on behind them?

The taxi turned into a wide boulevard which seemed familiar. Wasn't Carol's now empty place in this *quartier*? He was looking forward to picking up the keys to look at it again later. And soon he would be in there for real, tucked up with Rachel, private Parisians.

He still felt a bit guilty, being here just for fun. But if Hardman was giving him time to make the decision and offering a free trip, he might as well make the most of it. He had the whole day. It was good that Laura had agreed to keep the kids until tomorrow morning even though it was his weekend in charge. OK, it was hedged with a stipulation that he picked them up early as Tristran wanted to take her somewhere for the weekend. But he needed to do that anyway – the 10K run started at half ten. And overall, she was definitely more conciliatory these days, since his apology. It hadn't happened immediately, but he had sensed a gradual thawing of relations over the last few weeks. Although he could guess how she would react if he moved here and couldn't guarantee to pick them up regularly on a Friday evening.

The driver pulled up in front of the Hotel Méridien. As he stepped out, the aroma of the sea from the shellfish under the red awning triggered the memory of that caffeine-deprived first morning of Schmaltz Europe. Was it really only the start of this year? He had harboured a secret ambition to return here ever since that moment when they'd filed out from Hardman's first haranguing, gawping enviously at the rich Parisians in the dining room, living their happy Schmaltz-free existences. Now he was returning – on his own terms.

That was also the day he'd first met Salvatore. So an appropriate venue to meet him today. They had come through so much together this year. Yes, he could be pompous and infuriating, and yet his breezy confidence had been transformational. He deserved to be told first-hand about Hardman's job offer. And Stephen always valued the Italian's highly individual perspective on events. But would he be envious?

Salvatore had taken a table by the window, having stepped straight out of a fashion magazine as usual. What was it with Italians? How come the midnight blue jacket and crisp white shirt were so clearly stylish compared with his own Middleton High Street casual? Glancing up from behind his dark-framed glasses, Salvatore smiled warmly as he approached. And as Stephen offered his hand, his friend pulled him closer and kissed him on both cheeks. Stephen caught a subtle spicy scent. As per usual, slight envy morphed into man crush.

'I ordered us a *kir royale*, and then we'll have a bottle of Pouilly-Fumé. And we must eat seafood here,' Salvatore pronounced. The aperitif was already sparkling in front of Stephen. Before he'd met Salvatore, he'd always seen kir as a girly drink – it wasn't exactly *de rigueur* with Danny Allsop on a Friday night in the Crown.

'Stephen, this is nice; just a lunch with no meeting to follow. A great suggestion.'

'Yes, I'm glad you could make it at short notice.'

'Naturally – for my friend. When you told me you had some important news,' he said, while beckoning the *sommelier*.

'Yes, much to discuss. But first, have you heard about Carol?'

'Of course. Good for her.' He paused, with a little smile of recollection. 'I think she may be my greatest triumph.'

'What do you mean?'

'Me persuading that agency Oyster Inc to offer her a place on their board after all.'

'What?' Stephen exclaimed. Why was he surprised by this? Was there no end to Salvatore's manoeuvrings? 'Hang on, Salvatore, are you telling me you negotiated to get her a new job already? I heard she only just resigned.'

'Negotiate? I would say it's more an *intercessione*. A little prayer maybe.'

'But wait a minute, you were always telling me how incompetent she was.'

'Yes, that is why it needs an *intercessione*, my friend. But then they are incompetent too, judging from that ridiculous nibble advertising idea for Schmaltzy Bars.' The Italian shook his head again. 'So it's a wedding made in heaven,' he chuckled.

'A *marriage* made in heaven, it's a *marriage*,' Stephen said irritably. He always had this urge to correct Salvatore when he was being particularly exasperating. 'How much are they paying her? I suppose you know that too.'

'Not as much as she was earning here, that is for sure. But she will not go hungry. Unlike us in this place,' he scowled, raising a finger to get the waiter's attention.

'Negotiate your fee too, did you?'

Salvatore frowned at this scurrilous suggestion. The waiter arrived, and he ordered something which Stephen didn't catch.

The waiter turned to Stephen expectantly. He hadn't even looked at the menu yet.

'I'll have what you're having, Salvatore.'

The Italian looked impressed and said, '*pour deux*' to the waiter.

They talked a little more about Carol; Salvatore disparagingly, Stephen more sympathetically now. He argued that she did have talent; he'd seen that in those early years at Grimley's, but she'd been promoted in Schmaltz Europe far too quickly. And as he defended her, he realised, with relief, that the Carol infatuation had gone. He still thought about her apartment, but another woman was inhabiting it in his mind now.

Salvatore sloshed the white wine around in his glass and sniffed it. 'But Stephen, you didn't get me here just to talk about Carol Coolidge, I think. What is the news you wanted to tell me?'

'Well, even as I'm telling you this, I'm thinking you probably already know – you normally do – but Hardman has offered me her job.'

Salvatore was frozen, glass close to his lips. 'Oh, really?'

Just for once, Stephen was sure he had surprised him. 'Yes, he got me in earlier this week. Seems like he wants me to take over from her in Paris and sort out the rest of Europe like I have the UK. And you have in Italy,' he added quickly.

Salvatore hesitated for a moment, but then his face broke into a warm smile. 'Stephen. Congratulations. What a victory, after all they have put you through this year.' He raised his glass for a celebratory clink. 'When do you start? That's a great exchange, Middleton for Paris.' Somehow, his complacent certainty rankled.

'Yes, I think it's a good exchange. I'm pretty sure I'll take it.'

This prompted the sort of pitying look he hadn't received from Salvatore for a while.

'Pretty sure? What is this pretty sure? You English can be so difficult to understand sometimes.'

The waiter returned. '*Les fruits de mer, messieurs,*' he announced, placing a seafood platter ceremoniously on the table in front of them. God, was this what they'd ordered? A small mollusc on the third rung was still showing signs of life, and about to make a slither for it.

'It's not completely straightforward, Salvatore. There is Rachel to think about,' Stephen said, trying not to be distracted by the dining task ahead of him.

'Oh, is there? Give me an update on Rachel?'

'Well, it's great, we are definitely an item now. I know it won't be easy for her to move, but...'

'Stephen, this is fantastic.' Now Salvatore looked genuinely delighted. 'This is an even bigger cause for celebration. Not only has the madman offered you a big job, but a good woman wants to be with you. And the timing is perfect, yes? You told me last time we talked that she would be out of a job anyway. I mean that's a big shame. I looked at the website for, what is it, Action Stations, and what they do – it's great work. But maybe, how do you say, it's meant to be.'

Now *he* was sounding like bloody Conrad.

'It's not quite that simple, Salvatore. Action Stations isn't dead yet. In fact she, we, are doing this run tomorrow to raise money.' That wasn't looking too clever on a bed of seafood. 'And we'd need to work out what Rachel would do – in Paris. Or whether she might still need to stay in Middleton and we'd spend the weekends together. That could be very romantic.'

'We are talking about weekends in Paris, yes, not weekends in Middleton? No, she must come to Paris permanently. She wouldn't need to work. Every woman wants to live in Paris,' Salvatore asserted, his eye evidently caught by a particularly plump prawn on the top floor.

'And then there are my kids to think about,' Stephen added sharply.

'Of course, but with respect, Stephen, you only see them once every fortnight anyway. You should tell Hardman he needs to pay to fly you home every two weeks or fly them to you.' His eyes lit up at his own ingenuity. 'That would be brilliant. What an experience for them, coming to Paris every fortnight.'

Tell Hardman this, tell Hardman that. Sometimes Salvatore could be a bloody expert in telling you what to say to Hardman.

Stephen snapped a crab's claw with malice aforethought. 'For once, Salvatore, you seem to agree with the madman. He too tells me it will be a great experience for my kids.'

'Ah, what is it they say, even a fool is right once,' Salvatore said, twirling a mussel on a small fork. 'And what's more, if you had turned this down, what would you have done? What is there for you in the UK?'

An uneasy and uncharacteristic silence descended between them as they cracked and picked their way through the platter. Until Salvatore laid down his weapon, resting his elbows on the table, fingers laced.

'Sorry, I think I have offended you. My friend, naturally, it's up to you. You must decide.'

Stephen demolished the last prawn. 'All right, since you say we English aren't direct enough, yes, I am a bit offended. I mean, you ask what is there to do in the UK? Don't you realise what I've done, Salvatore? Do good among the carnage, Rachel said. Well, I certainly have. I've helped find a new job for everyone I had to fire in Middleton – most of them considerably easier than what I've had to put up with for the last year. I even found a cushy job for my drain of a deputy with some fair trade chocolate maker in leafy Devon. Come to think of it, he's probably on paternity leave cooing over his newborn by now, down in some small town on the edge of Dartmoor. Now that's what I call an *intercessi* – intercession. Knocks your efforts with Carol into a cocked hat. And I've saved the UK brands, for God's sake, and therefore a whole bloody factory.'

He realised it was a bit of a rant. But Salvatore looked at him sympathetically now. 'Of course, I know this, Stephen. You have done brilliantly. But what is there left to do in the future?'

It seemed he had said his piece, rinsing his fingers in the finger bowl and washing his hands of the problem. But as he wiped them gently on the napkin, he came back again.

'I just say this, my friend. Wherever you go, you want to wake up with her in your bed. You want to smell her perfume in your house. You need to be there for her on an evening when she has had a bad day. You need her to be there for you when you have a bad day. This idea you meet up every two weeks – it's fine maybe for a twenty-year-old. But you aren't a twenty-year-old.' He patted Stephen consolingly on the arm. 'I'm sure you will make it work in Paris.'

Stephen sighed. 'You might be right. You sometimes are. I did say I plan to take it.' He smiled. 'I certainly can't imagine being a marketing operative any longer. And with respect, *signore*, I'm also not sure I could stay in Middleton and take orders from you. And as I've said before, good jobs around Middleton aren't exactly two a penny, even for the East Midlands Marketing Personality of the Year. So, all in all…'

'What?'

'Didn't I tell you? I got an award. Only the East Midlands, but still…'

'No, not that, whatever that is. What you said before about taking orders.'

'I'm sorry, I know it's not very noble-minded, but as we've become such good friends these last few months, I would find it difficult if I had to now take orders from you. I haven't told you this, but if I don't take it, he'll offer it to you. Maybe that changes your mind about encouraging me to take it. Presumably Giulia and the children will be very happy to come to Paris with you, as it's so easy.'

Salvatore was laughing and shaking his head.

'Stephen, don't worry, I am not touching this job with a barge pole.' He sipped the remainder of his glass of wine and placed it firmly on the table. 'There, I think that's the right expression, yes?'

'Well, based on your logic that it's the only decent job in Schmaltz marketing, maybe *you* will have to resign.'

'I will not need to do this,' Salvatore said. 'Now, please excuse me for just a moment while I visit the restroom. And then I will explain why.'

It was typical Salvatore, leaving him in suspense. The waiter returned with the dessert menu, and the cheese board being circulated on a trolley around the room looked magnificent. Time for both maybe before he went to pick up the keys, but in which order? Cheese first, perhaps? When in Paris...

'*Et voici, monsieur.*' The waiter was showing someone to a table nearby. The man made eye contact with Stephen for a second, and they exchanged a polite '*bonjour*'. He looked strangely familiar. Stephen wasn't sure if he was French – but he definitely wasn't English. Something about the dark green jacket was just too stylish.

While Stephen had his nose back in the dessert menu, Salvatore returned, but remained standing, suddenly looking a little agitated.

'OK, tell me all,' Stephen smiled. 'This is a great restaurant too. Did you notice the cheese board?'

'No, I think maybe let's go for a little promenade,' Salvatore said softly, reaching for his wallet. 'Lunch is on me. We'll take coffee and cognac elsewhere.'

Chapter Thirty-Two

Salvatore rebuffed Stephen's attempt to find out what was going on with a sharp 'shush', as he led him at a brisk pace past a flower stall daubing exotic reds and oranges on the grey backdrop of the Place des Ternes. Here they took a sharp left into the Boulevard de Courcelles, where the low December sun had slipped behind the austere façades.

Stephen shivered. He was regretting not bringing a warmer coat. Then again, he hadn't signed up for a guided winter walk of the local neighbourhood. On Salvatore pounded, still wearing the shades he had slipped on as they left the restaurant.

'Salvatore, I don't know if you noticed, but it isn't actually sunny along here. And where the hell are we going?'

'I know exactly where I'm going,' he replied tersely, without breaking stride.

'I'm very happy for you, but can you tell me?'

'Not yet.' Salvatore's jaw tightened into a stern grimace while the shades stayed firmly in place. 'I'll let you know when it's OK to talk,' he whispered.

As they passed yet another inviting café, which to Stephen looked perfect for a coffee and a cognac, his patience broke.

'OK, Carnevale. You need to explain yourself. I feel like

I've stepped into a spy novel. I keep expecting "White Bear" to turn up.'

'Who?' The Italian's brow furrowed.

'It's a joke. You know, a code name for a secret agent. Never mind.'

'Stephen, this is serious.' Salvatore was looking around again, as if White Bear now provided an extra worry.

'Well in that case, you've got five minutes to explain what's going on, or I'm getting a taxi back to the letting agency and picking up the keys to Carol's apartment.'

'OK, OK, keep your hat on,' Salvatore said, while still pressing on at the same pace. 'Tell me, as we left the restaurant, did you notice that man, dark green jacket, on his own, who had just arrived?'

'Yes, he came in while you went for a pee.'

'Do you know who he is?'

'Can't say I do,' Stephen replied.

'No, I thought not.' Salvatore had the air of a disappointed schoolmaster hoping for better from his pupil – but not really expecting it.

Stephen indulged him. 'So, come on then, who was he?'

'His name is Gigi Peronace. Ring any bells?'

'Nope, does he play for Inter Milan? Looked a bit old.'

'Pah,' the Italian retorted disdainfully. 'He is in fact the leading financial reporter for *La Stampa*,' he announced. 'I noticed him on the plane this morning.' Salvatore's eyes darted around again.

'It's not exactly a celebrity spot, is it? You're talking to a man who sat next to Jessica Ennis-Hill on a flight back from Paris last month. You know, she won the gold medal…'

'Yes, and then I saw him at Charles de Gaulle, two behind me in the queue for a taxi.'

'Wow, business journalist travels to Paris and gets a taxi.'

'And then he comes into the restaurant, on his own.'

'Salvatore, does this man know you?'

The Italian was indignant. 'I am very well known in the business community in Milano.'

'Have you had a conversation with him – ever?'

'Stephen, I'm sure he knows who I am.'

'OK… I find this hard to fathom, but I think you're implying that he followed you to the restaurant.'

'Of course.'

'Can I suggest it may just be coincidence?'

'Why would an Italian journalist travel to Paris to dine on his own?'

'Maybe he was meeting someone. You had me out of there so quick, we'll never know. He's probably sipping an aperitif with some French banking bigwig by now.'

'I'm sure this isn't true, Stephen,' Salvatore said with an air of certainty, 'whatever a bigwig is.'

'All right, all right, if I go along with your hypothesis, just to humour you, can I ask the obvious next question? Why are you worried? What do you have to hide?'

Salvatore stopped and glanced around once more, seemingly still seeking confirmation that they were alone. They were outside a rather dowdy café which looked distinctly less welcoming than any they had passed in the last half hour.

'OK, this will do,' he said.

In the shadowy, deserted interior the Italian finally seemed to relax, perhaps convinced he had given Gigi Whatshisname the slip at last.

'Remember, Stephen, when we spoke earlier in the week and you asked if we could meet, I said it was good timing?'

'Yes, of course.' Stephen had forgotten; he'd been so keen to impart his own news.

'It's because I too have news. I do not need to resign, as you suggested at lunch, because I am already fired,' he announced matter-of-factly.

'What? Salvatore, that's terrible. I'm sorry, I've been so full of my own news.' Stephen was stunned. His friend must have been rumbled. All that dodgy business with Nutters only making the Italians fart in the product test. Those Carnevale chickens had finally come home to roost.

Salvatore looked bemused. 'Terrible? You must be joking. It's fantastic. Exactly what I planned.' He leant forward conspiratorially. 'They give me a very nice, how shall we say, *arrivaderci.*'

'Really?' Stephen said. This seemed very unlikely.

'Yes, a *very* nice *arrivaderci,*' Salvatore emphasised.

Stephen shook his head. 'How exactly have you managed this, Salvatore, given the ogre has had me pushing people out for a pittance all year?'

'Because things have changed, my friend,' the Italian pronounced gnomically.

'How exactly?'

Salvatore waited a moment until the waiter had placed two *petits cafés* on the table and returned behind the bar.

'Your friend Oscar Newte, how well do you really know him?'

'Newte? Friend? Please, not in the same sentence. But what's he got to do with it anyway?' This cloak-and-dagger behaviour was increasingly irritating. Especially as Salvatore was clearly still revelling in it.

'We had a little dinner – Mr Newte and I – in Auvois.'

'Auvois? At Pietro's? Salvatore, how could you? I thought it was somewhere only we know.' Stephen tried to look disappointed.

Salvatore continued unabated. 'Yes, it was actually he who suggested dinner. We were in Paris at a meeting, a few weeks ago. I had an idea what he might want to discuss, so I thought I would take him somewhere I felt comfortable, where nobody would see us.' He paused. 'My home ground, if you like. Yes, my home ground.' As usual he looked appreciative of his own choice of idiom.

'And what did he want to discuss?'

'Oh, he had a theory on our market research results, where we showed how our brands beat the American ones so clearly. He thought it was odd that only the Italians get wind from Nutters. What was it he said? Did I have an explanation for this funny business?'

'And did you?'

'Of course not,' Salvatore looked offended.

'So... that was it? I still don't know where your friend Gigi comes in. Is he nosing into this market research funny business too?'

'No, he chases a bigger story. Signor Peronace writes a blog, called *L'alveare*. It means, let me think, it's like where buzzing insects live.'

'The hive?'

'Yes, that's it. The idea is he reports on what is buzzing in business.'

'Bit odd. You know that's what our office space is called?'

'I don't think that's important.' Salvatore waved this away. 'But he is very clever, Signor Peronace. In his blog, he always calls himself *L'Ape Regina*, the Queen Bee, and just a few days before my dinner with Newte, *L'Ape Regina* says he, er, she notes that overall across Europe, our profits so far this year look quite nice. And she is surprised by this, as she knows about the strikes in France and Spain, and the poor sales in many countries. Now I know this bee, Stephen. When she says she is surprised, it means she suspects – and when she suspects, she starts to buzz, to look around.' Salvatore leant across the table and lowered his voice even further. 'So it turns out there is a little, how do you say, pokey jiggery, about Schmaltz Europe profits.' He surveyed the café once more, still empty but for the disinterested waiter checking his phone.

'Oh yeah? What sort of pokey jiggery?'

'It's the right idiom, yes?'

'It'll do – go on.'

'So, after Newte is trying to interrogate me at our dinner, I think maybe I turn the tables on him. He likes his Barolo, doesn't he, Mr Newte? Even more than you.' He chuckled. 'But, my friend, he doesn't take it so well.'

'You mean you got him pissed?'

'Pissed?' Salvatore shrank away from this indelicacy. 'I simply get him a little, how should we say, more open than is normal.' He summoned the waiter. 'Now, I haven't bought you that digestif.'

'What did he say?'

Salvatore examined the drinks menu. 'Two Armagnacs, maybe?'

'Anything. Look, I'm out of here if you don't tell me what he said.'

'Calm down, Stephen. So, Newte is drinking quite quickly, and I simply suggested that he didn't seem very happy. I say that maybe he should cheer up. I am thinking about what my Queen Bee writes. I say that, given how disastrous the sales have been around Europe, except for Italy and UK of course, the first half year profits are OK. In fact, quite hard to understand. But that just seemed to make him more miserable.'

'What do you think is going on, then?' Stephen was captivated now. But Salvatore continued to lay out his cards at the pace of an elderly lady playing a game of patience.

'Well, Newte says that, just between him and me, the true financial results for Schmaltz Europe's first six months of trading are indeed a disaster. It's obvious to me when they demote people who know what they are doing, and promote idiots like Coolidge and Newte, who could not organise a...'

'Piss-up in a brewery?'

'Yes, this is it. Then Newte tells me Hardman is under big pressure from the US already. The results would be enough to destroy Schmaltz value on Wall Street and Hardman would be sliced into little pieces by his bosses in Chicago. And it seems Hardman responds to the problem of poor profits as he does with any problem. By, as you would probably say, shitting on the person who sits below him. He just told Newte results need to improve and fast. You can imagine it, yes?' He did a weird imitation of Hardman's Texan drawl. 'You're the fucking Finance Vice President. Fix it.' His grin turned more malign. 'Then I hang the little fly on my fishing line. I am very friendly with Mr Newte, explain that in the Italian business we are always quite – let me find the word – creative in managing our profits, always legal of course, so if he does need any help, I may be of service. But then I also flatter him. I'm sure, I say, that an organisation like Schmaltz knows all the tricks too.' Salvatore suddenly rapped the table with his hand in recall of his triumph. 'And now the silly fish bites.'

Stephen shook his head. 'How do you do it? How do you get people to tell you everything?'

'The Carnevales have a long tradition in the priesthood, Stephen. I think maybe I have a face which invites confession,' Salvatore said, at his most pompous, before his face broke into a smile. 'And of course, we are well into the second bottle of Barolo by now. Or at least he is. I am only drinking *acqua minerale*. So Newte admits it was necessary to, you know, hide the losses a little, shuffle some money around.' He paused to sip his Armagnac.

'I don't know. I've never shuffled anything around in my life, except my kids unfortunately. Salvatore, this sounds like dynamite. The bastard. Sorry, but I mean, I had always thought that man was a self-promoting little shit, but I never really believed he would be involved in financial jiggery pokery – or even pokey jiggery. I was even beginning to feel a bit sorry for him. So what's he done? How much and where?'

'As I said, I don't know exactly – yet. Maybe I will find it later,' Salvatore replied nonchalantly, as if the money might appear under a sofa somewhere. 'But I encourage him to explain a little more. And he helpfully confides in me that he found a way to hide some of the costs which should really be on the books for Schmaltz Europe and present them in the profit report as costs for the individual countries instead. I think in a period of transition like this, it's not that difficult. Vassos in Greece in particular seems to have found a lot of nasty brown things on his balance sheets which should really be in Hardman's bed.'

'Blimey, poor Vassos,' Stephen said. Whenever he thought of that poor lad, he pictured him at the end of another crap week, head in hands. 'And I suppose that suits Hardman, doesn't it? If the Schmaltz Europe profits don't appear too bad, and the local companies like Greece look like they are truly in the deep stuff, it justifies his plans to bring all power to the centre.' Stephen felt rather satisfied that he was catching up.

'Ah, but it's not that simple, my friend.'

Stephen's head was spinning. Apparently he wasn't catching up after all. 'But presumably the trail leads back to Hardman? He must have put Newte up to it?'

'Ah, yes, you might think so, but it turns out, no.'

'Are you sure?'

'I am sure, because Newte told me. He said that when he showed Hardman how the profit figures had improved so much in July, Hardman sniffed it out. I told you all along. He may be a bastard, but when it's a question of money, he is not a stupid bastard. Even he can see it's strange as he knows how peach-shape things go still in the business. He challenged Newte and the idiot admitted that he might have moved the money around a little.' Salvatore smiled at such ineptitude. 'He probably thought Hardman would be pleased with him, improving the Europe profits and making Greece look bad. Just as you did.' Salvatore shook his head over their naivety.

'But Hardman wasn't pleased?'

'No, Hardman goes crazy, even crazier than Newte has ever seen him.'

'Mm, maybe not the reaction I would have expected.'

Once again, Salvatore offered him that look of mild disappointment. 'Think about it, my friend. Do you know anything about the history of Schmaltz?'

'No, Salvatore, I don't.' Schmaltz present was quite enough to worry about without delving into Schmaltz past. 'But I sense you're about to tell me.'

'The company was started by Manfred Schmaltz, a German Jewish immigrant who moved to Chicago at the start of the twentieth century. A very moral man, I am told. And there are still two descendants of his on the main board in Chicago. I hear it is a matter of honour to them that they deal fairly in business, maintain the philosophy of Manfred. I don't think this matters to Hardman personally. He is just a greedy pet food salesman who will do anything to make money. But I assume he knows how important it is to his bosses. To lose money for his bosses is bad, yes. But to damage their reputation by trying to hide those losses and being caught, it would be unforgivable.'

Stephen realised that for the second time in a week he was doing a passable imitation of a guppy.

Salvatore relaxed back in his chair and sipped his Armagnac, his tale apparently complete.

Stephen puffed out his cheeks. 'There's still a number of things I don't get. Firstly, why isn't Newte out of the door? I mean, Hardman gives every impression of thinking he's an imbecile.'

'Think about it, my friend.'

'Salvatore, please stop saying that. I'm thinking about it so hard my head's exploding.'

'OK, so Hardman is in a hole, yes? If the profit situation doesn't improve soon, he will probably lose his job. But if the pokery jig comes out, he will *definitely* lose his job, even if he didn't start all of it. Which is why he's furious. But Newte, the cause of his problems, is maybe at the moment the only hope of solving them. He told me that Hardman wants him to put it right so that when the profits for the full year are declared next spring, the true figures can be revealed. So Hardman has Newte by the short and curly things, running around Europe, working like a dog, trying to find other ways to save money. The results of our little market research test are the best bit of news they've had in months. Think how much they planned to spend launching Schmaltzy Bars and Munchy Moments. Stopping this crazy launch might be enough to save the profits – or at least help. Just as well we told them their products were too sweet.'

'And that your fellow Italians farted so much.'

Once again, Salvatore shrugged his innocence. He was like one of those veteran Italian defenders in the World Cup, who had just committed the most cynical of fouls but was pretending to the ref that it wasn't him, it was the other guy.

'OK, so if Hardman doesn't sack him, why doesn't Newte just leave? Surely he has some self-respect left.'

'It's obvious. If he leaves, and this gets out, he's in jail. Probably only a short sentence,' Salvatore said insouciantly. 'So he has to stay and try to make things better.'

Manfred Schmaltz probably had a beard, Stephen thought. He could see him now, back from the dead, in Schmaltz HQ in Chicago, dangling Brad Hardman upside down from a top-floor window. And Hardman's wrist was hanging onto Oscar Newte's wobbling foot.

'Any more questions, my friend?'

'Does anyone else know?'

'I believe the rest of the board are in the dark and fed something unpleasant – you know, like you explained to me about mushrooms once,' he smiled. 'Nobody else knows for certain, except me – and now you.' He winked.

Stephen's mind went back to another restaurant in Paris, that evening in La Belle Époque with Rachel when Hardman was bullying Newte, just before the red wine incident. 'I'm not fucking happy about this,' he'd bawled. Maybe he was referring to Newte's financial foul play. He recalled Newte's desperate expression when Stephen suggested he get out of the business – *Would that it were so simple.* And then he remembered another character from that evening: the suave continental-looking gent sat eating seafood on his own at a nearby table. He tried desperately to recall his face.

'But if your man in the restaurant, Gigi Peroni, is onto something, Newte's indiscretions might come out anyway.'

'Hah, I see you believe me now.' Salvatore banged the table joyfully. 'Gigi Peron – aa – chay,' he enunciated. 'Peroni is a beer. Surely you know this? I don't think he finds out much yet. But this is why we need to give him the slip today. We don't want anyone else to know, do we? Knowledge is power, Stephen. I always like this saying,' he smiled benignly. 'Of course, if Newte does sort it so the true profit figures are revealed at the end of the year, and they are still not very good, then he will probably be sacked anyway.'

Stephen shook his head. 'Yep, in the inimitable words of my Scottish colleagues, I can see that Oscar is truly up shit creek without a paddle. Don't attempt that idiom for a while yet, Salvatore.'

They sat ruminating over the last drop of their Armagnacs, Stephen trying still to take it all in, until Salvatore raised his glass delicately by the stem. 'Ah well. *Salute*, my friend. To you and Rachel in Paris.'

'What? Ah, yes, thanks.' Stephen raised his glass in response, albeit with less brio than at the start of the afternoon. 'But what about you, Salvatore? We still haven't got around to what you're going to do.'

'Me? I told you. I leave. As for Mr Newte, I don't do anything else – at least, certainly not at the moment. I keep the information up here.' He tapped his temple.

'You're not going to be the whistle blower then?'

'Certainly not, Stephen.' He appeared surprised at the very thought of it. 'And anyway, where is the power of forgiveness for him?' He held out his hands in a plea.

Stephen felt a little ashamed. 'I suppose so, but—'

'I mean, I too suggest to him that maybe he could make amends – perhaps some sort of reverse money shuffling in the future. But for the moment, when I told him I was planning to resign, we both agreed that it would be nicer for the company to make me redundant with a little *arrivaderci*, as I mentioned.'

'So, I might deduce that Brad Hardman isn't the only one who has hold of Oscar Newte by the short and curly things.' Stephen shook his head yet again. 'And it's a done deal that you're going?'

'Yes. For the last two months in fact.'

'What? You didn't tell me.'

'My friend, I wanted to, but I am sworn to secrecy.'

'Where will you go?'

'If I tell you now, you must promise not to tell anyone.'

'What, or you'll be forced to kill me? That was a joke, by the way. OK, fair enough.'

'I am going to Ciao Cioccolato – as Head of European Marketing.' He looked immensely proud.

'Wow, the opposition. You know as soon as you announce this Hardman will have you out the door before you can say, er, *ciao*. He won't want you gathering any more info to pass on to the oppo before you go.' The penny dropped. 'Which is why you haven't told anyone. So you can take a few more state secrets with you. Silly me. And then a drunken Newte plays into your hands, so you can leave when you've collected everything you want to collect, and with a pay-off too.'

Salvatore shrugged again, those deep blue eyes craving understanding.

'You think I have done the wrong thing – a bad thing?'

Stephen exhaled. 'I don't think you're standing on the highest of moral ground, *signore*. But if I've learnt anything this year, it's that trying to do good isn't that easy.'

Salvatore gripped his hand intently. 'Don't judge me too harshly, my friend.' His eyes brightened. 'Maybe even I will find a way to do some good, as your Rachel suggests.'

They walked down to the Champs-Élysées and stood watching the flow of late afternoon traffic ducking and weaving on the broad avenue.

'Just think, Stephen, when you take this job in Paris, we will be competitors. You will be Head of European Marketing for Schmaltz and I for Ciao Cioccolato. Not a bad year's work for both of us when I think back to January.'

Stephen put an arm around Salvatore's shoulder. 'That would certainly be true.'

'It will be fun. I promise a fair fight,' Salvatore said.

'I doubt that very much,' Stephen said, 'particularly with what you have in here now.' He tapped his own temple. They both laughed, although Stephen felt Salvatore did so with more abandon.

The very last vestiges of the sun created a crimson glow behind the Arc de Triomphe in the distance. 'It's a magnificent city, Paris,' Salvatore said, echoing Stephen's thoughts.

The Italian hailed a taxi for the airport, but Stephen decided not to share it. His flight wasn't for another four hours. It definitely wasn't far from here to that apartment. Too late to get the keys to look around maybe, but still time to walk there and gaze again from the outside, to imagine. And now he welcomed the cold fresh air blowing against his face. He needed to clear his head.

Chapter Thirty-Three

The wind was strengthening and coming straight at him as he turned onto the towpath, passing another banner reminding him this was the Middleton 10K Fun Run. One kilometre to go. His hamstring was tightening with every stride now. He'd overdone it again in the gym with Madison last week. And an all-afternoon drinking session with Salvatore probably hadn't been the ideal preparation.

He could see Rachel waiting for him as he approached the finishing line, her bright yellow vest one of several such beacons. She had enrolled plenty of friends to her cause, all sporting the same colour *SAS – Save Action Stations* tops. Her friend Greg sprinted past him in the last two hundred metres with a contented look on his face – retribution at last for the car puking a year ago, presumably. And Greg was being hugged by Rachel as Stephen crossed the line to what felt like a rather modest spattering of applause from the spectators.

'Well done,' she said as she came up to him, with just a hint of condescension, he thought. It was probably a fair cop, after his patronising offer at the starting line to keep her company. She tossed her head back to swig a bottle of water, and then offered it to him. 'Don't forget warming down is just as important as warming up,' she said, as she leant forward into a graceful knee lunge, like she could do the whole thing again.

Stephen flopped onto his back on the damp grass and thought he might not get up for some time.

'Are you all right, good sir?' a man's voice asked him.

He opened his eyes to see Greg and Jane both looking down at him with anxious expressions.

'Fine, thanks,' he muttered.

'Hasn't Rachel done fantastically, getting so many sponsors?' Jane enthused. 'I love this town when it pulls together like this.'

Rachel returned and looked down at him as well, with less concern than her friends.

'I'm going to find Kate,' she said.

'Has she finished already?' he asked.

'Oh, yeah,' she said, making it clear this was a dumb question.

'OK, I'll come with you.' He felt that hamstring again as he picked himself off the ground.

Kate was wearing the same bright yellow top, and a pair of sporty leggings which looked like the ones Rachel had advised him to buy for her last Christmas. They were short on her now, tight to her calves and revealing a couple of inches of bare skin above her running shoes. That was this year's Christmas present sorted then. She was talking to a boy of about the same height, again in a *SAS* vest, and they were laughing about something, her cheeks with more colour than usual.

'Oh, hi Rachel, hi Dad,' she said. She was trying to be nonchalant, but Stephen could spot the satisfied little smile.

'Hi Kate,' Stephen said. 'So, you put me in my place.'

'It's not a competition, Dad,' she said, grinning.

'Well at least not a close one,' Rachel added.

The young man took a photo of the three of them together, Kate in the centre, arm in arm with Stephen and Rachel, and then with a cheery 'See you on Monday, Kate,' he left them alone.

'So who was that? He seemed a nice lad,' Stephen asked.

'Oh, just someone in my class.'

'Does he have a name?'

'Stephen!' Rachel gave him a sharp dig in the ribs. 'Why don't we focus on Kate's time. Go on, Kate, tell us.'

'Just under fifty. I don't think I paced it quite right but that was my target. How about you?'

'Wow, Kate, that's amazing,' Rachel said. 'I was just over fifty-nine, which I'm very happy with.' She turned to Stephen, with more concern in her eyes now. 'Seemed like you were struggling a bit towards the end, there, hon.'

She had started to call him 'hon' recently. He liked it.

'Yes, we'll draw a discreet veil over my time, I think, but hey, think of the money we raised.'

'I know. You are both wonderful. I need to go and thank the others.' Kate had met another young man she knew, and Rachel went to seek out the other Action Stations volunteers or supporters who had taken part. Seb and Keira and other bright young things he recognised from the church were there, and she exchanged hugs with all of them. But he could share her now. He knew what he meant to her now. Recovering his breath, he watched her, his heart full of affection but tinged with sadness. No matter how much they raised, it felt like her charity was coming to an end.

Kate was loping back towards him. She appeared to have grown another couple of inches just this morning.

'My brilliant girl, I'm so proud of you,' he said.

'Thanks, Dad,' she said, with the brightest smile he could remember. And then she popped a kiss on his cheek. 'I'm proud of you too.'

*

'Respect,' Jake said through a mouthful of hamburger in Donny's Diner, as Kate told him her time. It was the first time Stephen could remember Jake showing his big sister any respect for a while. 'I wonder what time I could do it in?' he added.

'Considerably slower than your sister,' Stephen said. 'She's been practising hard for weeks.'

'More like months,' Kate said, and Stephen caught her glancing appreciatively towards Rachel.

'It sounds like a good sporting morning all round,' Rachel said. 'What score did you win, Jake?'

'Four-one. Easy,' Jake replied gruffly, shrugging his shoulders. It seemed like his voice had dropped an octave in the last month. As Rachel gallantly tried to extract more detail, Stephen remained silent, watching her operate. And felt love envelop his whole being.

Eventually, she said she needed to go, as he had known she must. He accompanied her to the door.

'Thank you,' he said, kissing her.

'For what?' she asked.

'Well, pretty much everything, but in particular for how you've helped Kate. For discovering this gift she has and – nurturing it. Sorry, that sounds pretentious.'

'No, it doesn't. It sounds lovely,' she said, smiling at him. 'If anything, I should be thanking her. I reckon practising with her has taken minutes off my time. Under an hour, Mr Carreras. Just saying. Some of us have just got it.'

He laughed. 'Yes, some of you just have.'

Rachel was looking back towards Kate. 'Seriously, though, she is a glorious runner – it's like her whole body just flows in one movement.'

How did he not know that? The truth was he did, he had just forgotten. He thought back to a little girl, her lovely limbs running across the sand with a bucket full of seawater and not a care in the world. Maybe Kate had forgotten it too – until now.

'You look sad,' Rachel said.

'I was just thinking, I haven't been very good at keeping my kids in balance, have I? All this year, I've been ardently following Jake and his Saturday morning football, while my daughter has been in a trough of gloom, and I didn't know what to do. That's why I'm thanking you.'

'Don't be too hard on yourself,' Rachel said. 'It's been nice for me, getting to know her more on these Saturday morning runs. And you really try, Stephen. That's what counts.' She held him tight. 'I've got to go, hon. I need to be on a train to Newcastle in a couple of hours. Can't keep my monks waiting.'

He didn't want to let her go. 'I won't see you now until Friday. And I've so much to tell you. I haven't even had time to tell you yet about yesterday in Paris with Salvatore.'

'It's OK,' she said. 'I know you might not believe this, but a few days apart will help, I promise you. It means we'll both have time to think. And you can tell me then what you've decided. And then we can have a lovely weekend, wherever you're taking me. I've packed for all eventualities.' She seemed so cheery and relaxed, but slipped in the big question as she nodded back towards Kate and Jake.

'When are you going to talk to those two about Paris?'

Jake was spooning ice cream into his mouth and sharing something on his phone with Kate. Whatever it was, she was giggling uncontrollably.

'I don't know,' Stephen said.

Chapter Thirty-Four

'OK people, how are you all doing out there this morning? Got the Christmas spirit yet? It's Tuesday, the first of December. Let me see, how many shopping days to—'

He turned the prattling DJ off.

Peace. Apart from the vents blowing warm air onto his windscreen, and the intermittent swish of his wipers.

What sort of peace was Rachel experiencing right now? Something a bit more substantive, no doubt. On her own in a monastic bedroom? Or maybe at breakfast prayer with a monk or two. Would she ask him on retreat some time? He wanted to be there now, so close he could feel her every breath. Although presumably that would never do, in a monastery.

She wasn't responding to any of his texts. She had told him it was a mobile-free zone, but surely they came up for air from time to time? It seemed that with Rachel, silent retreat meant just that. Once again, she wasn't doing things by halves. Had she even taken her phone with her? This felt like the most important decision of his life. And now she felt like the most important person in his life. And he couldn't share his thinking with her. But he remembered again her parting words as they stood outside Donny's Diner together.

When she had told him, once again, that she trusted him to make the right decision. He was trying so hard to relearn the language of trust.

The traffic was light and he was at work quicker than he had hoped this morning. Another fifteen minutes in a traffic jam, wrapped up in warm thoughts about Rachel, would have been very welcome. But he was here and he couldn't procrastinate any longer. This whole year had been one hurdle after another at work, and now here was one whacking great water jump to finish with. John Motson tried to interject but Stephen didn't let him – that guy needed to be retired.

He parked and started walking across the concourse towards the office, still lost in thought. By now, deep down, he knew what he wanted from this meeting. The trick was to get what he wanted, what was right. What would Salvatore do in this situation? He thought about his friend recounting his artful manoeuvring of Oscar Newte in Pietro's trattoria. *And now the silly fish bites*, he had said. If only he could take a leaf from the Italian book of angling this morning. Trouble was, Hardman was a bigger and smarter fish than Oscar Newte.

He became aware of raised voices – an altercation, just in front of the revolving door. Taylor had been drawn out from the sanctity of reception and, clad in a high-vis yellow jacket over her usual chocolate brown uniform, had mislaid her customary composure. She was confronted by a small band of women, all muffled against the cold and several of them holding the hands of small children. They were also holding a variety of placards, of which one in particular shouted to him.

LISA SAYS
DON'T SUGAR COAT CHRISTMAS
Life is Sweet Already

The women of LISA had landed in Middleton. And it was a fair bet Taylor hadn't bargained on having to deal with anything like this when she'd moved over from Orlando to be the face of Schmaltz UK's front desk.

'Sorry, ladies, but you can't come in here,' she shouted above the hubbub. 'This is private estate.'

'We don't want to come in,' retorted an elderly spokeswoman wearing a green woolly hat and scarf, in a country tweed voice. 'We are just going to stand here and protest peacefully. And we've got an interviewer from Good Morning Midlands turning up at nine o'clock to talk to us outside your offices.'

'That's out of the question,' Taylor said, eliciting further boos and protests.

'You try stopping us, love,' a gruffer northern voice countered.

Stephen needed to leave them to it and steel himself in readiness for Hardman. But as he tried to slip unnoticed past the melee, Mrs Country Tweed barked at him.

'Young man, do you work here?'

He was amused by the 'young man'. But there was something of the schoolmistress in her voice which felt naughty to ignore.

'I do indeed.'

She was clutching the hand of a little girl who looked about six, wrapped up in a warm red duffel coat. Her granddaughter? She was the spitting image of Kate at the same age.

'And what do you do?' the schoolmistress asked stridently.

'I do my best to sell our chocolate, madam. I'm afraid it's rather a busy day, so I can't—'

'Do you sell Little Monkeys?' the little girl piped up, looking up at him, nose wrinkled.

'I do actually.'

'I like Little Monkeys.'

'Well, that's good to hear.' Stephen couldn't resist winking at her. She wasn't exactly toeing the LISA party line with that one.

Mrs. Country Tweed sighed. 'Young man, I am not trying to stop my grandchild from eating this ghastly stuff. I understand children like chocolate. We just want you to make an effort. To do *something* about the sugar. Do you understand?'

She had an intelligent face. It was tempting to explain that if it weren't for him saving the old faithfuls like Little Monkeys, this and every other child in Britain would have been munching twice as much sugar next year after the Schmaltzy Bar and Nutters invasion. And possibly farting a lot more for good measure, although he remained unconvinced about that. But the little girl continued to stare up at him, with an enquiring expression.

'I do understand. And I promise you we'll do something,' he said.

*

Predictably, Brad was not in the lightest of moods.

'Fucking LISA,' he spat, as he waved Stephen into his office. He was staring out at the car park, from where the first strains of '*What do we want?*' were audible.

'What do these women want, Carreras?' Hardman looked accusingly at him.

Stephen could hear '*Hardman out*' but Brad didn't seem to have clocked it.

'They want us to reduce the sugar in our products, Mr Hardman.'

'I know that. It was a fucking rhetorical question. Anyway, sit down. You brought the contract with you? You should be thanking me extra for giving you the chance to escape these harpies.'

So the chair was still here. Stephen sat down and took a deep breath.

'I have brought the contract, Mr Hardman, but I haven't signed it – yet.'

Hardman remained standing, fists on hips in his sumo wrestler pose, eyes narrowing.

'Why the fuck not? I told you I wanted you to do this for me. Have you been to damn Paris since we talked last week?'

Stephen held a picture in his mind. It was a picture of Rachel, Kate, Jake and himself at six o'clock on a Saturday in the San Remo Pizzeria. He needed to hold it right there. And he needed to play this as if he held the whip hand. Keep out of his mind the possibility of Hardman firing him on the spot. That wasn't easy.

'I did go to Paris, Mr Hardman. And I've given this a lot of thought in terms of what's the best option for – the business.' That's right, frame it in terms of the business.

'I'm not in the habit of discussing options,' Hardman replied, but Stephen thought there was a trace of engagement in his eyes.

'I met with Signor Carnevale while I was there, just to review our brand plans for next year.'

'I suppose you told him I'd offered you this job?'

As ever with Hardman, he needed to get to the point.

'I did. He was typically gracious about it. But we spent more time talking about something else, something more important. You know those Italians, Mr Hardman. They always seem to have a way of discovering things.' Flatter him, get him on side. You and I, we understand these things, Brad. 'Signor Carnevale follows a very respected Italian journalist, a man called Gigi Peronace, and it's evident from this journalist's blog, that he is – for some reason – questioning Schmaltz Europe profits. Saying they are maybe not quite as good as has been reported?'

Hardman fixed him with those intimidating, piercing eyes. Would he deny it? Would he tell him where to go, and never to darken his doors again?

And then, he sat down. 'Do you believe him?' he said quietly.

The big fish had nibbled. Start reeling him in now; slowly, slowly.

'Yes, I do believe Signor Carnevale when he says that this journalist is sniffing around. Obviously I've no reason to believe his investigations will lead to anything.'

Hardman didn't look so bullish as normal, more pensive. 'Why do you believe Carnival? The fella's slippery as shit in my opinion. He could be making it up.'

It didn't seem like Hardman knew about Salvatore's planned imminent departure with Newte's generous *arrivaderci*. Oscar was sailing close to the wind trying to keep that quiet.

'Signor Carnevale was prompted to tell me about the journalist because we had arranged to meet in a restaurant in Paris, and he turned up at the same place – on his own.'

Hardman fidgeted, but said nothing.

'And then I don't know if you remember back in August, when I happened to be in La Belle Époque in Paris, with my new, er, partner, and you came in with Mr Newte?' Not surprisingly, Hardman's expression darkened at this damp recollection. 'I'm fairly certain the same reporter was there, at the next table, on his own again.'

Hardman stood up again and walked back towards the window. It seemed like he wanted to avoid eyeball to eyeball now. In the silence, the chants of the women in the car park below rang out more clearly.

'Give me an L!'

'L!'

'Give me an I!'

'I!'

'Fuck!' Hardman roared.

Stephen must have heard him use that word a thousand

times in the last year. But this one felt more desperate, that of a trapped man. Hardman turned to face him again.

'What do you propose we do about it, then, this Peroni guy?'

Typical, Brad, putting the onus on me. But exactly what I wanted. It's our shared problem now, isn't it? You need my help.

'Well, as I said, obviously I don't know whether he is really onto something, investigating our profits. But I just wanted to tell you something about me, Mr Hardman. I've worked in this business for a long time now, over ten years. I'm very proud of our reputation, and I'd hate to think of it being dragged through the mud. I'd like to do all I can personally to make sure that by next spring when we declare the final profits for the year, we're turning in numbers without a whiff of suspicion.'

He thought Hardman looked jaded, on the point of surrender. He needed to keep going.

'And I've worked with Mr Newte since he came into the business, just a couple of years ago. I'm sure I can help him to ensure we turn the profits around in future. If, of course, they need turning around.'

Hardman emitted a grunt. But nothing more. It was time to net the bastard.

'So, to go back to your generous offer to be VP Marketing for Schmaltz Europe, I'd really like to accept, but there is just one tweak I'd like to suggest.'

'Go on.'

'I'd like to do the job from Middleton. I mean, thanks for the offer of Paris, but for personal reasons I need to be here. And in the circumstances, if we do need to tighten our belts a little to hit the profit targets, and so this meddling journalist can't hold anything against us, it will be a good saving if I stay here. I don't need that apartment in Paris.'

There it was. He'd said it.

Hardman scrutinised him again. What was he thinking? It was

a fair bet nobody had tried to negotiate him *down* on salary before.

There was a loud crack.

'What the—' Hardman started, and took a step away from the window. Behind him, an eggshell was clinging to the pane, while its yolky content dribbled slowly downwards.

'What do we want?' they chanted.

'Hardman out!' It was nice and clear this time.

'When do we want it?'

'Now!'

The women of LISA had just provided the mallet with which Stephen could give this whopper a final whack on the head.

'That's the other reason I should be here. We need to combat LISA here first, Mr Hardman. Before they create a bridgehead and spread out across Europe. And believe me, I'm the best man to lead the fight.' It was hard in truth to believe that the woolly-hatted women standing outside would be invading Europe any time soon. But you never know. And Hardman would enjoy playing soldiers.

For the first time in the conversation, the American made that disgusting noise at the back of his throat. But his eyes were still not those of a dead fish. No, they were the beady eyes of a thoroughly live rat.

'OK, Carreras, I understand where you're coming from. You want to stay in this shithole.' Then that unsettling smile. 'But you know what? I don't want you to do this fucking marketing job after all.'

Chapter Thirty-Five

The sing-song voice of the station announcer heralded her coming.

'The train now approaching platform four is the 15:17 arrival from Newcastle, calling at London King's Cross only.'

'In the words of the Temptations, I'll be there.' That's what she'd said. He hadn't been able to resist pointing out it was the Four Tops, and she had deferred to his age, although he reminded her it was well before his time too. His heart was racing, eyes straining along the track for the first sign. A tiny dot of light appeared, slowly diverging into two distinct headlights. Then the low portentous drone of the engine, growing in intensity. She would be reaching up to the overhead luggage rack now, heaving down that tattered red bag, almost as big as she was.

As the carriages rolled slowly past him, he peered in for a first glimpse. Without success. Squealing brakes brought the train to a complete halt. In their own time, the steps automatically descended to the platform edge and the doors slid open. He realised he was standing outside a first-class compartment when two suited businessmen stepped down, in animated conversation. She wouldn't be in here. Further along the platform, other passengers were descending from second class. Where was she? Maybe she wouldn't be here after all. After a week of contemplation with those bloody monks, had she been put off by all this talk of moving to Paris? Maybe he hadn't been sensitive enough to her needs. He was now.

The doors were closing; the guard's harsh whistle blowing time.

That black and white striped jacket. Right at the far end of the platform. Thanking some guy who had helped her with the bag, laughing with him.

Putting the bag on the ground next to her, she turned to look along the platform. And now she was running. And now he was breathing her in.

*

'I was beginning to think you'd decided to become a nun.'

'Hardly likely. I was at a monastery, not a nunnery. But don't get too complacent. A couple of those young men were decidedly athletic.'

'You told me women weren't allowed to sleep in the monastery itself. I thought you were in the block next door.'

'Just adds to the fun. Anyway, Mr Carreras, Peterborough. An interesting choice. You clearly know the way to a girl's heart.'

Her teasing made him feel safe and loved. He leant over to kiss her throat.

'I can see I must go away more often.' She leant her head back, inviting more, until the car behind hooted a rude hurry-up. 'But first I think you need to insert ticket as instructed and get us out of this car park.'

'OK, OK.' He laughed, easing out into the afternoon traffic, feeling light-headed. 'But please don't,' he said, turning to her as they stopped at the first red light.

'Please don't what?'

'Please don't go away more often.'

She smiled, checking her appearance in the vanity mirror.

He didn't need the help of Satnav Alice here. She would give the game away.

'So, in case you hadn't worked it out, Peterborough is not our ultimate destination.'

'Oh no!' She affected a despondent look. 'Well, where are we going?'

'You'll just have to wait. We might be going on retreat again.'

She hit him on the knee with a rolled-up copy of *Cosmo*.

'Ouch. Don't worry, we aren't,' he added quickly. 'Well, not one like you've just been on. Although I suppose you might call it a retreat of sorts. It's only about forty-five minutes' drive.' He was quite enjoying teasing her now.

She laughed. 'That's a relief. I've had enough silence and isolation to last me until next year.' But then she looked at him more seriously.

'So?' she asked.

'So what?'

'I assume you've been to see the big boss again?'

'I have. But that can wait a little while.'

There would be time enough for bigger conversations. Just for now, he simply wanted to be next to her; next to her and back in her day to day life. Driving out of town, he steered the conversation towards understanding the rhythm and daily routine of her week away. And the words poured out from her after a week of silence. Soon they were turning off the A14 towards Cambridge. For the first time in the journey, Rachel seemed to become aware of the world outside.

'Oh, Cambridge. Is that where we're heading?'

'It might be.'

'That's exciting,' she said, wide-eyed.

He smiled. Even if it had been Peterborough, she would have made a fist of it.

'Do you know it?' he asked.

'No. I came here in sixth form once. Our head of year suggested I should apply. But at the time I thought it was too establishment for the northern Christian rebel socialist I was struggling to be.'

'Wow, that sounds like a challenging role.'

'It was. At least one too many adjectives there, I think.'

He sensed a little knot of sadness in her expression. 'Do you regret it at all?'

'I'm kind of working on not regretting things. But trying to learn from them instead. Regret has not always been my friend in the past.' She placed a hand tenderly on his knee.

The flow broken, they travelled in companionable silence for a few minutes.

'What was the breakfast like?' he asked eventually.

'Enough now,' she laughed. 'The muesli was cracking. I want to know why Cambridge.'

'When we met – at the party, a year ago – the day before, I'd been at some awful board meeting in a hotel somewhere round here. Grimley's was in its death throes. And Oscar Newte seemed to know everything there was to know about the Schmaltz takeover. I drove into town after the meeting finished. I don't know why, just something to do rather than go back to my house, I think.'

They had come to a roundabout. The roundabout. He looked to his right. The low flat roof of the Molitor Hotel was caught by the late afternoon sun. It looked almost beautiful.

'Go on,' she said. He followed the sign to the city centre.

'There was this young woman singing, from a room in one of the colleges. Clare College, actually. At first, I could just hear her, before I saw her. I didn't know what she was singing at the time – a hymn, very beautiful, haunting. And when she came out after rehearsing, her boyfriend met her.' He paused, capturing the image in his mind again. 'The hymn. I heard it again at that first church service you invited me to. I think it's an Advent hymn.'

Rachel sang quietly under her breath.

'O come, O come, Emmanuel
And ransom captive Israel
That mourns in lonely exile here
Until the Son of God appear.'

'Yes, that's it.' He swallowed hard. 'So I checked out Advent carol services in Cambridge, and there's one this evening – at Clare – at seven thirty. That's where we're going. And then we're staying in a very classy hotel, so not the Hotel Molitor. I hope that's all right?'

The look on her face told him it was.

'As long as we can go dancing sometime this weekend?'

'Dancing? Well, I'll see what I can do. Not sure there's a lot of punk revival in Cambridge.'

'Nah, I don't want punk. I want soul, baby.'

'Oh, do you? I didn't know you were a soul diva too.'

'There's still a lot you don't know about me,' she said.

*

He stretched out on the white duvet cover, hands behind his head, taking her in. She was perched at the foot of the bed, her back to him, looking at herself in the large mirror which stretched across the wall in front of them, carefully edging bright red lips. Then she lightly brushed powder across her cheeks, glancing at his reflection, basking in the glow of his admiration.

Only as she put on a gold necklace did she break the intimate silence.

'So, I have some news for you, Mr Carreras, from my deliberations over the muesli.'

'Oh, I see. Well, I have some news for you too.'

'But as you've been keeping me on tenterhooks, you're just going to have to wait now. I got in first.' She swivelled round and threw herself down next to him, lying on her stomach, head resting on folded arms.

'I need to tell you about the important stuff from my week – as opposed to the quality of the breakfast. Although when I say from my week, I really mean last weekend. Because something weird and wonderful happened after I left you on Saturday afternoon, just before I set off into my mobile-free zone. I thought I'd check the JustGiving page, to do a final reccy on how much we made from the run. And I discovered there was one late additional donation.'

'Oh, that's nice,' Stephen said. He kissed the nape of her neck. She smelt just as she had the night he had met her.

'Mm, yes, a bit more than nice. When I say a donation, well, actually, a hundred-thousand-pound donation.'

'Bloody hell.' He stopped kissing the nape of her neck.

'I see I have your full attention now.'

'But, I mean, who from?'

'So that's the odd thing. Well, the other odd thing, apart from it being a hundred thousand pounds, obviously. It was anonymous.'

'Do you have any idea? I mean have you had some rich backer in the past?'

'No, we're normally scrabbling to get money from trusts, local churches, the mosque, bless them. But nothing like this. The only thing was, it came with a message. It said, "Someone tells me that you do good among the carnage."'

It took a moment, then the penny dropped.

'Good grief, it's Salvatore.'

Rachel laughed. 'No, surely not. Why would Salvatore give us money? He's never even met me. And is he really that wealthy?'

'I think he feels like he knows you. I've talked a lot about you. He's always very interested in Action Stations. In fact, come to think of it, I might have even mentioned the run. And he's the only person I've ever told about the "good among the carnage" thing. And as for him being wealthy – I'm coming to this, I promise you – he has suddenly come into quite a lot of money.' He was now wondering again just how much. It really must have been an extremely nice *arrivaderci*. 'And I think he must have decided a little redistribution of wealth was a good thing.'

Rachel shook her head in apparent wonder. 'He does sound like the most remarkably good man.'

'Salvatore – a remarkably good man.' He paused. 'Remarkable, definitely. And unconventional. And infuriating. But yes, I think you're right. A good man.'

He got up from the bed and went over to the window, still trying to take it in.

'Does this mean Action Stations is safe after all?'

'Well, incredibly, it does. At least for the next two years.' She came up behind him to put her arms around him. 'But I've been thinking so much about Paris. I don't think I could properly absorb it all last week – how amazing your proposal was. There have been times in the past few days when I've fantasised over chucking it all in anyway and coming with you.' She sighed, and he felt her warm breath on his neck. 'But I just don't think I can desert Action Stations right now.'

The moment had come.

'Mm. So if I were to offer an alternative to a Parisian apartment, such as a three-bedroom semi-detached with marvellous potential in Middleton, how fantastic would that be exactly?'

She whispered in his ear. 'Can I take it from this, Mr C, that you too have had a week of quiet reflection?'

'Reflection, yes. Quiet, hardly. I even tried praying once, though I'm not sure I've got the hang of it yet.'

A playful smile lit her face, as she put her hands on her hips.

'Middleton instead of Paris, eh? I would have thought that's every woman's dream. Although my demands will include a weekend in Paris every year. And I don't mean in the Hotel bloody Splendid. I can only take so much.'

*

The footpath skirted a meadow which encroached incongruously into the city centre. They walked arm in arm past the hulking shadow of a cow, distinguishable in the gloom by its loud, purposeful chewing of grass. Rachel nestled her head against his shoulder.

'Of course, I'm relieved, deep down. I don't know what I would have done in the short term if we hadn't got a reprieve. If you had decided on Paris, maybe I would have come with you. I have no idea how I would have worked there, but I really would have given it a go. But now I'm worried that it was the silver-tongued Salvatore who talked you out of it.'

'Salvatore? No, he was absolutely convinced I should take it – but inadvertently he did talk me out of it, or rather he clarified things for me without knowing it.'

'How come?'

'I told him about the job offer and the fact that you and I were together, and that I'd asked if you would consider coming with me. And he was happy for me on both counts. But it was the look in his eye when he congratulated me on finding you

– that's what stuck. And made me think again about what the important thing was here.'

He stopped walking to look at her.

'Rachel, over the last few weeks a notion has started to form in my fuzzy brain. About the people I want to be close to. And those people don't include Brad Hardman. But last week when he offered me this job in Paris, I was so caught up in the triumph of being offered it, that notion got mislaid again. Earlier in the year I thought a thirty-mile commute to FastGro would be a challenge, aside of course from the bigger fact that I really, really don't want to work in fertiliser. Now here I was trying to convince myself I could easily manage my relationship with you and with the children from 400 miles. But good old Salvatore inadvertently helped me on that one too. Although he was delighted that we've got together, at the same time he seemed to ride roughshod over what might be important for you. He sounded a bit complacent, like Conrad, saying you might as well come with me as your job was disappearing. To be honest, I had been guilty of the same thought. But when Salvatore said it, somehow it made me realise what you were facing in giving up your work here, if you came to Paris.'

Her eyes were full of affection. 'I thought if I said I couldn't move to Paris, you would still go, and opt for the commuting option – coming back every two weeks to see the children, and hopefully me. You know I would have tried to make that work too.'

Salvatore was right on one thing. He wanted to wake up with her in his bed every day now, to smell her scent in every room of his house. He wanted to be there every evening when she had a bad day.

'I know you would have tried. But the idea of meeting up with you every two weeks – it's OK maybe for a twenty-year-old. But I'm not a twenty-year-old.'

'Darn, and there was me thinking…'

They walked up onto the Silver Street Bridge and stood there in silence. He drew her closer to him, against the cold. A low mist hung over the river and the punts were lying dormant. Students cycled purposefully past them, hooded against the cold damp air. The reverie was broken by two squealing teenagers running ahead of their parents.

'Something else has happened too. Here again Salvatore was useful in a way he didn't intend. He said what a great experience it would be for my kids, going to Paris for a weekend so regularly, instead of me always coming back here. Hardman said something similar. Rather than rely on their expert advice about what my kids would like, I had finally decided to talk to them about it after the run last Saturday. But when I went round to pick them up on Saturday morning, Laura asked if she could talk to me privately first. I was going to tell her about the offer anyway and see what she thought. As I've told you, we're trying very hard to be kinder to each other these days. But she had some news too. Turns out both the children have been asking if they can spend more weekends with me, and she actually thinks it would be a good idea as well. Basically, they just can't stand Tristran. A view I wholeheartedly endorse, of course, but that's another story.'

'Wow. And how did that make you feel? Sorry, I sound like a counsellor.'

'No, it's all right. I think a few months ago I'd have felt annoyed. I used to think Laura liked palming the children off on me, so she could be alone with lover boy, and now here she was suggesting they were more reliant on me, scuppering my dream of Paris. But I didn't feel like that at all. A whole mix of emotions really. Genuinely sorry for Laura, as I could sense it was hurting her, that they wanted to spend less time with her and more with me. Delight that I might see more of my kids, be a bigger part of their lives. But also aware of the responsibility. Laura is still quite anxious about Kate struggling with friendships, and whether she's showing one or two signs of a possible eating disorder. My daughter might not be out of the woods yet. In fact, I suspect your children are never out of the woods completely.'

Rachel looked pensive, and he squeezed her tight. 'But I have to say, I think you getting her into running is the best thing that's happened to her for a long time. I just felt she was transformed last weekend.'

'And you obviously noticed that a series of fit young men were forming an orderly queue to talk to her afterwards,' she said. 'So come on, what did you say when you talked to them about Paris?' she asked.

'I didn't talk to them about Paris. After you'd gone, they were just messing about together, sharing stuff on their phones that made them laugh. They were as happy as I'd seen them together in ages. I thought about discussing it with them. I even imagined how they would react if I did move. I pictured dragging them round some art gallery in Paris on a Saturday morning, trying to convince them they were having a good time, trying to convince myself I was having a good time. And then I thought about how much I look forward to watching Jake play football, driving him into town after, finally extracting a post-mortem from him and meeting Kate for lunch. With him in particular, it's like I've found this thing, Rachel, after five years, something that feels really important and connects me to him, and I would have to just pack it all in. And now I hope that maybe Kate will get into running every weekend too. So I never mentioned Paris. And honestly, I'm not being selfless. I've just understood who's important. Them – and you.'

They heard the steady wingbeat of incoming aircraft – a swan, landing on the river, rippling the surface. He searched her face for reassurance. 'I suppose at some level I'm a bit anxious about how the kids being around more might affect us – but I just hope we'll work it out.'

'I'm sure we will – over pizza. And if Kate *is* experiencing eating disorders, I've read the book and seen the movie on that. I'll try to help.'

'I'm not sure I deserve you, Rachel Pearson.'

She laughed dismissively. 'I'm sure we both deserve much better, but hey, we're all we've got. But does this mean you're just staying in your current job – for us?' she asked.

'Well, I'll stay in Middleton for you – and me. But the current job? No way. I need to tell you what else Salvatore said.'

Past the entrance to Queens' College, they turned to follow the path along the Backs. And as she held him close and they walked in step together, he recounted everything that Salvatore had told him about the mysterious Signor Peronace, Oscar Newte's money shuffling, and how the crafty so-and-so had used this information to arrange a very nice *arrivaderci*. And then how Salvatore thought Hardman was paranoid about observing Manfred Schmaltz's moral code. As usual when Stephen told Rachel anything about Salvatore, her reaction was a mix of fascination and incredulity. But then that pretty much summed up his own feelings.

They paused again to take in the view, over to the vast outline of King's College, the lights within transforming it into a cruise ship docked in the bay.

'So, this money that Salvatore sent. It's part of his pay-off?' Rachel asked.

'I assume so. I don't know how you feel about that. I mean, him squeezing a deal out of Oscar like that.'

'Don't worry about that, sunshine.' She sounded like a gangster's moll. They both laughed.

'Something else odd has just occurred to me,' Stephen said. 'When do you think Salvatore pledged his money?'

'It looked like it was midweek, before the race. But then the pledges get transferred weekly. So it's safely in the account now, before you ask.'

Once again, Salvatore's trickery was leaving him open-mouthed. 'OK, so he'd already made this donation, which he must have known would help you survive, when I met him on the Friday. In which case all his noises about what a shame it was that Action Stations was closing, and how that made it obvious that you should come to Paris – it was all a sham.'

'Ooh, yeah, I see what you mean.'

Stephen shook his head in puzzlement. 'You remember when you were trying to explain to me what you thought God was like – you know, all that stuff about we can never really understand him, or her, and that he, or she, exists outside time. I'm beginning to think Salvatore operates on a similar plane.'

Rachel laughed, clearly less concerned by the intricacies of it all than Stephen was. 'Ah well, there we go. But you still haven't told me what you're going to do.'

'No, I haven't, have I? Well, one of Salvatore's strongest arguments for Paris was that there's nothing left for me in Middleton. But after he left me, I went for a walk. I was going to try and find the apartment, but I didn't have the address. So I wandered the streets for a while, just reflecting. I knew he was wrong. It had dawned on me already that all the people I love are here. But I thought about work too, and how Salvatore was playing Newte to finance his own exit. And it occurred to me that maybe I could use what Salvatore had told me to manoeuvre Hardman too. To persuade him to let me stay in Middleton.'

'How? I thought he had insisted you did this job based in Paris or not at all.'

'He had. But when I went to see him this week, although I stressed again how flattered I was to be offered the job, I told him that I really wanted to do it in Middleton, and that he should think about all the money he'd save. I did also slip into the conversation what Salvatore had told me about Peronace and intimated that all the pokery jiggery might be exposed – that's an Italian expression, by the way – unless I sorted things out for him. That concentrated his mind. As I think did the women of LISA,' he smiled.

'OK, you've lost me again now.'

'They were protesting outside the office. You know, I think Hardman's just worn down by all the flak. I don't think he realised their campaign was going to be such a big deal, but now they're literally manning, er – womanning the barricades. So, I guessed that when I suggested doing the job from the UK, so I could help rid Hardman of this turbulent LISA, sort out our position on sugar, he would jump at the chance.'

'So you're still going to be the European Marketing Vice President – note I've got the lingo by the way – but based in Middleton. You're a genius.'

'Er, not so fast. That's what I was pitching for, and where I thought the conversation was going. But then he suddenly told me he didn't want me to do that job after all. I must admit that was the moment when I thought my strategy was unravelling and I might have to join Danny in the fertiliser. But it turned out he had another offer.'

'What?'

'Vice President, Schmaltz UK.'

A duck quacked on the river, rather mockingly Stephen thought. But Rachel hugged him.

'Well, Mr Carreras, I can see that you haven't been letting the grass grow under your feet in the last week. That sounds good to me.' And then she said, more doubtfully, 'Is it? Does Vice President Schmaltz UK trump European Marketing Vice President?'

'It does for me. Maybe Hardman thinks he's pulled a fast one on me, calling me a VP for the UK, not a president. But who cares? The main thing is I get to look after everything in the UK, not just marketing. And of course doing a UK job not a European job means I'll miss those exotic stays in the Hotel Splendid. I imagine Solène will be devastated not to see me. But it's effectively what I was hoping for a year ago, until Oscar announced the Schmaltz takeover. I was lying in bed last night thinking about all the other things I want to do in this job. I haven't felt this excited about work for years. I do think we need to get the sugar levels down. And after Hardman's reign of terror this year, I need to try and find a proper role for some of the people I've told you about, like Jerry Collins and Jennie Jacobs.' He laughed. 'I might even have a go at persuading him to go back to calling the business Grimley's instead of Schmaltz UK, although that might be too big an ask.'

He laughed at another recollection. 'One thing Salvatore always said was that Hardman might be a b— but surely he wasn't a stupid b—. I suppose he has shown enough self-awareness to realise that he personally might not have the core diplomatic skills to parley with LISA. And it frees him up to focus completely on his major ass-kicking tour of Europe. I don't know if I can do anything to restrain him on that one.'

Rachel winced. 'I'm thinking about Vassos,' she said.

'Mm, I know. But he's a grown-up. I'm sure he'll tunnel his way out – or Hardman will set him free.' He put his arm round her once more. 'But there's something else more important.'

'What's that?'

'I'm going to be living in the same place as the people I love.'

He wanted to kiss her again, but Rachel was still contemplating.

'And what are you going to do about Oscar and his pokery thingummy?'

The question hung in the evening mist. She was not easily satisfied, Rachel, always raising the bar; asking him again to do the right thing. And for reasons he couldn't explain, it was exhilarating to be listened to, loved, but still challenged.

'I've been thinking about that too. I need to help Oscar put things right, for everyone's sake, but I haven't worked out how yet. Or whether he'll even open up to me. Maybe I need Salvatore to arrange dinner for three at Pietro's next time. But I'll tread carefully, I think. I know Salvatore says Hardman wants nothing to do with Oscar's financial antics because of keeping the bosses happy – but the cynic in me wonders if it's simply because Hardman doesn't want to end up in jail. I don't want to overreach myself and find myself at the bottom of Middleton canal tied to a block of cement.'

'OK, I think you might have read too many political thrillers, but I do agree that's not going to help anyone.'

They started to stroll again. 'There's one other rather interesting twist,' Stephen said. 'Once he'd offered me the job as Head of Schmaltz UK, Hardman grunted in that delightful way of his and said he was going to offer the European marketing job to the effing Italian after all.'

'But Salvatore's leaving.'

'Is he? I didn't know that,' he said mischievously. 'It's obvious Oscar's deal with Salvatore hasn't come to Hardman's attention yet. Lovely, isn't it? I'll leave Hardman to offer it to him. It will be interesting to see how he reacts – he might backtrack. You never know with Salvatore. Although I suppose it's unlikely given that he's pinched some of our state secrets and I now know he has already paid you a considerable amount of his *arrivaderci*.'

'Which, as I said, is tucked safely in our account,' Rachel said firmly.

'I'm sure when it comes to that money, he'll be a man of honour – not in all things, but definitely in this.' He held her close again. 'I'm just so pleased that at least the next two years are sorted for you.'

'Yes, it's great,' Rachel said, but with a note of hesitation. 'As I said, I had a lot of time to think about it last week. I do definitely want to secure the future of Action Stations and that probably will take two years. But at some point, I think I should pass it on to someone else. And do something different. I don't like being defined for too long.' She laughed. 'One of the monks thought I should go into the church.'

Stephen withdrew slightly, so he could check if she looked serious.

'But I thought you were still trying to find God – isn't that a job for someone who's not still struggling with the satnav?'

'Well, you may be right.' Her face broke into a smile. 'On the other hand, I can think of a certain beardy evangelist currently residing in Malawi who would suggest that not being sure about God puts me in line with many other vicars in today's Church of England.'

'Wow, so when you say enter the church, you're considering becoming a vicar?'

'Don't worry, it's only a whimsical notion at the moment – you've got Mr Anxious face on, by the way.' She grinned again. 'But you never know. Ironic double twist. Bishop's daughter runs away from church – only to end up as vicar, shock.'

Her eyes scrutinised him. 'I have told you I'm in it for the long haul, trying to find God?'

He gave her a squeeze of affirmation.

'And I hope I'm in it for the long haul with you too,' she said softly into his ear.

They had come to the back gate of Clare College, a church bell calling them from across the bridge. This was where he had shared that moment with the Chinese tourist, both quietly admiring the beauty, a moment that felt almost religious. And where he had decided to go through the gate.

'That evening, a year ago, I cried,' he said. 'Not when I was in Cambridge, but when I got back home.'

She remained silent, inviting him to continue.

'That girl and boy made me cry. They just seemed to have – a future. And I felt I had no future. All I could see was this American takeover and I just knew it was going to be bad. But now I have a future again, Rachel. You've given me that. The fact that I don't know exactly how it's going to work out seems gloriously irrelevant. Or maybe the most relevant thing of all.'

She turned her head, inviting the kiss now. Her mouth enveloped his. He had a curiously erotic thought about her as a vicar, wearing nothing under a flowing white robe. The only sound was of the insistent church bell.

'Shit, we need to go.'

'What?'

'We really need to go. This service starts in fifteen minutes.'

*

They were squashed in at the end of a bench, his legs brushing against the red-haired girl in front of him. And the bony knees of a bespectacled young man, who had to be reading physics, formed a less than perfect back support. At the last minute, another gawky student, who smelt in need of a shower, squeezed in next to him, forcing him into ever closer union with Rachel's thigh.

'Ringside seats. Clever you,' she whispered, as if he'd booked them in advance, and pressed even closer. They were seated side on in the chancel, facing five more rows of congregation opposite them, with the still empty choir stalls to their left, between them and the altar. Everyone was clutching a small unlit white candle in a flimsy cardboard holder, handed to them as they entered.

A solemn voice bid them stand, and around the bare, cold stone chapel, the lights went out, one by one, until they were in near darkness. Only one tall, proud candle remained lit, burning brightly from a wreath in front of the altar.

The gloom was broken not by a light but a voice: a young woman's voice at the back of the church, slowly rising as she moved gradually down the aisle towards them, her face bathed in the light of the single candle she held.

'O come, O come, Emmanuel
And ransom captive Israel
That mourns in lonely exile here
Until the Son of God appear.'

A young female priest just in front of them took the lighted candle from the wreath at the altar and offered its delicate flame to those holding candles at the end of each row. The young man with questionable hygiene, his candle now lit, held it nervously towards Stephen, who in turn nudged his candle into the flame, and then retracting it, found that the flame had taken. He turned to Rachel, and their candles embraced in the same way. All around them, faces were being illuminated.

The whole choir, robed in white, took up the second verse, as they shuffled past the congregation towards the choir stalls. For the first time, Stephen tried to join in, hymn sheet in one hand, candle in the other, but it was tricky. It beguiled you this harmony, going one way and then another.

In the third verse, he felt her hand on his lower back, sliding gently south. What would the students think? He couldn't stop her; he had both hands full, one with a hymn sheet, the other with a candle. He didn't want to stop her. He turned to look at her. She was focusing not on him, but gazing into the space ahead of her, maybe at the stained-glass window on the other side of the nave. Her eyes were smiling and her lips enunciating every word. She didn't need to hold a hymn sheet. She knew it off by heart, how to bring words and harmony into step.

'*O come, Thou Dayspring, from on high,*
And cheer us by Thy drawing nigh;
Disperse the gloomy clouds of night,
And death's dark shadows put to flight.
Rejoice! Rejoice! Emmanuel
Shall come to thee, O Israel.'

It was a difficult but glorious rhythm.

Singing lessons next year. Now wouldn't that be a thing?

Acknowledgements

This novel started to form in my head over fifteen years ago, and I then embarked upon it for real in September 2014, on the inaugural Creative Writing MA course at St Mary's University in South-West London. So it has been a long time in the writing, and required support from many people along the way, all of whom have been generous with their time, and so helpful with their feedback.

Firstly, I'd like to pay tribute to my dear mother, Thelma Howden, who always encouraged me to write from being a small boy growing up in Middleham, a village in Wensleydale. It has only taken me until her hundredth year to finally finish this, but we got there in the end. I am very worried that she will not approve of the swearing, but I can't be responsible for Brad Hardman's behaviour. Caroline, my wife, was then the person who told me to stop threatening to write a novel and start doing it, and without her I would probably never have applied for the MA, or found the discipline to progress. Caroline, along with my daughter Sarah, has also been a patient and sympathetic reader of endless excerpts and drafts, and the two of them, along with my son Chris, have been a source of encouragement and inspiration throughout.

Acknowledgements

David Savill initiated the MA at St Mary's, before moving on to become Programme Leader in Creative Writing at the University of Salford. I owe him a huge debt of gratitude for having the vision to make the course happen, and for how much he taught me throughout its duration. He and the other course leaders, Scott Bradfield and Russell Schechter, challenged and helped us to 'just write better', and I hope to have made some progress on that score – athough as with Little Monkeys, there is clearly still room for improvement.

Since then, many others have contributed to the novel's evolution. Alison Taft, working with Cornerstones, helped me enormously with thinking through the structure. Cathie Hartigan, from Creative Writing Matters, gave me positive approval at a point when I most needed it. And Alison Baverstock, Professor of Publishing at Kingston University, not only understood what I was trying to achieve with this novel but advised me on how best to get it published. Over the last few months, Kate Berens at Ondine Editorial has been a brilliant editor, first by helping me find ways to fine-tune the characterisation, and then through a forensic and yet collaborative copy-editing process. And I am grateful now to Joe Shillito, Lauren Bailey, Philippa Iliffe and the rest of the team at Matador who have turned my vision into hard reality and demonstrated calm expertise in doing so.

Beyond this professional help, I owe so much to many others. Nine hardy souls embarked on that MA back on an autumn evening six years ago. Everyone supported each other as we all realised how much we didn't know about writing, and a small band of us have continued to encourage each other ever since – Louise Fein, Jennifer Small, Magdalena Duke, Gwen Emmerson and, from across the water, Lara Dearman. I am especially thankful to these talented writers for their friendly and always constructive comments. In addition, a host of other friends or family, who know me and my world only too well, have generously agreed to read complete drafts or important excerpts at various points over the last five years. In particular, I would like to thank Martin Howden, Liz Howden, Tony Franco, Alison Boulton, James Boulton, Andrew Lane, Julie Lawes, Adrian Stokes, Simon Brocklehurst and David Gapp. If I have missed anyone, I apologise and ask you to please remember that the book is, at heart, an exploration of forgiveness!